Morris Joseph Fuller

The Life, Times and Writings of Thomas Fuller, the Church Historian,

1608-1661

Morris Joseph Fuller

The Life, Times and Writings of Thomas Fuller, the Church Historian, 1608-1661

ISBN/EAN: 9783337000059

Printed in Europe, USA, Canada, Australia, Japan

Cover: Foto ©Raphael Reischuk / pixelio.de

More available books at **www.hansebooks.com**

THE

LIFE, TIMES AND WRITINGS

OF

THOMAS FULLER, D.D.,

THE CHURCH HISTORIAN (1608-1661).

BY THE

REV. MORRIS FULLER, M.A.,

Rector of Ryburgh.

AUTHOR OF "THE LORD'S DAY; OR, CHRISTIAN SUNDAY," "OUR ESTABLISHED CHURCH,"
"A VOICE IN THE WILDERNESS," "THE COURT OF FINAL APPEAL," &C.

VOL. I.

SECOND EDITION.

LONDON:

SWAN SONNENSCHEIN, LE BAS & LOWREY,

PATERNOSTER SQUARE.

—

1886

CONTENTS OF VOL. I.

PREFACE.

WHEN the writer of this work was a student at Cambridge, now many years ago, the Rev. Mr. Russell, Vicar of Caxton, Cambridgeshire, and author of the " Memorials of Fuller," called upon him, as a descendant of the Old Worthy, and presented him with a copy of the said work, which, at that time, was the only modern biography of his ancestor, Dr. Thomas Fuller. During his residence at the University, the writer saw a good deal of Mr. Russell, both in his own rooms and at Caxton Vicarage, and from these interviews he has carried away with him vivid recollections of Mr Russell's enthusiastic admiration for the subject of the " Memorials." It was there that Mr. Russell was always putting before him the example of his illustrious ancestor as an ideal churchman and clergyman, and model of true moderation—the via media of the Church of England,—at the same time urging him to expand the " Materials " some day, should an opportunity present itself, and make them the point of departure for a new biography. The duties of a Master in a Public School, and subsequently the responsibilities of one of the largest parishes in England—where much time had to be devoted to building and working school-chapels, restoring churches, and rebuilding a rectory house—precluded the idea of carrying out the proposal of composing a new biography of the celebrated Church Historian. But the writer never laid aside the intention which had been formed in his undergraduate days at Cambridge, and through life he had been collecting his materials. A change of residence during the last five years, bringing him within easy distance of the treasures of the British Museum, has enabled him at last to externalize this desire ; nor must he omit to notice the great assistance he has received from Mr. Bailey's exhaustive work, to whom he takes this opportunity of acknowledging his great indebtedness. But if the " Materials " were too dry for the ordinary reader, the book just referred to was too minute and tedious. The design of the present work, then, is to hold a middle position between these two, and its endeavour is to avoid the Scylla of baldness on the one hand, and the Charybdis of prolixity on the other.

The object of this " Life, Times and Writings " of Dr. Fuller is to add one more effort to stir up an interest in the life and works of this quaint old Worthy. Much as he is valued by the learned, he is not yet known, as he deserves to be, by the general public. In "Good old Fuller the Worthy " we have set before us an inspiring model of a good English Churchman and Clergyman all-round ; the Parish Priest, the Divine, the Preacher, and Lecturer ; and a better ideal of a good sound Anglican Divine, of the good old type, it would be difficult to find. There is the ring of the true metal about him. For he was not only a good Parish-Priest, he was likewise the cultured scholar, the courteous gentleman, the kind neighbour and companion, the loving husband and father, and the true patriot both in Church and State— in short, the type of excellence every clergyman should endeavour to reach unto. Here, then, is a model for all our Parish Priests, and there were giants in those days.

"But I speak of the number of Anglican divines of this period" (said the Archdeacon of Middlesex on the occasion of the unveiling of a window to his memory at St. Clement's, Eastcheap, on New Year's Day, 1878) "whose works of pen, or of life, or of both (for good men we are told 'lived their sermons' in those days) have come down to us. They differed, of course, in various respects, representing, as they did, the various lines of thought which existed then as now in the English Church." ("Address," p. 13.)

The character of Fuller is a remarkable illustration of this. As the quaint epitaph on his monument states, he spent his life in making others immortal, and thereby attained immortality himself—a sentence which is true of him in a double sense, for though the reference is there first to his great work, the "Worthies of England," it also holds good to the work he performed as a *clergyman*, and especially to that part of his work which he performed in the Savoy, and among the predecessors of the congregation who still assemble where he for the last time preached the Gospel of Peace.*

Besides which, the subject of these memoirs was a model of true moderation, holding precise dogmatic truth; a true Catholic, yet withal Protestant, as against the intruded mission of Rome on the one hand, and the fanaticism of the Sectaries on the other, keeping to the old paths of Scripture and Primitive Antiquity. But what we mean by *Moderation*, we must refer the reader to his *Essay on Moderation*, which is well worth reading at the present day, and in this age of extremes. He defines *Moderation* in a few admirable

---

* "Memorials of the Savoy," p. 181.

sentences : " It is not a halting between two opinions, neither is it a lukewarmness in those things wherein God's glory is concerned; but it is a mixture of discretion and charity in one's judgment. ' The lukewarm man,' he continues, ' eyes only his own ends and particular profit : the moderate man aims at the good of others and the unity of the Church.' "

Lastly, the object of this Biography is to inspire hope respecting the Church of the future. We belong to the same historical Church as Fuller did, and let us compare the present position of the National Church with what it was under the Commonwealth. It is true that the relations of Church and State don't even yet work smoothly ; that there is much friction and tension ; and there are still great searchings of heart. We have, unhappily, drifted into an " Ecclesiastical Dead-lock ; " but, at all events, our authorities in Church and State are trying to feel their way out of the difficulty, and doing their best to remedy the errors of the past. The appointment of a Commission for enquiring into the working of the Ecclesiastical Courts is a step in the right direction, in endeavouring to repair the luckless and hapless legislation of 1832-3. And if we compare the state of public feeling ; the hold the Church has generally upon the affections of the people ; the beauty and frequency and earnestness of the Church's services, there is much cause for gratitude. Look on this picture, when under the Commonwealth (according to the Diarists of the period) there was not a single Church service to be found in all London on Christmas Day, and on this (say the last Christmas Day under Queen Victoria), the efficiency of the Church in every parish in the kingdom, the beauty, heartiness and simple grandeur of the Church's functions; her restored Basilicas all over the country; the piety and devotion of her members, and the crowds of Communicants. Things may in some respects be bad, but they might be, as they have been, worse. One single clergyman has indeed been incarcerated, owing to the temporary confusion of the Regale and Pontificale, for the last twelvemonths, but in those days, the Parochial Clergy, almost to a man, were sequestrated all over the country. Had it not been for the City *Lecturers*, the Church's voice would not have been heard even in London. The Church had almost collapsed. In fact, Dr. Fuller wrote these words at the beginning of his "Church History" (1655) in his Epistle to the Reader : "An *Ingenious Gentleman*, moneths since, in jest-earnest, advised me to make Hast with my 'History of the Church of England,' for fear (said he) lest the Church of England be ended before the History thereof." Yet the Church rose like a Phœnix from her ashes, and the learned Doctor could add subsequently, "And blessed be God, the Church of England is still (and long may it be) in being, though disturbed, distempered, distracted. God help her, and heal her most sad condition."

Matters have much improved since those days. There have been the two great revivals in the Church 'during the present century—the one at Cambridge, and the other at Oxford—subjective and objective, making a complete and germane totality of re-formation. If the Church is still 'disturbed, distempered, and distracted,' and has trials to undergo from divided councils, opposing factions, false friends, and cruel adversaries, we must yet hope in God's good time all will come right, and eventuate in the salvation of souls and glory of God. Only let us be faithful and patient.

To conclude, in Fuller's own words: "Many things in England are out of joint for the present, and a strange confusion there is in Church and State: but let this comfort us, we trust it is confusion in tendency to order; and, therefore, let us for a time more patiently comport therewith."*

---

* The following extract from Fuller's " Occasional Meditations " is a good illustration of Longfellow's " Excelsior ":—It is headed *Upwards! Upwards!* "How large houses do they build in London on little ground, revenging themselves on the narrowness of their room with stores of storeys. Excellent arithmetic From the root of one floor to multiply so many chambers. And though painful the climbing up, pleasant the staying there, the higher the healthfuller, with clearer light and sweeter air. May I mount my soul the higher in heavenly meditations, relying on Divine Providence. Higher! my soul! higher! In bodily buildings, considering the garrets are most empty, but my mind, the higher mounted, will be the better furnished. Let perseverance to death be my uppermost chamber, the roof of which, grace, is the pavement of glory."

THE LIFE, TIMES AND WRITINGS

OF

THOMAS FULLER, D.D.

CHAPTER I.

INTRODUCTION.

" *Fuller* of faith than of fear,
 Fuller of resolution than pains,
 Fuller of honour than of days."
Inscription on monument in Westminster Abbey.

"QUAINT Old Fuller," " Old Tom Fuller," " The great Tom Fuller," " Good Old Fuller, the Worthy," such are some of the kindly epithets which have been lavished upon this wittiest of Caroline divines, this raciest of pre-Restoration writers. Witty he was rather than quaint, for " wit " was, according to Coleridge, " the stuff and substance of Fuller's intellect ; " and " old " did not refer to length of days, but may be regarded as a familiar form of endearment, as, for example, the " Venerable Bede." He is the *beau ideal* of a Church-and-State man, " that stout Church-and-King man Tom Fuller," as Coleridge calls him. Admirers he has had in abundance, and among them some of the greatest names in the annals of literature. The seventeenth century saw the first account of his life, " the life of that reverend divine and learned historian, Dr. Thomas Fuller ; " in the eighteenth was published the life of Fuller in the *Biographia Britannica;* and the present century has .witnessed the publication of the "Memorials of Dr. Fuller's Life and Works," by my friend the Rev. Arthur Russell, Vicar of Caxton, Cambridgeshire, whose presentation copy now lies before me ; some lives in biographical dictionaries, and the principal work on the subject by J. E. Bailey, "The Life of Thomas Fuller, D.D." But his critics have been both numerous and enthusiastic. Charles Lamb made an appreciative selection from the works of the genial old prebendary, who was at that time scarcely known except to antiquarians. From some similarity of genius he literally revelled in the "seria" and "joca," in the "golden works" of one, whom he called his "dear, fine, silly old angel." Coleridge speaks of him in no measured terms : "Next to Shakespeare, I am not certain whether Thomas Fuller, beyond all others, does not excite in me the sense and emotion of the marvellous . . . Fuller was incomparably the most sensible, the least prejudiced great man of an age that boasted a galaxy of great men." "Shakespeare ! Milton ! Fuller ! Defoe ! Hogarth ! As to the remaining host of our great men, other countries have produced something like them ; but these are unique. England may challenge the world to show a correspondent name to either of the five. I do not say that, with the exception of the first, names of equal glory may not be produced in a different kind. But these are genera, containing each only one individual." Fuller was the "prime favourite author" of the poet Southey, whose writings contain many notices of his works. Professor Rogers, in his essay, which he first published in the *Edinburgh Review*, January, 1842, expresses his conviction that posterity had dealt hardly by

Fuller's memory, and that "there are hundreds who have
been better remembered, with far less claims to that honour."
"Thus," he remarks, "it is singular that even Mr. Hallam,
in his recent 'History of European Literature,' should not
have bestowed upon him any special notice, but dismisses
him with only a slight allusion in a note upon another subject (vol. iii. p. 104). Yet Fuller was not only one of the
most voluminous — an equivocal indication of merit it
must be allowed —but one of the most original writers in
the language.   Like Taylor and Barrow and Sir Thomas
Browne, he wrote with a vigour and originality, with a
fertility of thought and imagery, and a general felicity of
style, which, considering the quantity of his compositions,
and the haste with which he produced them, impress us
with wonder at his untiring activity and preternatural
fecundity."   And again, "In a moral and religious point of
view, the character of Fuller is entitled to our admiration,
and is altogether one of the most attractive and interesting
which that age exhibits to us."

A writer in the *Retrospective Review* says of him, "His life
was meritoriously passed, and exemplary throughout; his
opinions were independently adopted and unshrinkingly
maintained.   In the darkest and gloomiest periods of our
national history he had the sense and the wisdom to pursue the
right way, and to persevere in an even tenour of moderation,
as remote from interested lukewarmness as it was from
mean-spirited fear.   Unwilling to go all lengths with either
party, he was of consequence vilified by both; willing to
unite the maintainers of opposite and conflicting sentiments,
he only united them against himself.   Secure in the strength
of his intellectual riches, the storms and hurricanes which

uprooted the fabric of the Constitution had only the effect of confining him more to his own resources, and of inciting him to the production of more numerous treatises and compilations, for which he received from his contemporaries respect and reputation, and for which posterity will render him its tribute of unfailing gratitude."

CHAPTER II.

"THE FULLER FAMILY."

"Ager Fullonum—Fullers Field."
Pisgah-sight, iii. 310.

THE very name of Fuller is suggestive of a pun, and we find that the changes of many a pun were rung upon it, both by the subject of our biography himself and his compeers both friend and foe alike. According to a Roman proverb, the name of "Old Fuller," as he was facetiously called, is both nomen and omen.

"Though Shakespeare asks 'What's in a name?'
(As if cognomens were much the same),
There's really a very great scope in it."
HOOD.

A *fuller* is one employed in woollen manufactures to mill or scour clothes, to *full* them, *i.e.*, to render them compact, thick, and durable. For this purpose *Fuller's earth* is required, and good cloth can hardly be made without it. Dr. Fuller having once asked his companions to write his epitaph, one of them suggested, "Here lies Fuller's earth."

As the industrious author of so many worthy, solid, and sterling works, he certainly answers to his name. Thus Nuttal, in his introduction to the "Worthies of England," comparing his writings with others, says, "They are not only Fuller in useful matter and varied interest, but (as a punster in his own day would have said) *fuller* in spirit, *fuller* in wit in fact, Fuller throughout." Deriving them from the origin of his name, Fuller made various puns—

"My soul is stained with a dusky colour,
Let thy Son be the sope, and I'll be the Fuller,"

is a prayer taken from his "Epigrams." Again, in his "Appeal of Injured Innocence," he prays, "As for other stains and spots upon my soul, I hope that He (be it spoken without the least verbal reflection) who is the Fuller's sope (Malachi iii. 2) will scour them forth with His merit that I may appear clean by God's mercy."

Again, in his witty work entitled "A Pisgah-sight of Palestine," he makes a jocular use of his surname, and in the map of Jerusalem which accompanies it, and which is evidently the author's handiwork, instead of writing "Fuller fecit," he has put in the left hand corner "Ager Fullonum" —"Fullers' Field," which clearly indicates the source of the pun, or, at all events, that he had secured an engraver who entered into the spirit of it.

A story is extant to the effect that on one occasion Dr. Fuller asked a Mr. Sparrowhawk, in whose company he happened to find himself, "what was the difference between an owl and a sparrowhawk?" from whom he received the unexpected reply, "An owl is *fuller* in the head, *fuller* in face, and *Fuller* all over." Dr. Peter Heylin, who was Dr. Fuller's antagonist all through life, and with whom he was perpetually breaking a lance, a disciple of Laud, and a leader of the advanced Church party, tells a story of our Fuller in his "Examen Historicum." "I have heard a story of a lady too, to whose table one Mr. Fuller was a welcome, though a frequent guest; and being asked once by her whether he would please to eat the wing of a woodcock, he would needs put her to the question how her lady-ship knew it was a wood*cock* and not a wood*hen*. And this he pressed with such a troublesome importunity that at last the lady answered, with some show of displeasure, that the woodcock was *fuller*-headed, *fuller*-breasted, *fuller*-thighed, and in a word every way *fuller*. Whether this tale be true or false I am not able to say, but *being generally believed*, I have set it down here."

But this constant punning on his name did not at all dis-concert the bearer of it. " I had rather," said this genial-hearted divine, "my name should make *many* causelessly merry, than *any* justly sad, and seeing it lieth equally open and obvious to praise or dispraise, I shall as little be elated when flattered " *Fuller* of wit and learning," as dejected when flouted " *Fuller* of folly and ignorance."

Fuller's name appears to have been the occasion of some mirth in connection with the Keeping some Act at Oxford University about the year 1656, and his constant opponent Heylin alludes to the fact of his having been ridiculed within a year or two afterwards ; to which Fuller replied, " I heard nothing thereof at Oxford, being then sixty miles distanced thence. Sure I am I did not there *male audire* deservedly, and if undeservedly, *mala fama bene parta delectat.* Secondly, I have heard since that one in the Act was bold to play on my own name, and *Church History*. But for the seventeen years I lived at Cambridge, I never heard any Prevaricator mention his senior by name ; we count such particularising beneath a University. Thirdly, I hope it will not be accounted pride but prudence, in me, to believe myself above such trifles, who have written a book to Eternity. Fourthly, I regret not to be anvil for any inge-

nious hammer to make pleasant music on ; but it seems my
traducer was not so happy. Lastly, I remember a speech
of Sir Walter Raleigh. "If any," saith he, "speaketh
against me to my face, my tongue shall give him an answer ;
but my back-side is good enough to return to him who
abuseth me behind my back." *

Even after his death Fuller's name continued to be played
upon. Thus, underneath the portrait which forms a frontispiece to his life by an anonymous author, but friend of the
subject of his biography, are these lines—

> "Bodie and mind do answer well his name,
>   Fuller, comparative to 's bliss and fame."

"Bliss covets to be *fuller* and complete" is also found in
Heath's elegy upon Dr. Fuller.

And in the chapel of St. Paul, in Westminster Abbey, is
a monument to Sir John and Lady Fullerton, with an
inscription stating that the former died "*fuller* of faith than
of fear, *fuller* of resolution than of pains, *fuller* of honour
than of days."

All through life Heylin continued to ridicule the name of
his great antagonist, who, however, replied in these words,
"All his jeering on my name shall not make me go to the
herald's office to endeavour the altering thereof. I fetched
it from my great, great grandfather, and hope I shall leave
it to my great, great grandchild : a name which no doubt
was originally taken from that useful trade, without which
mankind can neither be warm nor cleanly. The like is fre-

----

* "Heylin's Examen : Appeal," pt. i. p. 321.

quent in many respectful families in England, as the antiquary hath observed—

"From whence came Smith, albe he knight or squire,
But from the *smith* that forgeth at the fire."

Yet considering the narrowness of my name, it is inferior to
few, having produced the best of English pilots, Thomas
Fuller, who steered Captain Cavendish round the world ;
the best of English critics, Nicholas Fuller, so famous in
foreign parts for his "Miscellanies ;" and none of the worst
of English benefactors, John Fuller."

We will say a few words about each of these worthy
bearers of the name of Fuller, of whom our hero was so
justly proud.

About Thomas Fuller, the pilot, in the dedication of the
closing section of his work on "Church History," Fuller
thus writes: "I find that my namesake, Thomas Fuller,
was pilot in a ship called the *Desire*, wherein Captain
Cavendish surrounded (sailed round) the world." In his
"Worthies" of Suffolk, Fuller alludes to this Cavendish
having taken to the sea, and made the *third* circumnaviga-
tion of the globe in 1580. "Mr. Thomas Fuller," he adds,
"of Ipswich, acted as pilot, and made charts of the voyage,
which proved of much service to those early mariners." *

Nicholas Fuller, the theologian, was a man after Fuller's
own heart, and he has a place in the "Worthies" and
"Church History" of his namesake. Born about 1557, he
afterwards settled at Allington, near Amesbury, Wilts, where
he had a benefice rather than a living, so small the revenues

---

* "Appeal of Injured Innocence," ii. 533.

thereof.   But a contented mind extendeth the smallest
parish into a diocese, and improveth the least benefice into
a bishopric.   Here a great candle was put under a bushel
(or peck rather), so private his place and employment.
Here he applied his studies in the tongues, and was happy
in pitching on (not difficult trifles but) useful difficulties
tending to the understanding of Scripture.   He became an
excellent linguist, and his books found good regard beyond
the seas, where they were reprinted.   Drusius, the Belgian
critic, grown old, angry and jealous that he should be out-
shined in his own sphere, foully cast some drops of ink upon
him which the other as fairly wiped off again." This alludes
to his "Miscellanies." Good Bishop Andrews came to him as
the Queen of Sheba to Solomon, to pose him with hard
questions, " bringing with him a heap of knots for the other
to untie, and departed from him with good satisfaction."
Anthony Wood says of him (who has been sometimes confounded with our Fuller) that " he surpassed all the critics
of his time ;" and Fuller himself says, "he was the prince
of all our English critics . . . by discovering how much
Hebrew there is in the New Testament Greek, he cleareth
many real difficulties from his verbal observations."*

There is also another member of the Fuller family who
bears the same name as the linguist-critic ; this is Nicholas
Fuller, a bencher of Gray's Inn, and of Chamberhouse,
Berks, who also finds a place in the " Church History."
Fuller thus speaks of the character and attainments of his
kinsman.   " Be it reported to the Jesses of Gray's Inn (I
mean such benchers as pass among them for old men, and

---

* "Appeal " ii. 532.

can distinctly remember him) whether he hath not left a precious and perfumed memory behind him of one pious to God, temperate in himself, able in his profession, moderate in his fees, careful for his client, faithful to his friend, hospitable to his neighbour, pitiful to the poor, and bountiful to Emmanuel College in Cambridge." He died in 1619, and his son-in-law, Sir John Offley, Knt., of Madely Manor, was executor. "He left behind him the reputation of an honest man, and a plentiful estate to his family." This estate, which was in Berkshire, consisted of large landed property, which passed to his son, Sir Nicholas Fuller, Knt., who married Maria, daughter of George Douse, of Mere Court, Hampshire. This is the Douse Fuller, of Hampshire, Esquire, to whom Fuller dedicates one of the early editions of his "Church History," whom he claims to be a kinsman of, although he cannot say certainly, he "is near of kin unto us," as Naomi did to Boaz. (Ruth ii. 20.)

Of "John Fuller," the third of the illustrious Fullers mentioned in the "Appeal of Injured Innocence," we have the following particulars :—"One of the Judges in the Sheriff's Court in London, who built and endowed an almshouse (two according to his will) for twelve poor men at Stoken-heath, and another at Shoreditch for as many poor women. Besides, he gave his lands and tenements, of great yearly valuation, in the parishes of St. Benet and Peter (Paul's Wharf), London, to feoffees in trust to release prisoners in the Hole of both Compters, whose debts exceeded not twenty shillings eight pence." His lands in the parish of St. Giles were left to Francis Fuller, Gent.

Having thus referred to three illustrious members of his family, Thomas Fuller, who became more distinguished and better known than all, then enumerates with some degree of pride others of the same name who were then living (1659), and who were either dignitaries of the Church, or graduates in Divinity and Arts " of no contemptible condition," and concludes thus : " Pardon, reader, this digression done *se defendendo* against one (Heylin) to whom my name is too much undervalued by ironical over-valuing thereof." Against Heylin's ironical recapitulation of these four gradations of Fuller's : bad, worse, worst, worst of all, which our author wittily translates into "good, bad, better, best of all." And having summed up the characteristics of three first, he thus modestly answers for himself. " For the fourth and last, I will make the animadverter the self-same answer which the servants of Hezekiah returned to Rabshakeh, " But they held their peace, and answered him not a word."

There have been various readings of the surname of this family. It is written Fuller, le Fuller, Fuler, Ffooler, Fulwer, Ful-war, and the arms of the family are argent and gules. This coat (still used by the Fullers of Sussex) is ascribed by our Fuller to Douse Fuller ; it was also borne by Dr. William Fuller, Bishop, first of Limerick, then of Lincoln. (2) A second variation was barry of six argent and gules, a canton of the last. Other forms were (3) three barulets and a canton gule ; and (4) barry of six argent and gules without the canton. These (1) are also the arms of Dr. Thomas Fuller, of Sussex, and M.D. of Queens' College (1672), which are still used by the writer's family, the Sussex branch.

The original spot—" the hole of the pit from whence they were digged"—whence the family are found, is in the south-eastern counties. Perhaps *Suffolk* may claim to be the home of the original stock, where they obtained some

importance. This was the seat of the great woollen manufactures, of which the county town (Ipswich) was the
headquarters, and with this trade fullers (whence came the
name) were everywhere connected. The name is still to be
found in several parts of the county, as if locally correlated
with that manufacture, which has made the county famous.
There are also several families of Fuller to be met with in
Essex. Some of these claim to be descendants or connections of Robert Fuller, last Abbot of Waltham Abbey, where
our Fuller was curate just one hundred years after. The abbot
was also Prior Commendatory of St. Bartholomew, West
Smithfield. With regard to this abbey, Fuller tells us that
though the Abbot could not prevent its dissolution in the
time of Henry VIII., he preserved its antiquities from
oblivion in the "Ledger-book" which he himself collected.
This ecclesiastic died in 1540. In the extracts given from
the churchwardens' accounts by Fuller in his history of
Waltham Abbey, is entered a sum of £10, as received from
the executors of this "Sir Robert Fuller," according to his
will.

Although the clerical element in the Fuller family was
very strong in our Fuller's time, yet we find among the
section of the family settled in Cambridgeshire, about a
century later, the name of the celebrated Baptist Divine,
Andrew Fuller, with whom our author has been frequently
confounded. He, too, was a learned biblical critic, and still
holds, we believe, a revered position among the modern,
more moderate, and least Calvinistic section, of the Baptist
persuasion.

Other branches of the family are to be found in Berks,
Surrey, Kent, and Sussex. To this last branch belongs Dr.

Thomas Fuller, a physician of some eminence, and the author of several learned medical treatises. Strange to say, this worthy has also been sometimes mistaken for our hero. He was born at Uckfield, in Sussex, and entered the family college of Queens' College, Cambridge, in 1672, taking his M.D. in 1681. He wrote also some moral works, and, like his kinsman, made collections of proverbs, wise saws, maxims, and aphorisms. His arms are the same as the other members of the Fuller family, argent, three bars and a canton gule : the crest being a lion's head out of a ducal coronet, and on the coat is an escutcheon of pretence, showing his wife was an heiress or co-heiress. He was honorably distinguished for his kindness to the poor, and died 1734, having written a tetrastic epitaph for himself.

Some of these different sections also settled in London, and became merchants, and it was doubtless in the metropolis that our hero's father, " Thomas Fuller the elder," first saw the light. He is principally celebrated as being the father of the illustrious Church Historian, and was entered at Trinity College, Cambridge, 1583, taking his B.A. degree the same year as the renowned Cabalistic divine and orientalist, William Alabaster, of Trinity, 1587. He was present at the celebrated disputation between Dillingham, a controversial divine of the period, and Alabaster, in a Greek act, "a disputation so famous that it served as an era or epoch for the scholars in that age to date their seniority." * He became Fellow of his College, 1590, having been a pupil of the erudite and learned Dr. Whitaker, whose portrait in "The Holy State" of "the

---

* Holy State," 47.

controversial Divine" is drawn out of admiration by Dr. Fuller himself. Fuller's father then became a parish priest, and was presented by the second Lord Burghley, and first Earl of Exeter, to the rectory of St. Peter's, Aldwinckle, near Oundle, Northamptonshire, in 1602. In his dedication of "Pisgah-sight of Palestine" to Lord Burghley, our author wittily says, "Now the first light which I saw in this world was in a benefice conferred on my father by your most honorable great father, and therefore I stand obliged in all thankfulness to your family. Yea, this my right hand, which *grasped the first free aire* in a Manor to which your Lordship is Heir-Apparent, hath since *often been catching at a pen* to write something in expression of my thankfulness, and now at last dedicates this book to your infant honour. Thus as my obligation bears date from my *birth*, my thankfulness makes speed to tender itself to your *cradle*."

In alluding to his clerical parentage, and in reply to the then attacks of the Church of Rome against the children of clerics, Fuller avers in one of his works that such have been as successful as the children of men of other professions; they may have been more *observed*, but not more *unfortunate*.

CHAPTER III.

FULLER'S FATHER, FAMILY, AND FRIENDS.

" He was born at All-Winckle, . . a place now equalled to, and vying honour with, any seed-plot (in that county) of virtue, learning, and religion ; and of which hereafter to its glory it shall be said '*that this man was born there.*'"—*Anonymous Life.* p. 2.

THE subject of this biography—the celebrated Church-Historian, the witty writer and laborious Antiquary, was born at St. Peter's Vicarage, Aldwinckle, between Thrapston and Oundle, in 1608, and baptised June 19th of the same year, being the elder of the two sons of Dr. FULLER, Rector of St. Peter, Prebendary of Sarum, and formerly Fellow of Trinity College, Cambridge.   He was proud of his native county, which was Northamptonshire, and which he considers to be " as fruitful and populous as any in England." Lord Palmerston used to say a man should be enthusiastic, not only about his native country, but his county, and even town or village ; *Civis Romanus sum* should be his motto. Fuller would have answered well to this description.   He gloried in his native county—the county town, and his own birthplace.   " God in His providence fixed my nativity in a remarkable place.   I was born in Aldwinckle, in Northamptonshire, where my father was the painful preacher of St. Peter's ;" and again, " If that county esteem me no *disgrace* to it, I esteem it an *honour* to me." *

---

* " Mixt Contemplations," 43.

Aldwinckle, or the Aldwinckles, for there are two of them, is situate in the north-eastern part of the county, and in the valley of the river Nene. It is surrounded by rich pastures and well-wooded fields, the fields in this locality being un-usually large. The village of Aldwinckle stands on a sloping ground, near the old forest of Rockingham ; and in the com-fortably thatched vicarage of All Saints, Dryden, the poet, was born, and spent the early part of his life, twenty-three years after the birth of the subject of this memoir. The poet was in all probability baptised by the rector in the grey old turreted church of Aldwinckle All Saints, although there is no record of the same, the parish registers of that period being no longer extant. The other church of Ald-winckle, which is more intimately connected with the early days of the subject of this biography, St. Peter's, carries with it a more venerable air, and is pleasantly situated not far from the road, and is surrounded with trees. It boasts of some architectural beauty, and is chiefly remarkable for its spire, which gracefully rises to the height of ninety-five feet, the tower and spire being harmoniously blended.

Northamptonshire is great in spires, and the inhabitants have a saying that the county is famed for its " squires and spires, its springs and spinsters." Dr. Fuller thus speaks of it in his " Worthies :" " It is as fruitful and populous as any in England, insomuch that *sixteen* several towns with their *churches* have at one view been discovered therein by my eyes, which I confess none of the best ; and God grant that those who are sharper-sighted may hereafter never see fewer." He adds in a note, " Other men have discovered two and thirty." This gives point to a remark in Coleridge's "Friend," that an "instinctive taste teaches men to build

B

their churches in flat countries with spire steeples, which, as they cannot be referred to any other object, point up with silent finger to the sky and stars." There are several fine spires in the county of Northampton—Oundle, Wellingborough, Thrapston, Kettering, Kingsthorpe, Higham Ferrers, Denford, and the Aldwinckles, all which have been much admired for their elegance and beauty. It is supposed there were even more in Dr. Fuller's time. It has been well remarked that Quakers must have learnt to call churches "steeple-houses" from this county.

The interior of St. Peter's, Aldwinckle, is even more interesting than the exterior. It has a nave and two side aisles, with a spacious chancel, lighted with long decorated windows, and a very large east window of five compartments. There are some stained-glass windows, and around the border of one of them is a dog and hare alternately. The dog seems to suggest that this window was the gift of one of the Lords Lovell. In heraldry a white dog is called a "*lovell*;" and it was by this very cognizance that in the celebrated satirical verses upon Richard III. reference was made to one of the lords of this manor, Francis Viscount Lovell.

These well-known verses are thus given by Fuller :

> "The Rat and the Cat, and *Lovell the dog*,
> Do govern all England under the *Hog*," *

i.e. Ratcliffe and Catesby under King Richard "who gave a boar for his crest."

Under an altar tomb on the south-east side is buried Margaret Davenant, some time wife of John Davenant, Esq.,

---

* "Worthies" (Northampton), p. 287.

Citizen of London. She departed this life March 30th, 1613.

Upon the tomb is the following epitaph :—

"Many and happy years I lived a wife,
Fruitful in children, more in godly life.
And many years in widowhood I past,
Until to heaven I wedded was at last.
In wedlock, children, widowhood ever blest,
But most in death, for now with God I rest."

This Margaret was daughter and co-heir of John Clarke, of Farnham, Surrey : her husband was John Davenant, descended of the ancient family of that name settled at Sible Hedingham, Essex, as early as the reign of Henry III., and was the second son of William Davenant, and Joan, his wife. He was a merchant-tailor, lived in Watling-street, London, and accumulated a vast estate. By his wife Margaret he had two daughters, Judith, wife of Thomas Fuller the father of the celebrated author, and Margaret, wife of Dr. Townson, Bishop of Salisbury. He had also by the same Margaret four sons. The eldest, Edward, married Anne, daughter of John Symmes, of London, and by her had two sons, Edward Davenant subsequently D.D., and secondly Dr. John Davenant, successor to his brother-in-law, Dr. Townson, in the see of Salisbury.

Dr. Thomas Fuller, the subject of this biography, "first saw the light," as he himself says, in the old glebe house at the upper end of the village. But the rectory was pulled down some eighty years ago, by the first Powys, owner of the property. And yet it seems to have been a building of considerable interest, and if not so famous as Shakespeare's house at Stratford-on-Avon, in degree, yet the same kind of interest attached to it, as is the case with the birthplaces of remarkable men.   There are none living who remember it, but there is still the traditional history of it current ; that it stood on the glebe close to the village street, and contiguous to a well, which now exists, and out of whose waters he must often have drunk, seems clearly attested.   The well appears to have been close to the back door, and no doubt suggested his remark, that, " the mischief of many houses was where the servants must bring the well on their shoulders."   But irrespective of these considerations, the old Parsonage seems to have been a well-built house, in Fuller's language a " substantive able to take care of itself." It possessed a remarkable staircase, broad and massive, with great posts and timbers, " almost like the pillars in the church," and no doubt from this peculiarity may be dated back to the time of Queen Elizabeth.   People " used frequently to come on purpose to see the old house, it was so curious. "

From the description of this Parsonage, there can be no doubt that Fuller had his eye upon it, when he wrote his essay " On Building," which also illustrates his fondness for his home.   It was built, as he there says, " in the wholesome air," commended for a house, and wood and water were also "two staple commodities."   "The former, I confess," he says, "hath made so much iron, that it must now (1640) be bought with the more silver, and grows daily dearer. But 'tis as well pleasant as profitable to see a house cased with trees like that of Anchises in Troy. (Æn. ii. 299).

' Quanquam secuta parentis
Anchisæ domus arboribusque obtecta recepit.'

The worst is, where a place is bald of wood, no art

can make it a periwig. As for water, begin with Pindar's beginning, ἄριστον μὲν ὕδωρ."

"Tho' deep in shade
My father's palace stood embayed."—(CONINGTON.)

The Rectory had also the "pleasant prospect" requisite for a house, and it was a substantial building, as he says, "Country houses must be substantives, able to stand by themselves : not like city buildings, supported by their neighbours." And in this building "beauty was last to be regarded," being made "to be *lived in*, not *looked at*." Nor did it "look asquint on a stranger but accosted him right at the entrance."

It was in this parsonage the elder Fuller began to devote himself to the duties of a parish priest, his life varied only by visits to his Alma Mater, in his official capacity as head lecturer at Trinity College. This was in 1605. The great event in his pastoral life would be the progress of Queen Elizabeth's successor through the kingdom, "by many small journeys and great feastings, from Scotland to London," and the king passed close by the neighbourhood of Aldwinckle. Fuller gives a graphic description of this progress, and of the many entertainments, and especially of that at the house of Master Oliver Cromwell, which seems to have distanced and eclipsed all others.

Two years after his appointment to the Rectory of Aldwinckle, Mr. Fuller, in 1607, married Judith, daughter of John Davenant, a citizen of London. The celebrated Church historian was their eldest son, being born in June of the following year, 1608, and baptized June 19th, in St. Peter's Church.

This brings me to say a few words about the history of Dr. Fuller's mother's family, the Davenants, a name also honoured, and well-known in ecclesiastical circles.

The Davenants were of an ancient and honourable family, and were descended from Sir John Davenant, who the time of Henry III. settled at Davenant's lands, in the parish of Heddingham, Essex. His descendants followed "in a worshipful degree," till we come to William Davenant, who married Joan, daughter of John Fryer, of Clare, in Suffolk. Their son was John Davenant, a merchant tailor, of Watling Street, who was, says Fuller, "wealthy and religious." His wife, Margaret Clarke, was the daughter and co-heiress of John Clarke, who resided at Farnham Castle, in Surrey. It was in this way that she became acquainted with Stephen Gardiner, and received kindnesses from him which were suitably acknowledged in "our author's gratitude to Stephen Gardiner."

It was this old lady's grandchild, Judith Davenant, who became the mother of Dr. Fuller, whose life we are considering. When his baptism took place at St. Peter's, as stated before, he had as godfathers his two uncles, Dr. Davenant and Dr. Townson. Of these, he says in his "Worthies," "Both these persons were my godfathers and uncles, the one marrying the sister of, the other being brother, to my mother." These two uncles are intimately connected with their nephew in his subsequent official career, and require some notice *en passant.*

John Davenant was a younger son of Mr. John Davenant, merchant, already alluded to, and was born in 1572. He was educated a fellow-commoner of Queens' College, Cambridge, and was elected fellow of that society in 1597,

It is highly probable that he was at that time a college associate of the elder Fuller. Davenant gave such an earnest of his future maturity, that the celebrated Dr. Whitaker, hearing him dispute, uttered the prediction, which afterwards came to pass, that he would prove to be the honour] of the University. He became subsequently president of Queens' (and no doubt Fuller thought of him when he wrote his " Good Master of a College," and " The Good Bishop," in " Holy State," p. 80), Margaret Professor of Theology, and Bishop of Salisbury.

There is a good anecdote anent tithes, told by Fuller in his " Church History," about Davenant, when Vicar of Oakington, near Cambridge (1612). " A reverend Doctor in Cambridge, and afterwards Bishop of Salisbury, was troubled at his small living at Oakington with a peremptory Anabaptist, who plainly told him, ' It goes against my conscience to pay you tithes, except you can show me a place of Scripture, whereby they are due unto you.' The Doctor returned, ' Why should it not go as much against my conscience, that you should enjoy your nine parts, for which you can show no place of Scripture ? ' To whom the other rejoined, ' But I have my land deeds and evidences from my fathers, who purchased and were peaceably possessed thereof by the laws of the land.' ' The same is my title,' saith the Doctor, ' tithes being confirmed unto me, by many statutes of the land, time out of mind.' Thus he drave that nail, not which was of the strongest metal or sharpest point, but which would go best for the present. It was *argumentum ad hominem* fittest for the person he was to meddle with, who afterwards peaceably paid his tithes unto him. Had the Doctor engaged in Scripture argument

though never so pregnant and pertinent, it had been endless to dispute with him, who made clamour the end of his
dispute, whose obstinacy and ignorance made him incapable
of solid reason ; and therefore the worse the argument, the
better for his apprehension."

Robert Townson, a native of Cambridge, was also
entered at Queens' College, and became a fellow of that
society, with his future brother-in-law, Davenant, in 1597.
He was afterwards beneficed at Wellingborough, in Northamptonshire, and married Margaret, elder daughter of John
Davenant, the merchant tailor of London, being born in
1585. Living in the same neighbourhood, the families of
Townsons and their cousins, the Fullers, both very numerous, would naturally have been thrown much together, and
there are proofs of an intimacy between the younger Townson and Fuller. To this period belongs Fuller's recollection
of his uncle, Dr. Townson, who was "of a comely carriage,
courteous nature, an excellent preacher," and "becoming a
pulpit with his gravity." Like Fuller himself, and the rest
of that family, Dr. Townson had a very retentive faculty,
for when made D.D. he could repeat the whole of the
second book of the *Æneid* without missing a single verse.
These two divines, being uncles of our hero, and beneficed
in the same county, were frequent guests at his father's
rectory, and Fuller not only saw much of them, but entertained for them the greatest regard.

Among the friends of Fuller's father at that time, and
who were in the habit of coming to the rectory, may be
mentioned the names of Sir Robert Cotton, Dr. Roger
Fenton, Dr. John Overall, Richard Greenham, Carey, and
Pykering. One or two of these deserve some notice. Dr.

Roger Fenton was one of the translators of the Bible, "than whom never a more learned hath Pembroke Hall brought forth, with but one exception" (*i.e.* Bishop Andrewes). Fenton was the faithful, pious, learned, and beloved minister of St. Stephen's, Walbrook, London. Fuller mentions the fact of their "being contemporaries, collegiates, and city ministers together, with some similitudes in their names, but more sympathies in their natures;" and he tells the following anecdote of these two divines: "Once my own Father gave Dr. Fenton a visit, who excused himself from entertaining him any longer. 'Mr. Fuller, hear how the passing bell tolls at this very instant for my dear friend Dr. Felton, now a-dying; I must to my study, it being mutually agreed upon betwixt us in our health, that the survivor of us should preach the other's funeral sermon.' But see a strange change! God, to whom belong the issues from death, was pleased (with the patriarch Jacob blessing his grandchildren) wittingly to guide his hands across, reaching out death to the living and life to the dying. So that Dr. Felton recovered, and not only performed that last office to his friend, Dr. Fenton, but died Bishop of Ely (1626)."

Dr. John Overall was also most intimate with Mr. Fuller. He wrote the sacramental part of the Catechism, and was also one of the translators of the Bible. He was called "a prodigious learned man." He was a Cambridge man, and succeeded Whitaker as Regius Professor of Divinity. He was appointed to preach before the Queen as Dean of St. Paul's, and professed to the elder Fuller, "he had spoken Latin so long, it was troublesome to speak English in a continued oration." Fuller calls him "one of the most profound school divines of the English nation." He was made Bishop of Norwich (1618), and was a "discreet presser of Conformity," and he had great influence, not only with the divines of his own, but with those of other countries.

The Church of England must always feel a debt of gratitude to this able divine, for the lucid and exhaustive exposition of its sacramental system.

It was here, then, at Aldwinckle,—a parish, with some of the Lecturers in its vicinity, and not altogether at ecclesiastical peace with itself,—the elder Fuller, a devoted Churchman, but not a bigot, laboured for thirty years, endeavouring to avoid every occasion of strife—theological and political— in that most disputatious period. We may safely conclude that the words which Fuller wrote would apply no less to the father than to his son, the author of them himself: " He (*i.e.* the faithful minister) is *moderate* in his *tenets* and *opinions*. Not that he gilds over lukewarmness in matters of moment with the title of discretion, but withal is careful not to entitle violence in indifferent and inconcerning matters to be zeal. Indeed, men of extraordinary tallness, though otherwise little deserving, are made porters to lords, and those of unusual littleness are made ladies' dwarfs, while men of moderate stature may want masters. Thus many notorious for extremities may find favourers to prefer them, whilst moderate men in the middle truth may want any to advance them. But what saith the Apostle ? 'If in this life only we have hope, we are of all men most miserable.' "

It is evident that the elder Fuller belonged to that class of men who (to use his son's own words) were pious, but not so eminently learned—" very painful* and profitable in God's vineyard."

---

* The word "painful" continually occurs in Fuller's writings, By "painful" is meant "taking *pains*," not giving pain. Thus the Archbishop of Dublin explains the word. Fuller, our Church historian, praising some famous divine, lately dead, exclaims : "Oh the *painfulness* of his preaching." How easily we might take this for an exclamation wrung out at the recollection of the tediousness which he inflicted on his hearers. Nothing of the kind : the words are a record not of the *pain* which he caused to others, but of the *pains* which he bestowed himself. Nor can I doubt, if we had more "painful" preachers in the old sense of the word, *i.e.*, who took *pains* themselves, we should hear fewer "painful" ones in the modern sense, who cause *pain* to their hearers. So, too, Bishop Grosthead is recorded as "the *painful* writer of two hundred books, not meaning hereby that these books were 'painful' in the reading, but (*Holy State*, p. 78) that he was laborious and 'painful' in their composition." *English Past and Present*, p. 200-1.

CHAPTER IV.

FULLER'S EARLY YEARS.

" Having under this tuition past the just time of adolescency in these puerile studies, at twelve years of age this hopeful slip was translated to Cambridge, where he first settled in Qyeens Colledge, of which a neer kinsman of his, Dr. Davenant, was then President."—*Anonymous Life*, p. 3.

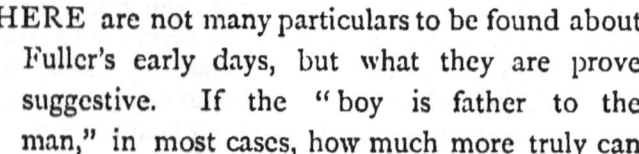HERE are not many particulars to be found about Fuller's early days, but what they are prove suggestive. If the "boy is father to the man," in most cases, how much more truly can these words be spoken of our hero. He was sent to a private school in his own village, which was kept by the Rev. Arthur Smith, who was probably of Emmanuel College, Cambridge. This Mr. Smith was for some time "Curat" of Mr. Brown, Rector of Achurch, the Brownist, and founder of the sect, which ultimately became the Independent. After leaving the national Church, and founding the Brownists, propagating his theories of Church Government —the autonomy of each several congregation—in Holland and subsequently at Norwich, where many Dutch were settled, he returned to the Church of his baptism (leaving however his mantle to one, Harrison, to carry on the schism), and was preferred to the rich living of Achurch, by his kinsman, one of the Cecil family. Mr. Smith was his "Curat" during Mr. Brown's absence, between 1617 and

1626, and as locum tenens his name frequently occurs in the parish registers.

This Mr. Smith was not a good schoolmaster, if we can trust the author of "An Anonymous Life," for he was not διδακτικὸς apt to teach, although he was "plagiosus," a pædagogue given to the rod. Fuller does not seem to have learned much under his tuition, with whom he spent about four years. Yet he had a very high estimation of the duties of a schoolmaster : witness his essay in the "Holy State," and his panegyric on Thomas ·Robertson. Anent the latter faculty for education, he says, "Every *boy* can teach a *man* ; whereas he must be a man that can teach a *boy*. It is easy to inform them who are able to understand, but it must be a masterpiece of industry and discretion to descend to the capacity of children." Speaking of the scholastic profession, he says, "There is scarce any profession in the Commonwealth more necessary, which is so slightly performed. The reasons whereof I conceive to be these : first, young scholars make this calling their refuge, yea, perchance before they have taken any degree in the University, commence schoolmasters in the country, as if nothing else was required to set up this profession but only a rod and a ferula. Secondly, others who are able, use it only as a passage to better preferment, to patch the rents in their present future, till they can provide a new one, and betake themselves to some more gainful calling. Thirdly, they are disheartened from doing their best, with the miserable reward which, in some places, they receive, being master to the children, and slaves to the parents. Fourthly, being grown rich they grow negligent, and scorn to touch the school, but by the proxy of an usher."

Doubtless we should never have heard of the schoolmaster,
Mr. Arthur Smith, but for the celebrity of his pupil, Dr.
Fuller.   But to quote from "the good schoolmaster" once
more, "Who had ever heard of R. Bond, of Lancashire, but
for the breeding of learned Ascham, his scholar; or of
Hartgrave, of Mundley School, in the same county, but
because he was first to teach worthy Dr. Whitaker. Nor
do I honour the memory of Mulcaster for anything so
much as for his scholar, that gulf of Learning, Bishop
Andrewes.   This made the Athenians, the day before the
great feast of Theseus, their founder, to sacrifice a ram to
the memory of Conidas his schoolmaster that first instructed
him.*"   The elder Fuller would seem to have devoted his
firstborn son to the service of that Church, in which so many
members of his family had engaged.   It was a father's best
gift, and he did· not begrudge such an offering, nor did he
know of that silly saying, which obtained in a past generation, that "any thing was good enough for the Church." And
it was with this view that his education was carefully
superintended by his father, who was fully qualified to take
it in hand.   He got on quickly enough when he was transferred from the tuition of Mr. Smith to that of the Parson of
Aldwinckle, for "in a little while, such a proficiency was
visibly seen in him, that it was a question whether he owed
more to his father for his birth or education."

The key-note of the boy's character at this time was
diligence, and a close attention to his studies.   "He was
admirably learned, before it could be supposed that he had
been taught." His progress was remarkable, and he literally

------

* (*Holy State*, p, 88).

devoured books, and his intense application to his studies followed him through his whole career. He was a very precocious lad, one who would be called an "old boy." He would have been called "ingenious and industrious" in that "Grammar of boys' natures," which he holds a good schoolmaster would soon be able to make of his scholar. "The conjunction of two such planets in a youth," he says, "presage much good unto him."

In " Aubrey's Letters " there is a memorial of Fuller's early days, by Aubrey, who was intimate with Fuller's cousin, and with other members of the family, to the following effect : " He was a boy of pregnant wit, and when the Bishop (Davenant, his uncle) and his father were discoursing he would be by, and hearken, and now and then put in, beyond expectation of his years. He was of a middle stature, strong set, curled hair, a very working head, insomuch that, walking and meditating before dinner, he would eat up a penny loaf, not knowing that he did it." We have then presented to our view, a lad (as prefiguring his after years) of " pleasant ruddiness," " grave and serious aspect," and " comely light-coloured hair," fond of the company and conversation of his seniors, which no doubt he did much to enliven. In the grave and witty society of his father's quaint parsonage, no doubt our hero imbibed his prolific and inveterate habit of punning—which he illustrated so freely in his subsequent writings as an author. Every one was a punster in those days both wit and poet, politician and theologian. Addison tells us in the *Spectator* (No. 61) that " the age in which the punn chiefly flourished was the reign of King James I. That learned monarch was himself a tolerable punster, and made

very few Bishops or Privy Councillors, that had not sometime or other signalized themselves, by a clinch or a *conun-*
drum. It was, therefore, in this age when the punn
appeared in pomp and dignity. It had before been admitted into merry speeches and ludicrous compositions, but
was now delivered with great gravity from the pulpit, or
pronounced in the most solemn manner at the Council-
table. The greatest authors, in their most serious works,
made frequent use of punns. The sermons of Bishop
Andrewes and the tragedies of Shakespeare are full of them.
The sinner was punned into repentance by the former, as
in the latter nothing is more usual than to see a hero
weeping and quibbling for a dozen lines together."

Fuller therefore followed the literary "form" of the age
in which he lived, but from his own natural predisposition
out of the alembic of his own mother wit—*crassa Minerva,*
as the Romans would have said—he raised the mere
fashion of punning and verbal alliteration, to the dignity
of genuine English wit. Surrounded by the quaint and
witty, the boy became quaint and witty too, and such was
the bent of his natural genius, he excelled them all in a
line in which they were all more or less famous. He "was
well learned, especially in history : *very witty* and very
pleasant in discourse. He would often give a smart jest,
which would make the place both blush and bleed where it
lighted. Yet this was the better taken at his hands,
because he cherished not a cowardly wit in himself to wound
men behind their backs, but played on them freely to their
faces : yea, and never refused the coin they paid him in,
but would be contented to be the subject of a good jest,
and sometimes he was well favourably met with, as the bes.

fencer in wit's school hath now and then an unhappy blow dealt him."*

Aubrey also tells us that Fuller had a most excellent appetite, and was blessed with a good and strong constitution. He was robust and broad shouldered, and when he was middle-aged thankfully acknowledged that he had never had a day's illness in his life. In this respect he has presented a remarkable contrast to that of most students, where the attenuated frame, the transparent hand, and the rose taken out of the cheek, attest the constant and painful worker, and the midnight oil.

Brought up by a studious father, and surrounded by learned theologians and wits, we are not surprised to find that young Fuller was very fond of books, and of books he chose the solid and the wiser sort, nor did the boy disdain pictures. On the contrary, he seems to have preferred them, and amongst his chief favourites was " Foxe's Book of Martyrs," illustrated, and folio edition. It is impossible to overrate the power of such a book as this, especially on the youthful imagination, and the telling effect of its pictures. " When a child I loved to look on the pictures in the ' Book of Martyrs ' " he says, in his " Mixt Contemplations." We can well picture to ourselves the precocious boy, with his ruddy cheeks, his light curly hair, and his witty expression of eye, sitting in the quaint old Parsonage at the feet of his aged but saintly grandmother, who had lived in the days of Mary, and stood in awe in the presence of Bishop Gardiner, at Farnham Castle. The old lady would be only too pleased to talk of those terrible days, to her witty and

---

* (*Holy Warre*, vol. ii., c. xxiv.)

intelligent grandchild for auditor.　Her influence and that
of his father's is seen in the "Life of Bishop Ridley," which
he wrote against those who have "cried down" the martyrs
of that age, but especially against "the author of the book
lately printed of '*Causes hindering Reformation in England,*'"
a John Milton, of whom Fuller says, "One lately hath traduced them with such language as neither beseemed his
parts, whosoever he was that spake it, nor their piety of
whom it was spoken." "When I was a child I was possessed of a reverend esteem for them (the Marian Martyrs),
as most holy and pious men, dying martyrs in the reign of
Queen Mary for the profession of the truth ; which opinion
having from my parents taken quiet possession of my soul,
they must be very forcible reasons which eject it." No
wonder, stimulated by such surroundings, he learned to
reverence the memories of "our first reformers, reverend
Cranmer, learned Ridley, downright Latimer, zealous
Bradford, pious Philpot, patient Hooper, men that had
their failings, but worthy in their generations."

The illustrations, rude and quaint though they were, made
such a vivid impression, that our author could well recall
them forty years afterwards, yielding them from the "mindful tablets of his memory."

> "Profuse in garniture of wooden cuts,
> 　　Strange and uncouth : dire faces, figures dire,
> 　　Sharp-kneed, sharp elbowed, and lean-ankled too,
> 　　With long and ghastly shanks—forms which, once seen,
> 　　Could never be forgotten."—*Wordsworth.*

Fuller never forgot his illustrated copy of "Foxe's Book of
Martyrs" all through life, and in writing his "Church
History," Foxe was always at his elbow.　He loved the

book, he revelled in it, and in his " Good Thoughts " he has
given us some idea of the childish thoughts which struck him.
" I thought that there (*i.e.*, in the pictures in the book) the
martyrs at the stake seemed like the three children in the
fiery furnace, ever since I had known them there, not one
hair more of their head was burnt, nor any smell of the fire
singeing of their clothes. This made me think martyrdom
was nothing. But, oh ! though the lion be painted fiercer
than he is, the fire is far fiercer than *it* is painted. Thus it
is easy for one to endure an affliction, as he limns it out in
his own fancy, and represents it to himself but in a bare
speculation. But when it is brought indeed and laid home
to us, there must be a man, yea, there must be God to
assist the man to undergo it."

His love for his Bible also was very strong. The Bible
is, as we know, a well of undefiled English, and has done
much in forming the style of many a writer by its terse,
vigorous, and Saxon language. Archbishop Sharpe said
that the Bible and Shakespeare had made him Archbishop
of York. Like Timothy, he must have known the Scriptures
from a child, which is proved by his so often quoting from
the Old Bibles used anterior to the translation of King
James. He could never forget the phrases and words he
had been accustomed to in his youthood, although he must
have prized the new version, if only from the fact that many
of his relations or connections assisted in its compilation.
We subjoin some of the alterations. The phrase "at
adventures," 1 Kings xxii. 34, is given in the new translation
"at a venture" in his "Pisgah-sight." We find also
pismire (for ant) as a quotation from Prov. vi. 6. (" Pisgah-
sight.") " Preach *you* on the housetops," as if quoted from

Matt. x. 27. Again, "His behaviour was as though he would go to Jerusalem," instead of "his face," was quoted from Luke ix. 53. The following words also occur, "clouts," which occurs in Jeremiah xxxviii. 11, 12, and "clods," which is given as a quotation from Luke xxii. 44. But then changes are inevitable in every new translation, and we, in our days, may witness something of the kind when the new revised translation comes into circulation and use.

When Fuller was about five years old, his grandmother, Margaret Davenant, who had apparently come to live with or near them, died, and was buried in St. Peter's Church. Three years later, a tablet was put up to her memory on the south wall, and an inscription, which we have already given. It contains the arms of Davenant and Clarke.

In the locality in which young Fuller spent his boyhood, there were many things observable and remarkable, and we may be quite sure that, under the stimulating tuition of his father, these would not be lost in forming his character. We have already alluded to Dryden, and his connection with Aldwinckle.

There was *Fotheringhay Castle*, near Oundle, and the tragedy which had been connected therewith, in the matter of Mary Queen of Scots. The room in which she was beheaded had been bought by Sir Richard Cotton, furniture and all, and set up in his house at Conington. The castle had been partly dismantled, but in his youth he had read in one of the rooms the verses penned by Queen Mary "in a window with a pointed diamond"—

> "From the top of all my trust,
> Mishap hath laid me in the dust."

This castle was also famous for being the birthplace of Richard Plantagenet (Crookback).

In the same direction, further on, near *Stamford*, was the magnificent mansion, turreted and quaint, built by Queen Elizabeth's great minister, Lord Burghley, which hospitable mansion had some years before opened its gates to entertain King James in his triumphant progress from Scotland to the metropolis, and the seat of Government. There were many other noble mansions in the vicinity. "No county in England," says Fuller, "yielding more noble men, no noble men in England having fairer habitations."

Young Fuller might have seen at *Geddington* village, the site of the ancient palace connected with many of our earliest Kings and Parliaments. And here too, at a place where three roads meet, is a perfect specimen raised by Edward I. in memory of Queen Eleanor. It is a triangular erection, and is still in the same preservation as it must have been in Fuller's time.

West of Aldwinckle is *Grafton-under-Woods*, which is associated with another Queen, Elizabeth Woodville, of whom every Queens' man ought to be proud, for she had much to do with the founding or finishing of the College of S. Margaret and S. Bernard, commonly called Queens' College, in Cambridge. Fuller believes she was born here. "Her memory," says he, "is most remarkable for the finishing Queens' College, in Cambridge, where I had my first breeding, and for it and all therein I shall ever have an unfeigned affection."

There were two notables in the neighbourhood in which young Fuller spent his early days. Brown, the founder of the Brownists sect, or Independents, and Francis Tresham so active with the Gunpowder plot. " God in His providence fixed my nativity," he says, " in a *remarkable place,* Aldwinckle. This village was distanced one good mile from Achurch, where Mr. Brown, the founder of the Brownists, did dwell, whom, out of curiosity when a youth, I did often visit. It was likewise a mile and a half distant east from *Siveden,* where Francis Tresham, Esquire, so active in the Gunpowder Treason, had a large demeasne and ancient habitation." The person of Brown was no doubt very familiar to both our author and his father, as he had been connected with the Church from 1591 to 1630. Fuller seems often to have gone over to Achurch, to see a man who had given so much trouble to those in authority. " For my own part," Fuller says, in his " Church History " (whose nativity placed within a mile of this Brown his pastoral care), " I have, when a youth, often beheld him." Fuller therefore had ample opportunities of knowing about one who was the founder of the modern Independents, introducing principles, and an ecclesiastical regimen, the most inimical of all to the claims of the National Church. From the position of his birthplace, between Brown on the one hand and Tresham on the other, Fuller imbibed the virtue of moderation, and hit the *via media* of the Church of England. In his " Thoughts " he says, " My nativity may mind me of *moderation,* whose cradle was rocked between two rocks. Now, seeing I was never such a churl as to eat my morsel alone, let such as like my prayer join with me therein; God grant that we may hit the golden mean, and endeavour to avoid all extremes—the fanatic *Anabaptist* on one side, and the fiery zeal of the *Jesuit* on the other—that so we may be true Protestants, or which is a far better name, *real Christians* indeed."

This moderation was one of the strong points of Fuller's character. It was his pleasant dwelling place, and in his excellent essay on the subject he endorses the apothegm of his friend Bishop Hall by quoting it ; " Moderation is the silken string running through the pearl chain of all the virtues."

The dialect of the district where Fuller spent his youth is as pure as any in England, which must have exercised a beneficial influence upon his speech and diction. It is remarkably pure even on the lips of ploughboys, and both Latham and other philologists acknowledge that the Northamptonship dialect in or near where Fuller was brought up is the purest in England, just as Tours and Blois are the parts where the purest French is spoken. This purity of diction is alluded to by Fuller himself in his " Worthies." The language of the common people is generally the best of any shire in England, a proof whereof, when a boy, I received from a hand-labouring man herein, which since my judgment : " We speak, I believe," said he, " as good English as any shire in England, because though in the singing Psalms some words are used to make the metre unknown to us, yet the last translation of the Bible, which no doubt was done by those learned men in the best English, agreeth perfectly with the common speech of our country." And again, " The English of the common people therein (lying in the very heart of the land) is generally very good."

Fuller's writings contain a great many old Bible words, and, like Dryden—who also received some of his early education in the neighbouring village of Tichmarsh—are remarkable for vigorous diction, which we can likewise trace to the dialect of the country. His style was massive and Saxon, full of a number of uncommon but expressive words which must have been acquired by lengthened intercourse with the people. If he uses words of a sesquipedalia character, or classical derivation, it is mostly for the sake of punning. And to this all agree. Marsh says "They, *i.e.*, our author and Sir Thomas Browne are both remarkable for a wide range of vocabulary, Fuller inclining to a Saxon, and Browne to a Latinised diction, and their syntax is marked by the same peculiarities as their nomenclature." Archbishop Trench, whom we have already quoted, says that few writers are more important than Fuller for the study of English, and Coleridge uses the following strong language : " Fuller's language ! Grant me patience, Heaven ! a tithe of his beauties would be sold cheap for a whole library of our classical writers, from Addison to Johnson and Junius inclusive." And Bishop Nicholson, a painstaking old charwoman of the antiquarian and rubbish concern ! " The venerable rust and dust of the whole firm are not worth an ounce of Fuller's earth."

Meanwhile Fuller's uncles were being preferred in the Church. In 1617 Townson was introduced at Court, and was made chaplain to King James. He was subsequently made Dean of Westminster, and in 1618 it was his melancholy duty to attend the execution of Sir Walter Raleigh, in Palace Yard, of whose last hours he has left a touching and graphic account. In 1620 he was appointed to the see of Salisbury, and consecrated July 9th, at Lambeth, but he did not long enjoy his preferment, as he died 15th May, 1621, prematurely of a fever, the result of a chill, and was buried in Westminster Abbey. The King (James) was very fond of both divines, and selected Davenant to succeed Townson in the see of Salisbury, which see he held for many years, and the tablet to his memory is still to be seen in Salisbury Cathedral. He had been President of Queens' College, and Margaret Professor of Divinity, Cambridge. In 1619 he had been elected one of the delegates to the synod of Dort. Hall and Carleton (afterwards Bishops) and Dr. Ward, Master of Sidney Sussex College, were his associates. Hacket says of him, " What a pillar he was in the synod of Dort is to be read in the judgments of the British divines inserted in the public Acts, his part being best in that work, and that work being far the best in the compliments of that synod." One of their acts was the order for the translation of the Bible. The British Divines returned after seven months' absence. They met with their reward—a liberal payment of the States, and early preferment at the hands of King James. A gold medal was struck to commemorate the event, representing the synod in session. Davenant returned to his lectures in the schools, the collegiate cure, until called away to his preferment in the Bishopric to which, " by an unusual rise," he was elected within a month of the death of his brother-in-law.

CHAPTER V.

COLLEGE DAYS (QUEENS').—1621-9.

" But this (then disqualifying Statute at Queens') gave him a fair occasion to transfer himself to *Sidney College*, whither by some of his choice and learned friends he had often been invited."—*Anonymous Life*, p. 4.

T the early age of twelve—the age among the Jews for becoming a "son of the law"—Fuller was removed from the parental roof, and sent up to Cambridge. Students entered the University much earlier in those days to what they do now, and it is said that Jeremy Taylor was entered even younger, so that going up so young need not be put down to any particular precocity. Still, it must be admitted that twelve is very early to begin student life, and be it remembered the number of students in those days exceeded that at the present time. He was entered at the ancient and loyal College of St. Margaret and St. Bernard, commonly called Queens', one of the three royal collegiate foundations of the University. This was about the time of the death of his uncle, Bishop Townson, Bishop of Salisbury. Fuller himself allows that the age was " very young," and in his " History of Cambridge " says of the Franciscans there, 1384, that they " surprised many when children into their order, before they could well distinguish between a *cap* and a *cowl*, whose time ran on from their admission therein, and so they became Masters of *Arts* before they were masters of *themselves*."

In the choice of a college—one of the most important steps in life, second only to a choice of a profession or a wife—no doubt Fuller's father had many friends in the University, and indeed himself was still connected with it, who would be in a position to advise him. Among others he would naturally consult his own brother-in-law (Davenant), at that time President of Queens' College, and Margaret Professor of Divinity. The Fullers were also on intimate terms with Dr. Ward, Master of Sidney Sussex College, and about this time (1620) Vice-Chancellor of the University. The result was that it was finally determined to enter him at his uncle's college—which has been always regarded as the family college—the college of the Davenants, the Townsons, the Fullers (both on the theological and medical side, for these seem to have been the two professions the family principally addicted themselves to), and he was accordingly entered on Friday, June 29th, 1621. Why he was entered at the end of the academical year, deponent sayeth not, for the Cambridge academical year begins in the October term, except it may have been to save a term.

It was endowed with revenues to the amount of £200 per annum for the support of a President and four fellows. The first stone of the chapel was laid, for the Queen, by Sir John Wenlock (afterwards slain at Tewkesbury), who caused the following inscription to be engraved on it : " Exit Domina nostra Margaretta Dominus in Refugium et lapis iste in Signum " (The Lord be a refuge to our lady, Queen Margaret, and this stone shall be a token thereof).

The civil wars soon after interrupted the work, but Andrew Dokett, the President, obtained, besides several other considerable benefactions, the patronage of Elizabeth Woodville, Queen of Edward IV., and the number of fellows was increased to nineteen, and forty-five scholarships were founded, recently consolidated into fewer. The Lady Elizabeth has since been annually celebrated as a co-foundress. The endowments were much increased by Richard III., and various benefactors.

The College of St. Margaret and St. Bernard, commonly called Queens' College, was so called from the two Queens, the one who began to build it in 1448, Margaret of Anjou, wife of Henry VI., and the other, Elizabeth Woodville, wife of Edward VI., to whom reference has been already made, and who completed it. Thus, as Fuller observes, "the two houses of York and Lancaster had their *first amity* in that foundation." It is entered by a lofty gateway, with a tower, upon which are emblazoned the arms of Queen Margaret. There is an air of antiquity about it, and the buildings are much admired. The gateway is said to contain the oldest brickwork in England, and no antiquarian or architectural enthusiast would dream of leaving Cambridge without having paid a visit to Queens'. From the first quadrangle, which is 96 feet long and 84 broad, there is a passage into the second, where most of the fellows reside, in an angle of which is Erasmus' tower and rooms. Through another passage we pass out into the Walnut-tree Court, one of the most charming learned retirements in the whole university. On the right hand of the quadrangle, to one entering, is the venerable chapel, lately restored, and opposite is the Hall and combination-room leading therefrom. The Hall is large, handsome, and well proportioned, and contains the following portraits : Sir Thomas Smith, the eminent Greek scholar, half-length and dressed in a fur cloak, leaning on a globe :

Elizabeth Woodville, Consort of Edward IV., a very fine painting ; the learned Erasmus, seated at a table writing, and dressed in a fur cloak. On the west side is a full-length portrait of Joshua King, LL.D., the late President. The large oriel window has recently been ornamented with the arms of the foundresses, presidents, and other distinguished persons, and the side windows with the arms of the Earl of Hardwicke, Earl of Stamford, and Sir Henry Russell. The combination-room contains a fine portrait of Dr. Milner, President, and Dean of Carlisle, who also left 3,000 valuable works to the Library. Between the Hall and Chapel is a splendid Library of 30,000 volumes, one of the finest in Cambridge, and the Librarian is selected from one of the undergraduates, who usually holds the Clark's scholarship with it. In the Library are all the Greek and Latin works of Sir Thomas Smith, a fine copy of the Antwerp Polyglot Bible in eight folios, above 100 volumes given by Henry Hastings, Earl of Huntingdon ; 60 folios given by Dr. Tindal, Dean of Ely ; 600 volumes bequeathed by the learned John Smith, 1650 ; 13 Persian and Turkish MSS., rare missals and Roman service books, and a perfect repertoire of old and choice works. The whole buildings are very striking, and when seen by moonlight have a quaint weird look about them. The President's Lodge, which is commodious and extensive, contains many valuable pictures, and an altar-piece from the chapel ; it is at the corner of the inner court, cloistered on three sides, each about 80 feet in length, which leads out from the Walnut-tree Court, and is entered by a door in the cloisters. It abuts on the river, and the front presents a neat oriel. Queens' now ranks as one of the smaller colleges, but in young Fuller's time it ranked fifth in point of numbers, having, including tutors, about 290 members resident.   One of its chief worthies is Erasmus, the celebrated reformer and writer of the "Colloquies," who came to this university to complete his theological studies, and for some time it was believed held the chair of theology (Margaret).   He selected Queens', although, as Fuller says, "no doubt he might have picked and chosen what house he pleased."   The south-west tower in the old court—we may borrow Fuller's words even now—"still retaineth its name." Erasmus' study is on the top of this tower, from which there is a pleasant prospect.   The writer's first rooms at Cam - bridge, before he removed to the Walnut-tree Court (Staircase H), were in this tower, so the reader will kindly excuse his dwelling so long upon them.   " Erasmus' walk " is to be found on the other side of the river, over the Mathe- matical Bridge, where are the College Gardens and grounds, for the Undergraduates of Queens', which are truly collegiate, adorned by some fine trees, overhanging a beautiful terrace on the banks of the river, stretching on to King's, with a pretty view of Clare College.   Queens' boasts of a number of eminent men, five Bishops, among whom are John Poynet, called the (*boy*) Bishop of Winchester, 1550, Anthony Sparrow, of Norwich, and Simon Patrick, of Ely. It is worthy of remark that the President, Fellows, and Scholars were, in 1642, without one exception, ejected for refusing to subscribe the covenant.

Erasmus "often complained of the college ale," says Fuller, "*cervisia hujus loci, mihi nullo modo placet*, as raw, small, and windy : whereby it appears (1) ale in that age was the constant beverage of all colleges before the innovation of beer (the child of hops) was brought into England ; (2) Queens' College *cervisia* was not *vis cereris* but *ceres vitiata.* In my time (when I continued member of that house) scholars, continued Erasmus' his complaint : whilst the brewers, having, it seems (prescription on their side for long time) little amended it. The best was, Erasmus had his lagena or flagon of wine (recruited weekly from his friends in London), " which he drank sometimes singly by itself, and *sometimes encouraged his faint ale with the mixture thereof.*" No one can complain of the Queens' College ale of the present day, as with King's and Trinity, the other two Royal Colleges, it has the privilege of brewing its own ale, and the strength of the "Audit ale" is notorious. As was natural, Fuller had a great respect and admiration for the great scholar, and frequently mentions him in his writings. He often quotes from his *Colloquia and Adagia,* which seem to have been his favourites. He considered Desiderius Erasmus to be a greater scholar than divine. A full length portrait of him, together with those of the foundresses, adorns the Hall.

When Fuller began his college days at Queens,' his uncle, Davenant, was still its President, although he was Bishop Designate of Salisbury, which appointment he had just received in May. He had been the head of his College for six years, and his qualifications for the post were of a high order. He took great interest in the students and their studies, and his departure was much regretted, for his influence with them was very great. His nephew relates that when "taking leave of the College, and one, John Rolfe, an ancient servant thereof, he desired him to pray for him, and when the other modestly returned that he rather needed his Lordship's prayers; 'yea, John,' said he, 'and I need thine

too, being now to enter into a calling, wherein I shall meet
with many and great temptations.'" Fuller says, "*Præfuit
qui profuit* was the motto written in most of his books, the
sense whereof he practised in his conversation."

His uncle, Davenant, would have a thorough knowledge of
his nephew's talents and powers, before quitting the Presidentship of the College for his Bishopric, and no doubt had made
every preparation for the supervision of young Fuller's
course of study, and arranged his curriculum. His interest
remained unabated during the whole of his nephew's career,
as his letters to Dr. Ward, Master of Sidney Sussex College,
when he had taken his B.A. degree some seven years afterwards, sufficiently testify.

Davenant was consecrated Bishop the following November 18th, and finally resigned the mastership of the College,
which he would fain have held with it. On the same day
were consecrated Laud to St. David's, and Carey to Exeter,
both appointments being mainly due to Lord Keeper
Williams, lately preferred to Lincoln. Fuller tells us that
his uncle, whom he regarded as a paragon of all clerical
excellence, received consecration at the hands of Archbishop Abbott, in spite of the irregularity under which that
prelate was supposed to lie, on account of his having
accidentally shot a gamekeeper, "by some squeamish
and nice-conscienced elects." After his consecration,
Fuller tells us, "being to perform some personal service to
King James, at Newmarket, he refused to ride on the Lord's
Day : and came, though a day late to the Court, no less
welcome to the King, not only accepting his excuse, but also
commending his seasonable forbearance." Davenant afterwards "magnified King James's bounty to him, who, from a

private master, without any other immediate preferment, advanced him by an unusual rise."

Aubrey tells us that many leases of the lands of the See " were but newly expired when Davenant came to this See, so that there tumbled into his coffers vast summes."

When he finally quitted Queens', and settled at Salisbury, he was joined by his widowed sister, Margaret, and her children, who took up their abode at the episcopal palace, finding there, as her epitaph records, "consolation and a home." From letters extant, the Bishop, we find, was anxious to advance these children, and to get his two nieces comfortably settled in life. The Bishop himself was never married, and it is narrated by Camden that King James, when he bestowed the bishopric upon him, forbade him to take a wife. Davenant was long enough connected with Queens', as its President, to give it a distinct theological tone, which we might have expected from his holding the Chair of Margaret Professor of Theology, whence he influenced the University with it. His reputation as a theologian was so great, that he was one of the English prelates selected to attend, as we have seen, the Synod of Dort. His Commentary on St. Paul's Epistle to the Colossians is a standard work. Like most of the divines in the reign of King James, he had strong Calvinistic tendencies, but these were much modified by his sound learning ; at the same time he shared the strong feelings against Popery, peculiar to that period. He treated the Puritans with tolerance and even kindness, being a gentle presser of Conformity when Bishop, but he was a great stickler for the old canonical ceremonies of that reign. His divinity was of a practical cast and moderate,

D

and he strongly held the doctrine of universal redemption. Fuller had the greatest respect for his uncle's character and attainments, being much thrown with him in his early days, and he followed the Bishop's churchmanship all through life, with a very large circle of his connections, which, indeed, did very much to perpetuate it. Mr. Russell sums up his character as "a man in whom piety and sound learning were united to a degree, perhaps, rarely excelled." (Page 303.)

Bishop Davenant was succeeded in the Presidentship by Dr. Mansel in 1622, which post he held for nine years, and was therefore Master of the College during the whole of Fuller's student life. There are no records concerning him of any moment : but to his eternal disgrace, or that of the College authorities, or both, Fuller, with all his brilliancy, was never elected Fellow of that House, in spite of all the Bishop's influence, nor did he, as a matter of course, receive a College living. Whoever may be at fault, it is a matter which has never been satisfactorily cleared up.

The two tutors, under which Fuller was placed at Queens', were Mr. Edward Davenant, and Mr. Thorpe. Mr. Davenant was the Bishop's nephew, and, therefore, Fuller's cousin. His father was a London merchant, a great mathematician, a better Greek scholar than the Bishop, and, according to Aubrey, "an incomparable man." Edward was educated at Merchant Taylors', and then sent up to Queens', where he proved himself a ripe scholar, with a strong bent and genius for mathematics. He was one of the Fellows of Queens', having taken his B.A., 1614. Aubrey knew him well, and obtained from him most of his memorials about Dr. Fuller. When his uncle became

Bishop of Salisbury, he received from him, first of all, a Prebendal stall, and subsequently the treasurership of the Cathedral (1630). He was also rector of Gillingham, in Dorset. He became Archdeacon of Berks, and received Paulshot Parsonage, near Devizes. Aubrey speaks of him in the highest terms, and calls him "*my* singular good friend, a man not only of vast learning, but great goodness and charity: he was very ready to teach and instruct: he did me the favour to inform me first in algebra; his daughters were algebrists." Mathematics was his favourite study, to which he would naturally direct young Fuller's attention, into which he entered "with great contentment, using it as ballast for his soul, yet to fix it, not to stall it, nor suffers he it to be so unmannerly as to jostle out other arts." (Holy State, Chapter vii.)

Under this tutor it was Fuller cultivated the art of memory, which brought him in after life such remarkable fame. He taught his pupils to repeat without notes what they had heard or just read, and Fuller may have got his method in his mind when he subsequently wrote his essay on "Memory." Much is not recorded of Fuller's other tutor, Dr. Thorpe, but he calls him "my ever-honoured tutor: not so much beneath him" (another Thorpe) "in logic, as above him in the skill of divinity and an holy conversation." What a bond of union there must have been between College tutor and student, when the pupil could so write of his instructor so many years after.

Among the celebrities connected with Queens' at that time was Dr. John Preston, one of the Fellows of that Society, and a tutor very successful with his pupils; John Goodwin, a great advocate of religious toleration, and an

uncompromising champion of the Independent cause ; and
Herbert Palmer, who became President in 1644, in place of
the ejected Dr. Martin.   He received the living of Ashwell
from Laud, and took many pupils, being very careful of
their religious training, as well as their education.
Subsequently, he became one of the assessors of the
Assembly of Divines.   John Weever, the antiquary,
another of the worthies of Queens', was also at the
College about this time.   And such were the tutors, and
such some of his associates, when Fuller commenced his
student life in the old royal foundation, in which he entered
with characteristic ardour.   College life and academical
habits were very different in those days to those which
obtain now, and our modern students affect.   Prayers were
said in the College Chapel every morning at *five* o'clock,
and then after breakfast began the regular work of the day.
"It consisted of two parts—the *College studies*, or the
attendance of the students on the lectures and examinations
of the College tutors, or lecturers in Latin, Greek, logic,
mathematics, physics, &c.   And the *University's exercises*,
or the attendance of the students, together with the students
of other Colleges, in the *public schools* of the University,
either to hear the lectures of the University professors of
Greek, logic, &c. (which, however, was not incumbent on
all students), or to hear and take part in the public
disputations of those students of all the Colleges, who
were preparing for their degree."   Dinner was at twelve
o'clock, after which a short attendance was given to the
disputations.   Students were expected to attend evensong,
and supper was served at seven o'clock, and they retired to
rest about nine or ten o'clock, this time being their own.

The course of studies in the "Liberal arts" took about seven years, the curriculum being divided into two periods of four and three years.

We cannot do better than give the course of study from the pen of Fuller himself, under the title of "The General Artist." "I know the general cavil against general learning is this, that *aliquis in omnibus est nullus in singulis :* he that sips of many arts drinks of none. However, we must know that all learning, which is but one grand science, hath so homogeneal a body, that the parts thereof do, with a mutual service, relate to, and communicate strength and lustre each to other. Our learning, knowing language to be the key of learning, thus begins :

1. His tongue being one by nature he gets cloven by art and industry. Before the confusion of Babel all the world was one continent in language, since divided into several tongues as several islands. Grammar is the ship by benefit whereof we pass from one to another, in the learned languages generally spoken in no country. His mother tongue was like the dull music of a monochord, which by study he turns into the harmony of several instruments.

2. He first gaineth skill in the Latin and Greek tongues. On the credit of the former alone, he may trade all over Christendom. But the Greek, though not so generally spoken, is known with no less profit and more pleasure. The joints of her compounded words are so naturally oiled that they run nimbly on the tongue, which makes them, though long, never tedious, because significant.

3. Hence he proceeds to the Hebrew, the mother tongue of the world. More pains than quickness of wit is required to get it, and with daily exercise he continues it. Apostacy

herein is usual to fall totally from the language by a little neglect.

4. Then he applies his studies to logic and ethics. The latter makes a man's soul mannerly and wise : but as for logic, that is the armoury of reason, furnished with all offensive and defensive weapons.   There are *syllogisms*, long swords : *enthymemes*, short daggers : *dilemmas*, two-edged swords that cut on both sides : *sorites*, chain-shot : and for the defensive, *distinctions*, which are shields : *retortions*, which are targets with a spike in the middest of them, both to defend and oppose.   From hence he raiseth his studies to the knowledge of *physics*, the great hall of nature, and *metaphysics*, the closet thereof : and is careful not to wade therein so far, till by subtle distinguishing of notions he confounds himself.

5. He is skilled in rhetoric, which gives a speech colour, as logic doth favour, and both together beauty.   Though some condemn rhetoric as the mother of lies, speaking more than the truth in hyperboles, less in her meiosis, otherwise in her metaphors, contrary in her ironies, yet is there excellent use of all these, when disposed of with judgment. Nor is he a stranger to poetry, which is music in words ; nor to music, which is poetry in sound.

6. Mathematics he moderately studieth.

7. Hence he makes his study into the progress of history.   Nestor, who lived three ages, was accounted the wisest man in the world.   But the historian may make himself wise by living as many ages as have past since the beginning of the world.   His books enable him to maintain discourse, who besides the stock of his own experience, may speed on the common purse of his reading.   This directs

him in his life, so that he makes the shipracks of others sea-
marks to himself : yea, accidents which others start from for
their strangeness, he welcomes as his wonted acquaintance,
having found precedents for them formerly. Without history
a man's soul is purblind, seeing only the things which almost
touch his eyes.

8. He is well seen in Chronology.

Then taking these sciences in their general latitude, he
hath finished the round circle or golden ring of the arts ;
only he keeps a place for the diamond to be set in : I mean
for that predominant profession of law, physic, divinity, or
state policy, which he intends for his principal calling hereafter."

This, then, is a sketch of the curriculum through which our
young student passed. By it he became " so general a
scholar that it was his insight into everything he had read
(together with his thinking and meditating nature, out of
which he could not be got sometimes for several hours
together) made his fancy so nimble that as soon as he heard
any subject, he was able to speak to it, taking not above two
hours' time to recollect himself for his sermons."

A student's life is generally uneventful. Fuller's undergraduate days sped their usual flight, the only events likely
to relieve their monotony being the royal visits, which happened from time to time, when the King was hunting at
Newmarket and Royston, and received invitations to Cambridge. On one such occasion "the young scholars, dressed
according to their degree, were placed in order from Jesus
College gates unto Trinity College gates." When the King
was feasted at Trinity, the King was greeted everywhere with
cries of " Vivat Rex," and no doubt our young student

joined in this demonstration of loyalty, being both loyal himself and belonging to a foundation remarkable for its loyalty.
Then there would be the rejoicings (1623) upon the return
of Prince Charles from his impolitic matrimonial tour to
Spain, when, as Mede says, "our bells rang all that day,
and the towne made bonfires at night." Fuller would seem to
have much enjoyed and to have taken a lively interest in the
private theatricals and the Latin plays, which at that time
obtained at the University, not only at the time of the royal
visits, but which were allowed to be repeated at other times.
He may have acted himself.   At all events, he made the
acquaintance of the dramatic works of that dramatic age, and,
of course, especially of Shakespeare.   Several attempts
were made to put down these histrionic eventuations, but
they continued to flourish, and in some Colleges more than
others.   Thus, Queens' appears to have taken a prominent
place among them, and a play was acted there, called
"*Senile odium*," by the undergraduates in 1631.   It was
composed by a friend and neighbour of Fuller's, Peter
Hanstead, born at Oundle, near Aldwinckle.

But, in spite of all these attractions, our student never
forgot the object for which he was sent to the University,
and diligently pursued those usual academic studies, which
can only be learned at one time in life, and at one place.
This diligence is proved by his taking his first or B.A. degree
at the early age of seventeen, in the year 1625.   For this
degree students had to take part in two disputations before a
Moderator.   Each candidate had to be respondent, and to
give in three propositions to be maintained in Latin.   Other
examinations were also required, including questions from
the old Stagyrite Aristotle.   These tests having been com-

plied with, the successful candidates were duly announced by the Proctor, on the Thursday before Palm Sunday. Thus Fuller took his B.A. degree, Commemoration Day, at the end of the Lent term, 1624, together with fifty-one other students of Queens', having passed through his exercises with great *éclat*, which is expressly stated, and signed his name in the University subscription book to the newly-introduced Thirty-nine Articles. The first period of his student life was thus as successful, as it had been assiduous.

Our student had now three years more to reside and spend in his academical studies before he could proceed to the superior degree. For this he had to perform fresh acts, both in the public schools and separate colleges. During this time he began to be surrounded by a numerous circle of friends, for his genial disposition, his *bonhommie*, his ready wit, his genuine humour, were bound to make him a general favourite with his compeers and College companions. Aubrey says, " He was a pleasant, facetious person, and a *bonus socius.*" The friendships he made at Queens' were lasting, and at the lapse of thirty years he could remember many of them. Amongst his friends and acquaintance may be mentioned William Buckley, one of the Fellows, whom Fuller speaks of as "my worthy friend, lately gone to God"; Stephen Nettler, another Fellow, who wrote a learned work in answer to Selden's "Divine Right of Tithes"; William Johnson, another Fellow, who took great delight in the plays acted in the College; Edmund Gourney, another fellow, "an excellent scholar, who could be *humorous*, and would be *serious*, as he was himself disposed: his humours were never prophane towards God, or injurious towards his neighbour : which premised, none have cause to be *displeased* if in his fancies he *pleased* himself. Coming to me in Cambridge, when I was studying, he demanded of me the subject on which I studied. I told him I was collecting the witnesses of the Protestant religion through all ages even in the depth of Popery, conceiving it feasible, though difficult, to evidence them, ' It is a needless pains,' said he, ' for I know that I am descended from Adam, though I cannot prove my degree from him.' And yet, reader, be pleased to take notice that he was born of as good a family as any in Norfolk." Among Fuller's other acquaintances we may notice Thomas Edwards, the author of " Gangræna "; Sidrach Simpson, one of the five Congregationalists in the Westminster Assembly, 1643; who were both at Queens'.

King Charles was proclaimed king 30th of March, 1625, and the town and University of Cambridge seem to have given themselves up to unbounded joy at such a succession to the Crown. Troublous times, however, were in store for the nation ; and the struggle, which was then going on in the political world, soon began to be felt both in town and college. The students in those days probably took a more spirited interest in politics and political questions than they do now, and Queens' appears to have played by no means an unimportant part in these struggles.

In the disputed election between the Earl of Buckingham, as Chancellor of the University, and the Earl of Berkshire, " loving and loved of the University," the members of Queens', especially the students, took a most active part in promoting the candidature of the latter, which, however, proved unsuccessful, the Court favourite winning by four votes. No doubt this and other similar conflicts were preparing the students for the important part which they had to play a few years afterwards, when the kingdom found itself divided between Royalist and Roundhead : a conflict which had even then begun.

Mr. Bailey (in his voluminous biography) gives us an account of an interesting episode which took place at Midsummer Eve, this year, as recorded by Fuller in his " Worthies." A book containing " A Preparation to the Cross," and two other treatises on religion, was found in the belly of a codfish, which had been brought to Cambridge for sale. The affair created a great sensation. The book " was wrapped about with canvas, and probably that voracious fish plundered both out of the pocket of some shipwrecked seaman. The wits of the University made themselves merry thereat, one making a long copy of verses thereon, whereof this distich I remember—

> " If fishes then do bring in books, then we
> May hope to equal *Bodlye's Library.*"

But whilst the youngsters disported themselves therewith, the graver sort beheld it as a sad presage ; and some who little looked for the *Cross* have since found it in that place."

Young Fuller, it may be confidently asserted, was foremost among these wits. We wonder whether any of the bad jokes which follow may be attributed to him : " A young scholar (who had in a stationer's shop peeped into the titles of the civil law) there viewing this unconcocted book in the codfish, made a quiblet thereupon, saying that it might be found in the *Code*, but never could be entered into the *Digest :* " Another said or wrote, "that he would hereafter never count it a reproach to be called *Cod's head,* seeing that fish is now become so learned an *helluo librorum,"* which signifies a man of much reading, or skilful in many books. Another said, " that at the act of commencement for degrees, two things are principally expected, good learning and good cheer, whereupon this seaquest against the very term of commencement brought his book to furnish the one, and his carcase to make up the other."

We have another recollection of Fuller's college days in the following passage, where he is speaking of Latimer's sermon on the Cards — blunt preaching, which was then admirably effectual, but ridiculous now. " I remember in my time a country minister preached at St. Mary's : his text, Romans xii. 3, 'As God hath *dealt* to every man a measure of faith.' In a fond (foolish) imitation of Latimer's card sermon, he prosecuted the metaphor of *dealing,* that men should *play above board,* i.e., avoid all dissembling, not *pocket cards,* but improve their gifts and graces, *follow suit,* wear the surplice, and conform in ceremonies, &c. All produced nothing but laughter in the audience. Thus the *same actions* are by several persons and times made not the *same actions;* yea, differenced from commendable discretion to ridiculous absurdity. And thus he will make but bad music, who hath the *instrument and fiddlestick,* but none of the *rosin* of Mr. Latimer."

Fuller's anonymous biographer relates that he would have been elected to a Fellowship at Queens' College, but that the statutes forbade two fellowships to be held together at the same time by natives of his county. The same writer adds, that he might have had a dispensation, but declined it. The following correspondence, however, of his uncle, Bishop Davenant, with his intimate friend, Dr. Ward, would lead us—as Mr. Russell says in his Memorials —to infer that this account was altogether unfounded : in fact the reason why he was passed over has always been a mystery to us.

SALUTEM IN CHRISTO.

July 27th, 1626.

GOOD DR. WARD,

    I hope you will make a journey this summer into these western parts and visitt us here in Salisbury in your way. Had not God taken from vs our worthy friend I might perchance have accompanied unto Wells: but now these viadges are with mee at an end. I would intreat you to cast about, wher I may have ye best likelihood for preferring my nephew Sr Ffuller, to a fellowship, yf hee cannot speed in Queens Colledg Dr. Mansel has yet givin mee no answer one way or other, but I think ere long hee will. I pray when you come down this way so cast your business yt I may enjoy your company as long as your occasions will p'mitt: you cannot doe me a greater kindeness. And thus with my harty commendations I committ you to God and rest alwaies.

Your very loving friend,

JO: SARU.

To ye right woorll. his very loving friend Dr. Ward, Master of Sidney Colledg, and one of the publicq readers in Divinity, give this.

The next letter in which Sr Ffuller's name appears is dated Sept. 23rd, 1627, and written at Lacham, a seat of the Montagus, near Chippenham, with whom the Fullers seem to have been upon very intimate terms.

SALUTEM IN CHRISTO.

GOOD DR. WARD,

    So soon as I have opportunity I shall think of those points which you mentioned unto mee in your last letter. But I am at

this present unfurnished of bookes and am like so to continew
till I return to Sarū.   The number of those who die weekly is not
great ; but ye danger is that ever and anon some new house is
infected.   I pray God wee may savely return thither at Christmas.   I am now going to ye Bath, to try yf I can gett away
ye noise in my head.   I have writt unto the Master of Queens'
Colledg (Dr. Mansel) to know what likelihood ther is for ye
preferment of my nephew Thomas Ffuller vnto a fellowship.
Hee is to bee Master of Artes next commencement, and therefore
I am resolved (yf ther bee no hope ther) to seek what may bee
doon els where.   And herein I must crave your favour and
assistance.   I pray therefore (yf you can preferr him in your
own colledg) let me intreat your best assistance therein : or yf
you have no means to doe it there, make trial what Dr. Preston
thinks may be doune in Immanuel Colledg.   In briefe, I should
bee gladd to have him spedd of a fellowship in any Colledg : and
should not be vnthankful towards that society, which for my
sake should do him ye favour.   I am unwilling to write vnto any
but your selfe, unles I first might vnderstand from you, wher is
ye best likelihood of prevailing, and then I should write willingly,
vnto, any whome you finde willing at my motion to doe him good.
Then with remembrance of my love, I comit you to God and rest
alwaies.

Your very loving friend,
JO : SARU.

The next letter on the same subject is dated October
25th, and is written from the same place.

SALUTEM IN CHRISTO.

GOOD DR. WARD,

   I have spent some time in considering those pointes concerning ffreewill, which you mentioned in your last letter.   But
I am altogether destitute of my bookes, and cannot possibly bee
furnished with them, unless myselfe (which I am yet loath to
doe) should goe over to Salisbury.   I am therefore loath to send
you my bare conceat of those questions : but so soon as I can

have ye help of my bookes to advise withall, you shall know my opinion.

Dr. Mansel has not yet given mee a resolute answer whether Sr ffuller bee in possibility of beeing chosen at their next election or no. But I have now writt unto him, and expect a ful and finall answer yf their bee no hope of speeding in Queens Colledg: I should think my selfe behoulding vnto you (as I formerly writt) yf you should take pains to inquire in what other colledg hee might be spedd. Whersomever that favour should bee donne him : I should not forgett to take some opportunity of requiting it: I once mentioned another matter unto you, which I would desire you still to think of. It was this, that when you know any Discreet Man, competently provided for, who intends marriadg, you would (as from your selfe) wish him to bee a suiter unto some of our maidens (*i.e.* the Townsons) wherof two are now marriadgable. My sister will give reasonable portions and I shall bee ready to doe somewhat for any woorthy man that shall match with any of them, as occasion is offered mee. The sickness contineus so at Salesbury, that I doubt I shall keep my Christmas here at Lacock. Thus comitting you to ye protection of ye Almighty I rest alwaies

Your very loving friend,

JO: SARU.

Nothing resolute having been done for our student by Dr. Mansel and the Fellows of Queens', although some promise had been given by the former, Bishop Davenant wrote to Fuller's father to go up to Cambridge, and see what could be done, as the following letter, dated 28th November, will testify.

Dr. Ward,

I hartily thank you for your mindefulness of my nephew Sr ffuller : what Queens' Colledg: will doe for him I know not : I have writt unto his father to make a jorney to Cambridg and to see if anything is likely to bee done for him in our own Colledg, yet yf bee no hope there, wee may seek abroad in time. As for my nieces, ye elder is seventeen yeer ould, a maide of a sober and gentle disposition, and every way fitt to make a good wife for a Divine. The next is but fiveteen yeer ould, not yet ripe for marriadg, but will bee by that time a good husband bee found for her, and I doubt not she will in all good qualities match her sister, &c.

The annual commencement took place July 1st, 1628, when Fuller proceeded to his degree of M.A. The Vice-Chancellor was Dr. Bainbrigge, Master of Christs College, where Milton was a student; and the usual ceremonies and rejoicings in connection with it began at St. Mary's Church. The Divinity Act (of which Dr. Belton, of Queens', and Mr. Chase, of Sydney, were the respondents) took place in the morning, and the Philosophical Act in the afternoon. Witty Dr. Brownrig (one of Fuller's friends) was the Prevaricator, and the whole proceedings, especially in the public schools, seem to have passed off with unusual *éclat* and brilliancy.

Fuller received his M.A. degree with marked applause, in company with 216 other graduates. We are told that both his degrees were " taken with such general commendation, and at such unusual age, that such a commencement was not within memory." He had once more to sign his name to the subscription book, and thus moved one step higher. He had now passed through the whole curriculum of his seven years' studies, and no doubt had made the acquaintance of those Fathers and classic authors, quotations from which abound in such a marvellous way, as was the case with the other giants of literature in that period.

But Fuller was still without his fellowship. There was another election this same year; but, in spite of the earnest entreaties of Bishop Davenant, he was again passed over, the reason not being given ; but it would seem to point to a want of inclination on the part of the President. Yet it was needful for something to be done, for being intended for the Church, five years more were required to qualify him for his degrees in Divinity. This would entail a burden upon his father, and if he had to remain in residence, it was needful for his friends to make some arrangement for his subsistence. Accordingly, we find Davenant once more writing to his "very loving friend," Dr. Ward, on the subject, dated October 21st, 1628.

SALUTEM IN CHRISTO.

DR. WARD,

I am informed they have made a late election at Queens' Colledg : and utterly passed by my nephew. I would the Master had but donne mee that kindenes, as not to have made mee expect some kindenes from him. I should have taken it much better, than his dooing of lesse than nothing, after some promise of his favourable assistance. I am loath Mr. ffuller should bee snatched away from the University before hee bee grown somewhat riper. His ffather is p'swaded to continew him there vntill I can provide him some other means: but hee think it will bee some disparagement and discouragement to his sonne to continew in that Colledg: where hee see many of his punies stept before him in preferment. In which hee is very desirous that hee should remoov vnto your colledg, there to live in fellowes comons, till hee should bee otherwise disposed of. Wee neither intend nor desire to make him fellow of yours or any other colledg: but only that hee may be conveniently placed for ye continuance of his studyes. I pray him doe him what kindenes conveniently you may in helping to a chamber and study, and in admittance into fellowes comons with as little chardg as ye orders of your howse will give leave. In Queens' Colledg, Mrs. of Arts had many times ye favour granted to come into Comons, without giving plate

E

or any such like burdens, which lay upon young gentlemen fellow comoners. I make no doubt of your readines to doe him any lawfull favour : but ye cheife thing which I am at in his removal is that hee may also have your supr'vision and direction bothe in ye course of his life and study. And thus with remembrance of my love I comitt you to God and rest alwaies,

Your very loving friend,

JO : SARU.

Thus Fuller's connection with the old royal foundation was severed once and for all. There is another account given of the reason why he did not obtain a Fellowship at Queens'. During his stay there, a co-fellowship fell vacant, and our student became a candidate for it,'" prompted thereto by a double plea of merit and interest, besides the desire of the whole house." But the College statutes forbade the election of more than one fellow from the same county, and Northamptonshire was already represented, probably by Fuller's cousin, Robert Townson, who required it more than he did, so Fuller accordingly " quitted his pretensions and designation to that preferment." It was proposed to alter the said statute in his favour, so as to allow him to accept a fellowship, but this " he totally declined," thinking it an unwise precedent to change a College statute, " not willing to own his rise and advancement to the courtesy of so ill a precedent, that might usher in more immodest intrusions upon the privileges and laws of the College."

Thus Fuller quitted the College of his family and connections ; the College of his choice, in which he had spent seven pleasant and profitable years. He left it with his M.A. degree and a good stock of solid learning, with a mind well-stored with general and special literature. In after

years he always looked back with loving and grateful remembrance upon the time he had spent within its own quaint
and venerable walls. "And thus," he said, in the annals of the
University, "I take my farewell of this foundation, wherein I
had my education for the first eight years [1621-8] in that
University. Desiring God's blessing to be plentifully
poured upon all the members thereof."

" Accordingly," says Mr. Russell, " Fuller was on the 5th
of November, 1629, admitted a *Tanquam-Socius* at Sidney-
Sussex College, under the tutorship of Dr. Ward, the Master,
and Mr. Richard Dugard."

CHAPTER VI.

COLLEGE DAYS (SYDNEY-SUSSEX).—1629-1631.

" He was chosen minister of *St. Bennet's* parish in the Town
of Cambridge, in whose church he offered the *Primitiæ* of his
ministerial fruits, which, like apples of gold in pictures of silver
(Sublime Divinity in the most ravishing elegancies), attracted
the audience of the University, by whose dilated commendations
he was generally known at that age at which most men do but
peep into the world."—*Anonymous Life,* p. 5.

ROM one end of Cambridge to the other, from
Queens' Lane to Jesus Lane, from Queen's
College to Sydney College, we must now
accompany our learned and studious hero to his
new rooms, in which he will now address himself to the
studies of Theology, Hebrew, and Divinity.   Mr. Bailey says
he was admitted to this foundation not as "*Tanquam
socius,*" as stated, but only *ad convictum sociorum, i e.,* as
fellow-commoner. Fuller says "a *Tanquam* it seems, is a
fellow in all save the name thereof," which he defines as "a
fellow's fellow."   To acquire this privilege higher fees had
to be paid, and no doubt Bishop Davenant defrayed the
extra expense incurred by this privilege.   But I fail to see,
if Fuller was neither a fellow or *Tanquam socius* at Sydney, the
reason of his migrating from Queens'.   There are to this
day fellow-commoners at Queens', and surely such a distinguished commoner as Fuller would have been allowed to
remain on that foundation, in which he had spent seven

years, in this new capacity. The expense would have been about the same, and the only way in which I can account for his migration is either pique at being passed over, or the friendship of so famed a theologian as Dr. Ward.

Sydney, or more correctly Sydney Sussex, commonly called "Sydney Sus" College, was a new college, comparatively speaking, when Fuller migrated to it, and had been founded by Frances, widow of the Earl of Sussex, and aunt of Sir Philip Sydney. It stood on the site of the old Franciscans, or Grey Friars friary, who established themselves on the spot 1274, and dated back to Edward I., its founder. Fuller observes in his day the area of their church was easily visible in Sydney College garden, where the depressions and subsidency of their bowling green, east and west, present the dimensions thereof : and I have oft found dead men's bones thereabouts." The site had been purchased from Trinity College, to whom it had been granted by Henry VIII., on the suppression of their house by the foundress, and the church had been used for public exercises as far down as 1507, being the largest in the University. When the new college was erected, the refectory of the old friary was utilised for a chapel, which continued as such till 1776. But there seems to have been a doubt as to its consecration, some averring that it had been a stable. For this it was "presented" among the visitation articles by Bishop Wrenn to Archbishop Laud, with which his Majesty was much displeased, and determined on its consecration. On the other hand, it was contended by many learned authorities (and Fuller evidently shared their opinion) that the continuous use of the building for public prayers for the space of 30 years did effectually consecrate it. He calls the foundation a *Benjamin* College, "the least, and last in time, and born after the death of its mother." Though "a little babe," Fuller says it was "well-batteled" under the fostering care of its early masters, and others who interested themselves in increasing its revenues.

The first master of the College was Dr. Mountagu, afterwards Bishop of Bath and Wells, who was a great benefactor to his College. He was a strenuous advocate of "Low Church" opinions, and gave the College a Puritanical tendency and reputation. He was a courtier, and translated King James's works into Latin, for which the King gave him rapid promotion. He died Bishop of Winchester, being succeeded by "that gulf of learning," Bishop Andrewes, in 1618. Among the other benefactors was Francis Cleark, Knt., who either pitched upon the foundation for the receipt of his charity because it was the youngest, or out of admiration for Dr. Ward and his scholars, their grave deportment and patient industry, whose commendable order he beheld on a visit of his to the University. Also Mr. Peter Blundell, of Tiverton, founder of Blundell's School, where Dr. Temple, the present excellent Bishop of Exeter, was educated, and laid the foundation of his future success.

Fuller tells us of one of the curiosities of Sydney College, a skull brought from a well in Candia (about ten feet beneath the soil) to England in 1621, which was *candied* all over with *stone*, yet so as the bone remained entire in the middle, as by a casual breach thereof did appear. He had been speaking of a spring which is conceived to turn wood into stone. "The truth is this, the coldness of the water incrustateth wood (or what else falleth into it) on every side with a strong matter, yet so that it does not transubstantiate *wood* into *stone;* for the wood remaineth entire within, until at last wholly consumed, which giveth occasion to the former erroneous relations. The like is reported of a well in Candia with the same mistake, that *quicquid incidit lapidescit."* He then mentions the skull at Sydney College. This skull was sent for by King Charles I., through Dr. Harvey, and whilst I lived in the house, by him safely returned to the College, being a prince as desirous in such cases to preserve other's property, as to satisfy his own curiosity." The teeth are white and sound and remain unchanged, but the other parts resemble a hard sandstone. It has, however, since been broken and some parts lost. The library, which is conveniently contrived as a study to the Master's Lodge, and is neatly fitted up with a choice selection of books, also contains a bust of Cromwell, executed by the celebrated Bernini, from a plaster impression, taken from Oliver's face after his death and sent to Italy. The countenance bears a great resemblance to the celebrated picture by Cooper.

The College is situated on the east side of Sidney Street, at the corner of Jesus Lane : its buildings enclose two small courts, much altered since Fuller's time, having recently undergone great restoration, under the direction of Sir Jeffrey Wyatville, in the Gothic style. The north court is embattled and gabled ; windows on the east side are transomed, without tracery, and the central portion projects beyond the rest with an arcade. The second or south court is gabled and embattled on the north and south sides ; the west, on which stands the library and chapel, is graced with pinnacles, an enriched porch, a bell-turret or rather bell-gable, in the hermitage or monastic manner, observable at Skelton Church, near York, and some few village churches in Rutland.

The chapel, which, as we have observed, was originally the Friars' dormitory, has been elegantly re-built. It contains a very handsome Altar-piece, viz : " a Repose during the Flight into Egypt." It was painted by Pittoni, a Venetian, and represents the Virgin with the infant Saviour in her arms reclining on some loose straw : on the right is Joseph sleeping in the clouds ; in the upper part are several cherubs, one of whom bears a fillet, on which an inscription, explanatory of the subject, is supposed to have been written ; but this was obliterated by the damage the painting sustained in the ship which brought it from Venice being leaky. Both the composition and the colouring are extremely fine.

Among other portraits in the Master's Lodge, is an original crayon of Oliver Cromwell, by Cooper. This is esteemed a very correct likeness and has been frequently copied. It was presented to the College in 1765. Oliver, who was born in Huntingdon, April 25th, 1599, was a member of this house. The time of his admission into the College is thus noticed in the register : "Aprilis 26, 1616, Oliverus Cromwell, Huntingdoniensis, admissus ad commeatum Sociorum Aprilis vicesimo sexto, 1616, Tutore, Mro. Ricardo Howlet." Among other eminent men are to be found the names of Dr. Ward, second master of the College, the friend of the Fullers ; Archbishop Bramhall, of Armagh(1661), Dr. Seth Ward, Bishop of Salisbury (1667), and Dean Comber, of Durham (1691), and Wollaston, author of "The Religion of Nature Delineated."

Dr. Samuel Ward—"my reverend Tutor, " as Fuller calls

him, had been Master of the College since 1609, and not only had he been for many years on terms of intimacy with his family, but from the letters which passed between Bishop Davenant and himself, with regard to young Fuller, and which we have already given at length, it is easy to see what an interest he must have taken in the young alumnus. In fact, there seems to have been a great intimacy existing between the master and his pupil—which would be only natural, from the fact that the Doctor knew his family so well—the interest he took in his pupils was quite a note in his character—and he was well acquainted with the brilliant promise of the new student.

Dr. Ward was born at Bishop's Middleson, in the county of Durham, and came of a good family. He was educated at Christ's and Emmanuel Colleges, and had the reputation of being a learned theologian. To him, as he was an exact linguist, was assigned a part of the translation of the Bible— some of the Apocryphal Books, upon the production of which he was much complimented by the revisers, and on account of his great theological attainments he was selected with Davenant and others to represent the English Church at the Synod of Dort, where he distinguished himself. When Davenant was made Bishop of Salisbury, he suc- ceeded him as Margaret Professor of Theology, in accord- ance with Davenant's wishes, which chair he held for twenty years ; his theses attest his readiness in the scholastic divinity of those times ; he inclined to the Calvinistic School. He became chaplain to Bishop Mountagu (a former Head of the College), and by him was introduced to the Court. The King seemed to have held him in great estimation, but his theology didn't synchronise with that of Laud and the

Court clergy: he was, however, enrolled among the Court chaplains. Some idea of his learning may be gathered from his letters to the elder Vossins, in which he animadverted upon his "History of Pelagianism." He was also the friend and correspondent of the indefatigable Ussher. Dr. Ward made an excellent Master of a College, and the College flourished under him, numbering some 140 students. He took great interest in the advancement of his pupils, who were much attached to him in consequence. One of them, Lloyd, thus speaks of him, "He was so good a man that he was tutor as well as master to the whole College; yea, kept almost as big a College by his goodness, as he governed by his place: more depending upon him there and abroad as a benefactor, than did as a governour. Being a great recommender, as well as an incourager of worth, he used to say that he knew nothing that Church and State suffered more from, than the want of a due knowledge of those worthy men that were peculiarly enabled and designed to serve both. And as another argument of his goodness, he went always along with the moderate in the censures of the preachers in the University, practices in the Courts that were under his jurisdiction: and, in opinions in the Convocation, whereof he was a member, much pleased with a modest soft way;" With regard to his College duties as Master, there are documents extant, which prove that he was morbidly sensitive in the discharge of these.

Fuller, who has gratefully memorialized Dr. Ward in his "Worthies" (Durham vol. 1. p. 334,) concludes thus, "He turned with the *times* as a rock riseth with the *tide*," and, for his uncomplying therewith, was imprisoned in St. John's College, in Cambridge. In a word, he was counted a *Puritan*

before these times, and *Popish* in these times : and yet being
always the same, was a true Protestant at all times.   He
died anno 1643, and was the first man buried in Sydney
College Chapel."   Touching his character his pupil again
writes " Yet was he a Moses not only for slowness of speech,
but otherwise meekness of nature.   Indeed, when in my private thoughts, I have beheld him and Dr. Collins (disputable
whether more different or more eminent in their endowments), I could not but remember the running of Peter and
John to the place where Christ was buried.   In which John
came first as the youngest and swiftest, but Peter first entered into the grave.   Dr. Collins had much the speed of him
in quickness of parts: but let me say (nor doth the relation
of a pupil misguide me) the other pierced the deeper into
the underground and profound points of Divinity.   Now as
high winds bring some men the sooner into sleep, so I conceive the storms and tempests of these distracted times
invited this good old man the sooner to his long rest, where
we fairly leave him, and quietly draw the curtains about him."

Dr. Ward's deportment was particularly grave, and the
intimacy between him and his pupil quite paternal, so that
the residue of Fuller's studies were conducted under his
direction.   Ward contributed the " Life of Mr. Perkins,"
which is appended to " The Faithful Minister," and on his
authority, Fuller tells us, "That Perkins would pronounce the
word *damn* with much emphasis as left a doleful echo in
his auditor's ears a good while after."

Fuller's other tutor was Mr. Richard Dugard, Fellow and
tutor of Sidney College, and B.D., in 1620.   Of Dugard, he
records : " He was chosen Fellow of Sidney College, where,
in my time (for I had the honour of his intimate acquaint

tance), he had a moiety of the most considerable pupils, whom he bred in learning and piety in the golden mean between superstition and faction. He held a gentle strict hand over them, so that none presumed on his lenity to offend, or were discouraged by his severity to amend. He was an excellent Grecian and general scholar; old when young, such his gravity in behaviour; and young when old, such the quickness of his endowments." He was an intimate friend of Milton, and died Rector of Fulletby, in Lincolnshire, 1653; being buried under a marble stone in the chancel.

Surrounded as he was with such excellent tutors, and having before him such bright examples as Heads of Colleges, no wonder our author found plenty of material, wherewith to write his essay on " The Good Master of a College." We might have expected Davenant or Ward would have provided the original of the sketch, which, however, is supposed to be that of Dr. Metcalf, Master of St. John's College, who counted the College as his own home." Not like those masters who, making their Colleges as steps to higher advancement, will trample on them to raise up themselves; and using their wings to fly up to their own honour, cannot afford to spread them to brood their College. But the thriving of the nursery is the best argument to prove the skill and care of the nurse." Metcalf counted among his pupils, Roger Ascham, author of the "Schoolmaster," and tutor of Lady Jane Grey, Lord Burghley, Sir John Cheke, and others.

Settling down to his new work at Sidney, and surrounded with such eminent men and incentives to study, we can picture to ourselves the young student buckling with redoubled industry to his new curriculum of Hebrew and Theology.

There are many facts to prove that Fuller did not neglect his Hebrew studies. It has been already alluded to in his sketch of " The General Artist," and elsewhere he speaks of the necessity of continuous application to this language. " Skill in Hebrew," he says in his " Holy State," " will quickly go out, and burn no longer than 'tis blown." In his earlier writings there are occasional references made to this language, but it is chiefly in his ·" Pisgah-sight of Palestine " we find most plentiful instances of his skill in that tongue. Both in his " Sermons " and " Church History " are to be noticed traces of, and discussion anent, Hebraistic literature. His copy of Sebastian Munster's Hebrew and Latin Bible, which contains his autograph and his style (D.D.) annexed thereto, is in the possession of a Dorsetshire clergyman, and was exhibited in the Archæological Society in that county in 1865. Fuller took the degree of D.D. in 1660, and he died 1661, so there is an antecedent probability that this was one of the last books he studied, and that he kept up his Hebrew to the end. At all events, he was not one of those who buy books to adorn their bookshelves, but to read them and make use of them, so we may assume he read the Bible in the original at that time.

A hearty welcome and a warm reception must have been given Fuller on his introduction to Sydney College, not only on account of his intimate relations with the master, but from the attractions of the young graduate himself—his solid learning, his conversational powers, his *bonhommie* and ready wit. He formed, of course, many

new acquaintances (and his presence had been eagerly
desired at the college, according to his biographer), and
these with the old ones left behind at Queens' (for though
severed in body he was not separated in spirit from his old
friends he had left behind) his circle of friends must have
been both numerous and yet select.　Nor was he cut off
from them by the political troubles of the age.　There were
Litton, his "chamber fellow," Sir George Ent, Clement
Bretton, Walter Mountagu, Joseph Mede, and Edward
Benlowes.　All these were members of the college.　These
solid facts and surroundings combined no doubt to paint his
life at that time with rose colour.　It was in fact his golden
age, this loving intercourse with true friends.　"The poets
called the first age of the world *the golden age*, not on
account of the abundance of gold, of which there was then
but little in use (inasmuch as 'riches, the incentives to evil,'
were not yet dug out of the earth), but on account of the
supreme simplicity of that time.　And in this sense indeed I
ought to consider college-life truly *golden ;* for I recall with
delight our life at the time when we formerly devoted ourselves to letters at Sydney College, I under the chief
direction of Dr. Ward, you under the tutorship of Master
Dugard, who have now both joined the ranks of the
blessed.　But besides this happiness, which was common to
me with others, it was my especial honour to be associated
with you in the same chamber, for that saying is well known,
'one is known by one's companion :' wherefore I hope
that my obscurity among my associates will be brightened
among posterity (as by a noteworthy sign) by the advantage
of your company."

It will be seen from the above that a student had not in

those days a separate bedroom to himself, but shared it with a chum or chamber fellow, who, from the nature of the case, must have assisted or retarded the studies of the other. But we have changed all that now.

In Fuller's case evidently they were " kindred spirits."

This Lytton was of Knebworth, in Hertfordshire, his father being M.P. for Herts, and was one of the Committee of Parliament sent to treat with the King at Oxford, 1643. He was the ancestor of the present Lord Lytton, whose family have always been more or less remarkable in politics and letters. Clement Bretton was D.D., and died Arch deacon of Leicester in 1669. He penned some laudatory verses to " his dear friend " Mr. Fuller for the "Holy War "—

> Thy quill hath wing'd the earth, the holy land
> Doth visit us, commanded by thy hand, &c.

Dr. George Ent, "my old friend," as Fuller calls him, became President of the College of Surgeons, was knighted by Charles II., and wrote in defence of the discovery of Dr. Harvey, his friend and contemporary at college. Walter Mountagu, brother to the Earl of Manchester, was also at the college, but he " went over " to the Roman Church, and for a time went against the king, but retraced his steps, and subsequently became Chamberlain. Mede became a fellow of Christ's. Fuller calls him "most learned in mystical divinity." He was a great friend of Ussher's, and was much given to abstruse biblical studies, his *magnum opus* being *Clavis Apocalyptica.* He gave Fuller much assistance in his literary studies, who called him " my oracle in doubts of this nature," *i.e.,* some historical subject. Elsewhere Fuller says of him, " Of one who constantly kept his cell (so he called his chamber) none travelled oftener and farther all over Christendom. For things past, he was a perfect historian ; for things present, a judicious novilant ; and for things to come, a prudential, not to say prophetical, conjecturer." (Worthies I.) To Edward Bendlowes, Fuller dedicates the 6th Part of the "History of Cambridge." Mr. Russell says of him, "he appears to have been benevolent without prudence, and to have suffered accordingly, but to have lived in the respect of those who perhaps knew not the exigences by which he was overtaken in his later years. He retained moreover to an unfashionable period for such a characteristic that aversion to Popery and to Arminianism which in his younger days was far from singular." (p. 32.)

Besides these members of his own College there were a number of "out College men" whose friendship Fuller had the honour of, some of whom were destined to make a conspicuous figure in the world of letters. There was Edmund Waller, studying at Trinity, whose poems he was familiar with. Then there was George Herbert, who, as Public Orator, came down to discharge his duty "with as becoming and grave a gaiety as any had ever before or since his time": he and Fuller often met. At this time Milton was pursuing his studies at Christ's—"the lady of Christ's College," as he was called—under the tutorship of William Chappel, remarkable for his skill in turning out good scholars, and the love of poetry on both their parts would naturally bring the young students together. Lastly, there was the celebrated Jeremy Taylor, a native of Cambridge, and a sizar of Caius College, who became Fuller's "respected friend." Of the author of "Holy

Living and Holy Dying," &c., it is reported that when Laud heard him first preach, his remark was that "it was too good a sermon for so young a man": "Please your Grace," said the young divine, "if I live I will quickly mend that fault."

Such were some of Fuller's compeers at the University at this time, and it is to be confessed that with such friendships in and out of College, and such academical surroundings, that period of his life must have been a "golden age" indeed. In truth, he must have made many friends, and been quite a conspicuous figure among the young graduates of the period. Certainly there is no life so fascinating as that of College days, the mixture of grave and gay, the peculiar atmosphere of the College life itself, the quaint mediævalism, the *bonhommie* of youth, the stimulating the different parts of our many-sided nature, now intellectual and now the physical, the friendship and happy meetings—all combine to make life a prolonged and charming poem—at that time.

This good feeling and respect in which Fuller was held manifested itself in an unexpected way. He was offered the perpetual curacy of St. Benet's (*i.e.*, Benedict's) Church, by the Master and Fellows of Corpus Christi College, its patrons. This was in 1630, and soon after his admission at Sydney, but we are not told that Fuller had any claims on Corpus.

Corpus Christi College differs in its origin from that of any other in the University, and was founded by the union and benevolence of two societies or guilds in Cambridge, termed " Gilda Corporis Christi " and " Gilda beatæ Mariæ Virginis." Guilds were of very early institution, and

F

consisted of a company of persons associated sometimes for particular, and at others for mixed, purposes. These societies were of the latter class, and at once embraced various objects, religious, charitable, and commercial. Through the instrumentality of Henry Plantagenet, Duke of Lancaster, their alderman, these guilds obtained, in 1352, a licence from Edward III. to convert their societies into a College, and they endowed it for a master and two fellows. The endowments have been since augmented by succeeding benefactors, and particularly by Archbishop Parker, who added two fellowships and eleven scholarships. He procured also a new body of statutes, gave many considerable bene-factions, and made a large addition to the library, by a collection of printed books and rare and valuable MSS.

The College formerly consisted of an old Court and Chapel, the latter built in 1578, at the expense of Sir Nicholas Bacon, Lord Keeper, in the reign of Elizabeth, and father of the illustrious statesman and philosopher of that name. The old Court, situated behind the Hall, still exists, and from it the ancient tower of St. Benet's may be seen. The walls and buttresses of these old buildings are covered with ivy, and seem to breathe an atmosphere of a bygone age. The old Hall is now the College kitchen.

The Library contains some valuable books, and most of the Reformation documents, and those connected with the consecration of Archbishop Parker, and consequent episcopal succession in the National Church. The manu-scripts contained in this Library are amongst the most valuable in the kingdom. They are very ancient, some of them being as old as the eighth century, but are chiefly remarkable as comprising a large and very rare collection of papers relating to ecclesiastical affairs, which had been collected on the dissolution of monasteries by Henry VIII., and amongst them are found interesting documents relative to the Reformation, and a copy of the Thirty-nine Articles, with the manuscript corrections of the compilers.

This matchless collection of MSS. was left to the College by Archbishop Parker, formerly Master, and is held under the following particular restrictions. " Every year, on the 6th of August, it is to be visited by the Masters of Trinity Hall and Caius College, with two scholars on the Archbishop's foundation. Upon the examination of the library, if twenty-five books are missing, or cannot be found within six months, the whole collection devolves to Caius. In that case the Masters of Trinity Hall and Corpus Christi College, with two scholars on the same foundation, are the visitors, and if Caius be guilty of the like neglect, the books are to be delivered up to Trinity Hall : the then Masters of Caius and Corpus, with two such scholars, become the inspectors, and in case of default on the part of Trinity Hall, the whole collection reverts to its former order." These valuable books, and most important historical documents, are so carefully kept, that even a Fellow of the College is not allowed to enter the library, except accompanied by another Fellow or scholar, who must attend him during his stay, according to the Archbishop's will. Here is also a portrait of the Archbishop, supposed to be original. The College is now entered by a superb entrance gateway, flanked by lofty towers, in the grand west front, which faces Trumpington Street, but it was formerly entered from St. Benet's Street, near the Church tower. Before the erection of the present Chapel—an elegant structure, in the ecclesiastical style of

architecture —the students "kept their prayers" in St.
Benet's Church, which gave the name to the College even
in Fuller's days. "It hath another *working day* name," he
said, "commonly called, from the adjoined Church, Bennet
College."

When Fuller was admitted to this foundation Dr. Henry
Butts was Master, and, after his melancholy death, was
succeeded by Dr. Richard Love, who afterwards sat with
the Westminster Assembly. There were eleven fellows on
the foundation, and Fuller thus records his indebtedness to
them. "I must thankfully confess myself once *a member
at large* of this house, when they were pleased, above
twenty years since, freely (without my thoughts thereof) to
choose me minister of St. Benedict's Church, the parish
adjoining, and in their patronage."

Some description of this Church—as being Fuller's first
pastoral charge—may prove interesting to the reader, which
we give in Mr. Bailey's words : "The Church to which
Fuller was thus appointed takes us back to Saxon times,
dating from 650. It adjoins the northern part of the
College, and is of rather small dimensions. It was originally the University Church ; and the Vice-Chancellor, &c.,
still officially attend it every Easter Tuesday. The main
portion of the Church seems to be Early English : but the
edifice is chiefly remarkable in having a square, lofty,
unbuttressed and unornamented Saxon tower, which was
restored many years ago by the Camden Society. The
tower contains a peal of six 'tuneable' bells, upon one of
which, dated 1607, is inscribed : OF . ALL . THE BELLS IN
BENNET . I . AM . BEST . AND . YET . FOR . MY . CASTING . THE
PARISH PAID LEST. A similar quaint sentiment runs round

another. Very worthy of notice is the internal massive western tower-arch, distinguished by its peculiar impost mouldings, jambs of what is technically called 'long and short' work, and pilaster strips—the two latter being an evident imitation in stone of the wooden construction of the Saxons. This arch has been described by competent authority as 'certainly one of the most noticeable Romanesque arches in the country.' The window opposite the arch is also seen in the exterior view of the tower, &c. The 'long and short' work again appears at the angles of this tower."

There seems to be some discrepancy about the time that Fuller received holy orders. It is supposed that upon receiving this important pastoral charge—the perpetual curacy, or, as we should now say, the vicarage of St. Benedict's—he received ordination from his diocesan, the Bishop of Ely (John Buckeridge), by whom he would be licensed to his cure of souls. But he surely could not have received this pastoral care till he was in priest's orders (a rule which obtains universally and for obvious reasons), and yet there is no mention of his ordination to the diaconate. Possibly he may have received deacon's orders about 1628, and been priested on his nomination to St. Benet's, before his institution and induction to the temporalities of the living. The register, however, of Ely—neither at Ely or London—contains no record of the ceremony. One of his biographers says he was ordained by his uncle, Dr. Davenant, but there is no proof of this. Aubrey again avers that "he was first minister of Broad Windsor," *i.e.*, in the diocese of Bristol, which must be incorrect. During the time Fuller served St. Benet's, he did not reside at Corpus, but kept on his rooms at Sydney, for which College he had an affectionate regard.

At St. Benet's Church at all events Fuller entered into his labours as parish priest. He there "offered the primity of his ministerial fruits, which like apples of gold in pictures of silver (sublime divinity in the most ravishing elegancies), attracted the audience of the University." His success as a preacher was most marked, and as his biographer says, " he was generally known at that age at which most men do peep into the world," so young was he for that position. But his ministrations were of short duration. For the plague, which had been brought to Cambridge by two soldiers of the King of Sweden's army, broke out in the University about April, 1630. The town was well adapted for assisting the scourge, as it was "situate in a low, dirty, unpleasant place, the streets ill-lighted, the air thick and infected by the fens." According to Evelyn, most of the Colleges were closed, only a few (Dr. Ward among the number) remaining at their post. " Our University is, in a manner, wholly dissolved," says Mede, " all meetings and exercises ceasing. In many Colleges almost none left. In ours, out of twenty-seven messes, we have not five. Our gates strickly kept, none but Fellows to go forth, or any to be let in without the consent of the major part of our society : of which we have but seven at home at this present. Only a sizar may go with his tutor's ticket upon an errand. Our butcher, baker, and chandler bring the provisions to the College gates, where the steward and cook receive them. We have taken all our officers we need into the College, and none must stir out : if he doth, he is to come no more. Thus we live as close prisoners, and, I trust, without danger. 'As the plague increased, all the Colleges were closed, the students to return the ensuing term. There was a great distress everywhere, to relieve which collections were made in various parts of the country, especially in London. There died 347 of the townspeople. Few students re-assembled the next, *i.e.*, October, term, and the plague didn't leave till the winter."

During all this time Fuller remained at his post as Vicar of St. Benet's, which the official registers of the parish, kept by him, will duly testify. A great many were interred from the "Spittal." As we have said, Fuller was not residing at Corpus, so the Master, Dr. Butts, was left almost alone. The effect upon the University was most disastrous, and it was long before the students assembled in their usual numbers. Many got their degrees without public exercises, much to the annoyance of those who had painfully gotten theirs. "Yea, Dr. Collins, being afterwards to admit an able man Doctor, did (according to the pleasantness of his fancy) distinguish *inter cathedram pestilentiæ*, and *cathedram eminentiæ*, leaving it to his auditors easily to distinguish his meaning therein."

One of the parishioners of St. Benet's parish was no less a person than the celebrated "Hobson the carrier." He was a great benefactor to the church and parish, and possibly Fuller may have had him in his eye when he wrote his "Good Parishioner." He left five shillings a year for an annual sermon. This Hobson was the first man who let out hackney horses, and was much patronised by the students of the period. He kept forty horses in his stables, and there was always one ready when wanted, but he considerately obliged his customers to take the one nearest the

door.   Hence the well-known proverb, "*Hobson's choice,*
this or none."   Fuller would naturally have taken a pride
in such a parishioner as the merciful old waggoner, being
one who cared for his cattle, whose "dumbness is oratory
to a conscientious man ; and he that will not be merciful to
his beast is a beast himself," to quote from his "Holy
State."   Hobson died of the epidemic, having "sickened,"
as Milton says, "in the time of the vacancy, being forbid to
go to London by reason of the plague."   It was feared
that the infection would be spread by his waggon journeys
to and fro to the metropolis.

> His leisure told him that his time was come,
> And lack of load made his life burdensome.
> —*Milton's Epitaph.*

He was buried in the chancel of his parish church at his
own request, and no doubt Fuller performed the ceremony, as there is an entry in the parish register to that
effect, signed by Fuller.   Hobson bequeathed lands for
the erection of a workhouse, and the still existing conduit,
which he presented to his fellow-townsmen.

At the time when the students were being distracted into
their several counties by the plague, a royal prince was
born (Charles II.), May 29th.   " Great," says Fuller, "was
the rejoicing thereat.   The University of Oxford congratulated his birth with printed poems : and it was taken ill,
though causeless by some, that Cambridge did not do the
like; for then the wits of the University were sadly distracted
into their several counties by reason of the plague therein :
and remember Cambridge modestly excused herself in their
poem, made at the birth of the lady Mary : and it will not

be amiss to insert one tetrastic made by my worthy friend Master John F. Booth, of Corpus Christi College, Cambridge :

> Quod fuit ad nixus Academia muta prioris.
> Ignoscat Princeps Carolus, œgra fuit,
> Spe veniente nova, si tunc tacuisset amores :
> Non tantum morbo digna, sed illa mori.

Fuller's translation runs thus :

> Prince Charles, forgive me that my silent quill
> Joy'd not thy birth : alas ! so sick was I,
> New hopes now come : had I been silent still,
> I should deserve both to be sick and die.

On the birth of the Princess Mary, the mother of William III., next year, November 4th, 1631, the poetically inclined Cantabs put out a volume of congratulatory verses, amongst which appears Fuller as a contributor, in a poem of six Latin verses. This is supposed to have been his maiden production as a poet, being composed before his " David." Among the contributors was Edward King (Milton's " Lycidas "), Hansted of Queens', Whelock of Clare, Randolph of Trinity, and James Duport, one of Fuller's great friends. He it was who wrote some verses for the " Holy War."

> Then Christians rest secure : ye need not band
> Henceforth in Holy leagues for th' Holy Land,
> To conquer and recover 't from the Turk :
> 'Tis done already : Fuller's learned work
> And pen more honour to the cause doth bring
> Than did great Godfrey or our Lion King.
>
> .   .   .   .   .   .
>
> Thus learned Fuller a full conquest makes ;
> Triumphs o'er time and men's affections ; takes
> Captive both it and them : his History,

Methinks it not a war, but Victory:
Where every line doth crown (such strength it bears)
The author Laureate, and a trophy rears.

About this time there was no small stir made about draining the fens of Cambridgeshire; and Fuller alludes to the early efforts of Dutchmen to compass this important work. But the Bailiff of Bedford, "as the country people called the overflowing of the Ouse," attended like a person of quality, by many servants, and undid all their work. Arguments *pro.* and *con.* were given anent the scheme. "But the best argument to prove that a thing can be done is actually to do it." The draining brought more commodities; and as it had got more earth, so it gained better air. "And Cambridge itself may soon be sensible of this perfective alteration. Indeed, Athens (the staple of ancient learning) was seated in a morass or fenny place (and so Pisa, an academy in Italy), and the grossness of the air is conceived by some to quicken their wits and strengthen their memories. However, a pure air, in all impartial judgments, is to be preferred for students to reside in." Again, in his "Holy State," "Some say a pure and subtle air is best; another commends a thick and foggy air. For the Pisans, sited in the fens and marsh of Arnus, have excellent memories, as if the foggy air were a cap for their heads." However this may be, Fuller was through life remarkable for his vigorous memory, which he cultivated at this time at Cambridge. And both his father and uncle Townson, who had also a remarkable retentive faculty, were likewise Cambridge men.

CHAPTER VII.

FULLER'S AUTHORSHIP AND PREACHING.—(1631.)

" Conceive him (the faithful minister) now a graduate in Arts and entred into orders, according to the solemn form of the Church of England, and presented by some Patrone to a pastorall charge, or place equivalent, and then let us see how well he dischargeth his office."—*Holy State* (The Faithful Minister) p. 73.

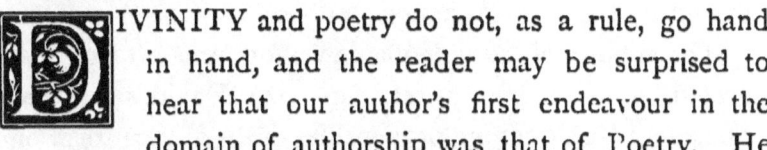IVINITY and poetry do not, as a rule, go hand in hand, and the reader may be surprised to hear that our author's first endeavour in the domain of authorship was that of Poetry. He who became a grave theologian and preacher made his first essay as the writer of verses. The *cacoethes scribenai* seems to have been strong upon him at an early age, and we have already noticed his first attempts, when, in company with a few of his friends, he wrote some congratulatory verses anent the birth of the Princess Mary. Yet Cambridge is not a place calculated to inspire a poetic feeling. Milton had to confess that the surroundings of his University were the very reverse. And Robert Hall, the great Baptist preacher, had no patience with the Cambridgeshire scenery, having neither river nor hill; and when one suggested that the fields gave an idea of plenty, "And so, sir," said Hall, "does a *meal* tub." However, this depressing effect is not visible in Fuller's case; for although in his maturer years he talked of the " pleasant but profitless

study of poetry," he seemed to have been carried away with the current *furore* then in vogue among the budding *literati*, and to have given himself up to verse making.

Most of our readers, who have heard of " Fuller's Church History," " Pisgah-Sight," " Holy War," " Holy and Profane State," will perhaps not even have heard of Fuller's first work, which is indeed quite forgotten. Yet even this work— we suppose because it was the first of so eminent an author —has fetched fabulous sums. A copy of it has lately been priced at eight guineas, and in the British Museum Copy there is a memorandum that it had sold for £17. Still we doubt if many of our readers ever saw a copy of it, except by the merest chance.

The subject of Fuller's maiden effort was no doubt suggested by his theological reading—viz.: 'David, sweet singer of Israel.' The punning propensities of the author are at once visible in the singular alliterative title, " David's Hanious Sinne, heartie repentance, heavie punishment." By Thomas Fuller, Master of Arts of Sidnye Colledge, in Cambridge. London, 1631. From the title, it is evident that the author endeavoured to gain a niche in the temple of fame, among the quaint poets of that quaint age—the ' metaphysical ' class of poets, as they may be termed, beginning with Lyly, culminating in Donne, and ending in Cowley. With the spirit of this class of poets, their peculiarities and manerisms, Fuller was thoroughly imbued.

The subject, which our author selected, has proved an attractive one to poets, but they do not appear to have been successful in it. George Peile had dramatized it in 1599. Cowley, about the same time as Fuller, wrote an " Heroical Poem on the troubles of David ": and Thomas

Ellwood, the Quaker, who is credited with the suggestion to Milton of his " Paradise Regained," also wrote on the same subject, but the poetry is conspicuous by its absence.

Fuller's first publication, then, is a modest and unpretending little book, compared with his later works, and consisted of three books, the books being divided into stanzas of seven lines each, and is comprised on forty leaves. As the work is scarce, we will quote a few lines, as a specimen of Fuller's versification. He begins by detailing the argument of the poem.

> How Zion's Psalmist grievously offended,
> How Israel's Harper did most foully slide,
> Yet how that Psalmist penitent amended,
> And how that Harper patient did abide,
> Deserved chastisement, &c.

After invocation for help, he then describes how David

> When on Bathsheba loose eyes
> He fixt, his heavenly Half did him dissuade.

After the storm struggle between flesh and spirit, the result is thus described :—

> Thus he that conquered men and beast most cruel,
> (Whose greedy paws with felon goods were found)
> Answer'd Goliath's challenge in a duel,
> And laid the Giant grovelling on the ground :
> He that of Philistines two hundred slew,
> No whit appal'd at their grisly hue,
> Him one frail woman's beauty did subdue.

Other incidents follow, and the attempt to make Uriah drunk.

> Abishay next is drunk-to, Joab's brother,
> And this cup to a second paves its way :

That orderly doth usher in another :
Then wine, once walking, knows not where to stay :
Yea, such a course methodical they take,
In *ordering* of cups, the same did make
Uriah quite *all* order to forsake".
His *false supporters* soon begin to slip :
And if his faltering tongue doth chance to light
On some long word, he *speedily doth clip*
The train thereof: yea, his deceitful sight,
    All objects paired doth present to him,
    As double faces, both obscure and dim,
    Seem in a lying looking glass to swim.

Then follows a prayer with a strong teetotal flavour,

My prayer for friend's prosperity and wealth,
Shall ne'er be wanting: but if I refuse
To hurt myself by drinking other's health,
O, let ingenuous natures me excuse.
    If men bad manners this esteem, then I
    Desire to be esteemed unmannerly,
    That, *to live well, will suffer wine to die.*

The plan not succeeding, he goes on to describe the treacherous letter to Uriah, who thus bears his own wittiness, and David sober worse than Uriah drunk.

Thus crafty maisters, when they mind to beat
A careless boy, to gather birch they send him :
The little lad doth make the rod complete
Thinking his maister therefore will commend him.
    But, busily employed, he little thought
    He made the net wherein himself was caught,
    And must be beaten with the birch he brought.

We come now to the besieging army, affairs in the town being thus described :—

Whilst in the town one with his friend did talk,
A sudden stroake did take his tongue away;
Some had their legs arrested as they walked,
By martial law commanding them to stay :
  Here falls a massy beam: a mighty wall
  Comes tumbling there : and many men doth maul
Who were *both slain* and *buried by the fall.*

After the death of Uriah, the second book opens with the anger of the Almighty, creation itself demanding David's punishment.

' Please it your Highness for to give me leave,
I'll scorch the wretch to cinders,' said the fire,
' Send me,' said Air, ' him of breath I'll bereave.'
' No,' quoth the earnest water, ' I desire
  His soily sins with deluge to scour.'
  ' Nay, but my Lord,' quote earth, ' employ my power
With yawning chaps I will him quick devour.'

God is represented as about to take away David's name from the book of life, but the Son intercedes, thereupon fire, air, earth, and water recant.

Plain-speaking Nathan is next introduced, this colloquy ends in David's repentance. Taking up his harp, David "makes one voice to sob and sing" the penitential Psalm (51st).

In the third part the death of Bathsheba is treated of, in which the following stanza occurs :—

As when a tender rose begins to blow
Yet scarce unswaddled is, some wanton maide,
Pleased with the smell, allured by the show,
Will not reprive it till it hath displayed
  The folded leaves : but to her breast applies
  The abortive bud, where coffined it lies,
Losing the blushing dye before it dies
So this babe's life, newly begun, did end.

These lines prove that Fuller had some power as a poet, but after the quaint "forms" of the age, he cannot resist punning in his rhyme.

The tragedy of Ammon follows, in which the praises of Rebecca are sung.

> Rebeka was esteemed of comely hew (hue)
> Yet not so nice her comlinesse to keepe
> But that she water for the camels drew:
> Rachell was faire, yet fedd her father's sheepe :
> But now for to supply Rebeka's place,
> Or doe as Rachell did, is counted base :
> Our dainty dames would take it in disgrace.

In the following stanza, Fuller descants on the doings of "Fame" just as Virgil had done before him in a well-known passage in the Æneid.

> She (Fame) gets by going, and doth gather strength,
> As balls of snow by rolling more doe gaine,
> She whisper'd first, but loudly blaz'd at length,
> *All the king's sonnes all the king's sonnes are slain.*
> The pensive Court in doleful dumps did rue,
> This dismal case, till they the matter knew :
> Would all bad news like this might prove untrue.

This he said in his Holy State, " Absolom killed one of David's sons " " but Fame killed all the rest." The following describes Absolom's death :—

> The graceless son was plunged in deep distress,
> For earth his weight no longer would endure :
> The angry heavens denied all access
> Unto a wretch so wicked, so impure:
> At last the heavens and earth, with one consent,
> *A middle place* unto the monster lent,
> Above the earth, beneath the firmament.

We have been induced to make rather lengthy quotations from this poem of "David," to give the reader some idea of Fuller's early poetical powers, and to bring before him specimens of a work now very rarely to be met with. The author himself doesn't allude to it, and most of the fanciful ideas and expressions were subsequently worked-up in his " Pisgah-Sight."

In guaging Fuller's merits as a poet, we must not look at him from a nineteenth century standpoint, for even in this materialistic age the spirit of poetry is not extinct. We must not put him in the same category as Tennyson or Coleridge, but, comparing him with the poets of his own age, we find the same blemishes in the works of his compeers, the quaint conceits, the everlasting pun, the endless alliterations, the far-fetched metaphors, the incongruous allusions, the word quibblings, verbal hobbies ridden to death—so that he does not come out of the comparison unfavourably. It was so in Cowley's poems, witness Addison's remarks on him :—

> One glittering thought no sooner strikes our eyes
> With silent wonder, but new wonders rise.

And in Dryden's; nor is Milton free from the same in his earlier poems.

Fuller, however, did not cease to try his hand in verses. Throughout his voluminous works are to be found scraps of poetry, and ready translations from the numerous classic authors, whom he so frequently quotes, done into the terse and most nervous English. There are also original couplets, telling epigrams, and poetical odds and ends, scattered up and down his larger works, as in his "Church History," for example, broadcast, in prodigal confusion.

G

We append some specimens of his verse translation: thus he renders,

> Tres sumus imbelles numero, sine viribus uxor,
> Laertesque senex, Telemachusque puer.

> Three weaklings we, a wife for war too mild,
> Laertes old, Telemachus a child.

In Queen Elizabeth's repartee to the Spanish Ambassador,

> Ad Græcas, bone rex, fiant mandata calendas,

Is translated

> "Worthy King know this your will,
> At *Latter Lammas* we'll fulfill.

Speaking of Perkins, a writer against Rome, who like Ehud was left-handed,

> Dextera quantumvis fuerat tibi manca, docendi
> Pollebas mira dexteritate manu.

> Though nature thee of thy right hand bereft,
> Right well thou writest with the hand that's left.

In his "Pisgah-Sight," he translates the Horatian lines, which he applies to Dagon,

> Desinit in piscem, mulier formosa superne:

> Upwards manlike he ascended,
> Downwards like a fish he ended.

And in the quotation from Horace:

> Naturam expellas furcâ licet, usque recurret,

> Beat nature back, 'tis all in vain,
> With tines of fork 'twill come again.

Again, illustrating his axiom "it is the life of a gift to be done in the life of the giver,"

Silver in the *living*
Is *gold* in the *giving*.
Gold in the *dying*
Is but *silver* a *flying*.
Gold and *silver* in the *dead*
Turn too often into *lead*.

There are many epigrams to be found in his other books, as well as couplets. Here are one or two instances on Peter's sinking :—

Cephas, what's that? a stone? Yea, so I think,
A heavy stone, for it began to sink.

And again on Peter's succession :—

If in the sea the Popes durst him succeed,
Where he was *duckt* they would be drowned indeed.

The following lines show a knowledge of human nature :—

And every man whereof himself is free,
That he conceives the only sin to be.

It is evident from the numerous quotations in all his works, more or less, the " itch of versification " remained on him to the last. He made no great flights as in his " David," but he " kept on singing " all through life. His hand never lost its cunning. Poetry and music, to use his words, " were excellent sauce, but they have lived and died poor that made them their *meat*."

The poem of Fuller was dedicated to the three sons of Lord Mountagu, of Boughton, one of whom at least was at Sidney College at the time of the publication. But there can be no doubt that the Fullers knew the Mountagus at

their home at Boughton, which was not far from Aldwinckle.
The Mountagus were descended from Thomas Mountagu
(sixth in descent from Sir Simon de Montacute, the
younger brother of the third Earl of Salisbury), who
married Elizabeth Boughton, of Boughton, Northamptonshire. Edward, their son, was brought up to the law, and
became Lord Chief Justice. He was a Privy Councillor,
and one of the sixteen councillors and guardians to Edward
VI, whose will he drew up, and signed the articles of
succession in favour of Lady Jane Grey, for which offence
he was dismissed from his office the following reign.
Fuller speaks of him as a "worthy patriot and bountiful
housekeeper, blessed in a numerous family." He was a type
of the old English Baron for patriotism and hospitality.

Sir Edward's eldest son, Edward, represented his shire in
Parliament, and was a man of decided piety and justice.
Indeed, his household formed a picture of the old English
piety. He had prayers daily offered, from the Book of
Common Prayer, and the Scriptures read in the Great Hall,
and two hymns sung after supper. The family were exemplary
in their attendance at church winter and summer, before
nine in the morning and one in the afternoon, and "he
never forced minister or people to weary themselves to wait
for his coming." On Sunday evenings the notes of the
sermon were repeated by the servants in their master's
presence. He belonged to the same school of thought as
his brother, the bishop. "So long as the truth was preached,
old Mountagu cared not who preached it; and his own
chaplain had no sinecure of it in his house, where that
reverend official, on Sunday afternoon, assembled the
servants, and put them through their Catechism. He was

as hospitable as pious. His cottagers found him a kind and generous 'lord,' and he patronised men of letters, his mansion being thrown open to many a divine and poor clerk. Two scholarships were founded by him at Sidney College, and ' of his work,' Fuller says, ' I will say nothing because I cannot say enough.' "

Our author then dedicated his poem to this worthy nobleman's three sons in the quaint style of the age and person, to the Honourable Mr. Edward, Mr. William, and Mr. Christopher Montagu, sons to the Right Honourable Edward Lord Montagu, of Boughton, addressing them thus :—

> Faire branches of a stocke so faire,
> Each a sonne, and each an heire :
> Two Joseph-like from sire so sage,
> Sprung in Autumne of his age :
> But a *Benjamin* the other,
> Gain'd with loving of his mother.
> This fruit of some spare hours I spent,
> To your Honours I present.
>
> *   *   *
>
> Whilst your father (like the greene
> Eagle in his scutcheon scene,
> Which with bill his age doth cast),
> May longer still and longer last.
> To see your vertues o're increase
> Your years, ere he departs in peace.
> Thus my booke to make an end
> To you, and you to God, commend.

Edward was a member of Sidney College. William took to the law, and was made by Charles II. Lord Chief Baron of the Exchequer, and Attorney General to Queen Catherine, and Christopher was educated at Sidney, but died in early manhood. Edward's lady " was biassed," Mr.

Russell says, "in favour of the Puritans and against the liturgy, wherefore her faithful and honest father-in-law (the first Lord Mountagu) who had the common prayer read daily in his house morning and evening, said to her, 'Daughter, if you come to visit me I will never ask why you come not to prayers; but if you come to cohabit with me, pray with me, or live not with me.' The second Lord Mountagu, her husband, was a most devoted friend of Fuller in his troubles, and provided at his own cost for the education of his elder son, a kindness which he acknowledges in a dedication to his son Edward in his map of Jerusalem, that accompanies his 'Palestine.'"

But advancement in the Church came quickly to Fuller. It must not be supposed that he was neglecting his clerical duties, while he was engaging in writing these poetical prolusions. He was still discharging the responsibilities and official duties of his pastoral charge at St. Benet's, and we are not surprised to find that his uncle Davenant gave him one of the earliest pieces of preferment at his disposal. On the death of Dr. Rawlinson, Prebendary in the Cathedral of Sarum, the vacant post was bestowed on Fuller. The Stall was that of Nertherbury-in-Ecclesia Beaminster, Dorsetshire, and was considered valuable preferment. Alluding to its value, Fuller says that it was "one of the best prebends in England." In the Bishop's register are to be found his subscription to the Articles in his own handwriting, and in the record office his composition for First-fruits, &c.

About this time, it appears, Bishop Dr. Davenant had got into some trouble with the "powers that be." He was preaching before the Court, and in continuation of his sermon preached the year before, launched out into the subject of Predestination, taking the moderate Calvinistic view. This was considered a violation of the wording of His "Majesty's declaration," which is prefixed to the articles. "It was drawing the article" aside one way; it was "putting his own sense and comment on the meaning" of the article, and not taking it in the "literal and grammatical sense." This was considered a grave offence, and for it he was "had up" before the Privy Council. Presenting himself on his knees before that august assembly, he had so continued, says his nephew, "for any favour he found from any of his own function then present. But the *Temporal Lords* bade him arise and stand to his own defence, being as yet only accused not convicted." Archbishop Harsenet (deputed by the King) "managed all the business against him (Bishop Laud walking by all the while in silence spake not one word). The heads of the Bishop's defence, spoken with much warmth, are given in the Church History, and a long letter from Davenant to Dr. Ward clearing and defending himself. Next day he kissed the King's hand. Fuller alludes to this episode at some length, showing his desire to vindicate his uncle's good fame. The party of Laud was now in the ascendancy at court, so there was little chance for the more moderate school of Davenant, who from this time forward seems to have kept to his diocese.

Fuller did not resign St. Benet's when he became Prebend of Salisbury, but kept it on for some years. At all events, he took his degrees in Divinity before finally quitting the University, which were taken seven years after his M.A. degrees. &c., about the year 1635. He may possibly, about this time, have gone to "read himself in," and take possession of his Sarum prebendary, and naturally a good deal of the time, which he could spare, would be spent in the company of his uncle, the Bishop.

Fuller thus alludes to his position in the Cathedral of Sarum, in his controversy with Peter Heylin: "My extraction—who was Prebendarius Prebendarides and relation (as the animadvertor knows) to two (no mean) bishops, my uncles—may clear me from any ecclesiastical antipathy. I honour any man who is a bishop: both honour and love him, who is a religious and learned bishop."

Speaking of Salisbury Cathedral and its elegant spire, the highest in England (where much of his time was now spent), he says that the doors and chapels therein equalled the months, the windows the days, the pillars and pillarets the hours of the year. "Once walking in this church (whereof then I was Prebendary) I met a countryman wondering at the structure thereof. 'I once,' said he to me, 'admired that there should be a church that should have so many pillars as there be hours in the year, and now I admire more that there should be so many hours in the year, as I see pillars in this church.'"

Fuller has a "meditation" upon Salisbury Cathedral: "Travelling upon the Plain (which, notwithstanding, has its risings and fallings) I discovered Salisbury Steeple many miles off. Coming to a declivity I lost the sight thereof, but climbing up the next hill the Steeple grew out of the ground again: yea, I often found it and lost it, till at last I came safely to it, and took my lodging near it. It fareth thus with us whilst we are wayfaring to heaven: mounted on the Pisgah-top of good meditation, we get a glimpse of our celestial Canaan (Deut. xxxiv., 1). But when, either on the flat of an ordinary temper, or in the fall of some extra-ordinary temptation, we lose the view thereof. Thus in the sight of our soul heaven is discovered, covered and recovered, till, though late, at last, though slowly, surely, we arrive at the haven of our happiness."

The King and Queen visited, the Town of Cambridge March, 1631, and were right royally received—feasting, speeches, and comedies being the order of the day. The play selected to act on this occasion was that of the "Rival Friends," by Hansted, of Queens' College, born at Oundle, in Northampton, a friend and compeer of our author. This Hansted became a Chaplain in the army, and met his death at the siege of Banbury. He was also Vicar of Gretton.

It was at St. Benet's Church his "Lectures on the Book of Ruth" were preached which Fuller published in 1654, that it might not be done by other hands from the imperfect notes which had been taken by some who heard them. In the Epistle Dedicatory he observes, "they were preached in an eminent place, when I first entered into the ministry, above twenty years since." Of this book "The first chapter," he saith, "sheweth that many are the troubles of the righteous, and the three last do shew that God delivereth them out of all."

"Perhaps there are few instances," says Mr. Russell in his memorials, "which so strikingly illustrate the great design of Scripture—that it should bear witness to Christ—than this book, few more striking instances how events, apparently the most private, and to the eye of the world unimportant, are all included in the Divine purposes, and made in their place subservient to that eternal wisdom which disposes all the hearts and ways of men. Fuller doesn't fail to notice that but for this Book genealogists had been at a loss for four or five descents in deducing the genealogy of our Saviour, and that under the conversion of Ruth, the Moabitess, and her reception into the ancestry of the Son of David, is typified the taking of the Gentiles into the sheepfold of the great Shepherd.

The lectures include only the first two chapters, and are not unworthy the author of " The Holy State." They evince that moderation, that benevolence, and that practical piety which ever characterised their author." Indeed, earnestness, plain speaking, moderation and piety are the characteristics of this production. His wit, too, breaks out, as if even sacred themes could not keep it back The following extracts will possess a double interest as being the first-fruits of one so ingenious :—" Bear with patience light afflictions when God afflicteth His children with long lasting punishments. Mutter not for a burning fever of a fortnight : what is this to the woman who had a running issue for twelve years ? Murmur not for a twelvemonth's quartan ague : 'tis nothing to the woman that was bowed for eighteen years, nor seven years' consumption, to the man that lay thirty and eight years lame at the pool of Bethesda."

> Many men have had affliction, none like Job :
> Many women have had tribulation, none like Naomi,

" This was the privilege of the people of the Jews, that they were styled God's people, but now Ammi is made Lo-Ammi, and Ruchama Lo-Ruchama, and we Gentiles are placed in their room. Let us therefore remember the words of St. Paul (Rom. xi. 21) : " Be not high minded, but fear, for if God spared not the natural branches of the olive, fear that He will not spare thee also." " O that He would be pleased to cast his eye of pity upon His poor Jews, which, for 1,500 years and upwards, have wandered without law, without lord, without land. And, as once they were, so once again to make them His people."

That Fuller walked along the true *via media* of the Church of England, the " old paths " of the Bible and Primitive antiquity, the word of God and the " old Fathers and Doctors " —steering between the Scylla of Rome on the one hand and the Charybdis of Geneva on the other, is proved by the following passage on the commemoration of the dead. " It is no Popery, nor superstition to praise God for the happy condition of His servants departed: the ancient patriarchs, the inspired prophets, the holy apostles, the patient martyrs, the religious confessors. When the tribes of Reuben, Gad, and half Manasses erected the altar E D (*i.c.*, a witness, the altar of testimony) at the passage of Jordan, it startled all the rest of the tribes as if under it they had hatched some superstitious design, whereas, indeed, the altar was not intended for sacrifice, but was merely an altar of memorial, to evidence to posterity that those two tribes and a half (though divided from the rest by the River Jordan), were conjoined with them in the worship of the same God. In like manner, when some ministers (probably in the Bidding Prayer) thank God for the departure of His servants, some people are so weak, and some so wilful to condemn such for passages of Popery, as if superstitious prayers were made for their departure, whereas, indeed, such congratulation, on the contrary, speaks our confidence in their present bliss and happiness, and continueth the Church militant with the Church triumphant, as the completing one entire Catholic Church of Jesus Christ." (p. 67).

Most characteristic of their author are the following passages selected from these lectures :—

"The monument less subject to casualty is, to imitate the virtues of our dead friends : in other *tombs* the dead are preserved, in these they may be said to remain alive."

"Always preserve in thyself an awful fear lest thou shouldst fall away from God. Fear to fall, and assurance to stand, are two sisters, and though Cain said he was not his brother's keeper, sure I am that this Fear doth watch and guard her sister Assurance. *Tantus est gradus certitudinis quantus sollicitudinis.* They that have much of this fear have much certainty; they that have little, little certainty; they that have none have none at all." (p. 86).

"Oh that there was such an holy ambition and heavenly emulation in our hearts, that as Peter and John ran a race which should come first to the grave of our Saviour, so men would contend who should first attain to true mortification.'

"After proof and trial made of their fidelity, we are to trust our brethren without any further suspicion. Not to try before we trust, is want of wisdom ; not to trust after we have tried, is want of charity" (p. 112).

Ruth ii. 20. "Naomi never before made any mention of Boaz, nor of his good deeds ; but now being informed of his bounty to Ruth, it puts her in mind of his former courtesies. Learn from hence, new favours cause a fresh remembrance of former courtesies. Wherefore, if men begin to be forgetful of those favours which formerly we have bestowed upon them, let us flourish and varnish over our old courtesies with fresh colours of new kindnesses ; so shall we recall our past favours to their memories" (p. 206).

"If envy and covetousness and idleness were not the

hindrances, how might one Christian reciprocally be a help unto another; all have something; none have all things; yet all might have all things in a comfortable and competent proportion, if seriously suiting themselves as Ruth and Naomi did, that what is defective in one, might be supplied in the other " (p. 223).

Again, after a quaint colloquy between Elimelech and "a plain and honest neighbour," dissuading him from his departure into Moab, the author asserts that to travel in a foreign country is lawful for (1) merchants, (2) ambassadors, and (3) "private persons that travel with an intent to accomplish themselves with a better sufficiency to serve their king and country; but unlawful it is for such to travel which, Dinah-like, go only to see the customs of several countries, and make themselves the lacqueys to their own humourous curiosity. Hence cometh it to pass, when they return, it is justly questionable whether their clothes be disguised with more foolish fashions, or bodies disabled with more loathsome diseases, or souls defiled with more notorious vices; having learned jealousy from the Italian, pride from the Spaniard, lasciviousness from the French, drunkenness from the Dutch. And yet what need they go so far to learn so bad a lesson, which (God knows) we have so many schools where it is taught here at home? Now if any do demand of me my opinion concerning our brethren, which of late left this kingdom to advance a plantation in New England, surely I think, as St. Paul said concerning virgins, ' he had received no commandment from the Lord;' so I cannot find any just warrant to encourage men to this removal; but think rather the counsel best that King Joash prescribed to Amaziah, ' Tarry at home.' Yet

as for those that are already gone, far be it from us to conceive them to be such, to whom we may not say 'God
speed' (as it is in 2 John v. 10), but let us pity them and
pray for them; for sure they have no need of our mocks,
which I am afraid have too much of their own miseries.   I
conclude, therefore, of the two Englands, what our Saviour
saith of the two wines (Luke v. 39), 'No man having tasted
of the old, presently desireth the new; for he saith, the old
is better.'"

We must now retrace our steps to Aldwinckle, and peep
into the quaint old Rectory of St. Peter's.   Here, in all
probability, Death, which comes to all sooner or later, laid
his icy hand on the revered father of our author, who, for
upwards of a quarter of a century, had been its painful and
pious parson, or parish priest.   It is not certain whether he
died here, or at Salisbury, where he was prebendary of the
Cathedral, or among his London friends, as there is no record
can be found of the place of his sepulture.   But his successor
(John Webster, B.A.) was instituted April, 1632.   He died
intestate, and probably poor, and he left his son, Thomas
Fuller, his executor, 10th April, 1632.

"The faithful minister lives in too bare a pasture to die
fat," is a sentiment which will be echoed by many a poor
parson, whose benefice is often called a "living" by a sort
of grim satire.   "It is well if he hath gathered any flesh,
being more in blessing than in bulk," remarks Fuller.

The painstaking regularity with which he made the entries
in the parish registers, even to the very last, as far as 1631,
is a proof how assiduous he was in the discharge of his
duties as parish priest; and this in spite of his official
duties connected with the prebendal stall of Highworth, in

the Cathedral of Sarum. He, too, " lived sermons," for he was a man of a blameless and as private life, who spent himself in the discharge of his pastoral office,—the best epitaph for the Christian pastor.

The prebendal stall thus vacated was conferred by Bishop Davenant (ever mindful of his family) upon his nephew, Robert Townson, and upon his death, a few months afterwards, upon John Townson, who, after sequestration, was repossessed of his stall at the Restoration, holding it fifty-four years. The death of the elder Fuller broke up the family household at the quaint old parsonage at St. Peter's ; which is an additional trial to the bereavement in case of the death of clerics, for the glebe house must be quitted at once. The widow, her son John, her daughters, of whom the youngest was sixteen, were now dependent upon others ; and no doubt our author, as the eldest son, took upon himself the burden of the family. The widow died in 1638, and John was entered of Sydney College, where he pursued his studies, taking his B.A. in 1635-6. About two years after the death of the elder Fuller, his sister-in-law, Margaret Davenant (wife of the former Bishop Townson, who died about thirteen years previously), died at her brother's palace at Salisbury, October 29th, 1634. She, like her sister, was remarkable for her circumspection and sanctity of life. She was buried in the Cathedral, near the south wall of the eastern transept, where a mural tablet was set up to her memory. The oval escutcheon contains the arms of Townson and Davenant, and both the monument and in-scription are of a simple character. Most of her daughters married " clergie-men," the Bishop conferring upon the husbands prebends and other dignities of the Church, which shows that he was neither unmindful of the temporal interests of his family, nor forgetful of his promise about "our maidens."   Margaret married a prebend and archdeacon; Ellen's husband became successively Bishop of Sarum and London; Maria married a prebend, who became Dean of Westminster and Bishop of Salisbury; and Judith married another prebend of Salisbury; all, it will be seen, with very clerical surroundings,—prebendal, archidiaconal, decanal, and episcopal.

The death of the elder Fuller may be connected with the resignation of his son of the perpetual curacy of St. Benet's, Cambridge, for there is no trace of his connection with it after March, 1632-3, when he made his last entry in the registers of the parish.   One of the fellows of Corpus, Edward Palgrave, was appointed his successor on July 5th, same year.   The Chapter Book of the College about this time being lost, no record can be found of the exact date.

The resignation, however, of this cure doesn't necessarily prove that Fuller's connection with the University was at this time severed.   More time, perhaps, may have been given to his uncle at Salisbury, but it is difficult to predicate exactly as to the date of his leaving Cambridge.   He says himself, in his "History of Cambridge": "At this time (1633-4) I discontinued my living in the University, and therefore crave leave here to break off my history, finding it difficult to attain to certain intelligence.   However, because I meet with much printed matter about the visitation of Cambridge in these troublesome times (though after some years' interval), I shall for a conclusion adventure to give posterity an impartial relation thereof" (p 162).   Fuller, however, must have been in nominal residence up to June, 1635, when he took his degree; and he calls Sydney College his mother up to 1636 or 1637, still later. In the summer of 1633 the King visited Scotland with Laud in his company, and on this occasion was crowned. His return was made the opportunity of penning congratulatory verses at Cambridge, and among the 140 contributors our author is credited with two poems. At this time the influence of Laud was making itself felt in the University, and there was quite a Catholic revival. Chapels were restored, organs introduced, College services improved, and a more reverent celebration of the Eucharist encouraged, which some thought then as they do now, that these things mean superstition and necessarily lead on to Popery.

Fuller comported himself with becoming gravity at this crisis, and showed his usual good sense, although he stuck through life to the moderate school in which he had been bred—the theology of his early days. He used the ritual customary in his time, not changing for fashion's sake, contented with that in which he was brought up, discarding neither surplice, litany, or decent ceremonial: his views on these subjects are clearly seen in "the true Church antiquary." "He is not zealous for the introduction of old useless ceremonies. The mischief is, some who are most violent to bring such in, are most negligent in preaching the cautions in using them: and simple people like children in eating of fish, swallow bones and all to their danger of choking. Besides, what is observed of horsehairs, that lying nine days in water they turn to snakes, so some ceremonies, though dead at first, in continuance of time, quicken, yet stings may do much mischief, especially in an age when the

meddling of some have justly awaked the jealousy of all.
Again, not that I am displeased with neatness or plead
for nastiness in God's service.   Surely God would have the
Church His spouse, as not a harlot, so not a slut: and indeed
outward decency in the Church is a harbinger to provide
inward devotion to follow after.   But we would not have
religion so bedaubed with lace that one cannot see the cloth,
and ceremonies which should adorn, obscure the substance
of the sacraments and God's worship.   And let us labour to be
men in Christianity, and not be allured to God's service by
the outward pomp and splendour of it.   But let us love
Religion not for her clothes, but for her face : and then we
shall affect it, if they should chance (as God forbid) to be either
naked through poverty, or ragged through persecution : in a
word, if God hath appointed it, let us love the plainness of
His ordinance, though therein there be neither warm water,
nor strong water, nor sweet water, but plain water of Jordan."

But Fuller did not censure all the practices of the Laudian clergy ; on the contrary, he says : " In mixt actions where
good and bad are blended together, we can neither choose
nor refuse all, but may pick out some and must leave the rest.
But they may better be termed *Renovations* than *Innovations*,
as lately not new forged, but new furbished.   Secondly, they
were not so many as some complain.   The suspicious old
man cries out in the comedy, that 600 cooks were let into his
house, when there was but two ; jealousy hath her hyperboles
as well as her flattery.   Thirdly, some of these innovations
may easier be railed on than justly reproved, viz. ; such as
concerned adorning of Churches.   Fourthly, if these gave
offence, it was not for anything in themselves, but either
because (1) they were challenged to be brought into without

law, (2) because they seemed new and unusual, (3) because they were multiplied without any set number, (4) because they were pressed in some places without moderation, (5) because they were pressed by men, some of whose persons were otherwise much distasted."

Would that these weighty words had been "marked, learned, and inwardly digested," during the Catholic revival and ritual recoveries of the last few years. A little more of Fuller's common sense would have saved us from many a trouble, many a mistake, in settling our religious difficulties, and ecclesiastical controversies, consequent on a revival of spiritual life and activity.

CHAPTER VIII.

" FAREWELL TO CAMBRIDGE AND REMOVAL TO BROAD WINDSOR " (1634).

"Then our minister compounds all controversies betwixt God's ordinances by praysing them all, practising them all, and thanking God for them all. He counts the Common Prayers to prepare him the better for preaching, and as one said, if he did not first toll the bell on one side, it made it afterwards ring out the better in his sermon."--*Holy State* (The Faithful Minister), p. 74.

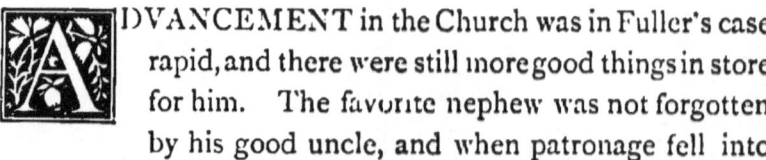DVANCEMENT in the Church was in Fuller's case rapid, and there were still more good things in store for him. The favorite nephew was not forgotten by his good uncle, and when patronage fell into his hands, Bishop Davenant at once offered it to him, and once again evinced his paternal kindness on his behalf. "That Prebend of Salisbury was a commodious step to another more profitable place," says his biographer. This was the Rectory of Broad Windsor, near Beaminster, in the County of Dorset, to which he was collated in 1634. Fuller did not immediately accept the proffered living "till after a serious scrutiny of himself, and his abilities to discharge the requisite duties the place called for: and after a very full and satisfactory enquiry of his Parishioners," he then became a " country parson."

The parish of Broad Windsor, consisting for the most part of a rich vale of meadows and orchards, watered by small brooks and bounded by bold hills (of which Lewesdon, 960 feet, and Pillesdon, 940 feet, are well known), is from five to six miles in length, and from two to three in breadth. It is situated between Bridport and Lyme Regis, and is not far from Somersetshire, taking its name from the *winding* nature of the border which separates the Counties. Fuller appreciated the County very highly, saying that it possessed all commodities necessary for man's temporal well-being. The two hills are used as landmarks at sea, and are called the Cow and the Calf, from their apparent likeness to those animals. "Lewesdon Hill" has been rendered classical by the poem of the Rev. W. Crowe, public Orator of the University of Oxford, the friend of the poet Rogers, and Rector of Stoke Abbott. Fuller quotes a local proverb, "as much akin as Leuson Hill to Pilsen Pen," it is no kin at all. "It is spoke of such who have vicinity of habitation of neighbourhood without the least degree of consanguinity and affinity betwixt them. For here are two high hills, the first wholly, the other partly, in the parish of Broadwinsor, whereof once I was minister."

Leaving Lyme Regis—famous for its three things—its pier, made of loose stones and rubble without mortar, its sea walk, and the house where Monmouth slept after landing (kept just as it was, furniture and all), and passing to Charmouth, a charming watering place (whence Charles II. attempted to escape after his defeat at Worcester), one has to keep this Lewesdon Hill in front to get to Broad Windsor. Ascending this hill is a good view, and the village and church connected with our author come suddenly into view and are seen to advantage. The prospect is all one can desire, with its undulating fields and scattered homesteads, the distant view of the sea, and the bathing crags of the shore—all blending with the deep blue sky above : Crowe speaks of it as

A variegated scene of hills
And woods and fruitful vales, and villages
Half-hid in tufted orchards, and the sea
Boundless, and studded thick with many a sail.
From this proud eminence on all sides round,
Th' unbroken prospect opens to my view,
On all sides large : save only where the head
Of Pillesdon rises, Pillesdon's lofty Pen :
So call (still rendering to his ancient name
Observance due) that rival height south-west,
Which like a rampart bounds the vale beneath.
There woods, there blooming orchards, there are seen
Herds ranging, or at rest beneath the shade
Of some wide-branching oak : there goodly fields
Of corn and verdant pasture, whence the kine
Returning with their milky treasure home,
Store the rich dairy : such fair plenty fills
The pleasant vale of Marshwood.

The village is both picturesque and neat, containing a population of about 1,400, partly engaged in agricultural pursuits and dairy produce, and partly in the trade of sail-cloth. There doesn't seem to have been much change in the occupation of the inhabitants since Fuller's time, although many of the old houses are still standing, the old Rectory in which Fuller wrote or projected some of his principal works has long since disappeared. The old house, which was very ruinous, described as a cottage, stood on the site of the present schools, which were erected by that famous champion of National Schools, Archdeacon Denison, the incumbent in 1843. It had two sitting rooms, four bed rooms, and built in the form of a carpenter's square.

The Church—the only remaining feature of interest now connected with Fuller—is of an ancient period, probably about the beginning of the thirteenth century. It is partly in the Norman and partly in the Gothic style, and was dedicated to S. John the Baptist, consisting of a nave, aisles, chancel, and a lofty western tower, embattled with a turret at one corner. Here are some old bells, which belong to a pre-reformation period, and the old tower is a resting place for birds. The building looks like so many churches of the West—thoroughly weatherbeaten. Fuller thus speaks of it, " Birds we see (Psalm lxxxiv. 3) may prescribe an ancient title to build in our steeples, having time out of mind taken the same privilege in the tabernacle and temple ; yea, David in exile, debarred access to God's public service, doth pity his own, and prefer the condition of these fowls before him. And although no devotion (whereof they were uncapable) but the bare delight in fair fabrics brought them hither, yet we may presume, according to their kind, they served God better than many men in that place, chirping forth morning and even praises to the honour of their Maker." (Pisgah-sight II. 365.) In the north aisle are two altar-tombs, which belong to the old family of Champernowne, members of which family resided there in Fuller's time, who are said to have come over with the Conqueror, and with whom Sir Walter Raleigh was related. The interior of the Church has been much altered at various times, as is shown by the want of harmony in its arrangement. It is spacious, and contains many styles of architecture, including the Norman. The pulpit remains the same as that in which the witty and accomplished preacher delighted his rustic audience. " It is very old," says Mr. Russell, in 1844, " but its carvings

disfigured by sundry coatings of paint:" no doubt these
blemishes have been removed at the recent restoration. "It
has a double row of panels, divided by a horizontal roll,
which are enriched by arabesque work of carved foliage.
At the angles, and dividing perpendicularly, are crocketed
buttresses, which below the roll are continued by a round
moulding, enriched with foliage of a semi-classical
character," is the description in Hutchins' "Dorset." (330.)

When the young Rector took up his abode in his new
parish as a "country parson," he had with him his unmarried
sister and his mother, who died between this date and 1637.
He very soon gained the general love and goodwill of his
people, which is the first step in realising the portraiture of
of "the faithful minister," which he penned about this time.
"*He is strict in ordering his conversation.* As for those who
cleanse blurs with blotted fingers, they make it worse. It
was said of one who preached very well and lived very ill,
'that when he was out of the pulpit, it was a pity he should
ever go into it, and when he was in the pulpit, it was a pity
he should ever come out of it,' but our minister lives
sermons." So of Perkins, "He lived sermons, and as his
preaching was a comment on his text, so his practice was a
comment on his preaching." (Abel Redevivus.) He is
"grave, courteous to his people, not too austere and
retired. Especially he detesteth affected gravity (which is
rather on men than in them), whereby some belie their
register-book, antedate their age to seem far older than they
are, and plait and set their brows in an affected sadness.
Whereas, St. Anthony, the monk, might have been known
among hundreds of his Order by his cheerful face, he
having ever, though a most mortified man, a merry coun-

tenance." *He doth not clash God's* ordinances *together about precedency*, not making odious comparisons betwixt prayer and preaching, preaching and catechising, premeditate prayer and extempore. Fuller must have been a diligent "catechist" to judge from the following: "*He carefully catechiseth his people in the elements of religion.* Except he hath (a rare thing) a flock without lambs, of all old sheep ; and yet even Luther did not scorn to profess himself *discipulum catechismi*, a scholar of the catechism. By this catechising, the Gospel first got ground of Popery : and let not our religion, now grown rich, be ashamed of that which first gave it credit and set it up, lest the Jesuits beat us at our own weapon. Through the want of this catechising, many who are well skilled in some dark out-corners of Divinity have lost themselves in the beaten road thereof." The care Fuller took with his sermons is evidenced in these words, "*He will not offer to God of that which costs him nothing :* but takes pains* aforehand with his sermons. Demosthenes never made any oration on the sudden ; yea, being called upon, he never rose up to speak, except he had well studied the matter : and he was wont to say *that he showed how he honoured and reverenced the people of Athens, because he was careful what he spake unto them.* Indeed, if our minister be surprised with a sudden occasion, he counts himself

---

* Speaking of a clergyman (Symmons), who was very conscientious in discharging his calling, he says, "being once requested by me to preach for me, he excused himself for want of competent warning, and when I pleaded that mine, being a country parish, would be well pleased with his performance," "I can," said he, "content them, but not my own *conscience* to preach with so little preparation." ("Worthies.")

rather to be excused than commended, if premeditating only the bones of his sermons, he clothes it with flesh extempore. As for those, whose long custom hath made preaching their nature, that they can discourse sermons without study, he accounts their example rather to be admired than imitated."

The whole essay on "The Faithful Minister," in the Holy State, is deserving of the most careful study, as well as the "Life of Mr. Perkins," on the part of those, who are endeavouring the ministry of the National Church. It gives us an epitome of George Herbert's "Country Parson." George Herbert had left the Court, and taken the living of Bemerton, near Salisbury, in 1630, where he was *living* sermons. The two grave divines were, therefore, neighbours, clergymen of the same diocese, and must often have met. Dr. Stoughton well sums up the points of them both : "Fuller had nothing of the poetical pensiveness of Herbert—nothing of that unearthly tone, which was so real in the Salisbury canon : nothing even of the High Church-manship of Dr. Hammond, yet he cordially loved the Church of England. If any one will take the trouble to compare the portraits of Herbert and Fuller, he must confess that Herbert's gravity would look as foolish in the face of Fuller, as Fuller's archness would be most unseemly if it could be fixed on Herbert's sedate countenance."

Fuller must have found a great difference between the social surroundings of a country village, some distance from the market town, and those of the University, more especially as he had made such proficiency in his academical studies, and seemed almost to belong to Cambridge. There are some men, who from their very natures, may from their very physique and appearance, seem cut out for country parsons, or hedge parsons, as they are facetiously called, rough, rubicund, almost bovine, suited for the company of farmers and bucolics : while others, as Herrick, of Dean Prior, near Dartmoor, from their gentler natures, their intellectual proclivities, are quite the reverse. Yet how often do the round pieces get into the square holes, and the square into round, in a sort of ecclesiastical hurly-burly.

Soon after settling in Broad Windsor, Fuller was induced by his numerous College friends, to pay a visit to Cambridge, to take his degree of Bachelor of Divinity, for which his studies and standing had duly qualified him. We can well believe he was by no means disinclined to fall in with their suggestion, and revisit his " Alma Mater," for which he had a sincere affection. He prepared to carry out these intentions, but he didn't omit to provide a suitable and efficient *locum tenens*, to whose temporary guardianship he could leave " his few sheep in the wilderness " with confidence. " Having taken care to supply his place for the time of his absence," says his anonymous biographer, " at his setting forth he was acquainted that four of his chief parishioners, with his good leave, were ready to wait on him to Cambridge, to testify their exceeding engagements : it being the sense and request of his whole parish. This kindness was so present, and so resolutely pressed, that the Doctor, with many thanks for that and other demonstrations of their love towards him, gladly accepted of their company, and with his customary innate pleasantness entertained their time to their journey's end."

The welcome accorded to Fuller on his return to Cambridge partook almost of the nature of an ovation. His old

friends and associates gave him a hearty welcome.   He was
visited, so we are informed, " almost by all considerable persons of the University and town, and the greeting of his old
parishioners to their beloved pastor was most cordial, fame
and love vieing which should render him most addresses, to
the great delight and satisfaction of his fellow travellers and
neighbours, in having a minister who was so highly and yet
no less deservedly honoured."   The visits both received and
paid must have been both gratifying and numerous.

But all these social pleasantries were the πάρεργον—the
by-work of the visit.   The work he had come to do was the
taking the B.D. degree, which (such was his acknowledged
skill and critical scholarship in the disputations and consequent reputation) he took with general applause and commendation, 11th June, 1635, in company with six other
graduates.   His signature in the University subscription
book is Thomas Fuller (only one " f " this time).

When the academical ceremonies were over, the young
bachelor gave the usual expected *feast*, in honour of the occasion, which put him to a considerable expense.   His biographer thus alludes to it : " At this commencement there
proceeded with him in the same degree of Bachelor of
Divinity three (there were six) other reverend persons, all
with general applause and commendation, and, therefore, to
do them no wrong, I forbear to give the deceased Doctor his
particular due.   Only thus much, by the way, may be added
that this commencement cost the Doctor for his particular,
the sum of seven score pounds, an evidence of his liberality
and largeness of mind, proportionable to his other capacities,
and yet than which nothing " was less studied."   This
apology for our author's extravagance is evidently from the

pen of a friend, who may have shared in the banquet.
These feasts certainly led up to extravagance, and sometimes no doubt to dissipation, and they were finally
abolished under the Puritan rule in 1647. It is said of
Williams, by Hacket, on taking his M.A. degree in 1605,
" he feasted his friends as if it had been his wedding,"
having plenty of 'cash at his disposal.

Commencement and feast being now over, Fuller took his
" farewell of Cambridge," and returned to his flock and
country parsonage. " At his departure he was dismissed
with as honourable valedictions, and so he returned in the
same company (who had, out of their own purse, contributed another condition of honour to that solemnity), to his
said Rectory of Broad Windsor, resolving there to spend
himself and the time of his pilgrimage amongst his dear and
loving charge."

Fuller's connection with Cambridge after this must have
been only nominal, but five more years (and usually of residence) were required before taking his D.D degree. He
would naturally qualify in every possible way for that ecclesiastical eminence which lay before him, being now already
firmly placed on the ladder of preferment. He speaks of
his connection with Sydney College till 1637, and of the
seventeen years he spent at Cambridge, which cost him less
than the seventeen weeks he passed at Oxford, where he
lost his all. This fact is again alluded to in his Appeal.
But he may have been speaking roughly. At all events, for
any practical purpose we may consider his farewell was
taken about this time, and this is his prayer for his College
and University, in what he calls "a child's prayer for his
mother." " It is as yet but *early days* with his College (which

hath not seen sixty years), yet hath it been fruitful of working men, proportionably to the age thereof, and I hope it will daily increase. Now, though it be only the place of the parents, and proper to him as the greater to bless his childe (Heb. vii. 6), yet it is the duty to pray for his parents, in which relation my best desires are due to this Foundation ; my mother, for the last eight years in this University, may her lamp never lack light for the oil, or oil for the light thereof. ' Zoar, is it not a little one ? ' Yet, ' who shall despise the day of small things ? ' May the foot of sacrilege, if once offering to enter the gates thereof, stumble and rise no more. The Lord bless the labours of all the students therein, that they may tend and end at His glory, their own salvation, the profit and honour of the Church and Commonwealth." (Hist. Camb. viii. 155).

Fuller's love for his Alma Mater was most enthusiastic, and in his portraiture of " The Good Bishop," in his " Holy State," he makes love for his College, which bred him, one of the cardinal notes of this episcopal character :—" *He is thankful to that College whence he had his education.* He conceiveth himself to hear his mother-college always speaking to him in the language of Joseph to Pharaoh's butler : ' *But think on me I pray thee, when it shall be well with thee* ' (Gen. xl. 12). If he himself hath but a little, the less from him is the more acceptable ; a drop from a sponge is as much as a ton of water from a marsh. He bestows on it books, or plate, or lands, or buildings, and the houses of the prophets rather lack watering than planting, there being enough of them if they had enough." (p. 228).

What a contrast are these lines in his " Holy State " to those of Dryden, who was born and reared in the same village in Northamptonshire :

Oxford to him a dearer name shall be
Than his own Mother-University :
Thebes did his green, unknowing youth engage,
He chooses *Athens* in his riper age.

Fuller showed his love for *his* "Mother-University" by writing an exhaustive history of Cambridge and its separate Colleges, exhibiting zeal for its reputation, and offering up prayers for its welfare.

We must not, in quitting Cambridge, omit to mention the sermon on the "Doctrine of Assurance," which Fuller preached there in 1634, but which was not "exposed to pub-licke view by the importunity of Friends" till 1648. "This grace of Assurance," he observes, "is not attainable with ease and idleness—Christianity is a laborious profession." After various illustrations of this topic, he lays down, as the plain doctrine of the text (2 Peter, i., 10), that assurance of one's calling and election may, without any miraculous reve-lation, be in this life acquired : secondly, that such assur-ance is a separable fruit or effect not of every tree, but only of some strong faiths, whereby the party is persuaded of the certainty of his calling and election. "I say separable, to manifest my dissenting from such worthy divines, who make this assurance the very being, essence, life, soul and for-mality of faith itself." Whence these, our author admirably observes in this sermon, "All heavenly gifts, as they are got by prayer, are kept, confirmed and increased by praises." "Presumption," he remarks, "is hot poison, it kills its thou-sands, makes quick riddance of men's soul to damnation. Despair, we confess, is poison, and hath killed its thousands, but the venom therefore is more curable, as more cold and faint in the operation thereof. Take heed, therefore, of presumption, lest the confidence *of the assurance of thy calling* betray thee to spiritual pride, that to security, that to destruction."

"Now we must with sorrow confess that this doctrine of the Spirit dwelling in the hearts of God's servants, is much discountenanced of late, and the devil thereupon hath improved his own interest. To speak plainly, it is not the fierceness of the lion, nor the fraud of the fox, but the mimicalness of the ape, which in our age hath discredited the undoubted truth. But what if the apes in India, finding a glow-worm, mistook it to be true fire, and heaping much combustible matter about it, hoped by their blowing of it thence to kindle a flame. I say, what if that animal γελωτόποιον, that mirth-making creature, deceived itself, doth it thence follow that there is no true fire at all? And what if some *fanatical Anabaptists* by usurpation have entitled their brain-sick fancies to be so many illuminations of the spirit, must we presently turn Sadducees in this point, and deny that there is any Spirit at all? God forbid!"

"The third and last witness we shall insist on," says our author, "is that comfort and contentment, the conscience of the party takes in doing good works, and bringing forth the fruits of new obedience; that, though he knows his best good works are straitened with corruption and many imperfections, yet, because they are the end of his vocation, and the justifiers of his faith—because thereby the Gospel is graced, wicked men amazed, some of them converted, the rest confounded, weak Christians confirmed, the poor relieved, devils repining at them, angels rejoicing for them, God Himself glorified by them; nay, because of these and other reasons, He doth good deeds with humility and cheerfulness, and findeth a singular joy in his soul, resulting from the doing thereof." Two opinions as false as dangerous, must of necessity be inferred, first, that everyone who hath true faith, and is eternally to be saved, hath *always* some measure of this assurance ; secondly, that such who are devoid of this assurance, are likewise deprived of all sincere faith for the present. But God forbid any preacher should deliver doctrines so destructive to Christian comfort on the one side, and advantageous to spiritual pride on the other, such will prove *carnificinæ*, the racks and tortures of tender consciences. And as the careless mother killed her little child, for she overlaid it, so the weight of this heavy doctrine would press many poor but pious souls : many faint but feeble infant-faiths to the pit of despair, exacting and extorting from them more than God requires—that every faith should have assurance with it, or else be ineffectual to salvation.

He then proceeds to state the proper ground of assurance, which he does in a syllogism.

"THE MAJOR."

" He that truly repenteth himself of his sins, and relieth with a true faith upon Christ is surely called, and by consequence elected before all eternity to be a vessel of honour."

"THE MINOR."

" But I truly repent myself of my sins, and rely with a true faith on God in Christ."

"THE CONCLUSION."

" Therefore I am truly called and elected."

To arrive at such an assurance, we must have, he adds, the testimony of our conscience to the truth of our repent-

I

ance and sincerity of our faith ; secondly, the witness of the Holy Spirit (Rom. viii. 16).

"Such faithful preaching," Mr. Russell adds, "is but too unfashionable, yet, what but presumption is likely to ensue in those congregations which are always cloyed with cordials? What other effect is likely to attend the facile labours of those, all whose looks are smiles, and whose preaching a perpetual canticle, who are ever wooing their congregation, thus abusing that much misquoted precedent of Him who became all things to all men that He might save some ; Him who as sternly rebuked hypocrisy and worldly compliances, as he tenderly consoled the dejected, and condescended to the weak." (p. 62).

Return we now from the Cambridge commencement to Broad Windsor with worthy Master Fuller, where he settled down among his neighbours, who soon became his friends and acquaintances. Our space will not permit us to do more than enumerate some of the more prominent among them. Fuller seems to have been on terms of intimacy with the illustrious *Rolle* family, which was seated at Bicton, the head of his house being *Dennys Rolle*, Esq. He was buried in Bicton Church, in the chantry, on the south side of the chancel. On a slab of black marble are the effigies of himself and wife, and underneath it that of a child. Prince, in his "Worthies of Devon," says the inscription in letters of gold on black marble, was made by Dr. Fuller." The epitaph is as follows :—

> " The Remains of Dennis Rolle, Esquire,
> His earthly Part within this Tombe doth rest,
> Who kept a Court of honour in his Breast :
> Birth, Beauty, Witt and Wisedome sat as Peeres,
> Till Death mistooke his virtues for his yeares :
> Or else Heaven envy'd Earth so rich a treasure,

Wherein too fine the Ware, too scant the measure,
His mournfull Wife her love to show in part,
This Tombe built here : a better in her heart.
Sweete Babe, his Hopefull Heyre (Heaven grant this boon)
Live but so well : but oh ! dye not so soon."

Through the Rolle family, Fuller became acquainted with the Pouletts, of Hinton St. George, Somerset. John, first Baron Poulett, was active on the King's side in the civil wars, when our author often met him. Fuller was also at this time probably acquainted with Gerard Napier, Esquire, of Middlemarsh Hall, Dorsetshire. He was created a baronet in 1641, and was a member of the Long Parliament till 1644.

Fuller's neighbour, Hugh Windham, Bart., of Pilsden Court, was a patron of his " Pisgah-Sight," and among his clerical neighbours we may mention Rev. Gilbert Ironsides, Rector of Winterbourne ; his name is returned as one who had not paid ship money; and Rev. Robert Gomersall, Vicar of Thorncombe, who was not only a florid preacher, but a composer of tragedies and poems. The following laudatory verses were composed by him, and prefixed to the second edition of the " Holy War." " To his worthy dear friend, Thomas Fuller, B.D., upon his excellent work." :—

" *Peace* is thy calling, Friend, thy title Warre :
What doth thy Title with thy calling jarre?
The Holy Warre: this makes the wonder cease:
A holy Warre becomes a man of peace.
Tasso be silent: my friend speaks: his storie
Hath robb'd thy poeme of its long liv'd glorie.
So rich his vein, his lines of so high state
Thou canst not figure so well as he relate.

> Godfrey first entered on this warre, to free
> His Saviour's Tombe from Turk's captivitie :
> And too too meanly of himself he deems,
> If thus he his Redeemer not redeems.
> A glorious end ! nor did he fear to erre
> In losing life, to gain Christ's sepulchre.
> But I dare say, were Godfrey now alive,
> (Godfrey, who by thy penne must needs survive)
> He would again act o're his noble toil,
> Doing such deeds as should the former foil :
> If for no other reason, yet to be
> Delivered unto time and fame by thee :
> Nor would he fear in such exploits to bleed,
> Then to regain a tombe, now not to need."

At the further end of the county, his former tutor at Queens' and relation—the great mathematical " coach "—Edward Davenant was beneficed at Gillingham, near Shaftesbury, a living he received from his uncle, the Bishop of the diocese, in 1626. Fuller would naturally from time to time be a visitor at the vicarage, and he certainly was there in 1656, when he preached the assize sermon at Shaftesbury. Here a numerous family was born to him, and after holding the vicarage fifty-three years, he died. Walker has an account of his trials and sufferings during the political troubles by the sequestration of the living.

"Another nephew of the same Bishop, Edward Davenant, on whom was bestowed not only the treasureship of the Cathedral, 'the best dignity,' but the valuable living of Gillingham, besides other preferments. He is described by Aubrey as not only 'a man of vast learning, but of great goodness and charity.' He was executor to Bishop Davenant's will, and also the inheritor of most of his property, insomuch that it was said that ' he gained more by the

Church of Sarum than ever any man did by the Church since the Reformation.' "* (p.202).

In Fuller's parish there also dwelt the descendants of the great sea-king, Sir Francis Drake, whose life Fuller appended to his essay on "The good sea-captain," one of whom "his dear and worthy parishioner," died in 1640. In his "Worthies," mentioning those who had raised themselves in the reign of Elizabeth by sea-service and "letters of mark," he says "that such prizes have been best observed to prosper whose takers had least of private revenge, and most of public service therein. Amongst these, most remarkable, the baronet's family of Drakes in Devonshire, sometime sheriffs of that county."

About this period Fuller must have entered into the holy estate of matrimony, but we are not informed by any of his biographers who the lady was. Such a grave Divine would no doubt make a prudent choice, especially if he put in practice the injunction attributed to him by Smiles (character p. 215) "take the daughter of a good mother." His "Holy State" begins with an essay on "The good wife," which forms a sort of frontispiece, and he enumerates a decade of good qualities or characteristics, which portraiture the wives of the 19th century would do well to study, based on Colossians iii. 18. He here depicts her more as a good housekeeper (" the house is the woman's centre ") than as a companion. In his commentary on Ruth he describes the marriage state as one of rest, so we may venture to hope that his premarital expectations became a realized fact in his domestic life. Her christian name appears to have

---

* S.P.C.K. Diocesan Histories (Salisbury) by W. H. Jones.

been Ellen, but as to her surname we are not told, except
that " she was a virtuous young gentlewoman." No record of
the marriage has yet been found, nor has the date been
ascertained. Bishop Davenant writing in 1638, makes
mention of her as being his nephew's wife, so he must have
been married before that year. It has also been surmised
that she was a Seymere or Seymour, as Fuller dedicates one
of his books in 1655 to Richard Seymere " my kinsman "
(*necessario meo*), which would point to the fact of his having
married into the family of Seymours of Dorset, or Devon.
His age at the time of his marriage would be about thirty,
and in addition to his cultured mind, his refined character
and cheerful disposition, he had a handsome and comely
person. He had an open countenance, blue eyes, florid
complexion, and light curly hair. He was a kind and
indulgent husband, and the marriage was a happy one.
But the stormy troubles, both in Church and State, were
soon to attract the notice of the " country parson " at
Broad Windsor, despite his happy social and domestic
surroundings. Government without parliament was coming
to an end, and about this time the agitation of the people
of Lyme Regis, anent the ship money, with which they were
heavily taxed, would be felt in that neighbourhood. In
matters ecclesiastical there was the Sabbatical controversy,
and that connected with the sacredness of holy places,
churches, adoration towards the altar, which name Fuller
observes now began to " out " God's Board, or Communion
Table. To a moderate man like Fuller the accommodation
of such matters " had been easy with a little condescension
on both sides." The injunction of Bishop Davenant on
this subject in the church, which was discovered by my

friend (Rev. J. Bliss) in the register, and printed at the end of his Oxford Edition of Laud's Works (Anglo-Catholic Library), is now, thanks to his industry, well-known. This document, which bears on the position of the " Holy Table," of Bishop Davenant's, respecting the church and parish of Aldbourne, in North Wilts, is of so much importance as throwing light on what was deemed the proper position of the Holy Table in 1637 (the period we are considering) that we venture to give a copy of it.

Bishop Davenant's order is as follows :—

John, by Divine providence, Bishop of Sarum.

To the Curate and Churchwardens with the parishioners of Awborne, in the county of Wilts, and our diocese of Sarum, greeting.

"Whereas his Majestie hath been lately informed that some men factiously disposed have taken upon themselves to place and remove the Communion Table in the Church at Auborne, and thereupon his highness hath required me to take present orders therein :—These are to let you know, that both according to the injunctions given out in the raign of Queene Elizabeth for the placing of the Communion Tables in Churches, and by the 82 canon agreed upon in the first yeare of the raigne of King James of blessed memory, it was intimated that these Tables should ordinarily be sett and stand with the side to the east wall of the Chancel, I therefore require you, the Church-wardens, and all other persons not to meddle with the bringing downe or transposing of the Communion Table, as you will answer it at your own perill. And because some doe ignorantly suppose that the standing of the Communion Table where altars stood in time of superstition, hath some relish of Popery, and some perchance may as erroniously conceive that the placing thereof, otherwise when the Holy Communion is administered, savours of irreverence, I would have you take notice from the fore named injunction and canon, from the Rubricke prefixed before the administration of the Lord's Supper, and from the first article not long since inquired of in the Visitation of our most reverend Metropolitan, that the placing of it higher or lower in the chauncell or in the Church is by the judgment of the Church of England a thing indifferent, and to be ordered and guided by the only rule of convenientie.

"Now, because in things of this nature to judge and determine what is most convenient belongs not to private persons, but to those that have ecclesiasticall authority, I inhibit you the Churchwardens, and all persons what-soever to meddle with the bringing downe of the Communion Table, or with altering the place thereof at such times as the Holy supper is to be administered, and I require you herein to yeeld obedience unto what is already judged most convenient by my chauncellor, unless, upon further consideration and viewe it shall be otherwise ordered. Now, to the end that the Minister may neither be overtoyled, nor the people indecently and inconveniently thronged together, when they are to drawe neire and take the Holy Sacrament, and that the frequent celebration thereof may never the lesse be continued. I doe further appoint that thrice in the yeare at the least, there be publique notice given in the Church for fower Communions to be held upon fower Sundaies together, and, that there come not to the Communion in one day, above two hundred at the most. For the better observation wherof, and that every man may know his proper time, the curate shall divide the parishioners into fower parts, according to his discretion, and as shall most fittingly serve to this purpose. And if any turbulent spirits shall disobey this our order, he shall be proceeded against according to the quality of his fault and misdemeanour!

"In witness whereof I have hereunto sett my hand and scale, Episcopall, this seventeenth day of May, 1637 and in the yeare of our Consecration the sixteenth."

This injunction is entered in the Aldbourne Parish Registers, and is printed in the Oxford edition of Laud's works by the Rev. J. Bliss (vol. vi. p. 60). It is referred to by the Archbishop himself in Laud's "Speech at the Censure of Basterwick." Ibid., 11, p. 80. See also Wilts Arch. Mag. vii. 3.

The direction contained in it, to the effect that Holy Communion should be administered on four successive

Sundays, and that no more than *two hundred* persons should communicate at one time, is to say the least a re- markable one respecting a parish, which we can hardly think was ever a very populous one.

Fuller seems, however, now to have settled down to his books and writing, in the quiet retirement of his country parsonage, which indeed has also in many other cases proved itself—as in that of Hooker and Herbert—a most congenial sphere for the pursuit of literary investigation. Here at Broad Windsor he laid the foundation of his great literary fame, and began to collate and systematise the results of his reading at Cambridge. Here too he got together the materials of two works, which made his literary reputation at one bound, and found for themselves a niche in the temple of fame, among the classics of the language, viz., " The Holy War," or " A History of the Crusades," and a " Pisgah- Sight of the Holy Land."

The " History of the Holy War " is dated from Broad Windsor, March 6th, 1639, and is dedicated to Edward, Lord Montagu, of Boughton, and John, Lord Poulett, of Hinton St. George, in Somersetshire. The " Pisgah-Sight," however, was not published till some time afterwards, the Epistle Dedicatory being dated at Waltham Abbey, July 7th, 1650. Fuller's anonymous biographer acquaints us that in the retirement of Broad Windsor, he prepared his " Pisgah-Sight," a work abounding with interest, and for the time in which it appeared, of no common value. "In the amenity and retirement of his rural life, some per- fective was given to those pieces which soon after blest this age. From this pleasant prospect he drew that excellent piece of his ' Holy Land,' ' Pisgah-Sight,' and other tracts

relating thereto : so that what was said bitterly of some
tyrants, that they made whole countries vast solitudes and
deserts, may be inverted to the eulogy of this Doctor, that
he in these recesses made deserts—the solitudes of Israel,
the frequented path and track of all ingenious and studious
persons." (Life, p. 12.)

The " Historie of the Holy Warre," being a history of the
Crusades, although dated at Broad Windsor, was published
at Cambridge, in folio, same year—which shows the interest
he still felt in, and the desire to retain his connection with
his old "Alma Mater." At this time there seems to have
been a feud between the London and Cambridge booksellers,
the former of whom disputed the right of the latter to
publish, which, however, they were entitled to, by Royal
grants. Fuller evidently took the side of the Cambridge
men, and several editions of this work, as well as the " Holy
State," were published there by a celebrated University
printer of the period—Roger Daniel. Fuller's works,
especially his early ones, are adorned with engravings and
wood-cuts, which look exceedingly quaint to us, living in
such a marvellous age of artistic culture. His engraver was
William Marshall, a man of reputation in his day, who designed
the title-page. It depicts a scene in which persons of all
ranks and conditions are seen marching out to war from
Europe, going out full and returning empty. In the
foreground is the temple of the Sepulchre, and oval-shaped
portraits of Baldwin, King of Jerusalem, and Saladin, are in
the two topmost corners ; and opposite are the arms of
Jerusalem and the Turkish Crescent; and at the end of this
volume is a curious map of the Holy Land. In his
dedication, Fuller makes the following remarks on Learning

and History : " Now, know, next Religion there is nothing accomplishes a man more than Learning. Learning in a Lord is a diamond in gold. And if you fear to hurt your tender hands with thorny school-questions, there is no danger in meddling with History, which is a velvet study and recreative-work. What a pity it is to see a proper gentleman have such a crick in his neck that he cannot look backward. Yet no better is he, who cannot see behind him the actions which long since were performed. History maketh a young man to be old, without either wrinkles or gray hairs ; privileging him with the experience of age, without either the infirmities or inconveniences thereof. Yea, it not only maketh things past present, but inableth one to make a rational conjecture of things to come. For this world affordeth no new accidents, but in the same sense wherein we call it *a new moon,* which is the old one in another shape, and yet no other than what hath been formerly. Old actions return again, furbished over with some new and different circumstances." Elsewhere he says, "Our experimental knowledge is in itself both short and narrow, and which cannot exceed ' the span of our own life.' But when we are mounted on the advantage of History, we cannot only reach the year of Christ's Incarnation, but even touch the top of the world's beginning, and at one view oversee all remarkable accidents of former ages."

The customary poetical commendation of our author and his book are prefixed, after the custom of the period, many being from the pens of his old college friends.

We subjoin a few specimens—the first by Robert Tyrling—

> " Of this our author's book, I'll say but this
> (For that is praise ample enough), 'Tis his :
> Nor all the Muses and Apollo's lays,
> Can sing his worth : be his own lines his bays."

Of our author's " excellently composed history," Booth (of Corpus), " his worthy and learned friend," says—

> " Captain of Arts, in this thy holy war,
> My muse desires to be thy trumpeter,
> In thy just praise to spend a blast or two:
> For this is all that she (poor thing) can do."

Reading the book—

> " Methinks I travel thro' the Holy Land,
> Viewing the sacred objects on each hand.
> Here mounts (me thinks) like Olivet, brave sense :
> There flows a Jordan of pure eloquence.
> A Temple rich in ornament I find
> Presented here to my admiring mind,
> To testify her liking, here my Muse
> Makes solemn vows, as Holy Pilgrims use :
> I vow dear friend the Holy War is here
> Far better writ than ever fought elsewhere.
> Might I but chose, I rather would by far
> Be author of thy book, than of that war.
> Let others fight, I vow to read thy works,
> Prizing thy ink before the blood of Turks."

H. Hutton, fellow of Jesus, says the book would make his memory as famous as his style—·

> " Thy style is clear and white : thy very name
> Speaks pureness, and adds lustre to the frame.
> All men could wish, nay long, the world would jar
> So thou'dst be pleased to write, compose the war."

Henry Vintener, of King's College, a friend of Pearson's, has some stately lines—

> " The Temple razed and ruined seems more high
> In his strong phrase than when it kiss'd the sky.
> And as the viper, by those precious tears
> Which Phaethon bemoan'd, of Amber wears

A rich (though fatal) coat : so here inclosed
With words so rare, so splendent, so compos'd
Ev'n Mahomet has found a tomb, which shall
Last when the fainting loadstone lets him fall."

There are also several other laudatory poems, all attesting the great popularity to which the work so speedily attained.

Fuller's " History of the Holy War," and " The Crusades," comprises five books, the first four of which contains the actual history which is thus summed up, " Thus after an hundred and ninety years, and four years, ended the Holy War : for continuance the longest, for money spent the costliest, for bloodshed the cruelest, for pretences the most pious, for the true intent the most politic, the world ever saw, and at this day, the Turks to spare the Christians their pains of coming so long a journey to Palestine, have done them the unwelcome courtesy to come more than half the way to give them a meeting." The fifth book is called a " Supplement, " and is said by Fuller to be " voluntary and over-measure, *only to hear the end of our history that it ravel not out.* " He now feels himself " discharged from the strict service and ties of an historian : so that it may be lawful for me to take more liberty and to make some observations on what hath passed." He thereupon treats of the fates of the Templars and other orders of Knights : of superstition in the war: of the Christians breaking faith with the infidels: of the hindrances to success: of the military position of Jerusalem : of the incredible numerousness of the armies : of the merit attaching to each nation for their military valour : of the influence of the war on heraldry : of subsequent proposals for a crusade ; of the fortunes of Jerusalem since the war ; of the pretenders to the kingdom ; of the greatness and wants

of the Turkish, Empire : " with some other passages which
offered attendance on these principal heads."

The Turk, though moribund, takes a long time in dying.
It may be interesting to some of our readers, who take an
interest in the " Eastern Question" as it is called, and would
like to drive the Osmanlis, " bag and baggage," out of
Europe, to know what Fuller thought of their possible deca-
dence, even when it was a mighty empire. " The Turk's
head is less than his turbant, and the turbant less than it
seemeth ; swelling without, hollow within. If more seriously
it be considered, this state cannot be strong, which is a pure
and absolute tyranny. His subjects under him have nothing
certain but this—that they have nothing certain, and may
thank the Grand Signor for giving them whatsoever he
taketh not away from them. We have just cause to hope
that the fall of this unwieldy empire doth approach. It was
high noon with it fifty years ago ; we hope now it draweth
near night ; the rather because luxury though late, yet at last
hath found the Turks out, or they it. Heaven can as
easily blast an oak, as trample a mushroom, and we may expect the ruin of this great empire will come : for of late it
hath little increased its stock ; and now beginneth to spend
of the principal. It were arrant presumption for flesh to
prescribe God His way : or to teach Him, when He meaneth
to shoot, which arrow in His quiver to choose. It is more
than enough for any man to set down the fate of a single
soul: much more to resolve the doom of a whole nation,
when it shall be. These things we leave Providence to
work, and posterity to behold. As for our generation, let
us sooner expect the dissolution of our own microcosms
than the confusion of this empire : for neither are our own

sins truly repented of, to have this punishment removed from us: nor the Turk's wickedness yet come to the full ripeness, to have this great judgment laid upon them." (p. 301.)

Mr. Bailey, in Fuller's life observes, "This unique history, Fuller's *first* ambitious effort, at once introduces us to Fuller's very felicitous way of writing. No work better displays the wealth of the Author's mind. It has all his genuine wit, his peculiar quaintness, his irresistible drollery, his skilfully constructed antithesis, and his incongruous allusions, —in very much of which there is always something more than mere ingenuity. He seems to revel in his composition, as if his favourite study, history, and not divinity, were his proper sphere. It is full of passages worthy of remembrance or quotation." The following is a specimen of some of them, "Mariners' vows end with the tempest." "It is charity to lend a crutch to a lame conceit." "The best way to keep great Princes together is to keep them asunder." "Charity's eyes must be open as well as her hands." "Slander (quicker than martial law) arraigneth, condemneth, and executeth all in an instant." "Hell itself cannot exist without Beelzebub, so much order there is in the place of confusion." "No opinion so monstrous, but if it had a mother, it will get a nurse." "A friend's house is no home." "*Mercenaries;* England has best thrived without them : under God's protection we stand on our legs. Let it be our prayer, that as for those hirelings which are to be last tried and least trusted, we have never want of their help and never have too much of it."

Fuller's great narrative power comes out in this work, and like a magician, or word-painter, he has a marvellous faculty of relating old stories in a novel and attractive manner. Vigorous liveliness is the backbone of his style, and in this work especially he may well earn the commendation of his fervent admirer Charles Lamb, who says, "Above all his way of telling a story, for its eager liveliness, and the perpetual running commentary of the narrator, happily blended with the narrative, is perhaps unequalled." This praise is well merited.

Professor Rogers in his essay in the *Edinburgh Review* writes sympathetically thus, "The activity of Fuller's suggestive faculty must have been immense. Though his principal characteristic is wit, and that too so disproportionate, that it conceals in its ivy-like luxuriance, the robust wisdom, about which it coils itself; his illustrations are drawn from every source and quarter, and are ever ready at his bidding. In the variety, frequency, and novelty of his illustrations, he strongly resembles two of the most imaginative writers in our language, though in all other respects still more unlike them than they were unlike one another, Jeremy Taylor and Edmund Burke . . . . We have said that Fuller's faculty of illustration is boundless : surely it may be safely asserted, since it can diffuse over the driest geographical and chronological details, an unwonted interest. We have a remarkable exemplification of this in those chapters of his ' Holy War,' in which he gives what he quaintly calls ' a Pisgah-sight or short survey of Palestine in general,' and a still stronger, if possible, in his ' Description of the Citie of Jerusalem.' In these chapters, what in other hands would have proved little more than a bare enumeration of names, sparkles with perpetual wit, and is entwined with all sorts of vivacious allusions."

The learning contained in this work is prodigious, and the authorities he consulted and collated, ancient and modern, are both various and numerous. These he cites, he often acknowledges, but sometimes he omits to do so, excusing himself for not doing so, in the following address "to the Reader," "If everywhere I have not charged the margin with the author's names, it is either because the story is author for itself (I mean generally received), or to avoid the often citing of the same place. When I could not go abroad myself, then I have taken air at the window, and have cited authors on others citations : yet so that the stream may direct to the fountain. If the reader may reap in a few hours, what cost me more months, just cause have I to rejoice, and he (I hope), none to complain." At the end is a chronological table, with a preface on chronology from A.D. 1095 to 1290, Pope Urban II. to Boniface VIII.

This book naturally engaged public attention, and became most popular, in fact this and the " Holy State" were the most popular of his works. It secured him at once his literary reputation, and much κῦδος as well as κέρδος. Next year (1640) saw a second edition, and 1647 a third : it was re-published in the Aldine edition of 1840, from which we have quoted : but its popularity seems to have waned after the Restoration, yet probably no books than the two quoted, ever had a larger circulation in that age of great writers and clever authors.

Fuller gives us some incidental allusions to its popularity, when discussing the question of second editions. "Here let me humbly tend to the reader's consideration that my 'Holy War,' though (for some design of the stationer) sticking still, in the title-page, at the third edition (as some unmarried maids will never be more than eighteen), *yet hath it oftener passed the press*, as hath my 'Holy State,' 'Meditations,'

K

etc., and yet never did I alter line or word in any new impression. I speak not this by way of attribution to myself, as if my books came forth at first with more perfection than other men's." ("Appeal," p. 293.)

Mr. Nicholl observes of the influence of the "Holy War" and "Holy State," that they "made a strong impression on the public mind, and for some years exercised an influence that might be distinctly traced in many affairs connected both with the Council and the Field, as the reader will perceive by my copious preface to Fuller's ' Holy War.'"

In this year (1639) Fuller's brother, John, took his M.A. at Sydney, and turned to the profession of the civil law, by permission of his good uncle (Bishop Davenant), who had otherwise evidently destined him for the Church ; and about this time our author visited Norwich, and speaking of the Cathedral, writes (in 1660) : "The Cathedral therein is large and spacious, though the roof in the cloisters be most commended. When some *twenty* years since I was there, the top of the steeple was blown down ; and an officer of the church told me 'that the wind had done them much wrong, but they meant not to put it up ;' whether the wrong or the steeple, he did not declare." Again : "As for the Bishop's Palace, it was formerly a very fair structure, but lately unleaded, and now covered with tile by the purchasers thereof ; whereon a wag, not unwittingly—

' Thus palaces are altered : we saw
  John Leyden, now Wat Tyler, next Jack Straw.'"

On Tuesday, April 14th, the Convocation assembled in the Chapter House of St. Paul's, and proceeded thence to hear the sermon in the choir. It was preached by Dr. Turner, Canon-residentiary of St. Paul's, and one of Laud's chaplains, in Latin, from St. Matthew, x. 16 : "*Behold I send you forth as sheep in the midst of wolves.*" Towards the close of the sermon he animadverted upon such of the Bishops as followed not closely in the steps of his patron, and held not the reins of Church government with an even hand, in pressing conformity strictly ; upbraiding them as seekers of popularity, by whose lukewarm courses the other Bishops were unjustly exposed to the charge of tyranny. After the service, Dr. Richard Stewart, Dean of Chichester, was chosen Prolocutor, *i.e.* chairman or "speaker" of the house. On Wednesday (15th) the Convocation met in that memorable chapel of King Henry VII., Westminster ; and when Sheldon presented the new Prolocutor to Laud, the Archbishop, in a Latin speech of three-quarters of an hour's length, deplored the calamities of the times, thus described by Fuller, consisting of "most of generals, bemoaning the distempers of the Church ; but he concluded it with a special passage, acquainting us how highly we were indebted to his Majesty's favour, so far entrusting the ability and integrity of that Convocation, as to empower them with his Commission, the like whereof was not granted many years before, to alter old, to make new canons for the better government of the Church." Fuller remarks that the appearance of Laud's eyes during the delivery of this speech was almost tearful, being but one remove from weeping ; and he alludes to the suspicions of thoughful men, lest that Convocation should over-act its part "in such distracted, dangerous, and discontented times."

CHAPTER IX.

THE CONVOCATION OF 1640 AND THE CANONS.

" He baits at middle antiquity, but lodges not till he comes at that which is ancient indeed. Some scoure off the rust of old inscriptions into their own souls, cankering themselves with superstition, having read so often *orate pro anima,* that at last they fall a praying for the departed ; and they more lament the ruine of Monasteryes, than the decay and ruine of Monk's lives, degenerating from *their* ancient piety and painfulnesse. Indeed, a little skill in antiquity inclines a man to Popery, but depth in that study brings him about again to our Religion."– *Holy State* (The True Church Antiquary), p. 62.

E come now to the memorable Convocation of 1640, in which Fuller sat, and approach the troublous age of internal politics. It is one of the most interesting and critical episodes in the history of our Church. It was convened at the time of that now known as the *Short Parliament,* April 14th, 1640, and was composed, to use Clarendon's words, of " sober and dispassionate men ; " it contained also, according to Cardwell, men " remarkably zealous for the rights of the Church," and " the most eminent assertors of those rights that our Church or nation has known." " We have the relations," says Mr. Perry, in his " History of the Church of England,"* " of several who were present at the meeting to guide us ; but not so full and copious as they might have been written ; for, says Fuller (who was one of

---

* Perry's " History of Church of England," vol. i. p. 600.

the proctors), 'it was ordered that none present should take any private notes in the house; whereby the particular passages thereof are left in great uncertainty. However, so far as I can remember, I will faithfully relate, being comforted with this consideration, that generally he is accounted an impartial arbitrator who displeaseth both sides.' "* Fuller was elected to represent the clergy of the diocese of Bristol, wherein he was beneficed; and it shows the esteem he must have been held in by his brother-clergy, for there is no greater honour or mark of respect and confidence, which can be bestowed on a beneficed clergyman by the clergy of a diocese than this, to depute him to represent them "and vote straight" in the Convocation of the province to which they belong.

His colleague in the representation was his friend and neighbour Gilbert Ironsides, Rector of Winterborne, a future Bishop of Bristol. There also attended this Convocation, Fuller's uncle, Bishop Davenant, and also Dr. William Fuller, the Dean of Ely.

Dr. William Fuller belonged to the Essex Fullers, and was son of Andrew Fuller, of Hadleigh, in Suffolk. Some authorities say he was one of Fuller's uncles, but this fact does not seem to be substantiated. He was a Cambridge man, Fellow of St. Catherine's Hall, D.D., and well known for his multifarious acquirements. After holding the living of Weston, Notts, and St. Giles's, Cripplegate, he was made Dean of Ely, 1636. He is described as a "notable, prudential man, a pathetic preacher, and of a nimble wit and clear expression." He was troubled by his

---

* "Church History," vol. xi. ch. iii. p. 1.

parishioners, but the Lords would not entertain the petition " against so revered a person, whose integrity is in so good an esteem with the Lords." He, however, felt the full brunt of the political troubles of the age, and suffered severely.

Another notable member of this Convocation was Dr. Peter Heylin, Fuller's doughty antagonist all through life ; the great High Church writer, and the consistent and persistent exponent of the Laudian school of thought. He sat as proctor for his College of Westminster. He was educated at Oxford, and was author of several works; his lectures at Oxford, called " Microcosmos ; or, A Description of the Great World," and a book of travels in France, which Southey characterised as " one of our liveliest books of travels in its lighter parts, and one of the wisest and most replete with information that was ever written by a young man."

In this Convocation, Dr. Heylin comes before us as the firm and unflinching opponent of the Puritan element, both within and without the Church, and he maintained his principle with much spirit and consistency. Southey says of him, " He was an able, honest, and brave man, who stood to his tackling when tested." He, as well as Fuller, published notes of this Convocation; but the two historians and literary athletes had been trained in different schools of thought—one moderate, and the other extreme. The consequence was, they were often found on opposite sides, and as antagonists, some smart, but bitter writing passed between them ; and although our author hit hard sometimes, as, for example, when he twitted Heylin for delighting to derive himself from the ancient kings of Wales in his

"Appeal of Injured Innocence," we must allow he was always most courteous, and readily acknowledged his opponent's skill in Church Law, and other legal acquirements which had not been so much in his line.

Fuller's history of this Convocation is to be found in his "Church History and Appeal," and is remarkable for its usual historical accuracy. It was, however, written from memory, as the members were not allowed, by a decision of the house, to take any notes, but he assures the reader that the work is honestly done, as far as his memory served him. Still, wonderful as was Fuller's retentive faculty, it was all but impossible that mistakes, especially in details, should not be made. This is not to be wondered at, considering the difficulty of the task of reporting memoriter, giving our author credit for the most conscientious painstaking. It must, however, be remembered that Fuller's, if brief, was the *first* complete account of this assembly, and that he had no authentic records to refer for verifying his own impression. Dr. Heylin's account, which is found in his "Life of Archbishop Laud," did not appear till many years afterwards, in 1668.

When Fuller's "Church History" appeared, containing his account of the Convocation, Dr. Heylin at once selected that for his animadversion, and boldly challenged its accuracy. Fuller accounts for this apparent discrepancy in a very ingenious way in his "Appeal," as following: "No wonder if some (I hope no great) variations betwixt us in relating the passages of this Convocation, each observing what made most for his own interest. The reader may be pleased also to use his own discretion, and to credit him, whom he believeth most probable of the two, exactly to observe, firmly to remember, and faithfully to relate what we saw done (both of us being there), and since borrowing help of our friends then present, where we fall short in our intelligence."[*]

Heylin's longer account is allowed to be more minute in its details, but is not free from a strong party bias. The most complete is that of Dr. Nalson's "Impartial Collections," drawn up at the instigation of Archbishop Sancroft, in answer to Rushworth's series of State Papers. Between the three accounts, it is possible to arrive at a resultant, which will give an approximation to the truth of a Convocation, memorable as to its session—both in regard to the critical time and the learned men who sat in it—momentous in its issues, and as being the first provincial council of which there is a full account.

" For as water long dammed up ofttimes flounce, and fly out too violently, when their sluices are pulled, and they let loose on a sudden, so the judicious fear, lest Convocation should now overact its part. Yea, they suspected, lest those who formerly had *outrun* the canons with their additional conformity (ceremonising more than was enjoined), now would make the canons *come up* to them, making it necessary for others, what voluntarily they had pre-practised themselves." (" Church History," bk. xi. cent. xvii.)

Five canons were made in this Convocation, before the dissolution of Parliament. The first (according to Heylin), concerning the regal power, appears not to have been considered till after the dissolution. That which is reckoned the third was first treated of, for *suppressing* the *further*

---

[*] "Appeal," pt. iii. p. 597.

growth of Popery, and *reducing Papists to the Church*. But this was suddenly withdrawn for revision : the Convocation proceeding with the second, *for the better keeping* of the *day* of *his* Majesty's most *happy inauguration*. For the reduction of the Papists, conferences were to be appointed to which they were to be compelled to come. Recusants were to be excommunicated, and prosecuted in the High Commission Court, and to be forbidden to keep school. Another canon was passed to check Socinianism, which appears to have increased in this reign more rapidly than in former years, when the services were more slovenly conducted. This canon was followed by another *against Sectaries*, Anabaptists, Brownists, Separatists, Familists, and depravers of the Liturgy, and against their books, and the printers and publishers of them.

But while the Convocation was in full session, suddenly the King took the ill-advised step of dissolving the Parliament. "His Majesty," says Hacket, "had been forewarned by a worthy counsellor, and a dying man against that error in the Christmas before, cujus mortem dolor omnium celebrem fecit." It was Lord Keeper Coventry, who made but one request with his last breath to the King, and sent it by Mr. James Maxwell, of the bedchamber, *that his Majesty would take all distastes from the Parliament summoned against April with patience, and suffer it to sit without an unkind dissolution.* But the barking of the living dogs was sooner heard than the groaning of a dying lion : for that Parliament ended in a few days, in its infancy and in its innocence, but the grief for it will never end." "From this very time," records Fuller, "did God begin to gather the twigs of that rod (a civil war) wherewith he intended soon after to whip a wanton nation."

The Parliament was dissolved Tuesday (May 5th), and on Wednesday the Convocation met, with the general impression that it would dissolve too—the spiritual Parliament following the temporal one, which it usually does *pari passu* —which it probably would have done, but that one of the clergy (Heylin), made the Primate acquainted with a precedent to the contrary, in Queen Elizabeth's time, for the granting a subsidy or benevolence by Convocation, to be taxed and levied by *synodical* Acts and Constitutions, without help of the Parliament, directing to the records of the Convocation where it was to be found. *

Soon after this a new commission was brought from his Majesty, "by virtue whereof," says Fuller, "we were warranted still to sit, not in the capacity of a Convocation, but a *synod*, to prepare our canons for the royal assent thereof. But Dr. Brownrigg, Dr. Hackett, Dr. Holdsworth, Mr. Warmistre, with others (of whom Fuller was one), to the number of thirty-six (the whole house consisting of about six score), earnestly protested against the continuance of the Convocation."

Amongst these was Fuller himself, but they did not enter a record of their protest, which he acknowledges to have been an oversight in his "Appeal." However, they importunely pressed that it might sink with the Parliament, it being ominous, and without precedent, that the one should survive, when the other expired. To satisfy these, an instrument was brought into synod, signed with the hands of the Lord Privy Seal, the two Chief Justices, and other Judges, "justifying our so sitting in the nature of a synod, to be legal,

---

* Fuller's " Church History." Book xi., cent. xvii., p. 458.

according to the laws of the realm." "This," says our author, "made the aforesaid thirty-six dissenters (though solemnly making their oral protests to the contrary) yet, not to dissever themselves, or enter any act *in scriptis* against the legality of this assembly ; the rather, because they hoped to moderate proceedings with their presence. Surely some of their own coat, which since have censured these dissenters for cowardly compliance, and doing no more in this cause, would have done less themselves if in their condition."

Now, because great bodies move slowly, and are fitter to be the consenters to, than the contrivers of business, it was thought fit to contract the synod into a select committee of some six and twenty, besides the Prolocutor, who were to ripen matters, as to the propounding and drawing up of forms to what should pass, yet, so that nothing could be accounted the act of the House, till thrice (as I take it) publicly voted therein. * Then the canon was passed, touching the regal power, affirming the order of Kings to be of Divine right, the ordinance of God Himself: that the Government of the Church belongs, in chief to Kings, as also the power to call and dissolve Councils, both national and provincial ; that the assertion of any co-active power, either papal or popular is treason, as well as against God as against the King; that for subjects to bear arms against their Kings, either offensive or defensive, is contrary to Scripture ; that the right of the King to all manner of necessary support and supply, and of the subject to his property, are not contrary but agreeable the one to the other.

---

* Heylin's "Life of Laud," Part ii., 403.

This canon not only provoked the indignation of the Parliament at a subsequent period, but at the time the populace testified its feelings against the clergy by assaulting the Archbishop's house, and the King was forced to appoint a guard to protect the members of the synod from the mobs which threatened them. Heylin thus describes the state of things, "To such extremities were the poor clergy brought during these confusions, in danger of the King's displeasure if they rose, of the people's fury if they sate, in danger of being beaten up by tumults when they were at their work of being beaten down by the following Parliament when their work was done. Everyone must have his blow at them."

Forasmuch as we are given to understand that many of our subjects being misled against the rites and ceremonies now used in the Church of England, have lately taken offence at the same, upon an unjust supposal that they are contrary *to our laws*, the declaration goes on to assert that they were used by the Reformers, but had lately begun to fall into disuse, and then having recited the powers given to this Convocation to make canons, it "ratifies and confirms the canons made." Sparrow's Collection, 337-344.

Next this assembly adopted an oath, obliging the Clergy not only obedience to the then constitution of the Church, but to maintain it without seeking directly or indirectly any alteration in the hierarchical form. This oath was to be taken by members of the Universities, schoolmasters, &c.

In the declaration concerning some rites and ceremonies, it was affirmed that the standing of the Communion Table sideway under the east window of every chancel or chapel, is in its own nature indifferent, but that it is judged fit and convenient that all churches and chapels do confine themselves in this particular to the example of the cathedral or mother churches, saving always the general liberty left to the bishops by law during the time of the administration of the Holy Communion. "And we declare that this situation of the Holy Table (the Greek, ἀγια τράπεζα) doth not imply that it is, or ought to be esteemed a true and proper altar, whereon Christ is again sacrificed : but it is, and may be called an altar by us, in that sense which the Primitive Church called it an altar and no other. The altar was to be railed about to prevent the irreverent use of it, the putting of hats upon it, common amongst those who abhor reverence in worship."

Obeisance is also commended to all upon entering and leaving the Church or the chancel, "according to the most ancient custom of the Primitive Church in the purest time, and of this Church also for many years of the reign of Queen Elizabeth. The receiving therefore, of this ancient and laudable custom we heartily commend to the serious consideration of all good people, not with any intention to exhibit any religious worship to the Communion Table, the East or Church, or anything therein contained, in so doing ; or to perform the said gesture in the celebration of the Holy Eucharist upon any opinion of the corporal presence of the body of Christ on the Holy Table, or in the mystical elements, but only for the advancement of God's Majesty, and to give Him alone that honour and glory that is due unto Him and not otherwise. And in the practice or omission of this rite, we desire that the rule of charity prescribed by the Apostle may be observed, which is, that they which use this rite, despise not them who use it not, and that they who use it not, condemn not those who use it."

Heylin tells us that there had also been "a design in deliberation touching the drawing and digesting of an *English Pontifical* to be approved by this Convocation, and tendered to his Majesty's confirmation, which said *Pontifical* was to contain the form and manner of his Majesty's coronation, to serve for a perpetual standing rule on the like occasions; another form to be observed by all archbishops and bishops for consecrating churches, churchyards and chapels, and a third for reconciling *penitents*, as either had done open penance, or had revolted from the faith to the law of *Mahom t*, which three together with the form of Confirmation, and that of ordering *Bishops, Priests, and Deacons,* which was then in force, were to make up the whole body of the book intended." Heylin also seems to intimate that another scheme for introducing the service in Latin in all colleges and halls, at least in the morning service failed.

These Canons were disallowed in the following parliament, and the oath was allowed to drop, Sanderson being of opinion that it would possibly endanger the Church. But after the twenty-six sessions, May 29th, the whole of the seventeen Canons were subscribed to, "every man's heart, says Heylin, going along with his hand, as it is to be presumed from all men of that holy profession." Laud, fourteen bishops (including Davenant), and eighty-nine other members (including Fuller), subscribed their names, for he talks of *our* subscription in the *Appeal.* The acts were then sent to the Convocation of York, which also adopted them, and they were then set forth by royal assent, June 30. Fuller and his party signed the document " suffering ourselves to be included by the majority of the votes, after the practice of Councils and Synods, that the whole body should subscribe to those acts that are passed by the major part, as to synodical acts, notwithstanding their private dissent."

No doubt the acts of this Convocation provoked the hostility of the popular party. The Canon, touching the King's majesty, gave especial umbrage, and that touching the oath* was not approved of by even many of the Bishops themselves. Some refused to tender it, as Hall and the Puritan Bishops, while the London and Lincoln clergy openly ignored it. Yet some of the Bishops were zealous in pushing it, and Fuller declares that to his knowledge, some of the clergy were compelled to take it on their knees. Be this as it may, the Canons of this Convocation were the principal agents in separating King and people, and divorcing Church and State. The impeachment of Laud was due mainly to them, as he was regarded as the *fons et origo*, the concrete embodiment of the whole synodical action on the part of the Clergy.

---

* The oath known as the Et Cetera Oath :—"I, A. B., do swear that I do approve the doctrine and discipline or Government established in the Church of England, as containing all things necessary to salvation; and that I will not endeavour by myself, or any other, directly or indirectly, to bring in any Popish doctrine contrary to that which is so established, nor will I ever give my consent to alter the government of this church by Archbishops, Bishops, Deans, and Archdeacons, &c., as it stands now established, and as by right it ought to stand, nor ever yet to subject it to the usurpations and superstitions of the See of Rome. And all these things I do sincerely acknowledge and swear, according to the plain and common sense understanding of the same words, without any equivocation, or mental evasion or secret reservation, whatsoever. And this I do heartily, willingly, and truly, upon the faith of a Christian, so help me God."—*Perry's "Church of England,"* i., 615.

CHAPTER X.

FULLER'S "JOSEPH'S PARTI-COLOURED COAT."—(1640.)

"*The Sacrament, solemnly celebrated, doth re-present and set forth the death and Passion of Christ.* That is, Christ was so powerfully and pathetically preached unto them in the word, His death so done to the life in the solemn, decent, and expressive Administration of the Sacrament, that the tragedy of Christ's death, nigh *Jerusalem,* was re-acted before them. Say, not, then in thy heart how shall I get to Jerusalem to see the place of Christ's suffering. See, faith can remove mountains. Mount *Calvary* is brought home to thee, and though there be μεγα χασμα, a great gulf, or distance of ground betwixt England and Palestine, yet, if thou be'est a faithful receiver, behold Christ Sacramentally crucified on the Communion Table. Say not in thine heart how shall I remember Christ's passion ; it was *time out of mind* 1600 years ago. Christ here teacheth thee the art of memory ; what so long was past is now made present at the instant of thy worthy receiving. Stay, pilgrims stay (would your voyages to the Holy Land had been as farre from superstition as hitherto from successe), go not you thither, but bring Palestine hither, by bringing pure hearts with you when you come to receive the Sacrament, for there *the Lord's Body is shewed forth,* as on the Cross."—*Joseph's Party-Coloured Coat,* pp. 61-62.

THERE can be no doubt that this convocation was the means of bringing Fuller (one of the Clerks for the Diocese of Bristol), into prominence and notice, and introducing him to the primate, and London. Although the Archbishop and the Bristol proctor had not taken the same sides in the synodical debates, yet it is evident from the gratitude which Fuller betrays toward Laud on more than one occasion, that the Archbishop had done him some act of kindness, or paid him some delicate attention. Some think it may have been a permission to preach in another diocese, or that Fuller was surprised by some unexpected courtesy, who alludes to it in the following words : " I am much of the mind of Sir Edward Deering, that the roughness of his (Laud's) uncourt-like nature sweetened many men when they least looked for it, surprising some of them (and myself for one) with unexpected courtesies." Whatever they may have been, the fact points to some rapprochement between the two, which had evidently left a pleasing reminiscence behind it.

At this period, too, Fuller made his acquaintance with London, and during the sittings of the Convocation preached in many of the leading pulpits—"the voice'd pulpits "— as his biographer styles them—of the metropolis. He became known as an attractive and popular preacher, popular in a good sense, being known as eloquent in speech, of a ready imagination, a sound divine, a clever writer, and of engaging conversation and pleasing manners. He was quickly a favourite among his new circle of friends, and was as much "run after" in London as he had been at Cambridge and Broad Windsor. This new life would, especially with such a temperament as his, in the whirl of Town, with the circumambient friction of thought, the collision of mind with mind, the excitement of the day, the social surroundings, and the general political and ecclesiastical ferment, prove very attractive to this rising divine, and the contrast between it and the humdrum of a country parson's life would naturally force itself upon him. He was drawn on more and more. Great changes were pending both in Church and State, and the discussions and debates anent them would be full of feverish interest and excitement. Into these Fuller would have been insensibly drawn, so that his prospects became altered, or at least modified, till at last the idea of migrating to Town gradually assumed shape, issuing in a determination to remove to the metropolis, and take an active part in the struggles of the day, and allay the unnatural strife thereof. "He was very sensible" says his biographer, "whither those first commotions did tend, and that some heavy disaster did, in those angry clouds which impended over the nation, more particular threaten the clergy."

About this time Fuller took the opportunity of his visit to Town to publish a volume of sermons, which was eagerly bought, both at the time, and continued their popularity through his life, which much enhanced his reputation.

This publication consisted of a comment on the portion of St. Paul's Epistle to the Corinthians connected with the institution of the Lord's Supper (1 Cor. xi. 18 to 31 v.), and eight other sermons were appended to it. Fuller gave it the quaint appellation of "Joseph's Parti-Coloured Coat" and it was printed by John Williams. It is dedicated to the Right Worshipful the Lady Jane Covert, of Pepper Harrow, near Godalming, Surrey. Fuller observes in the dedication, whilst custom has licensed flattery in dedicating epistles, epitaphs and dedications, he will not follow the stream herein. "First, because I account it beneath my calling to speak any thing above the truth, secondly, because of you it is needless. Let deformed faces be beholding to the painter, art hath nothing to do when nature hath *prevented* it." The title of the book seems to have been suggested by the variety of topics introduced—the sermons in the latter part of the book being on the following subjects, "Growth in grace : How far examples may be followed : An Ill-Match well broken off : Good from Bad Friends : A Glass for Gluttons : How far Grace may be entailed : A Christening Sermon : and Faction Confuted." At this time Fuller's popularity was of the highest kind, for his sermons had the charm of truth about them. It did not commence among a swarm of butterflies, it grew not up amongst a crowd of itching ears. It was not owing to their defects, but in spite of them, that Andrewes, and Fuller, and others of the like kind were in such estimation. But it must be allowed that unseasonable as is wit in sacred things, men are everywhere caught by it in spite of themselves.

In these remarkable sermons, Fuller gives a definition of heresy drawn from St. Augustine, an error in the *essentials* of religion, and that *obstinately* maintained. " In the primitive church many were too lavish in bestowing the name of heretic on those which dissented from the church in (as I may say) venial errors. A charitable man would have been loth to have been of the jury to condemn Jovinian for an heretic, on no other evidence than that he maintained marriage in merit to be equal with virginity." Pointing out the evils of ignorance he says " To prevent these mischiefs, let the meanest-parted labour to attain to some competent measure of knowledge in matters of salvation, that so he may not trust every spirit, but be able to try whether he be of God or no. Believe no man with implicit faith in matters of such moment ; for he who buys a jewel in a case without ever looking at it, deserves to be cozened with a Bristol-stone instead of a diamond."

Speaking of the love feasts, (ἀγαπὴ) of the Primitive Church, Fuller observes " Yet mark by the way that St. Paul does not plant his arguments point-blank to beat these love-feasts down to the ground, wholly to abrogate and make a nullity of them, but only to correct and reform the abuses therein, that there might be less riot in the rich, and more charity towards the poor."

Most characteristic of his pen is the following ; " *What shall I say ? shall I praise you in this ?* " Pastors may and must praise their people wherein they do well.

1.—Hereby they shall peaceably possess themselves of this good will of their people, which may much advance the power and efficacy of their preaching. 2.—Men will more willingly digest a reproof for their faults, if praised, when they do well. 3.—Virtue being commended doth increase and multiply ; creepers in goodness will go, goers run, runners fly. Use. "Those ministers to be blamed, which are ever blaming, often without cause, always without measure, (whereas it is said of God, He will not be always chiding, Ps. ciii. 9.) "Do any desire to hear that which Themistocles counted the best music, namely themselves commended ? On these conditions, we ministers will indent with them. Let them find matter, we will find words. Let them do what is commendable, and blame us if we commend not what they do. Such work for us would be recreation ; such employ-ment a pleasure, turning our most stammering tongue into the pen of a ready writer. To reprove is prest from us, as wine from grapes ; but praises would flow from our lips as water from a fountain. But alas, how can we build, when they afford us neither brick nor straw? How can we praise what they do when they will not do what is to be praised ? If, with Ahab they will do what is evil, we must always pro-phecy evil unto them."

Speaking of the way corruptions will creep in even in the best Churches. "If Primitive Churches, whilst the Apostles which planted them were alive to prune them, had such errors in them, no wonder if the Church at sixteen hundred years of age may have some defaults. Moses said unto the Israelites, Deut. xxxi. 27, "Behold, while I am with you this day, ye have been rebellious against the Lord ; and how much more when I am dead." So, if while St. Paul survived, Churches were so prone to decline, what can be less expected in our days? It was therefore well concluded in the 39th session of the Council of Constance, that every ten years at the furthest, there should be a General Council held to reform such errors in the Church as probably in that time would arise."

Speaking of the Word of God being attested most clearly by His providence, " The providence of God plainly appears in the preserving of Scriptures against all opposition. Many a time from my youth up (may the Scriptures now say), yea, many a time have they fought against me, but they could not prevail against me, neither Antiochus before Christ, nor Julian the Apostate since Him, nor the force of tyrants, nor the fraud of heretics (though the world of late hath scarce yielded a wicked sharp-wit, that hath not given the scriptures a gash), could ever suppress them. Their treading on this camomile made it grow the better, and their snuffing of this candle made it burn the brighter. Whereas, on the other side the records of tradition are lost, and those books wherein they were compiled or composed aut incuriâ hominum aut injuria temporis (either by the negligence of men or by the ravages of time) or by some other sinister accident, are wholly miscarried and nowhere appear.

Papias is reported by Eusebius (Hist. lib. 4, c. 8.) in five books to have contained all the Apostolical traditions which they call the *Word not written :* but Bellarmine himself confessed that these are lost. Likewise Clemens Alexandrinus (as the same Eusebius lib. 6, c. 11.) storieth it, wrote in a book those traditions which he received from the elders, and they from the Apostles, which book the Papists this day cannot produce. I will conclude all with Gamaliel's words, Acts v. 39. 'But if it be of God ye cannot destroy it.' Had these books been inspired by God's Spirit, no doubt the same providence would have watched to preserve them, which hath protected the Scripture. Let us therefore, leaving uncertain traditions, stick to the Scriptures alone, trust no doctrine on its single bond, which brings not God's word for its security. Let that plate be beaten in pieces which hath not this tower-stamp upon it. From the words ' As often as ye eat this bread,' he proceeds to urge frequent communion " Under *as often* is *often* included : Whence we gather we must frequently celebrate the Lord's Supper. In the Primitive Church it was done everyday, (1 Euseb. lib. 1 Demonst Evang. c. 10,) and fit it was the aqua vitæ bottle should ever be at their nostrils, who were swooning every moment : and they needed constant cordials, who ever and anon had the qualms of temptation in the time of persecution." This homely figure is so expressive, as almost by its suitableness to atone for its homeliness. This frequency soon abated when peace came into the Church, which makes S. Ambrose (Lib. v. de Sacramentis c. 4.) reprove the negligence of the Eastern Churches who received it but once a year.

Our preacher proceeds to answer the objections that have

been invented to dissuade from the revival of the better and more ancient spirit. The first objection is taken from the Passover which was observed but once a year. To this he replies "The Passover by God was stinted to be used no oftener : in the Lord's Supper we are left to our own liberty. Finding therefore our continual sinning, and therefore need thereof to strengthen us in our grace, we may, yea, must oftener use it, especially seeing all services of God under the Gospel ought to be more plentiful and abundant than under the Law." (p. 59) The second objection is " things done often are seldom done solemnly." Then he replies, *sermons and prayers should be equally rare.* The third is, that long preparation is requisite to this action. To this he answers that often preparing lessen the difficulty of right preparation. He does not (with many) extenuate the guilt of the unworthy communicant. He speaks of this sin as "the highest of any pardonable sin, even guiltiness of Christ's blood itself." This is a true maxim, " To him to whom the sacrament is not heaven, it is hell." He observes that there were other sins amongst the Corinthians, factions, preference of pastors, connivance of incest, and going to law one with another before heathen judges, and denying of the resurrection. Of these he notes they were *felony*, robbing God of His glory, but the irreverent receiving of the sacrament was high treason against the person of Christ, and so against God Himself."

Of the discourses that follow, the two most worthy of their author are, the first, " On Growth in Grace," and the last, entitled " Faction Confuted." In the first we have this excellent apothegm, " Practice without knowledge is blind, and knowledge without practice is lame." Again, plants, he observes, "have their bounds, both in height and breadth, set by nature, but growth in grace admits of no such period." The latter part of the sermon is an answer to the doubts of those who are troubled with scruples and fears respecting their being in a state of grace.

" Others concern themselves not to be grown in grace when they are grown, and that in these four cases.

" Sometimes they think they have less grace than they had seven years ago, because they are more sensible of their badness ; they daily see and grieve to see how spiritual the law of God is, and how carnal they are ; now they sin both against God's will and their own, and sorrow after their sin, and sin after their sorrow. This makes many mistake themselves to be worse than they have been formerly ; whereas, indeed, the sick man begins to mend, when he begins to feel his pain.

2. " Many think themselves to have less saving knowledge now than they had at their first conversion : both because (as we said before of grace) they are now more sensible of their ignorance : and because their knowledge at their first conversion seemed a great deal, which, since seemeth not increased because increased insensibly and by unappearing degrees. One that hath lived all his life time in a most dark dungeon, and at last is brought out but into the twilight, more admires at the clearness and brightness thereof, than he will wonder a month after at the sun at noon-day. So a Christian newly regenerated, and brought out of the dark state of nature into the life of grace, is more apprehensive at the first illumination of the knowledge he receives, than of far greater degree of knowledge which he receiveth afterwards.

" Some think they have less grace now than they had some

years since, because a great measure of grace seems but little to him that desires more. As in worldly wealth, *crescit amor nummi quantum ipsa pecunia crescit* (the love of money increaseth as the money itself increaseth), so is there an holy, heavenly and laudable covetousness of grace, which deceives the eye of the soul, and makes a great deal of goodness seem but little.

" Many think they are grown less and weaker in grace, when indeed they are assaulted with stronger temptations. One saith, 'Seven years since I vanquished such temptations as at this day foil me, therefore surely I am decreased in grace.' *Non sequitur*, for though it be the same temptation in kind, it may not be the same in degree and strength, thou mayest still be as valiant, yet these enemies may conquer thee, as assaulting thee with more force and fury. When thou wert newly converted, God proportioned the weight to the weakness of thy shoulders ; bound up the devil that he should set upon thee with no more force than thou couldst resist and subdue. Now, thou hast gotten a greater stock of grace, God suffers the devil to buffet thee with greater blows."

"Some think grace is less in them now than it was at the first conversion, because they find not in their souls such violent flashes, such strong impetuous (I had almost said furious) raptures of goodness and flashes of grace and heavenly illumination. But let them seriously consider that these raptures which they then had, and now complain they want, were but fits short and sudden : *nimbus erat, cito præteriit*: not settled and constant, but such as quickly spent themselves with their own violence : whereas, grace in them now may be more solid, reduced, digested,

and concocted : *Bos lapsus fortius figit pedem,* more slow,
but more sure, less violent, but more constant : though
grace be not so thick at one time, yet now it is beaten and
hammered out to be broader and longer, yea, I might add
also, it is more pure and refined.   This we may see in Saint
Peter, when he was a young man ; in a bravery he would
walk on the water, yea, so daring was he in his promise :
though all forsake thee, yet will not I: but afterwards in his
old age he was not so bold and daring.   Experience had not
only corrected the rankness of his spirit, but also in some
sort quenched, surely tempered the flashes of his zeal for the
adventurousness of it : yet was he never a whit the worse
but the better Christian : though he was not so quick to run
into danger, yet he would answer the spur when need required, and not flinch from persecution when just occasion was
offered : as at last he suffered martyrdom gloriously for Christ.

"To conclude, grace in the good thief on the cross, like
Jonah's gourd, grew up presently, for he was an extraordinary example ; but in us it is like the growth of an oak,
slow and insensible, so that we may sooner find it *crevisse* than
crescere.   It must, therefore, be our daily task all the days
of our lives ; to which end, let us remember to pray to God
for His blessing on us.   Our Saviour saith, Matt. vi. 27,
" *Which of you by taking care is able to add one cubit unto his
stature in the corporal growth,*" much less able are we to add
one inch or hair's breadth to the height of our souls.   Then
what was pride in the builders of Babel will be piety in us,
to mount and raise our souls on high, till the top of them
shall reach to heaven.   Amen."

The fourth sermon, "Good from bad friends," is as excellent as it is ingenious.   2 Samuel xv. 31, "And one

told David, saying, Achitophel is among the conspirators
with Absalom." Our author observes how the treachery of
Achitophel was a just visitation on David for his treachery
to Uriah; how, when our friends forsake us, we ought to
enter into a serious scrutiny of our own souls. 2. The most
politic heads have not always the faithfullest hearts. 3.
False friends will forsake in time of adversity.

From the unfaithfulness of friends we may learn: 1. To
consider with ourselves whether we have not been faulty in
entertaining talebearers, and lending a listening ear unto
them: 2. If thy conscience accuse thee not, whether there
was not a false principle in the first invitation of thy love?
was it a friendship begun in sin? 3. If it did not begin in sin,
hast thou not committed many sins to hold in with him? Hast
thou not flattered him in his faults, or at leastwise by thy
silence consented to him? 4. Hast thou not idolatrized thy
friend? 5. Has thou not undervalued thy friend, and set too
mean a rate and low estimate on his love? 6. It may be God
suffers thy friend to prove unfaithful to thee, to make thee
stick more closely to Himself. Micah vii. 5.

The next sermon is headed, "A Glass for Gluttons."
Rom. xii. 13. "Not in gluttony." Our preacher calls
gluttony the sin of England. "For though without usurpation we may entitle ourselves to the pride of the Spanish,
jealousy of the Italian, wantonness of the French, drunkenness of the Dutch, and laziness of the Irish, and though
these outlandish sins have of late been naturalized and made
free denizens of England, yet our ancientest *carte* is for the
sin of gluttony." This sermon against gluttony is itself a
surfeit of wit. Yet was it intended for a wholesome
medicine, but alas! the glutton is not the man to be laughed

out of his disease. The danger of this sin our author illustrates first, from the very circumstance that it is not punishable by human laws, for as those offences are accounted the greatest which cannot be punished by a constable, justice, or judge of assize, but are reserved immediately to be punished by the King himself, so gluttons must needs be sinners in an high degree, who are not censurable by any earthly king, but are referred to be judged at God's tribunal alone.

2. " It is more dangerous because it is so hard and difficult to discern. Like to the hectic fever, it steals on a man unawares. Some sins come with observation, and are either ushered with a noise, or like a snail, leave a slime behind them, whereby they may be traced and tracked, as drunkenness. The Ephraimites were differenced from the rest of the Israelites by their lisping ; they could not pronounce H. Thus drunkards are distinguished from the king's sober subjects by clipping the coin of the tongue. But there are not such signs and symptoms of gluttony. This sin doth so insensibly unite and incorporate itself with our natural appetite, to eat for the preservation of our lives, that as St. Gregory saith *(lib* 30 *moral c.* 28 *ante medium)* it is a hard thing to discern what necessity requires, and what pleasure supplies, because in eating pleasure is mixed with appetite or necessity: what is the full charge of food which nature requires for our sustenance, and what is that surcharge which is heaped by superfluity.

3. " Because of the sundry dangers it brings, first to the soul. Luke xxi. 34. ' Take heed lest your hearts be oppressed with surfeiting.' And, indeed, the soul must needs be unfitting to serve God so encumbered. That man hath

ut an uncomfortable life who is confined to live in a smoky
ouse. The brain is one of these places of the residence
f the soul, and when that is filled with steam and vapours
rising from unconcocted crudities in the stomach, the soul
nust needs male habitare, dwell uncheerfully, ill accomo-
lated in so smoky a mansion. And as hereby it is unapt
or the performance of good, so it is ready for most evil, for
uncleanness, scurrility, ili-speaking.

"Secondly, this sin impairs the health of the body: the
outlandish proverb says, that the glutton digs his grave with
his own teeth. Must there not be a battle in the stomach,
wherein there is meat hot, cold, sod, roast, flesh, fish? and
which side soever wins, nature and health will be overcome,
when as a man's body is like unto the ark of Noah, containing all beasts, clean and unclean: but he is the most
clean beast that contains them. Our law interprets it to be
murther, when one is killed with a knife. Let us take
heed that we be not all condemned, for being *felos-de-se:*
for willingly murthering our own lives with our knives by
our superstitious eating. Thirdly, it wrongs the creatures
that are hereby abused. God saith (Hosea ii. 9) that He
will recover his flax and his wool from the idolatrous Jews,
Vindicabo, I will rescue and recover them as from slavery
and subjection, wherein they were detained against their
will: and in such like tyranny are the creatures, as bread,
wine, and meat, tortured under the glutton. Lastly, it
wrongeth the poor, for it is the overmuch feasting of Dives,
which of necessity maketh the fasting of Lazarus: and
might not the superfluous meat of the rich be sold for many
a pound, and given to the poor?"

He then proceeds to consider wherein gluttony doth consist. It consisteth either in the quantity of the meat, or in the quality, or in the manner of eating. Here he first admits that it is hard to define the proportion of meat for every man's stomach: "that quantity of rain will make a clay-ground drunk, which will scarce quench the thirst of a sandy country." It is well that our author did not live in these times; and what would he have said to the Malthusian regulations in these and other matters?

"Let this be the rule," says our not less and truly philosophical author, "he shall be arraigned and condemned before God for gluttony in the quantity of meat, who hath eaten so much, as thereby he is disabled, either in part, or wholly, to serve God, in his general or particular calling, be his age, climate, or temper whatsoever.

"Gluttony is in the quality of the meat: (1) when it is too young (Exod. xxiii. 19); (2) too costly; (3) an incentive to lust; (4) to increase appetite. It is in the manner of eating. 1. Greedily, without giving thanks to God: like hogs eating up the mast, not looking up to the hand that shaketh it down. It is said of the Israelites (Exod. xxiii. 6), the *people sat down to eat and drink;* there is no mention of grace before meat: *and rose up to play;* there is no mention of grace after. 2. Constantly. Dives fared deliciously every day: there was no Friday in his week, nor fast in his almanack, nor Lent in his year: whereas the moon is not always in its full, but hath as well a waning and a waxing: the sea is not always in a spring-tide, but hath as well an ebbing as a flowing: and surely the very rule of health will dictate thus much to a man, not always to hold a constant tenure of feasting, but sometimes to abate in his diet. 3. When they eat their meats studiously, resolving all the powers of their mind upon meat : singing Requiem in their souls with the glutton in the Gospel, ' Soul, take thine ease,' etc. And whereas we are to eat to live, these only live to eat."

The next discourse is entitled, " How far grace can be entailed," in Tim. i. 5. Here he enters upon the question, How can we tell that grace is in another ? Only he replies by long and intimate acquaintance, " Too bold are those men, who upon a superficial knowledge and short convers- ing with any, dare peremptorily pronounce that such an one hath saving grace and sanctity in him. These are professors of spiritual palmistry, who think that upon small experience they can see the life-line (the line of eternal life in the hands of men's souls), whereas, for all their skill, they often mis- take the hands of Esau for the hands of Jacob."

The Christening sermon is from 2 Kings v. 14—the history of Naaman. Here he observes the state in which Naaman came to Elisha ; and how, being repulsed, he fol- lowed the advice of his servants. He proceeds to enume- rate the several points of his text, but finding them too many for one discourse, likens this circumstance to Gideon, who, having too great an army for his use, sent most of his servants away; and so confines his remarks to the time after his servants had persuaded him : the simplicity of the means in preaching and in the sacraments : the sevenfold washing, in which we are taught patience ; the duty of ob- serving God's commandments, both in matter and manner, both in substance and circumstance ; and the resemblance between the washing away of leprosy and the washing of baptism, to cleanse our original corruption, yet not to cleanse perfectly, but in part, for " though the bane be

removed, the blot doth remain ; the guilt is remitted, the
blemish is retained ; the sting is gone, the stain doth stay :
which, if not consented to, cannot damn this infant, though
it may hereafter defile." In this dogmatic assertion our
author follows St. Augustine.

The discourse, " Faction confuted," from 1 Cor. i. 12, is
against the factious affecting of one pastor above another.
Here our worthy preacher, who was no lover of faction,
is quite at home. He meets this folly with abundance of
satire, and exposes it as well in the minister as in his " dear
hearers." He was not one of those who reproved only the
unpopular faults of his generation, and spared pleasing
follies by levelling at them inane platitudes.

"Such," says he, " is the subtlety of Satan, and such is the
frailty of the flesh, though things be ordered never so well,
they will quickly decline. Luther was wont to say he never
knew a good order to last above fifteen years. This speedy
decaying of goodness you may see in the Church of Corinth,
from which St. Paul was no sooner departed, but they departed from his doctrine. Some, more carried by fancy
than ruled by reason, or more swayed by carnal reason than
governed by grace, made choice of some particular, whom
they extolled to the great disgrace of his fellow ministers,
and greater dishonour of God Himself. Now St. Paul, not
willing to make these ministers a public example, concealeth
their persons, yet discovereth the fault, and making bold
with his brethren Apollos and Cephas, applieth to them
and himself what the Corinthians spake of their fancied
preachers, ' *Now this I say that every one of you saith, I am
of Paul, and I am of Apollos, and I am of Cephas, and I am
of Christ.*

" I need not divide the words, which in themselves are nothing else but division, and contain four sorts of people, like the four sorts of seed (Matt. i. 3), the three first bad, the last only (I am of Christ) being good and commendable." The mischiefs of factiousness he thus enumerates, first, it will set enmity and dissension betwixt the ministers of God's word. " It will anger not only Saul, a mere carnal man, but even those that have degrees of grace. He hath converted his thousands, but such an one his ten thousands: these discords betwixt ministers I could as heartily wish they were false, as I do certainly know they are too true. 2. It will set dissension among people, whilst they violently engage their affections for their pastors. 3. It will give just occasion to wicked men to rejoice at these dissensions, to whose ears our discords are the sweetest harmony. O, then, let not the herdsmen of Abraham and Lot fall out, whilst the Canaanites and Perizites are yet in the land. Let us not dissent whilst many adversaries of truth are mingled amongst us who will make sport thereat. Lastly, it will cause great dishonour to God Himself: His ordinance in the meantime being neglected. Here is such doting on the dish, there is no regarding the dainties. Such looking on the embassador, there is no notice taken of the King that sent him. Even Mary's complaint is now verified, ' They have taken away the Lord, and placed Him I know not where.' And as in times of Popery, Thomas Becket dispossessed our Saviour of His Church in Canterbury (instead of Christ's Church being called St. Thomas's Church), and whereas rich oblations were made to the shrine of that supposed saint, *summo altari nil*, nothing was offered to

M

Christ at the Communion Table ; so whilst some sacrifice
their reverence to this admired preacher, and others almost
adore this affected pastor, God in His ordinance is neglected, and the Word, being the savour of life, is had in
respect of persons.

" To prevent these mischiefs both pastor and people must
lend their helping hands. I begin with the pastor, and
first with those whose churches are crowded with the
thickest audience. Let them not pride themselves with the
bubble of popular applause, often as carelessly gotten as undeservedly lost. Have we not seen those who have preferred the onions and fleshpots of Egypt before heavenly
manna ? lungs before brains, and sounding of a voice before
soundness of matter ?

" Yea, when pastors perceive people transported with an
immoderate admiration of them, let them labour to confute
them in their groundless humours. When St. John would
have worshipped the angel, ' see thou do it not ' (saith he) ;
worship God. So when people post headlong in affecting
their pastors, they ought to waive and decline this popular
honour, and to seek to transmit and fasten it on the God of
heaven. Christ went into the wilderness when the people
would have made Him a king. Let us shun, yea, fly such
dangerous honour, and tear off our heads such wreaths as
people would tie on them, striving rather to throw mists
and clouds of privacy on ourselves, than to affect a shining
appearance. But know, whatsoever thou art, who herein art
an epicure, and lovest to glut thyself with people's applause,
thou shalt surfeit of it before thy death. It shall prove at
last pricks in thy eye, and thorns in thy side, a great affliction, if not a ruin unto thee, because sacrilegiously, thou hast

robbed God of His honour. Let them labour also to in-
gratiate every pastor who hath tolerability of desert with his
own congregation.

"I am come now to neglected ministers, at whose
churches *solitudo ante ostium* and within them too, whilst
others (perchance less deserving) are more frequented. Let
not such grieve in themselves, or repine at their brethren.

"One told a Greek statist, who had excellently deserved
of the city he lived in, that the city had chosen four and
twenty officers and yet left him out. 'I am glad,' said he,
'the city affords twenty-four abler than myself.' And let us
practice St. Paul's precept by honour and dishonour, by
good report and disreport."

Turning to the people our preacher gives this excellent
advice : " First, ever preserve a reverent esteem of the minister whom God hath placed over thee. Secondly, let them
not make odious comparisons betwixt ministers of eminent
parts. It is said of Hezekiah (2 Kings xviii., 5) that 'after
him was none like him of all the kings of Judah, neither
any that were before him.' It is said also of King Josiah
(2 Kings xxiii., 25) 'and like unto him there was no king
before him, that turned to the Lord with all his heart, and
with all his soul, and with all his might, neither after him
rose up any like him." The Holy Spirit prefers neither for
better, but concludes both for best, and so, amongst ministers when each differ from others, all may be excellent in
their minds." Such was the sound teaching (now too much
gone out of fashion), the earnest spirit of one who was a
truly popular preacher, a divine who brought out of his
treasures new and old (καινὰ καὶ πάλαια), and was not carried
about by the current theology of the times ; who in doctrine

belonged not to this party or that, and avoided extremes on either side, but was a true and faithful, loyal and devoted son of his spiritual mother, the Church of England, and proved himself not unworthy to take his place by the side of judicious Hooker, pious Hall, saintly Herbert, learned Pearson, apostolic Leighton, devout Jeremy Taylor, and other worthies of the National Church.

We subjoin a few poetical gems taken from these sermons : "Traffic makes those wooden bridges over the seas, which join the islands to the continent." "Woful was the estate of the world when one could not see God for gods." " It is an old humour for men to love new things, and in this point even many barbarians are Athenians." "The *number of seven* is most remarkable in holy writ and passeth for the emblem of perfection or completeness ; as well it may, consisting of a unity in the middle : guarded and attended by a Trinity on either side." " *The death of the Godly* in Scripture language is often styled sleep, and indeed sleep and death are two twins. Sleep is the elder brother, for Adam slept in Paradise, but death liveth longest, for the last enemy that shall be destroyed is death." *Etymology of compliment* "they are justly to be reproved which lately have changed all hearty expressions of love into verbal compliments, which etymology is not to be deduced from *a completione mentis* but *a complete mentiri*. And yet I cannot say these men lie in their throats, for I persuade myself their words never came so near their heart, but merely lie in their mouths, when all their promises—

> " Both birth and burial in a breath they have ;
> That mouth which is their womb, it is their grave."

Speaking of the sea, he says " Esau went to kill his brother

Jacob, but when he met him, his mind was altered; he fell a-kissing him, and so departed. Thus the waves of the sea march against the shore, as if they would eat it up; but when they have kissed the utmost brink of the sand, they melt themselves away to nothing."

In these sermons Fuller evidently followed as his models such preachers as Donne and Andrewes, though it may be at a measurable distance, both in his manner of handling his discourse, by his manifold and complicated division and sub-division, and his style was both homely as theirs, and charac·terised by the epithet of " quaint." It was Andrewes who said of his sermons, and what preacher has not felt this who is called upon to make a double homiletic effort every Sunday? "When I preach twice every Sunday I *prate* once." In these sermons we notice Fuller's fondness for alliterations, playing on the words and the first letters of them, antithe-sis, and antithetical periods, incongruous allusions, and the everlasting pun. All these peculiarities are sown broadcast over his work in prodigal confusion. But in spite of these eccentricities we can well imagine that his preaching must have been very impressive, and to thoughtful hearers most attractive. He had all the makings of a popular preacher in the best sense, for he was earnest, and his sermons breathe an atmosphere of practical piety. They are also remark-able for their outspokenness, which no doubt earned for him the soubriquet, which he deserved, of *downright* Fuller. They beautifully illustrate his own sketch of the faithful minister, who, having brought his sermon into his head, labours to bring it to his heart before he preaches it to his people, and who chiefly reproves the reigning sins of the time and place he lives in.

Fuller composed about this time the " Life of Dr. Colet " in a popular manual called *Daily Devotions;* or the *Christian Morning and Evening Sacrifice.* He calls Colet "a Luther before Luther for his doctrine," and praises him for his learning and shrewdness.   There is also a notice of him in his " Abel Redevivus " and his " Church History."   The publication of this manual, together with other remarks made in his other works, attests the value that Fuller set upon forms of prayer in general, and a pre-composed liturgy in particular, not that he despised the extempore mode, on the contrary, he highly valued it, but he regarded the set form as more reverent in the addresses of the creature to his Creator.   The free form of prayer was soon coming in, and forms of prayer were about to be abolished, and it is quite clear what Fuller's views were on this subject.   Indeed, he, in common with some of the dispossessed clergy, composed some of the forms which were used during the time of the prohibited liturgy.   Pearson preached a sermon at Cambridge in 1643 "On the Excellency of Forms of Prayer," and in the days of the Directory, Fuller defended " our late admired liturgy," which he, with other cavalier parsons, never gave up.   In his " Good thoughts in worse times " he shows that " prescript form of Prayer " of our own and others composing are lawful for any, and needful for some, to use.   " *Lawful for any :* otherwise God would not have appointed the Priests (presumed of themselves best able to pray) a form of blessing the people : nor would our Saviour have set us His prayer, which (as the town-bushel is the standard both to measure corn and other bushels by) is both a prayer in itself, and a pattern or platform of prayer. Such as accuse set forms to be pinioning the wings of the dove, will, by the next return, affirm that girdles and garter made to strengthen and adorn, are so many shackles and fetters which hurt and hinder free motion."

"*Needful for some :* namely, for such as yet have not attained (what all should endeavour) to pray extempore by the spirit. But many confess their weakness in denying to confess it, who, refusing to be beholding to a set form of prayer, prefer to say nonsense rather than nothing in their extempore expressions. More modesty and not less piety it had been for such men to have prayed longer with set forms that they might pray better without them."

"It is no base and beggarly shift (arguing a narrow and necessitous heart), but a piece of holy and heavenly thrift, often to use the same prayer again. Christ's practice is my Directory herein, who "the third time said the same words" (Matt. xxvi., 44). A good prayer is not like a strata-gem of war, to be used but once. No, the oftener the better. The clothes of the Israelites, whilst they wandered forty years in the wilderness, never waxed old as if made of perpetuano indeed. So a good prayer, though often used, is still fresh and fair in the ears and eyes of Heaven. Despair not, then, thou simple soul, who hast no exchange of raiment, whose prayer cannot appear every day at Heaven's court in new clothes. Thou mayest be as good a subject, though not so great a gallant, coming always in the same suit—yea, pur-chance the very same which was thy father's and grandfather's before thee (a well composed prayer is a good heirloom in a family, and may hereditarily be descended to many genera-tions), but know to thy comfort, thy prayer is well known to Heaven, to which it is a constant customer."

Thus our author synchronizes with Paley in his excellent

essay on " Forms of Prayer," and the argument is more than clenched when applied to the Liturgy, *i.e.*, the form of celebrating Holy Communion, as witnessed by the Primitive Liturgies of the sub-Apostolic age.

CHAPTER XI.

THE LONG PARLIAMENT AND SECOND CONVOCATION OF 1640. DEATH OF BISHOP DAVENANT.—(1641.)

"In all State-alterations, be they never so bad, the *Pulpit* will be of the same wood with the *Council-Board.*"—*Church History* iv. 153.

E have dwelt in the last chapter, at some length, on the early works of Fuller, to give the reader an idea of their literary merits, and it would appear that about this time he was engaged in collecting materials for other works which he was projecting, and which his visit to London enabled him to do. But the times were getting stormy, and for a time he had, like Milton, to relinquish those intellectual studies in which he took so much pleasure. These events forced him "to interrupt the pursuit of his hopes, and to leave the calm and pleasing solitariness, fed with cheerful and confident thoughts, to embark on a troubulous sea of noises and hoarse disputes from beholding the bright countenance of truth in the quiet and still air of delightful studies." ("Church Hist." xi., 172).

In the latter half of the year 1640 Fuller may have possibly returned to his country parish, and devoted himself to his parochial duties at Broad Windsor, but it must have been with sad forebodings, for the political outlook was indeed dark and stormy. Driven by his necessities the King summoned that Parliament known as the "Long lasting Parlia-

ment," so known to posterity for the remarkable actions
therein," not the least of them being the impeachment and
incarceration of Archbishop Laud. It met Nov. 3rd, 1640,
and convocation again met—its last sitting for many a long
year to come, and under the same Prolocutor.

But, as Fuller significantly states, "the Parliament and it
were unable long to keep pace together." In this Convocation Fuller does not seem to have sat, though most of his
friends were there. It met pretty frequently, but nothing
appears to have been done.

Early in the session the Acts and Canons (of the last Convocation) came under the censure of the House, as Clarendon puts it, "in that warm region where thunder and
lightning were made." They were discussed on the 14th December and following day, it being carried:—

"That the Clergy of England, convened in Convocation,
or synod, or otherwise, have no power to make any Constitutions, Canons or Acts whatsoever in matter of doctrine,
discipline, or otherwise, to bind the clergy or laity of the
land, without common consent in Parliament. That the
canons do contain in them matters contrary to the King's
prerogative, to the fundamental laws and constitutions of the
realm, to the rights of Parliament, to the property and liberty
of the subject, and matters tending to sedition and of dangerous consequences. That the several grants of the
benevolence or contribution granted to his most excellent
Majesty by the clergy are contrary to the laws, and ought
not to bind the clergy."

The consideration of the subject was again taken in hand
April 26th, 1641, and a Bill was brought in punishing and
fining the members of the Convocation of the province of

Canterbury. When the committee met, the fines were taken in hand, and the clergy of the Convocation were fined £200,000, which was as much, or more than their whole estates amounted to. Laud was fined £20,000, the Archbishop of York £10,000, Bishop Wren £10,000, Bishop of Chester £3,000, and so on in proportion. In Rushworth's list the entries under Bristol are given thus :—" Dean of Bristol £500, Proctor ——" *i.e.,* £500.

The penalties appointed for the other proctors was £200, and this was the sum levied upon Fuller, as he says in his Appeal. Upon Heylin twitting him at the fear of being unnoticed as a Clerk in Convocation, Fuller replied, " Dear honour, indeed, *honos onus* for which I *was fined*, with the rest of my brethren, two hundred pounds by the House of Commons, though not put to pay it : partly because it never passed the House of Lords : because they thought it needless to *shave* their hair, whose *heads* they meant to cut off : I mean they were so charitable as not to make *them* pay a fine, *whose* place in cathedrals they intended not long after to take away."

Dr. William Fuller, Dean of Ely, was fined £1,000. The principals of Convocation did not get off so well as the Proctors, for thirteen of them were impeached by the Commons. Among them were Hill, Warner, Skinner, Goodman, and Towers, and some like Wren were imprisoned in the Tower. Heylin found fault with Fuller for calling the Convocation a " younger brother " of Parliament, who thus excused himself for using the term, " The Parliament hath made a *younger brother* of the Convocation, and there being a priority in power, he in effect is the heir and elder brother who confineth the other to a poor pittance, and small portion as our age can well remember." (Appeal ii. 502).

Through the influence of Williams, a committee of the Lords was formed to settle matters and bring peace to the Church. It was agreed to draw up a scheme and submit it to Parliament. A *sub-committee* was also appointed, composed of quite moderate men, to prepare the agenda for them. Most of the Bishops and Divines must have been known to Fuller, who would have met about this time, Mr. Thomas Hill, Rector, of Titchmarsh, near the Aldwinckles, an old friend of the family, and also Stephen Marshall. Bishop Usher, Bishop Hall, and Bishop Morton were there, and likewise Drs. Ward, Hacket, and Saunderson. They met in the Jerusalem Chamber, but were entertained by Williams at the Deanery "with such bountiful cheer as well became a Bishop." "But this," said Fuller, "we may behold as the *last course* of all public episcopal treatments, whose guests may even now put up their knives, seeing soon after the *Voider* was called for, which took away all Bishop's lands, and most of English hospitality." But the meetings of the committee soon came to an end, as a Bill regarding Deans and Canons—the outworks of Episcopacy, as Fuller calls them, and which was to affect both him and many of his friends—was run through the Commons, and sent up to the Lords. Fuller observes concerning this Bill, that it put such a distance between these divines "that never their judgments, and scarce their persons, met after together." Great efforts were made by the "moderate cathedral men" to preserve their foundations, and a deputy from each chapter was to solicit friends on their behalf, and to solicit Parliament. But all their efforts were unavailing. The

cathedral establishments were suppressed, and their endowments appropriated to further piety and learning. It was
owing to this measure that Fuller lost his valuable prebendal stall, and for twenty years, according to Walker
(Sufferings of the Clergy ii. 67) he was deprived of its
profits. This measure was quickly followed by a Bill for the
abolition of Episcopacy.

The death of Bishop Davenant occurred on April 21st,
1641, and Fuller was summoned to Salisbury to witness the
closing scenes of the good Bishop's life. His nephew thus
writes about his last hours : " With what gravity and
moderation he behaved himself : how humble, hospitable,
painful in preaching and writing, may better be reported
hereafter, when his memory (green as yet) shall be mellowed
by time. He sate Bishop about twenty years, and died of a
consumption, Anno 1641, to which sensibleness of the
sorrowful times (which he saw were bad, and foresaw would
be worse) did contribute not a little. I cannot omit how
some hours before his death, having lyen for a long time
(though not speechless yet) not speaking, nor able to speak,
(as we beholders thought, though indeed he hid that little
strength we thought he had lost, and reserved himself for
purpose), he fell into a most emphatical prayer for half or
quarter of an hour. Amongst many heavenly passages
therein, he " thanked God for this his fatherly correction,
because in all his lifetime he never had one heavie affliction,
which made him often much suspect with himself whether
he were a true child of God or no, until this his last sickness."
Then he sweetly fell asleep in Christ : and so we softly draw
the curtains about him." Fuller says elsewhere, " We read
of the patriarch Israel that the time drew near that he must

die, (Gen. xlvii. 29) " *must*, a necessity of it. Such a decree
attended this Bishop, happy to die, before his order (for a
time) died April, 1641 ; and with a solemn funeral he was
buried in the south aisle of the choir of, his own cathedral.
Dr. Nicholas (now, 1661, Dean of St. Paul) preaching an
excellent sermon at his interment." This Dr. Nicholas was
at the time one of Fuller's colleagues, a Prebendary of
Salisbury Cathedral. An elegant marble monument was set
up, and is still to be seen against the south wall, flanked
with Corinthian pillars, and surmounted by the Bishop's
arms, with the following inscription :—" As a living example
of venerated antiquity, he discharged all the duties of a
primitive Bishop : and thus during his twenty years' oversight of this Diocese, he was honoured by all good men, and
even by his enemies."

The most remarkable feature in the Bishop's character was
his active piety. According to an old epitaph " *Regem
veneratur, sed et timeat Deum*." On one occasion being
called to preach at Court, he came a day late, because he
would not ride on Sunday. Such a proceeding was likely
to give great offence, but when the King (James) heard
thereof, he applauded him.

Davenant was regarded by his contemporaries as a model
Bishop, a good "all-round" Bishop, both as to the learning,
piety, and discipline. When Williams was preferred to the
see of Lincoln, he took him for his episcopal model. By
all parties he was treated with respect, so that he earned for
himself the soubriquet of "The good Bishop." In his
" Holy State," then on the eve of publication, Fuller is
supposed to be drawing the portrait from his uncle's life and
character " as Diogenes confuted him, who denied there

was any motion, by saying nothing, but walking before his eyes ; so our Bishop takes no notice of the false accusations of people against his order, but " walks " on " circumspectly " in his calling, really repelling their cavils in his conversation. A Bishop's bare presence at a marriage in his own diocese is by the law interpreted for a license, and what actions soever he graceth with his company, he is conceived to privilege them to be lawful, which makes him to be more wary in his behaviour. . . . He is loved and feared of all, and his presence frights the swearer out of his oaths or into silence, and he stains all other men's lives with the clearness of his own." There is an anecdote about Bishop Davenant a propos to the last remark. " Once invited by Bishop Field, and not well pleased with some roisting company there, he embraced the next opportunity of departure after dinner. And when Bishop Field proffered to light him with a candle down stairs, ' My lord, my lord,' said he, ' let us lighten ourselves by our unblameable conversation :' for which speech some since have severely censured him, how justly I interpose not. But let others unrelated to him, write his character, whose pen cannot be suspected of flattery, which he when living did hate, and dead did not need."

In Fuller's essay, " The Good Bishop " is careful and happy in suppressing of heresies and schisms—which illustrate the paternal discipline in Davenant's diocese : " He meddleth as little as may be with temporal matters, having little skill in them and less will to them. Not that he is unworthy to manage them, but they unworthy to be managed by him, yea, generally, the most dexterous in spiritual matters are left-handed in temporal business, and go but untowardly about them.   Heaven is his vocation, and therefore he counts earthly employments avocations."

In the same work Fuller also commends "worthy Bishop Lake," "whose hand had the true seasoning of a sermon with Law and Gospel," and "Reverend Andrewes" who was out of his element in civil affairs, and he thus alludes to his uncle, "In his grave writings, he (the good Bishop) aims at God's glory and the Church's peace, with that worthy prelate *the second Jewel of Salisbury*, whose comments and controversies will transmit his memory to all posterity."   Whose dying pen did write of *Christian Union* :

> How Church with Church might safely keep *communion*,
> Commend his care, although the cure do misse :
> The woe is ours, the happiness is his :
> Who finding discords daily to increase,
> Because he could not live, would die in peace.

The last lines referred to a book which the Bishop pub·lished a short time before his death, being an English translation of his *ad paternam communionem inter Evangelicas Ecclesias restaurandum exhortatio (1640)*.   But his chief works written in Latin, were "An Exposition of the Epistle to the Colossians" (1627), and his "Treatise on Justification."   As Divinity professor at Cambridge, Davenant's prelections obtained considerable renown.   Mr. Perry says of him "Though by no means free from the usual faults of commentators, and rather inclined to talk about a difficulty instead of fairly meeting it, these treatises display much talent and learning.   Bishop Davenant's Latin is not so classical or so vigorous as that of Crakanthorp or Hall, but his composition is clear, and his reflections valuable."— *Church of England* i., 636.

An extract of Bishop Davenant's will is given in Cassan's Bishops of Salisbury. The Davenants, Fullers, and Townsons are all mentioned, and suitable legacies left to each. Our author is not forgotten, and due recognition is made to his literary tastes. His brother John received a legacy, but of the five sisters, the names of Mary and Judith do not appear, and they were probably dead; Margaret was the wife of Matthew Huit, and to him the Bishop bequeathed a valuable copy of Whitaker's works. He also left one of his English books to each of his nieces, who seem to have been of a studious turn of mind, the distribution being made by Edward Davenant, his nephew. Bishop Davenant was succeeded by Dr. Duppa, Chancellor of the Diocese, who held the See for only a short time, and became a fugitive to Oxford.

A son was born to our author a few months after the death of the Bishop, and he was baptised in Broad Windsor Church. The baptismal register is as follows "June 6, (1641), John fil Thomas Ffuller Clerici." He was probably named after his great uncle, and lived to edit that part of the work left unfinished by his father. Some months after this Fuller's wife died, but where this event took place cannot be ascertained. The registers of Broad Windsor make no sign, nor can the record of it be traced to any London registers, nor is the date exactly known. The biographer merely states it was soon after the birth of her son, "and but a short time before the eruption of the civil wars."

It is probable that this bereavement had something to do with his removal to the metropolis, where he would get not only change of scene, but social intercourse, likely to

N

alleviate his trouble. Some think that his active and free genius was getting tired of the dulness and routine of a country parish, "which was framed by nature for converse and general intelligence, not to be smothered in such an obscurity." But this can be hardly correct, although perhaps containing an element of truth. Rather are we disposed to think that his session in Convocation had introduced him to London life, new clerical associations, and the stirring strife of the times. As the centre of the national feeling, the unquietness of the age, would, as a matter of course, come to a head there : his perfervid patriotism would naturally be enkindled to throw himself into the discussion, and to do what he could to heal the sad struggle between King and people, for the doing of which his eminent pulpit talents and the confidence reposed in him, eminently qualified him. It is not known the precise time when Fuller resigned the living of Broad Windsor. Walker in his sufferings of the clergy speaks of Fuller, and (sometime minister of Broad Windsor) being deprived of his prebend, and lectureship at the Savoy, and as the Dorsetshire Rectory is not mentioned, it may be supposed that he had resigned it. Yet no duly appointed successor seems ever to have been instituted, and his right to the living seems not to have been questioned at the Restoration. Fuller's *locum tenens* was in all probability that John Pinney, who was serving the Church at the time of the Restoration. He had made common cause with the parliamentary party, and was therefore left in peace and undisturbed possession. Things were going on quietly in his country parish, and Fuller saw no reason to disturb the general contentment with Pinney and his ministrations. But he received no fiscal benefit from it, for it was in reference to this benefice, and not the Savoy Lectureship, that he said for the sake of his "lord and master, King Charles," he lost "none of the *worst livings*, and one of the best prebends in England," the word *living*, though applied to Church preferment by a sort of grim satire, refers to a *legal* benefice, and not a lectureship. It was for this remark he was subsequently twitted by his antagonist Heylin. Be the cause however what it was of leaving his country cure, we must now bid adieu to Broad-Windsor and its broadening meadows and streams, and accompany our author to the Royal Chapel of the Savoy—being chosen by the Master and Brotherhood (as well as earnestly desired and entreated by that small parish), to accept the lectureship at their Church, or Chapel of St. Mary.

CHAPTER XII.

FULLER AT THE SAVOY.   HOLY STATE.

"As for the matter of this Book, therein I am resident on my
Profession; Holiness in the latitude thereof falling under the
cognizance of a Divine: For curious method, expect none,
Essays for the most part not being placed as at a *Feast*, but
placing themselves as at an *Ordinary*."—*Holy State* (To the
Reader).

T was about the year 1641, Fuller took up his per-
manent abode in the metropolis, and at first
mostly preached in the Chapels of the Inns of
Court—that "green oasis in the midst of a
wilderness of houses," as Lamb calls them.   Here he probably filled the office of lecturer, but there are no records
to that effect.   That a hearty welcome was accorded to so
witty a Preacher, and sound a Divine, there can be no
doubt.   But he was not long without preferment and a
definite cure, for he was invited to preach at the Chapel
Royal, Savoy, by the master and brotherhood.   His biographer says he was made lecturer, but more probably he
was the chaplain, with cure of souls, for he signs himself as
" Minister " of the parish, and speaks of " My dear parish,
St. Mary, Savoy."   Fuller is styled "Curate " in the manuscript in the possession of the present chaplain, the Rev. H.
White, and the technical meaning of curate is " one who
has cure of souls," as in the prayer for Bishops and *Curates*.
To understand the limits of Fuller's charge we must refer to
the history of the Savoy.

The Savoy Chapel stands on the south side of the Strand, within the precincts of the old Palace of the Savoy, of which it is the only relic. Henry VIII. had founded a hospital on the ruins of the palace as a lodging for poor persons, and religious services were held for them in the Church of St John Baptist. It was licensed by Henry VIII. in the early part of his reign on the completion of the foundation, and confided to the care of a master and four chaplains. In the next reign it was handed over to the Protector, who made extensive alterations in that neighbourhood, pulling down portions of the buildings and the Church of St. Mary-le-Strand. Queen Mary re-established it, and her maids of honour provided the hospital with bedding, blankets, &c., corporal works of mercy, for which Fuller makes special commendation in his " Church History," and speaking of these charitable ladies, says, that if they were still living this should be his prayer for them : "The Lord make all their bed in their sickness." After this time the Sovereign became their visitor, instead of the Abbot of Westminster, as heretofore. In Queen Elizabeth's reign, by the consent of the ecclesiastical authorities (Bishop Grindal), a part was carved out of St. Clement Danes (the mother parish of Savoy) with the Church of St. John's as the parish church of the new cure. The minister of the Savoy was therefore, as the patents call him, Curate of the Parish of St. Mary le Strand, serving the hospital Chapel of St. John's. The name of the chapel was St. Mary, Savoy, or St. Mary le Savoy, because the parishioners of St. Mary le Strand used to attend it, when the Protector deprived them of their own parish church. There are many interesting historical facts connected with this chapel. It is said that the liturgy was first used here, after it had been "Englished" in Elizabeth's reign. Part of the buildings was turned into a prison, and part into an agency for carrying on correspondence with foreign churches (Protestant I ween) by the Parliament. It was here also in 1658 that the faith and order of the congregational churches was agreed to. King William's chaplain, Dr. Hornecke, like Fuller, one of the foremost preachers of the day, predicated here the fire which took place in 1664, destroyed the handsome carved ceiling, paintings and blazonry, and left only the walls and tower remaining. It has been handsomely restored by the Queen, as a memorial to the late Prince Consort, the benefice belonging to her Majesty, in right of her Duchy of Lancaster. The appointment of these four chaplains who formed the brotherhood was in the hands of the master, but as their stipend was very small, they usually held other (more lucrative) benefices with them, on which they resided. The original object of the hospital fell into desuetude, and the hospital was dissolved in 1702, the statutes not having been kept within living memory. The master of the Savoy when Fuller was elected, was Dr. W. Balcanqual, one of the King's chaplains, which he had held since 1617, and the master paid the curate £20 per annum, who also received the voluntary offerings of the parishioners.

These parishioners were as eager to secure Fuller's services as the brotherhood, and he was "earnestly desired and entreated by that small parish." This cure naturally brought him under the notice of the Court, for his attractive preaching and loyal teaching quickly attracted a large congregation of the nobility and gentry, who chiefly affected Royalist principles. Many of them resided in the immediate vicinity, for the convenience of their attendance at Court. The Chapel of the Savoy became the great centre and rallying-point for the loyal churchmen of the period, and the congregation from without the precincts was larger than that within. It was here Fuller made the acquaintance of so many of the nobility, which appears from his various dedications, and it was through their timely assistance so many of the distressed and dispossessed clergy (Fuller included) were relieved. Among his friends and parishioners were James, Earl of Northampton and family; Frances Mountagu, Countess of Rutland; Sir Thomas Adams, founder of the Arabic professorship at Cambridge: Mr. Thomas Rich and Mr. Henry Barnard. "You are," writes Fuller to Rich, "the entertainer general of good men. Many a poor minister will never be wholly sequestered whilst you are living, whose charity is like to the wind, which cannot be seen but may be felt."

Fuller, with such sympathising and attractive surroundings, discharged his official duties with great effect and marked approval, and his ministrations lasted two or three years. It was August, 1643, when he is supposed to have left London, so that the time he spent in the metropolis was one full of stirring events and exciting topics. But he evidently laboured under some uncertainty as to his future, and wondered if he should be surrounded with suitable accessories in carrying on his literary work, but he expresses a resolve to "preach constantly in what place soever God's providence and friends' good will should place him." His misgivings were not without foundation, for there broke out about this time that strong feeling, and wish for the abolition of Episcopacy, and doing away with that regimen altogether. There broke out also a serious rebellion in Ireland, which embittered the feelings of many against the King's party. The uncertainty as to the King's intentions brought on "the Grand Remonstrance," which was presented to the King by Sir Ralph Hopton. Petitions were sent in for Church Reforms, and against the Bishops, in connection with which was the apprentices' riot, and their attack on the Abbey, which was courageously defended by the Dean, for no other reason, but because the late Convocation had held their meetings there.

Assent was given by the King at Canterbury, February 14th, 1642, to a Bill which had been passed by the Lords for the exclusion of the Bishops from the House of Lords. "Dying Episcopacy," said Fuller, "gave the last groan in Bishop Warner, of Rochester," who was one of good speech and a cheerful spirit, and (which made both) a good purpose, and (which made all three) a good cause. He alone of the Episcopal bench was left in the Lords to plead the cause of his order; he was its "best champion," and "pleaded stoutly" for it. Many of the lay Lords also made vigorous speeches on behalf of the Bishops, their efforts being seconded by the unejected clergy of the city, Fuller being one of them.

On his return from Scotland, in filling up the vacant sees, the King had been very careful to select sound, but moderate, men, and of blameless lives. Hall, Skinner, Duppa, who succeeded Davenant at Salisbury, were of the number but "all would not do." Fuller says "many who loved them in their *gowns*, did not at all like them in their *rochets*." (xi. 194.) Fuller was present on May 18, at the consecration of Dr. Ralph Brownrigg to the see of Exeter,

when Hall was translated to Norwich. The consecration
sermon was made by Brownrigg's good friend Dr. Young
("The waters are risen, O Lord, the waters are risen,")
wherein he very gravely complained of the many invasions
which popular violence made on the privileges of Church
and State. This Bishop himself, adds Fuller, was soon
sadly sensible of such inundations, and yet by the *procerity*
of his parts and piety, he not only safely waded through
them himself, but also when Vice-Chancellor of Cambridge,
by his prudence raised such banks that those overflowings
were not so destructive as otherwise they would have been
to the University." He was banished from Cambridge, for
the expression of his loyalty in an Accession Sermon, by
the Parliamentarians.

The King departed from Whitehall (Jan. 10) soon after
the attempted seizure of the five members, and then went to
York (March 19). He raised his standard at Nottingham
in August: the battle of Edge-hill in Warwickshire, was
fought in October, and began the Civil War, but it decided
nothing. Fuller alludes to the fight at Brentford in his
Worthies, and speaks with amazement of the quantity of
victuals sent out to feed the soldiers, being enough to have
feasted them for some days, and fed them for some weeks.
Although a Committee was appointed to enquire into the
condition of the plundered or ejected Ministers, there can
be no doubt that they suffered a good deal at this time
owing to their loyalty. Fuller records that the more moderate men of the Parliament party much bemoaned the
severity by which some clergymen, blameless for life, and
orthodox for doctrine, were only ejected on account of
their faithfulness to the King.

Fuller's success in preaching at this time was prodigious, and ofttimes it might be said as it was of Dr. Hornecke, " Dr. Hornecke's parish was much the largest in town, since it reached from Whitehall to Whitechapel." Fuller's eulogist thus alludes to it. " Witness the great confluence of affected hearers from distant congregations, insomuch as his own Cure were (in a sense) excommunicated from the Church, unless their timous diligence kept pace with their devotion ; the Doctor affording them no more time for their extraordinaries on the Lord's day, than what he allowed his habituated abstinence on all the rest. He had in his narrow chapel two audiences, one without the pale, the other within : the windows of that little church, and the sextonry so crowded as if bees had swarmed to his mellifluous discourse." "Life," p. 18. The influence of the pulpit is great in every age, but especially was it so at a time when litera- ture was not being disseminated as it is now, when papers and magazines were few and far between, and a daily press was unheard of. It is owing to this power that the Parliamentary party was quick to eject the Royalist clergy, and put in their place preachers after their own hearts. Fuller observes somewhere that it was generally observed that they who held the helm of the pulpit could generally stir people's hearts as they please. These tactics were employed with great effect after the loyal clergy had been turned out of the City benefices, and their tongues silenced. The new preachers openly broached ' doctrines of rebellion.' Clarendon speaks of these "Ambassadors of peace by their functions," who became "incendiaries towards rebellion." Hacket also speaks of those who " rang the pan in the pulpit, and the bees swarmed to rebellion." And Fuller in reference to these events speaks of "Ambitious clergymen, who reversing the silver trumpets of the sanctuary, and putting the wrong end into their mouths, make what was appointed to sound religion, to signify rebellion." ("Ch. Hist." iv. 153.)

The consequent excitement of all this was very great. The people forsaking their Pastors, if the pulpit was not tuned to their liking, plunged into all kinds of excesses. The congregations were fickle and unstable. Dr. Holdsworth seems to have been an exception. "It is truly observed that the people in London honour their Pastors as John Baptist for an hour or short time, (πρòς ὥραν) yet this Doctor had his hour measured him by a large glass" (alluding to the preaching hour glasses). Another instance to the contrary, was the devoted congregation at the Savoy, who came to listen to the words of their favourite pastor Sunday after Sunday with increasing interest. Yet Fuller, although an exceedingly effective and popular preacher, and none more so in his day, yet was popular in the best sense of the word. There was no claptrap, nor meretricious rhetoric, nothing that could pander to the weaknesses of his hearers. He *taught* his people with authority, he used his great predicatorial influence with moderation, he comported himself with becoming dignity, and his endeavour was to guide his people along the safe path of rectitude, and do his utmost to heal the breach which broadened out from day to day in threatening attitude. His ministerial life could bear inspection. "Many ministers," he used to say, "are most admired at a distance, major e longinquo reverentia, like some kind of stuff, they have the best gloss a good way off, more than a prophet in his own country."

During the course of 1642, Fuller put forth his "Holy

and Profane State," that work by which he has been more generally known than any other, as being of universal interest, a mixture of biography and parable, commending itself to all tastes, and adapted to all readers. This work was published in Cambridge and London, and it is worthy of remark, that this is the only one of his principal works without a dedication; it presumed, as its author puts it, "to appear in company unmanned." In his address 'to the Reader,' he commences " Who is not sensible with sorrow of the distractions of the age. To write books therefore may seem unseasonable, especially in a time wherein the press, like an unruly horse, hath cast off his bridle of being licensed, and some serious books which dare fly abroad, are hooted at by a flock of pamphlets," and concludes as follows, " Meantime I will stop the leakage of my soul, and what heretofore hath run out in writing, shall hereafter, God willing, be improved in constant preaching, in what place soever God's providence and friends' good-will shall fix."

These moral essays, which are characterised by Fuller's good sense and liveliness, are divided into five books—the first four contain the Holy State, and the last the Profane State—characters to be imitated, and those to be shunned. The first part refers to family relationships. The good wife, the good husband, the good parent, the good child, &c. The second book refers to portraitures of characters or delineations of callings, as the good advocate, the good physician, the true church antiquary, the good parishioner, &c. The third treats of general subjects; as hospitality, jesting, anger, recreation, trials; "general rules placed in the middle, that the books on both side may reach equally to them, because all persons therein are indifferently concerned." The fourth book returns to the miscellaneous characters, and the last to the Profane State, characters to be avoided. In Pickering's edition, the essays are simply divided into " The Holy State " and " The Profane State." This book belonged to a class of literature, which in the 17th century attained to great popularity. It was published at a very critical time, and the author's loyalty to Church and State was too pronounced to escape observation. What his feelings towards Episcopacy were is too evident in his essay on " The good Bishop ;" and his leanings towards the monarchy were illustrated by this remark that "subjects should be adjective, not able to stand without (much less against) their prince, or they will make but bad construction otherwise."

These sentiments, correlated with the Fullerian appellation, would naturally procure the disfavour of those who were in a state of antagonism to their king. The essay on " The King," beginning " He is a mortal God," gives seven delineations of the character of a good one, and bursts out in this loyal panegyric of the then reigning monarch. " Such a gracious Sovereign hath God vouchsafed to this land. How pious is he towards his God ; attentive in hearing the word, preaching religion with his silence. How loving to his spouse, tender to his children, faithful to his servants. How doth he, with David, walk in the midst of his house without partiality to any. How many wholesome laws hath he enacted for the good of his subjects. How great is his humility in so great height, which maketh his own praises painful to himself to hear. His royal virtues are too great to be told, and too great to be concealed." The whole essay concludes like Milton's, with a remarkable prayer.

Fuller's intense admiration for the King, be it remembered, never waned through life.

The popularity of this work was very great, and successive editions came forth from the press, appearing in 1648, 1652, 1663. Some of the copies were bound up with Fuller's "Holy War," and the various editions seem to have been put out as quietly as possible, so as to lull suspicion, and not rouse the antagonism of the ruling powers. Williams was his publisher, and he must have made a good thing out of our author's literary labours. For some unexplained reason, Fuller changed his publisher in after life; of this he says " I will not add that I have passed my promise (and that is an honest man's bond) to my former stationer, that I will write nothing for the future which was in my former books so considerable as to make them interfere with one another to his prejudice."

It is worthy of remark that in all the editions of his works, even in those troublous times, Fuller continues to style himself " Prebendary of Sarum," notwithstanding that "from and after 29th March, 1649," the name, title, dignity, function, and office of Dean, Prebend, belonging to any cathedral, was wholly abolished and taken away. The book was not suppressed from motives of policy; " books," to quote our author's words, " are most called on when called in, and many who hear not of them when printed, enquire after them when prohibited." The work has been twice reprinted in our time. Although the criticism on Fuller's works has been of a somewhat discrepant character, posterity has been united as to the merits of the work under consideration.

The writer in the *Retrospective Review* thinks that it is perhaps the best of his works, that it "certainly displays to better advantage than any his original and vigorous power of thinking." Reed notices that his essays are in wit and wisdom and just feeling not unlike the 'Elia' essays of Charles Lamb. Coleridge carefully read this work, and in the margin said of Fuller's wit that it was "alike in quantity and quality and perpetuity, surpassing that of the wittiest in a witty age," but that it "robbed him of the praise not less due to him for an equal superiority in sound, shrewd, good sense and freedom of intellect." And Mr. James Nichols in his editorial preface says, "This curious collection of essays and characters is the production of a man possessed of no ordinary grasp of mind, who lived in times of uncommon interest and excitement, and who wrote with the obvious intention to personate " a wise and witty moderator between the two great parties in the State that were then openly at issue." Archbishop Trench often quotes our author in his "English, Past and Present," and brings forth samples of his writing as illustrating the mean_ ing of the word he is endeavouring to point out ; and he draws attention to the many apophthegmatic sentences, alliteratively constructed, pithily pointed with shrewd sense, and so sententious, as to convey almost the idea of their being current proverbs of the day. No series of essays would be complete without reference to these, and the numbers of " wise saws," and " elegant extracts " culled therefrom is a proof of the estimation in which this work " so enamelled with figures and flowers of wit " has been held.

With regard to the authorship of this work, it is curious to notice that it was ascribed to one Nicholas Ferrar, of Little Gidding, Hunts, west of Fuller's birthplace, who mentions Ferrar's house and chapel as among the buildings of the county. "Here," he says, "three numerous female families (all from one grandmother) lived together in a strict discipline of devotion. They rose at midnight to prayers, and other people most complained thereof, whose heads, I daresay, never ached for want of sleep. But their society was beheld by some as an embryo nunnery," and as such the household received the attention of the Long Parliament. Fuller speaks as if he were intimate with the house, and willing to give it a good word, says of it, "Sure I am strangers were by these entertained, poor people were relieved, their children instructed to read, whilst their own needles were employed in learned and pious work to bind Bibles." In the catalogue of works found at Gidding were a number of *Liv's* essays, characters, &c., and many of them tallying with the heads of Fuller's essays. It was therefore put down erroneously for the work of Ferrar, who, however, died five years before the work came out, *i.e.*, in 1637. Most probably the manuscript referred to contained extracts from other works, which may have been culled by Ferrar for the benefit and instruction of the inmates, to which were added some of Fuller's essays subsequently taken, and transcribed by the ladies to be read in rotation, finding the Holy State so very suitable for their purpose. Hence the mistake may have arisen. "The nunnery was broken up," says Fuller, "by Parliament in 1648, making a great noise all over England." We subjoin a few extracts as specimens of the essays contained in this work. Speaking of the *Controversial Divine*, he says, "*He engageth both his judgment and affections in opposing falsehood..* Not like country fencers who play on to make sport, but like

duellers indeed ; as if for life and limb ; chiefly if the question be of large prospect and great concernings, he is
zealous in the quarrel. Yet some, though their judgment
weigh down on one side, the beam of their affections stand
so even they care not which part prevails." There are
twelve other points. Describing the *Church Antiquary*, he
says, " Some scour off the rust of old inscriptions into their
own souls, cankering themselves with their superstition,
having read so often ' Orate pro anima,' that at last they fall
a praying for the departed : and they more lament the ruin
of monasteries than the decay and ruin of monk's lives, degenerating from their ancient piety and *painfulness* (painful
is one of the words selected by Trench, which means
taking pains or suffering pain). " He (the true Church
Antiquary) " is not zealous for the introducing of old useless
ceremonies. The mischief is that some who are most
violent to bring them in are most negligent to preach the
cautions in using them, and simple people, like children in
eating of fish, swallow bones and all, to their danger of
choking." Of course it depends altogether what ceremonies
are to be regarded " old and useless," and the reasons for
arriving at such conclusions.

Speaking of the *faithful minister*, he says, "He doth not
clash God's ordinances together about precedency, not
making odious comparisons betwixt prayer and preaching,
preaching and catechising, public prayer and private, premeditate prayer and extempore. When, at the taking of
New Carthage, in Spain, two soldiers contended about the
mural crown (due to him who first climbeth the walls), so
that the whole army was in danger of division, Scipio, the
general, said he knew they both got up the wall together,

and so gave the scaling crown to them both. Thus our
minister compoundeth all controversies betwixt God's
ordinances, by praising them all, practising them all, and
thanking God for them all. He counts the reading of
Common Prayers, to prepare him the better for preaching ;
and as one said, "if he did first toll the bell on the one side,
it made it afterwards ring out the better in his sermons ; "
ever seasonable is that place of our author, where he intro-
troduces the faithful pastor, as "chiefly reproving the
reigning sins of the time and place he lives in." Preaching
is also called prophesying, and the Christian pastor is in the
place of a prophet, "boldly to rebuke vice." " We may
observe," says Fuller, "that our Saviour never inveighed
against idolatry, usury, Sabbath-breaking, amongst the Jews;
not that these were not sins, but they were not practised so
much in that age, wherein wickedness was spun with a finer
thread ; and therefore Christ principally bent the drift of
His preaching against spiritual pride, hypocrisy, and traditions, then predominant amongst the people." No reader
would like the following omitted, " He counts the success
of his ministry the greatest preferment. Yet herein God
hath humbled many *painful* pastors, in making them to be
clouds not to rain over Arabia the happy, but over the
stony, or desert. Yet such pastors may comfort themselves
that great is their reward with God in heaven, who measures
it, not by their success, but endeavours. Besides, though
they see not, their people may feel benefit by their ministry.
Yea, the preaching of the Word in some places is like the
planting of woods, where, though no profit is received for
twenty years together, it comes afterwards. And grant that
God honours thee not to build His temple in thy parish,

yet thou mayest with David provide metal and material for Solomon, thy successor, to build with."

Fuller's grateful spirit thus speaks of the fatherly affection of his now deceased uncle, Bishop Davenant. "In his grave writings, he (the good bishop) aims at God's glory and the Church's peace, with that worthy prelate, the second Jewel of Salisbury, whose comments and controversies will transmit his memory to all posterity." The character of the good bishop is so inimitably drawn by Fuller, that we may readily conceive that he would himself, had his life been spared, considerably outshone the witty Bishop Corbet, and have been transmitted to posterity as a second Toby Matthews, that cheerful prelate, never to be forgotten by those who have been acquainted with him through the pages of his friend, Sir John Harrington.

CHAPTER XIII.

FULLER'S SERMONS AT THE SAVOY.—1641-3.

" Having brought his Sermon into his head, he labours to bring it into his heart before he preaches it to his people. Surely that preaching which comes from the soul most works on the soul. Some have questioned *ventriloquie*, when men strangely speak out of their bellies, whether it can be done lawfully or not. Might I coin the word *cordiloquie?* When men draw the doctrines out of their hearts, sure all would count this lawful and commendable."—*Holy State* (The Faithful Minister), p. 75.

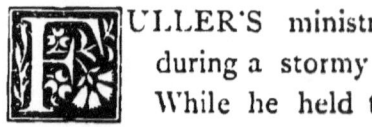ULLER'S ministry at the Savoy was passed during a stormy period of our national history. While he held the prominent position of one of the foremost preachers of the day, political troubles were thickening around him. And initial mistakes in the political sphere were rapidly developing their baleful crop of anarchichal miseries. Civil war had begun in earnest, and the patriotic party (as they called themselves) showed neither mercy nor pity to those who had the temerity to differ from them. The King, insulted and unprotected, had fled to York. This was in 1642. There followed him Lord Keeper Lyttleton, and many of the nobility, and amongst them the Earl of Northampton and Lord Paulet. The King removed his headquarters to Oxford, after the battle of Edgehill.

Three of Fuller's sermons, preached at this time, were

published, and they illustrate the line of conduct he adopted during the crisis, and they are a proof of his moderation,

"Moderation, the silken string running through the pearl chain of all virtues,"

and desire for a peaceful solution of the political problems of the day. From these three specimens we can gather a good idea of his opinions, and also of his preaching, when he was at the height of his predicatorial success. They were preached on feast days, or fast days, which shows that the Calendar of the National Church hadn't become the dead letter it subsequently became, when the observance of Saints' Days has fallen into desuetude, and it not only proves that the clergy said the office, but that the laity attended the service at all events in sufficient numbers to warrant the production of such deep and learned homiletic efforts.

There are three Holy days which are grouped round the cradle of Bethlehem : and on the three days following the Festival of the Nativity we have, first, St. Stephen's Day, protomartyr of the Christian Church, a martyr both in *fact* and in *intention:* then comes the Festival of St. John the Evangelist, martyr in intention but not in fact: last, the Holy Innocents' Day, martyrs in fact but not in intention. It was this last feast day in the following December (28th) which the Parliament ordered to be kept as a *fast,* peradventure as a religious mark of contempt for the institutions and observances of the Church of England. Upon this day Fuller preached a powerful sermon on Peace, from St. Matthew v. 9, "Blessed are the peacemakers," in reference to the Civil War. He notices the coincidences of the two observances, for he says "that a fast and feast justled together," but he reverts to the maxim of the Solomon, and urges his hearers to fast and not to feast, " and it may please God of His goodness so to bring it to pass, that if we keep a sad Christmas, we may have a merry Lent." He says also, " We use to end our sermons with a blessing : Christ *begins* His with the beatitudes, and of the eight my text is neither the last nor the least." He sees in the words *the best work*—" peacemaker :" and *the best wages*—they are "*blessed.*" He exposes the un-Christian nature of war : its opposition to the spirit of prayer, faith, and obedience. Wars are wicked. " But the worst," said he, " is still behind, for we are afflicted with *civil* war : many wars have done woefully, but this surmounteth them all. In civil war nothing can be expected but ruin and desolation."

He alluded to the miserable condition of the Irish Protestants, the desertion of whose cause must necessarily ensue in the continuance of the civil war at home. In the early part of this reign a monthly fast was held. "Our general fast," says Fuller, " was first appointed to bemoan the massacre of our brethren in Ireland." It was appointed January, 1642, the last Wednesday in each month being devoted to it, to continue so long as the condition of the country indicated that the Divine displeasure rested upon it. What would our author have said in these days of the Land League agitation ? Alluding to this, he says : " That harp which, when it was well tuned, made so good music, must now thereafter *be hung upon the willows* (a sad and sorrowful tree), and our distraction will hasten their final destruction." And again : "It is in vain to have a finger in the eye, if we have not also a sword in the other hand : such tame lamenting of lost friends is but lost lamentation. We must bend our

bows in the camp, as our knees in the churches, and second
our posture of piety with martial provision." He replied to
the objection, that the cause of truth would be sacrificed by
peace, " Before this war began, we had in England truth
in all essentials to salvation. We had all necessary and important truths truly compiled in our Thirty-nine Articles.
We had the Word of God truly preached (I could wish it
had been more frequently and generally), the sacraments
duly administered; which two put together doth constitute
a true Church." He proceeded to the objection, that errors
had crept into our doctrine, new ceremonies and innovations in discipline, " The best and only way to purge
these errors out is in a fair and peaceable way: for the
sword cannot discern betwixt truth and error; it may have
two edges, but never an eye. Let there, on God's blessing,
be a synod of truly grave, pious, and learned Divines: and
let them both fairly dispute and fully decide what is true,
what is false; what ceremonies are to be retained, what to
be rejected: and let civil authority stamp their command
upon it, to be generally received under what penalty their
discretion shall think fitting. But as long as war lasts, no
hope of any such agreement; this must be a work for peace
to perform." "So, then, under the notion of peace,
hitherto we have and hereafter do intend such a peace as,
when it comes, we hope will restore truth to us in all the
accidental and ornamental parts thereof, and add to it that
truth in essentials to salvation which we enjoyed before this
war began; and in this sense I will boldly pronounce,
' Blessed are the peacemakers.' "

He proceeds to the hindrances of peace, the many
national sins of our kingdom not repented of, sins not of one

army, or of one class of persons. "Think not that the
King's army is like Sodom, not ten righteous men in it ; and
the other like Zion, consisting all of saints. No. There be
drunkards on both sides, and swearers on both sides, and
whoremongers on both sides, pious on both sides, and profane on both sides ; like Jeremy's figs, those that are good
are very good, and those that are bad are very bad, in both
parties. I never knew or heard of an army all of saints,
save *the holy army of martyrs,* and those you know were
dead first ; for the last breath they sent forth proclaimed
them to be martyrs." " But it is not the sins of the army
alone, but the sins of the whole kingdom, which break off
our hopes of peace—our nation is generally sinful. The city
complains of the ambition and prodigality of the courtiers ;
the courtiers complain of the pride and covetousness of the
citizens ; the laity complain of the laziness and state
meddling of the clergy; the clergy complain of the hard
dealing and sacrilege of the laity ; the rich complain of the
murmuring and ingratitude of the poor; the poor complain
of the oppression and extortion of the rich. Thus, everyone
is more ready to throw dirt in another's face than to wash
his own clean. And in all this, though malice sets the varnish, sure truth doth lay the ground-work."

"Of particular hindrances, in the first place, we may rank
the Romish recusants. *Is not the hand of Joab with thee in all
this ?* was David's question. But is not the hand, we may
all say, of *Jesuits* in these distractions." The Papists, he
observes, discovered that the strength of England lay in
unity, and that it was impossible to conquer English
Protestants but by English Protestants. And to this end
they sowed dissension. Then he proceeds to speak of "the

schismatics," who had improved themselves upon the clemency and long-suffering of our state ; and of those who for their private interest supported the war, whose very being consisted of war. "*The truly noble English spirits desire a foreign foe, for a mark for their bullets.*"

He then advises petitions both to the King and to the Parliament, " the Gods on earth " (using the words of Tertullus to Felix, Acts xxiv. 3), the laying aside of odious party names and terms of contempt, and a serious and general repentance, perorating in the following pregnant style—" We are too proud hitherto for God to give peace to: too many of us are *humiliati*, but few made *lowly*, so that we are proud in our poverty, and as the unjust steward said, " To beg I am ashamed ; " for we are too stout, though half-starved, on the bended knees of our souls, with true repentance, to crave pardon of God for our sins ; which, till it be done, we may discourse of peace and superficially desire it, but never truly care for it, or can comfortably receive it." He then compared " the complexion of the war" with the recent " wars of Germany," which were " far lighter than ours," and which ended where ours began—in the winter—and, in allusion to a saying of our Saviour, and to the recent battle of Edgehill, he adds the comment " winter fights, woeful fights ; Sabbath wars, sorrowful wars." It had been, he said, " a great curse of God upon us, to make a constant misunderstanding between our King and his Parliament, whilst both profess to level at the same end." He gives reasons why he was not out of heart, but that there was no hope of peace. He therefore again exhorts his hearers to the devout observance of the fast, warns them from the prophet Amos, who complaining of the luxury of the Israelites, their sensuality and degeneracy, concludes all with this sharp close—"But they are not grieved for the affliction of Joseph."

Fuller in this sermon shows his moderation, and he confined himself within very strict limits.   He avoided everything of a strictly political nature, and so prevented the danger of turning a fast into an occasion of strife and debate.   He loved peace, and he was labouring in private and public to beget a right understanding among all men of the King's most righteous cause, which through seduction and popular fury was generally maligned.   His exhortations to peace and obedience were his constant subjects in the church (all his sermons were such liturgies), while his secular days were spent in vigorously promoting the King's affairs, either by a sudden reconciliation or potent assistance ("Life," p. 121).   But although he failed to bring others round to his views, he, with our peacemakers, was comforted in his conscience that "they may appeal to the God of Heaven how they have prayed heartily for peace, have petitioned humbly for peace, have been content to pay dearly for peace, and to their power have endeavoured to refrain themselves from sins, the breakers of peace ; and therefore they trust that Christian English Protestant blood which shall be shed, which hath been and hereafter may be shed in these woeful wars, shall never be visited on their score, or laid to their charge."   In his sermon the preacher strongly urged the sending a petition to the King, which was presented to his Majesty, January 7th, 1642-3. In connection with this petition the name of Dr. Fuller appears, but whether it was Fuller of the Savoy (as representing one of three loyal parishes of Westminster, St.

Martin's, and St. Clement Danes) or some other Dr. Fuller, is a question which has not been satisfactorily settled.

The Parliament professed (not with sincerity however) to desire to have a peace. Their irritating language, and demand that the King would sanction the utter abolition of the episcopal regiment, shewed of themselves that as they addressed him no longer as his subjects, they had no intention of again acknowledging his authority. And on the other hand there were those about the King who were as little inclined to make any concessions, or to treat with their enemies in any other light than that of traitors. Taking advantage of this juncture of affairs, Fuller took the opportunity of preaching a second public sermon, in which he inculcated the duties of submission. This was preached on the anniversary of the King's accession, March 27th, 1643, at Westminster Abbey, which was probably lent him for the occasion, through the kindness and influence of his friends with the Dean and Chapter. The anniversary fell on a Monday (two days before the monthly fast of Wednesday), but its celebration had been strongly recommended in one of the Canons of the Convocation of 1640, with which Fuller evidently heartily agreed.

His discourse shows that he took a sanguine view of affairs even at that time, although his text could not have proved very palatable to any revolutionary spirits. It was taken from II Samuel, 30, " Yea, let him take all, forasmuch as my Lord, the King, is come again in peace unto his own house." This sentiment of David's old friend was uttered to show the "hyperbole of his happiness, the transcendency of his joy, conceived at David's safe return ; joy which swelled up in him in full measure, pressed down, shaken together,

and running over.   Yet, lest the least drop of so precious a
liquor as this was (being the spirits of loyalty distilled)
should be spilt on the ground, let us gather it up with our
best attention to pour it in our hearts to practise it as it
flows from the text.   He says of the action of the civil
power, somewhat satirically, "perchance the wisdom of our
Parliament may suffer in the censures of such who fathom
mysteries of State by their own shallow capacities, for seeming to suffer sectaries and schismatics to share and divide
in God's service with the Mephibosheths, the quiet and
peaceable children of our church.   And, indeed, such
sectaries take a great share to themselves, having taken all
the Common Prayer out of most places, and under the
pretence to abolish superstition, have almost banished
decency out of God's Church.   But no doubt the sages of
our State want not will, but wait a time, when, with more
conveniency and less disturbance (though slowly, surely),
they will restrain such turbulent spirits with David in my
text, who was rather contented than well pleased to pass by
Ziba for the present."   He adds, with further reference to
his own time, "Pious princes can take no delight in victories
over their own subjects.   For when they cast up their audits
they shall find themselves losers in their very gaining.   Nor
can they properly be said to have *won the day*, which at
best is but a twilight, being benighted with a mixture of
much sorrow and sadness.   For kings being the parents of
their country, must needs grieve at the destruction of their
children.   I dare boldly say, that in that unhappy Aceldama
(Edge Hill, fought Oct. 23rd of the preceding year), wherein
the person of our Sovereign was present, *a sword did pierce
through his own heart* in the same sense as it is said of the

Virgin Mary (Luke ii. 35). For though (thanks be to God) Divine providence did *cover his head in the day of battle,* as it were miraculously commanding the bullets, which flew about and respected no persons, not to touch His anointed, yet, notwithstanding, his soul was shot through with grief to behold a field spread with his subjects' corpses, that scarce any passage but either through rivulets of blood, or over bridges of bodies. And had he got as great a victory as David got in the valley of Ephraim, yet surely he would have preferred peace far above it." In speaking of the peaceful clauses of the text, he censures those who would bring about a dishonourable peace. "Now-a-days all cry to have peace, and care not to have truth together with it. Yea, there be many silly Mephibosheths in our days that so adore peace that to obtain it they care not what they give away to the malignant Zibas of our kingdom. These say, 'Yea, let them take all, laws, and liberties, and privileges, and proprieties, and Parliaments, and religion, and the Gospel and godliness, and God Himself, so but that the Lord our King may come in peace. But let us have peace and truth together, both or neither; for if peace offer to come alone, we will do with it as Ezekiel did with the brazen serpent, even break it to pieces and stamp it to powder as the dangerous idol of ignorant people."

Fair are the professions of the Parliament, on the other side, and, no doubt, but as really they intend them. But these matters belong not to us to meddle with; and as for all other politic objections against peace, they pertain not to the pulpit to answer. All that we desire to see is, the King re-married to the State; and we doubt not, but as the bridegroom, on the one side, will be careful to have his portion paid—*His prerogative;* so the bride's friends entrusted for her, will be sure to see her jointure settled—*the liberty of the subject.*

Then applying the text to the occasion, he thus lauds the King: "Seeing now the servants of our Sovereign are generally gone hence to wait on their Lord, we may now boldly, without danger to make them puffed up with pride, or ourselves suspected of flattery, speak that in praise of their master, which malice itself cannot deny. Look above him : to his God, how he is pious ! Look beneath : to his subjects how is he pitiful ! Look about him : how is he constant to his wife, careful for his children ! Look near him : how is he good to his servants ! Look far from him : how is he just to foreign princes." Then enumerating the qualities of our sovereigns, from William the Conqueror down to Edward the Fourth, he proceeds : " But let malice itself stain our Sovereign with any notorious personal fault—for to wish him wholly without fault were in effect to wish him dead. Besides this, consider him as a King, and what favours he hath bestowed on his subjects."

In opposition to the Anabaptists, separatists, and schismatics whose pretended truth he calls " flat falsities, mere fooleries," the preacher, a loyal son of the Church, repeated the assertion that formerly "we had in our churches all truth necessary to salvation. Yea, let these that cry most for the want of truth show one rotten kernel in the whole pomegranate, one false article in all Thirty-nine. But these men know wherein their strength lieth, and they had rather creep into houses and lead away captive silly women, laden with infirmities, than to meddle with men and enter the lists to combat with the learned doctors of the Church."

He spoke very earnestly and unreservedly upon the duty of all to unite in accepting the peace, which the King now offered.

"There must," he says, "at least be a mutual confiding on both sides, so that they must count the honesty of others their only hostages. This the sooner it be done, the easier it is done. For who can conceive that when both sides have suffered more wrongs they will sooner forgive, or when they have offered more wrongs be sooner forgiven. For our King's part let us demand of his money what Christ asked of Cæsar's coin. 'Whose image is this?' Charles', and what is the superscription? 'Religio Protestantium, Leges Angliæ, Libertates Parliamenti,' and the same hath caused them to be cast both in silver and gold, in pieces of several sizes and proportions, as if thereby to show that he intends to make good his promise both to poor and rich, great and small, and we are bound to believe him, nor less. Next we insist on *his own house*, wherein the city is particularly pointed at. For if London be the Jerusalem of our David, then certainly Westminster is his Zion, where he hath his constant habitation. Here is the principal palace of his residence, the proper seat of his great council, the usual receipt of his revenues, the common courts of justice, the ancient chair of his enthroning, the royal ashes of his ancestors, the fruitful nursery of his children. You, therefore, the inhabitants of this city, have most reason to rejoice."

"But, alas! what have I done that I should not, or rather, what have I to do that I cannot, having invited many guests now to a feast, and having no meat to set before you? I have called courtiers and citizens to rejoice, and still one thing is wanting, and that, a main material one, the founder of all the rest, the King is not returned in peace. Then the sun is slipped out of our firmament, and the diamond dropped out of the ring of my text. I pretended and promised to make an application thereof to the time, and must I now be like the foolish builder in the Gospel, begin and cannot finish ? *Own house*, that is the bottom of the text, but this stands empty. *My Lord the King*, and that is the top of the text, but he is far off; and the words which are the side-walls to join them together, *He is come home in peace*, these, alas ! cannot be erected. In this case there is but one remedy to help us, and that prescribed by our Saviour Himself, John xxvi., **23**, 'Whatsoever ye shall ask the Father in My name, He will give it you,' and then that his courtesies might not unravel or fret out, hath he bound them with a strong border, and a rich fringe, a triennial Parliament." He then sums up the King's concessions, the abolition of the Star Chamber and High Commission Court, monopolies, and ship-money, and the King's offer of abolishing "burdensome ceremonies to tender consciences ;" and lastly, triennial parliaments settled, and the present indefinitely prolonged. Fuller hints at the *excess* of these concessions in his own happy way. "Do we not dream? Do I speak? Do you hear? Is it light? Do we not deceive ourselves with fond fancies? or are not these boons too big to beg? too great to be granted? *Such as our fathers never durst desire, nor grandfathers hoped to receive?* O no, it is so, it is sure, it is certain we are awake, we do not dream ; if anything be asleep it is our ingratitude, which is so drowsy to return deserved thanks to God and the King for these great favours."

"Next to the King comes *my Lord the King*, and this

peculiarly concerns the courtiers, and such Mephibosheths as eat bread at his table, who, under God, owe their being to his bounty, and whose states are not only made but created by him. These, indeed, of all others are bound most to rejoice at their Sovereign's return, being obliged thereunto by a three-fold tie: loyalty to a Sovereign, duty to a master, and gratitude to a benefactor; except (as some fondly hold that a letter sealed with three seals may be lawfully opened) any conceive that a three-fold engagement may be easiest declined."

" Let us pray faithfully, pray fervently, pray constantly, pray continually; let preacher and people join their prayers together, that God would be pleased to build up the walls, make up the breaches in application, that what cannot be told, may be foretold for a truth; and that our text may be verified of Charles in prophecy, as by David in history. Excellently St. Austin adviseth that men should not be curious to enquire how original sin came into them, but careful to seek how to get it out. By the same similitude (though reversed) let us not be curious to know what made our King (who next to God I count our *original good*) to leave this city, or whether offences given or taken moved him to his departure: but let us bend our brains and improve our best endeavours to bring him safely and speedily back again. How often herein have our pregnant hopes miscarried, even when they were to be delivered! just as a man in a storm swimming through the sea to the shore, till the oars of his faint arms begin to fail him, is now come to catch land, when an unmerciful wave beats him as far back in an instant as he can recover in an hour. Just so, when our hopes of a happy peace have been ready to arrive, some envious unexpected

P

obstacle hath started up, and hath set our hopes ten degrees backward, as the shadow of the sun-dial of Ahaz. But let us not be hereat disheartened, but with blind Bartimæus, the more we are commanded by unhappy accidents to hold our peace, let us cry the louder in our prayers, the rather, because our King is already partly come ; come in his offer to come ; come in his tender to treat ; come in his proffer of peace. And this very day being the beginning of the treaty, I may say he set his first step forward : God guide his feet, and speed his pace. O let us thriftily husband the least mite of hopes that it may increase, and date our day from the first peeping of the morning star, before the sun be risen. In a word, desist from sinning, persist in praying, and then it may come to pass that this our use may once be antedated, and this day's sermon sent as a harbinger beforehand to provide a lodging in your hearts for your joy against the time that *my Lord our King* shall return to his own house in peace."

This sermon got our preacher into trouble, for the " theme was so distasteful to the ringleaders of the rebellion, and so well and loyally enforced by him that drew not only a suspicion from the moderate misled party of Parliament, but an absolute odium on him from the grandees and principals of the rebellion." (Life, p. 17.) As an *apologia pro doctrinâ suâ*, he published this sermon to prevent any misrepresentation of his words. In his preface, which he added, he said, " Sermons have their dooms, partly according to the capacities, partly according to the affections of their hearers. I am, therefore, enforced to print my more pains, not to get applause, but to assert my innocency, and yet indeed he gaineth that can save in this age.

Read with judgment, censure with charity. As for those who have unmercifully persecuted me, my revenge is in desiring they may be forgiven."

Notwithstanding the displeasure of the Parliamentary leaders at this sermon, no steps seem to have been taken to eject him from his position at the Savoy. Many of the more pronounced Royalist clergy had been either driven out by the " committee for plundered and scandalous ministers," or taken themselves to the King's quarters, and Fuller was left alone, almost the solitary representative of loyal principles, amongst those with whom he had but little sympathy. It may seem strange that he should have been left unmolested when so many were compelled to leave, but his known moderation and attractive power as a preacher had rendered him a favourite, even with the more moderate of the Parliamentary leaders. He seems to have been allowed to do as he liked, and it is probable that the popular party were unwilling to convert him into an avowed open enemy. But his isolated position brought him into the more prominent notice of his opponents. " Their inspection and spyal was confined almost to the Doctor's pulpit as to public assemblies. But he went on labouring for peace in season and out of season, and although the most strenuous efforts were made to induce him to leave the Royalist cause, he remained, like Abdiel, true and faithful to his principles."

A third sermon was preached about this time by Fuller on occasion upon another Fast Day, which was ordered by the Parliament. Taking advantage of this, he preached a sermon at his own chapel at the Savoy on Reformation, which word was then in every body's mouth. Anent this subject there were several treaties put out by eminent men on Church matters.   Bishop Hall asserted *Episcopacy* to be *of Divine right* in 1641.   Jeremy Taylor followed on the same side in his *Episcopacy asserted*.   After the imprisonment of Laud, Hall wrote *his humble remonstrance to the High Court of Parliament* in defence of Episcopacy.   Milton followed with his essay of *Reformation* and the causes that hitherto have hindered it (1641), and there is evidence to prove that Fuller was one of the earliest readers of the work.   Heylin came to the assistance of Hall, harassed by many assailants, in his *History of Episcopacie* (1642).   Reformation and cognate subjects were as familiar to the auditors as the preachers, when everyone was talking about it.

The sermon is entitled "*A Sermon of Reformation*, from Heb. ix. 10, until the time of Reformation," and it was licensed by John Downam, and published the same year. Fuller begins his discourse by remarking that the word "Reformation" was long in pronouncing, and longer in performing, and insists upon the fact that Christians "living under the Gospel live in a time of reformation.   Ceremonies had been removed, manners reformed, and doctrine refined, so that our twilight is clearer than the Jewish noonday.   The Jews, indeed, saw Christ presented in a landscape, and beheld Him through the perspective of faith—seeing the promise afar off.   But at this day a dwarf Christian is an overmatch for a giant Jew in knowledge."   Freely confessing the "deformation" of the Church by Popery, Fuller says the reforming under Henry VIII. and Edward VI. was partial and imperfect.   But the doctrine established in the time of Elizabeth and her successors, and embodied in the Thirty-nine Articles, "if declared, explained, asserted from false glosses, have all gold, no dust or dross in them."

" Withal we flatly deny that Queen Elizabeth left the dust behind the door, which she cast out on the dunghill, whence this uncivil expression was raked up." He also says, " We freely confess that there may be some faults in our Church in matters of practice and ceremonies ; and no wonder if there be ; it would be a miracle if it were not. Besides, there be some innovations rather *in* the Church than *of* the Church, as not chargeable on the public account, but on private men's scores,—who are old enough, let them answer for themselves." He then proceeded to show the true character of such who are to be true and proper reformers. They must have a *lawful calling* to this work. It is plain, from the approbation bestowed on the kings of Judah for their interference in ecclesiastical affairs, that to reform the Church was their proper office. Private persons should help forward with their prayers. Their office is to reform themselves and their own houses. " A good man in Scripture is never called God's Church (because that is a collective term belonging to many), but is often termed God's temple : such a temple it is lawful for every private man to reform : he must see that the foundation of faith be firm, the pillars of patience be strong, the windows of knowledge be clear, the roof of perseverance be perfected." He omits not in the qualifications of a true reformer, discretion. " Christian discretion, a grace none ever spake against, but those that wanted it." Speaking much to the same effect, he says in his " Pisgah Sight," " Oh if order were observed for every one to mend his own house and heart, how would personal amendment by degrees produce family, city, country, kingdom reformation ! How soon are those streets made clear, where every one sweeps against his own door."

Besides Christian discretion, he sets forth piety, knowledge, true courage, and magnanimity as being proper qualifications in a true reformer.

In reply to the objection as to the preacher's own calling to meddle with this matter, Fuller replies with good reason : " I am, or should be, most sensible of mine own weakness, being ἐλαχιστότερος,. the least of those that dispense the Word and Sacraments ; yet have I a calling as good as the Church of England could give me. And if she be not ashamed of such a son, I count myself honoured with such a mother. And though mere private Christians may not inter-meddle with public reforming of a Church, God's prophets have in all ages challenged the privilege to tell necessary truths to the greatest. . . . We are Christ's Embassadors (2 Cor. v. 20), and claim the leave to speak Truth with soberness. And though I cannot expect my words should be *like nails fastened* by the Masters of the Assemblies (Eccles. xii. 11), yet I hope they may prove as tacks (!) entered by him that desires to be faithful and peaceable in Israel."

In this sermon, as in the last, he animadverts upon the turbulent spirit of the Anabaptists. " Very facile, but very foul is that mistake in the Vulgar Translation," Luke xv., 8. Instead of *everrit domum*, she swept the house, 'tis rendered *evertit domum*, she overturned the house. Such sweeping we must expect from such spirits, which, under pretence to cleanse our Church, would destroy it. The best is, they are so far from sitting at the *helm*, that I hope they shall ever be kept under the hatches."

Fuller then commends a due regard both to the *ancient* and to the modern Fathers. " Reformation is to be done with all reverence and respect to the ancient Fathers. These, though they lived near the fountain of religion, yet lived in the marches of Paganism, as also in the time when the mystery of iniquity began to work, which we hope is now ready to receive the wages. If, therefore, there be found in their practice any ceremonies smacking of Paganism or Popery, and if the same can be justly challenged to continue in our Church, I plead not for their longer life, but for their decent burial."

"Secondly, with honourable reservation to the memories of our first reformers, reverend Cranmer, learned Ridley, downright Latimer, zealous Bradford, pious Philpot, patient Hooper, men that had their failings, but worthy in their generation."

"And lastly, with carefulness not to give any just offence to to the Papists, though Papists forget their duty to us, let us remember our duty to them, not as Papists, but as professors of Christianity, to their persons, not erroneous opinions, not giving them any just offence."

He concluded by saying that there was a grand difference between the founding of a new church and reforming of an old ; that a perfect reformation of any church in this world may be desired, but not hoped for. In proving the fanaticism of some of the sectaries, he remarks, "And yet there are some now-a-days that talk of a great light manifested in this age, more than ever before. Indeed, we moderns have a mighty advantage of the ancients ; whatsoever was theirs by industry may be made ours. The Christian philosophy of Justyn Martyr, the constant sanctity of Cyprian, the Catholic faith of Athanasius, the subtle controversies of Augustine, the excellent Morals of Gregory the Great, the humble devotion of Bernard, all contribute themselves to the edification of us, who live in this latter age. But as for any transcendent, extraordinary, miraculous light, peculiarly conferred on our times, the worst I wish the opinion is this that it were true."

He then points out, in conclusion, the melancholy condition of England at this time: " O the miserable condition of our land at this time. God hath shewed the whole world that England hath enough of itself to make itself happy or unhappy, as it useth or abuseth it. Her homebred *wares* enough to maintain her, and her homebred *wars* enough to destroy her, though no foreign nation contribute to her overthrow. Well, whilst others *fight* for peace, let us *pray* for peace, for peace on good terms, yea, on God's terms and in God's time, when He shall be pleased to give it and we fitted to receive it. Let us wish both King and Parliament so well, as to wish neither of them better, but both of them best, even a happy accommodation."*

---

* This sermon, which was published, illustrates the true and only logical platform of the Anglican Church—the appeal to Primitive Antiquity—and was licensed by John Downam, youngest son of the Bishop of Chester, one of the licencees of the divinity publications. Williams was the publisher, and it was duly entered at Stationers' Hall. It brought about a sudden change in the preacher's prospects. Some condemned him as too hot a Royalist. Truth then his character for moderation was gone. And a contemporary writer says that Fuller "was extremely distasteful to the Parliament." We shall not therefore be surprised to find London became too hot for him, and to hear of his flight from the metropolis, and the cession of the Savoy chaplaincy.

CHAPTER XIV.

FULLER'S FLIGHT FROM LONDON—GOES TO OXFORD (1643).

" The Doctor was settled in the love and affections of his own
Parish (Savoy), besides other obligations, so that the *Covenant*
then tendered might seem like the bright side of that cloud
(promising security and prosperity to him, as was insinuated to
the Doctor by many great *Parliamentarians*) which showered
down, after a little remoteness, such a black horrible tempest
upon the Clergy—nay, the Church and the Three Kingdomes.
But the good Doctor could not bow down to his knee to that
Baal-Berith, nor for any worldly considerations (enough whereof
invited him even to fall down and worship, men of his great
parts being infinitely acceptable to them) lend so much as an ear
to their serpentine charm of Religion and Reformation."—
Anonymous Life. p. 21.

JUST four days after the preaching of the sermon
on Reformation the news came to London that
Bristol had surrendered to the Royalist forces,
and that Nathaniel Fiennes had capitulated, July 27th, 1643.
This was the second important victory secured to the
Royalist forces, the former having been gained by Hopton
near Devizes on the 13th of the same month.   Clarendon
says the direful news struck the Parliamentarians to the
heart.   To the King it was a full tide of prosperity, and
made him master of the second city of the kingdom, and
gave him the undisputed possession of one of the richest.
The position of the Royalist armies at this time generated
the triplet :

> " Bristol taking,
> Exeter shaking,
> Gloucester quaking."

The disputes, however, of Princes Maurice and Rupert

wasted the opportunities now open to the King. There was a debate in Parliament about this time, and an accommodation with the King was carried by a considerable majority. But on the following day, no longer held sacred by these hypocrites, the city preachers—now augmented by the assembly of Divines—sounded the tocsin to arms. The proposals were rejected, and at a council meeting, presided over by Lord Mayor Pennington, it was determined to continue the war. Fuller had been appointed with five of his brethren to carry up a petition for peace to the King, but was on the way remanded by Parliament. His conscience would not allow him to take the oath, and to avoid the consequences of his refusal, " I withdrew myself," said he, " into the King's parts, which (I hope) I may no less safely than I do freely confess, because punished for same with the loss of my livelihood, and since, I suppose, pardoned in the Acts of Oblivion."—(1651.)—(" Ch. Hist." xi., 20.)

It was at this juncture that many members of both Houses and several Royalists made their way to the King's quarters at Oxford, whose star at this time seemed in the ascendant. Although our preacher still remained at the Savoy, his days were evidently numbered. Clarendon says, " The violent party carried now all before them, and were well contented with the absence of those who used to give them some trouble and vexation." With renewed vigour the war was entered upon, and there seemed small hopes of peace.

Fuller's last sermon had given the greatest umbrage. His remarks anent the Papists classed him as a malignant. His idea of a Church was abhorrent to those who had cast aside the episcopal regimen, and his loyalty to the King and proposal for peace, brought down upon him the odium of the Parliamentarians. It was needful to tune all the London pulpits, and so it was thought advisable to break up the influential congregation which Fuller weekly addressed ; and it was now therefore his refusal to take the recent oath afforded the opportunity for driving the preacher away. Some who were present in the vestry, when Fuller had taken the oath, may have complained that he had not taken it in its entirety, Be that as it may, it was determined to make Fuller take the oath in the face of the congregation at the Savoy *in terminis terminantibus*, on Sunday, Aug. 20th, 1640. This he firmly refused to do, under the altered circumstances, as he could not conscientiously agree to its terms. His mind was made up ; his mission of peace was ended, and he forthwith withdrew.

We are not told in what way Fuller's flight was managed from London to the King's quarters, which were then at Oxford, but no doubt it was by a prearranged plan at the latter place, although communication between the two cities was very difficult, passes from either side being demanded. Nor do we know the exact date when his sudden disappearance took place, but it must have been just before the excitement consequent upon the siege of Gloucester, to the relief of which the trained bands marched under Essex (Aug. 21, 30). The battle of Newbury was fought on their return, "wherein the Londoners did show," says Fuller, "that they could as well use a sword in the field as a metward in the shop" (Sep. 20). The solemn league and covenant was taken five days after, which secured the assistance of the Scotch, at Westminster, by members of the House of Commons and the Assembly of Divines, it being subsequently signed by their adherents. The whole of the proceedings were regarded with aversion by many, like Walton, who says, "All corners of the nation were filled with Covenanters, confusion, committee-men, and soldiers."

It was said by some that Fuller had taken the solemn league and covenant, which he distinctly repudiated, but there can be no doubt that all sorts of wild stories got circulated after his departure from the metropolis. No doubt many were nettled at this act of self-sacrifice on the part of our author, which he willingly offered on the shrine of Episcopacy and Royalty—thus giving up his livelihood.

"A severe persecution," says Hallam, "fell on the faithful children of the Anglican Church. Many had already been sequestered from their livings, or even subjected to imprisonment, by the Parliamentary committee for scandalous ministers, or by subordinate committees of the same kind set up in each county within their quarters ; sometimes on the score of immoralities or false doctrine ; more frequently for what they termed malignity, or attachment to the King and his party. Yet wary men, who meddled not with politics, might hope to elude this inquisition. But the Covenant, imposed as a general test, drove out all who were too conscientious to pledge themselves by a solemn appeal to the Deity to resist the polity which they generally believed to be of this institution. What numbers of the clergy were ejected (most of them for refusing the Covenant and for no moral offence or reputed superstition) it is impossible to ascertain. Walker, in his "Sufferings of the Clergy," a folio volume, published in the latter end of Anne's reign, with all the virulence and partiality of the High Church faction of that age, endeavoured to support those who had reckoned it at 8000 ; a palpable overstatement upon his own shewing, for he cannot produce near 2900 names, after a most diligent investigation. Neale, however, admits 1600, probably more than one-fifth of the beneficed ministers of the kingdom. The biographical collections furnish a pretty copious martyrology of men the most distinguished by their learning and virtues in that age. The remorseless and indiscriminate bigotry of Presbyterianism might boast that it had heaped disgrace on Walton, and driven Lydiate to begging; that it trampled on the old age of Hales, and embittered with insult the dying moments of Chillingworth." ("Constitutional History of England," vol. 1, pp. 168-9.)

But the report has been traced to one William Lilly, the notorious astrologer and almanack maker of the time, in his address to the reader prefacing his true history of James the First and Charles the First. To this statement, however, Fuller makes a satisfactory refutation in his "Church History," where he says, "So much concerning the covenant, which, during three months after (Oct. 1st, 1640), began to be rigorously and generally urged. Nor have I aught else to observe thereof, save to add, in mine own defence, that I never saw the same except at distance, as hung up in churches, nor ever had any occasion to read, or hear it read, till this day in writing my History, whatever hath been reported and printed to the contrary of my taking thereof in London, who went away from the Savoy to the King's quarters long before any mention thereof in England." Then in a paragraph, which he terms *The author's plea in his own just defence*, he describes the oath which he did take, and which has been already referred to and quoted.

The anonymous biographer thus writes of this part of

the author's life : " The Doctor was settled in the love and affection of his own parish, besides other obligations to his numerous followers ; so that the covenant then tendered might seem like the bright side of that cloud (promising serenity and prosperity to him, as was mistaken by many great Parliamentarians) which showered down after a little remoteness such a black horrible tempest upon the Clergy, nay, the Church, and these kingdoms.

But the good Doctor could not bow down his knee to that Baal-Berith, nor, for any worldly consideration (enough whereof invited him to fall down and worship, men of his great parts being infinitely acceptable to them), lend so much as an ear to their serpentine charms of religion and reformation. Since, therefore, he could not continue with his cure without his conscience, and every day threatened the imposition of that illegal oath, he resolved to betake himself to God's providence, and to put himself directly under it, waiving all indirect means and advantages whatsoever to his security. In order thereunto, in April (August ?) 1643, he deserted the city of London, and privately conveyed himself to Oxford, to the no less sudden amazement of the faction here (London, who yet upon their recollection quickly found their mistake) than to the unexpected contentment and joy of the loyal party there, who had every day Job's messengers of the plundering, ruin and imprisonments of orthodox divines." ("Life," pp. 18-22.)

Oxford, the head-quarters of the Royalist party, the asylum of Charles himself after the drawn battle of Edgehill, was in 1643 (as the author of the "Worthies" describes it) "a court, a garrison, and a university," and so remained for about three years. Cambridge was in the hands of the

Parliamentary party, who retained possession of it during the struggle, but Oxford remained true to the King. Some of the students were enrolled as archers, and most of them laid aside the pen for the sword. Prince Rupert was quartered at Magdalen, which was especially loyal.

The King kept his court, thronged with numerous and influential adherents, at Merton College, " famous for schoolmen," and the Queen was the centre of great attraction. The city had undergone great changes, fortifications having been thrown up, at which the students worked with a will. Colleges were turned into barracks ; their inmates became cavaliers. There was an influx of persons in favour of the King's cause, soon after the King resorted here, and the Royalist adherents poured from every quarter. The biographer of Fuller describes it as " the common refuge and shelter of such persecuted persons as Fuller, so that it never was nor is it like to be a more learned university (one breast in Cambridge being dried up with Cromwell's visitation, the milk resorted to the other), nor did ever letters and arms so well consist together, it being an accomplished academy of both " ; adding, of the King's friends, that they came " like the clean beasts to the ark, when the waters increased." (" Life," pp. 22-23)

Fuller, now a fugitive, was lodged in Lincoln College, then reputed the least in the university. Dr. Sanderson was holding office in the university at the time and kept there, but the academic curriculum was much interrupted at this period by the demands made upon their time and hospitality by the refugees. The colleges were crowded by other than the usual class of inmates, and the price of living became very high. Amongst other residents in

College was Sir Gervase Scroop, who was miraculously saved after his twenty-six wounds received at the battle of Edgehill, where he and his tenants fought for the King, and a description of which he gave to Fuller—a monument of God's sparing mercy and his son's affection.

"He always after carried his arm in a scarf; and loss of blood made him look very pale, as a messenger come from the grave to advise the living to prepare for death. The effect of his story I received from his own mouth in Lincoln College." (Lincoln "Worthies," p. 170). Another of the residents was Sir Edward Wardour, the colleague of Dr. Fuller of the peace petition, occupying for the three last quarters of the year the low chamber of the west end of the new chapel. His death occurring here, he was buried in All Saints (the parish church of Lincoln College).

During his stay at Oxford, Fuller preached before the King in the university church: but his sincerity and moderation (as Russell says) did not shield him from the reflections of some whose zeal knew no bounds, although it was not so with their charity. Fuller sought to reconcile the animosities of unreasonable men on both sides, but if the Heylins took this ill, we may be sure the Sandersons and Halls did not. Bishop Hall owned his friendship in a most cordial spirit, subscribing himself his much devoted friend, precessor, and fellow-labourer, in his letter vindicating himself and his colleague in the Synod of Dort, from the aspersions of Goodwin, the author of the book entitled "Redemption Redeemed." And of Dr. Sanderson, who was of the same mind as our author, in respect of the much disputed Canons of

1640, our author writes "amongst the modern worthies of his College, still surviving, Dr. Robert Sanderson (late Regius Professor) moveth in the highest sphere, as no less plain and profitable, than able and profound casuist (a learning almost lost among Protestants) wrapping up sharp thorns in rosy leaves; I mean hard matter in neat Latin, and pleasant expressions." ("Ch. Hist." bk. x. p. 85).

Fuller remained at Lincoln College during his sojourn at Oxford, but he complained of the dearness of the place. Thus he writes in his "Church History," "I could much desire (were it in my power) to express my service to this foundation, acknowledging myself for a quarter of a year in these troublous times (though no member of) a dweller in it, I will not complain of the dearness of this University, when *seventeen weeks* cost me more than seventeen years at Cambridge, even all I had: but shall pray the students therein be never hereafter disturbed upon the like occasion."

Heylin, Fuller's old antagonist, himself a native of Oxfordshire, and upholding the honour of his alma mater, falls foul of him for his remark thus: "He hath no reason to complain of the University or the dearness of it, but rather of himself for coming to a place so chargeable and destructive to him. He might have tarried where he was, for I never heard he was sent for, and then this great complaint about the dearness of that University would have found no place." To whom Fuller replied: "As for my being sent for to Oxford, the animadvertor I see hath not heard of all that was done. I thought that as St. Paul wished all "altogether such as he was, except these bonds," so the animadvertor would have wished all Englishmen like himself,

Q

save in his sequestration, and rather welcomed than jeered such as went to Oxford." ("Appeal," p. 11, 144.)

Our Fuller would meet with at least two other Fullers refugees at Oxford for the Royalist cause. One was Dr. William Fuller, Dean of Ely, who had sat in the Conovcation of 1640. He seems to have come under censure very early in the troubles of the period in connection with some disturbance about the altar rails of St. Giles, Articles were exhibited against him in Parliament, both as to his action about lecturers and for some sermons preached by him, and he was adjudged a delinquent. He was sent to Oxford in exchange for another, and where he remained throughout the siege, acting as Chaplain in Ordinary to the King. It was said of him that " he preached there so seasonably that King Charles would say of him and some others there, that they were sent of God to set those distracted times in their wits by the sobriety of their doctrines and the becomingness of their behaviour. The Dean was not unlike our Thomas Fuller, whom the King learned to appreciate, ordering him to print more than one sermon preached before the Court: and Charles, according to the biographer was "the most excellent intelligent prince of the abilities of the clergy." On the death of Balcanqual the King conferred the Deanery of Durham on William Fuller, but he would not quit Ely. He was D.D. of Cambridge, became incorporated D.D. of Oxford, where he remained till its surrender.

Fuller would also meet another William Fuller, who ultimately became Bishop of Lincoln. We have alluded to him before, as he has been thought to be the uncle of our author, and indeed has been confounded with Thomas Fuller himself by some. He was educated at West-

minster School, afterwards entered Magdalen Hall, migrated
to Edmund's Hall, where he studied for fifteen years. He
became a "petty Canon of Christ Church," then Chaplain
to Lord Lyttleton, keeper of the Great Seal. He was
rector of Ewhurst, and in 1641 retired with his patron to
Oxford, where he remained till its surrender.

Our loyal and witty Thomas Fuller received a hearty welcome from King Charles and his adherents. With many of
his courtiers he was on terms of intimacy, and as they had
been formerly parishioners or members of his congregation
at the Savoy, were frequent in their invitations for him to
remove to Oxford. No doubt the King had often heard of
the attractive discourses of the Savoy lecturer, and also of
his deep attachment to the Royalist cause, which he, in
common with the rest of the Fullers, dutifully enforced. It
was suggested that Fuller's long continued services to the
Royal cause should not continue without some public acknowledgment, and accordingly the King vouchsafed the
Doctor the honour of preaching before him. Fuller willingly consented, and prepared a sermon specially for the
occasion. Here was an opportunity, had he been a time
server, of ingratiating himself in the Royal favour and advancing his popularity and preferment in the Church.
But no. He was true to himself as a minister of the Gospel.
A brilliant audience had been attracted to St. Mary's to
listen to the witty Divine, and he seemed to have preached
to, not *before*, his hearers, not to the satisfaction of all the
assembled courtiers. He attempted to discuss both sides of
the prevalent feeling which actuated the contending parties,
and professed a hope of arriving at some *modus vivendi*,
which would restrain the hostile factions from renewed

attacks and further effusion of blood. His biographer says "He laid open the blessings of an accommodation, as being too sensible (and that so recently) of the virulency and impotent rage, though potent arms of the disloyal Londoners, which, as the Doctor then Christianly thought, could not better be allayed than by a fair condescension in matters of Church Reformation."

The preacher then rebuked the injustice of the party in some respects, and made a side thrust against the godlessness of some of the Cavaliers, whose " heaven upon earth was to see the day that they might subdue and be revenged upon the Roundheads." Fuller evidently spoke out his mind, and was so intent upon doing good " that he minded neither his own estate, habit, or carriage." He saw the disturbing elements seething around him, but he would still, as a minister of the good news, " pray for the peace of Jerusalem," and recall the great Master's beatitude on the peacemakers. He saw there were good and bad on both sides, and so he would not indiscriminately blame the one, and praise the other. Thus he repeated at Oxford his London missive of peace, but his manly, outspoken, and sincere nature—his words of truth and soberness—pleased the Royalists no better than he had before the Parliamentarians.

"Some particulars in that sermon" were considered by " some at court" to have been far too lukewarm, having a tendency to damage the Royal cause, then as it appeared in a prosperous condition. But these censures came not from the King and the more moderate of the body, but from the hot-blooded zealots and those eager for war. Thus it came to pass that the same consistent Divine, who in London had been censured as " too hot a Royalist," was now at the Royal head-quarters condemned for not thoroughly owning the Royal cause. Consequently, he fell into disgrace again, "to the great trouble of the Doctor." But he was not the only Divine who gave offence by his too plain outspokenness, for he was kept in countenance by good company, by Ussher, who at this time was giving umbrage by his faithful preaching, and by Chillingworth, who in a sermon in the autumn of this year, exposed the follies of the times.

Fuller, by his moderation, then had contrived to offend the two contending parties in the State, or rather the extreme men on both sides. He offered the nation an *cirenicon* which was not accepted. But he regarded his own present position as presumptive evidence that he was right. His endeavours were not only unsuccessful, but they recoiled upon his own head, and militated against his advancement. His conduct can "only be ascribed to his moderation, which he would sincerely have inculcated in each party as the only means of reconciling both." But it was altogether a thankless task. In after life, Fuller thus sketches the fate of those who attempt to mediate between hostile parties : "Let not such hereby be disheartened, but know that (besides the reward in heaven) *the very work of moderation is the wages of moderation.* For it carryeth with it a marvellous contentment in his conscience, who hath endeavoured his utmost in order to unity, though unhappy in his success." It must have been galling and mortifying in the extreme to his frank and independent spirit to have thus undeservedly fallen into odium with the very party, with whom all his own personal and traditional sympathies were linked, for whom he had risked everything, on whose behalf he had quitted his post in the metropolis, and to whom he must ultimately look for protection in the troubles which were thickening around him. Writing upon the failure of conciliatory endeavours, he afterwards (1660) wrote in his *Mixt Contemplations*, " Had any endeavoured, some sixteen years since, to have advanced a firm peace betwixt the two opposite parties in our land, their success would not have answered their intentions ; men's veins were then so full of blood, and purses of money." (xviii., 28.) Pride and popular applause were the two great enemies to moderation. " And sure they who will sail with that wind have their own vain-glory for their heaven."

In answer to the charge of " lukewarmness " brought against him both in London and Oxford, our author is at some pains to point out the difference between it and moderation. He thus defends his conduct at this time : " I must wash away an aspersion generally but falsely cast on men of my profession and temper, for all *moderate* men are commonly condemned for lukewarm.

As it is true: *Sæpe latet vitium propinquitate boni,*
It is as true : *Sæpe latet virtus propinquitate mali,*
And as lukewarmness hath often fared the better (the more men's ignorance) for pretending neighbourhood to moderation, so moderation (the more her wrong) hath many times suffered for having some supposed vicinity to lukewarmness. However, they are at a great distance, moderation being an wholesome cordial to the soul, whilst lukewarmness (a temper which seeks to reconcile hot and cold) is so distasteful that *health* itself seems sick of it, and vomits it out (Rev. iii., 16). We may observe these differences between them : " First, the lukewarm man (though it be hard to tell what .

he is who knows not what he is himself) is fixed to no one opinion and hath no certain creed to believe, whereas the moderate man sticks to his principles, taking truth wheresoever he finds it, in the opinions of friend or foe, gathering a herb though in a ditch, and throwing away a weed though in a garden." "Secondly, the lukewarm man is both the archer and mark himself, aiming only at his outward security. The moderate man levels at the glory of God, the quiet of the Church, the choosing of the truth, and contenting of his conscience." "Lastly, the lukewarm man as he will live in any religion, so he will die for none. The moderate man, what he hath warily chosen, will valiantly maintain, at leastwise intends and desires to defend it to the death. 'The kingdom of heaven,' saith our Lord, 'suffereth violence.' And in this sense I may say the most moderate men are the most violent, and will not abate an hoof or hair's breadth in their opinions, whatsoever it cost them. And time will come when moderate men shall be honoured as God's doers, though now they be hooted at as owls in the desert." ("Truth Maintained." 'To the Reader')

Fuller's sermon on "Reformation" was about this time attacked by Mr. John Saltmarsh, M.A., of Magdalen College, Cambridge, and minister of Hesterton, Yorkshire. Fuller thus speaks of him in his "Worthies": "John Saltmarsh was extracted from a right ancient but decayed family in Yorkshire, and I am informed that Sir John Methan, his kinsman, bountifully contributed to his education. Returning into his native country, he was very great with Sir John Hotham, the elder. He was one of a fine and active family, no contemptible poet, and a good preacher, as by some of his profitable printed sermons doth appear. Be it charitably imputed to the information of his judgment and conscience, that from a zealous observer, he became a violent oppressor of Bishops and ceremonies. He wrote a book against my sermon on *Reformation*, taxing me for many points of Popery therein. I defended myself in a book called *Truth Maintained*, and challenged him to an answer, who appeared on the field no more, rendering the season thereof, that *he would not shoot his arrows at a dead mark*, being informed that I was dead at Exeter. I have no cause to be angry with Fame (but rather to thank her) for so good a lie. May I make this true use of that false report, *to die daily*. See how Providence hath crossed it : the *dead* (reported) man is still living (1661), the then living man, dead ; and, seeing I survive to go over his grave, I will tread the more gently on the mould thereof, using that civility on him which I received from him." " He died in or about Windsor (as he was riding to and fro in the Parliament army) of a burning fever, venting on his deathbed strange expressions, apprehended (by some of his party) as *extatical*, yea *prophetical*, raptures, whilst others accounted them (no wonder of outrages in the city, when the enemy hath possessed the castle commanding it) to the acuteness of the disease which had seized his intellectuals. His death happened about the year 1650." (" Worthies," Yorkshire, p. 212).

Saltmarsh's strictures were licensed by Mr. Charles Herle, a Cornishman, and B.A., of Exeter College, Oxford, who died 1655. The notification of licence is followed by an anonymous advertisement affirming that Mr. John Downam had received from Fuller a promise which the latter did not fulfil, to alter some passages in his sermon of Reformation.

Saltmarsh dedicated his "Examinations" to the Assembly of Divines : he professed that his thoughts took him *but one* afternoon, and they accordingly evince neither learning nor caution. Fuller replied to these animadversions in a work, *Truth Maintained,* or positions delivered in a sermon at the Savoy, since traduced for dangerous, now asserted for sound and safe (Oxford, 1643). After the dedication to the Universities is a letter from Mr. Herle, in which he vouches for the utility of Saltmarsh's rash censures in the licence he affixed to them. This was regarded by Fuller as endorsing the charges brought against him and Saltmarsh, which might have endangered him in those troublesome times. Then follows a letter to Downam, in which Fuller categorically denies the anonymous report that he had promised to answer some of the passages in the sermon under discussion. Then follows an epistle to Saltmarsh himself, and this is succeeded by another to his parishioners of St. Mary, Savoy. As a specimen of the verve and manly spirit which animate these epistles we will give the last in full :—

"MY DEAR PARISH—for so I dare call you, as conceiving that as my calamities have divorced me from your bed and board, the matrimonial knot betwixt us is 'not yet rescinded. No, not although you have admitted another (for fear and hope rather than affection) in my place. I remember how David, forced to fly from his wife, yet still calls her 'my wife Michall,' even when at that time she was in the possession of Phaltiel, the son of Laish, who had rather bedded than wedded her.

"This sermon I first made for your sakes, as providing it, not as a feast to entertain strangers, but a meal to feed my family And now, having again enlarged and confirmed it, I present it to you as having therein a proper interest, being confident that nothing but good and profitable truth is therein contained.

"Some, perchance, will object that if my sermon were so true why then did I presently leave the parish when I had preached it? My answer is legible in the Capital letters of other ministers' misery who remain in the city. I went away "for the present distress" (1 Cor. vii. 26), thereby reserving myself to do you longer and better service if God's providence shall ever restore me unto you again. And if any tax me as Laban taxed Jacob, 'Wherefore did'st thou flee away secretly,' without solemn tears? I say with Jacob to Laban, 'Because I was afraid,' and that plain-dealing patriarch, who could not be accused for purloining a shoe-latchet of other men's goods, confessed himself guilty of that lawful felony that he 'stole away' for his own safety : seeing truth itself may sometimes seek corners, not as fearing her cause, but suspecting her judge.

"And now all that I have to say to you is this : Take heed how you may imitate the wise and noble Berœans, whatsoever the Doctor or doctrine be, which teacheth or is taught unto you. Search the Scriptures daily, whether these things be so. Hansell this my counsel on this my book, and here beginning, hence proceed to examine all sermons by the same rule of God's Word.

"Only this I add also: pray daily to God to send us a good and happy peace, before we be all brought to utter confusion. You know how I, in all my sermons unto you, by leave of my text, would have a passage in praise of Peace. Still I am of the same opinion. The longer I see this war the less I like it, and the more I loathe it. Not so much because it threatens temporal ruin to our kingdom, as because it will bring a general spiritual hardness of hearts. And if this war long continues, we may be affected for the departure of charity. As the Ephesians were at the going away of St. Paul, 'Sorrowing most of all that we shall see his face thereof no more' (Acts xx. 38). Strive, therefore, in your prayers that that happy condition, which our sins made us unworthy to hold, our repentance may, through God's acceptance thereof, make us worthy to regain.

"Your loving Minister,
THOMAS FULLER."

This truly touching letter not only gives the authentic reason of Fuller's departure from the Savoy, but expresses his deep sorrow at this sundering of parochial ties, which, with buoyant hopes, he trusts may speedily be removed. He also delicately hints at the different doctrine now preached in his pulpit, and the Doctor alluded to is supposed to be Dr. John Bond, of the Parliamentarian party.

As these letters are comparatively unknown, we are tempted to give one more illustration of the raciness of his epistolary productions. It is addressed to "*the unpartial reader*," whom he requests to have no fear of his soi-disant "dangerous" positions. "The saints did not fear the infection of St. Paul, though he was indicted to be a pestilent fellow." He calls attention to the moderation he had practised—"I cannot but expect to procure the ill-will of many, because I have gone in a middle and moderate way, betwixt all extremities. I remember a story too truly applicable to me. Once a jailor demanded of a prisoner newly committed to him whether or no he was a Roman Catholic. 'No,' answered he. 'What then,' said he, 'are you an Anabaptist?' 'Neither,' replied the prisoner. 'What!' said the other, 'are you a Brownist?' 'Nor so,' said the man, 'I am a Protestant.' 'Then' said the jailor, 'get you into the dungeon : I will afford no favour to you, who shall get no profit by you : had you been of any of the other religions some hope I had to gain by the visits of such as are of your own profession.' "I," continues Fuller, "am likely to find no better usage in this age, who profess myself to be a plain Protestant, without welt or guard, or any addition—equally opposite to all heretics and sectaries.... yet I take not myself to be of so desolate and forlorn a religion as to have no fellow-professors with me. If I thought so, I should not only suspect but condemn my judgment, having ever as much loved singleness of heart as I have hated singularity of opinion. I conceive not myself like Eliah 'to be left alone'—having as I am confident in England more than seventy thousand just of the same religion with me—and among these there is one, in price and value, eminently worth ten thousand, even our gracious Sovereign, whom God, in safety and honour long preserve amongst us."

At the conclusion of these epistles, Fuller enters into a detailed examination of Saltmarsh's strictures, but he proves himself a fairer controversialist than his opponent. For whereas Saltmarsh selects isolated passages upon Fuller's sermons, and concretes his criticism upon them, Fuller takes the censures of Saltmarsh *en bloc* and goes through them *seriatim.* This habit he had learnt from his uncle, Bishop Davenant, who, in answering Hoard's " *God's Love to Mankind,*" incorporated the whole of it in his reply. Fuller thus alludes to his method of reply. " This disjointing of things undoeth kingdoms as well as sermons, whilst even weak matters are preserved by their own unity and entireness;" adding,"I have dealt more fairly with you to set down your whole examination." This is a proof of Fuller's fairness as a polemic. Notwithstanding the critical state of affairs, our author is as witty as he is sarcastic—" Some mirth in this sad time doth well."

There is no need to go into the details of this controversy, which, though it elicited the keenest interest at the time, would be perhaps wearisome to the modern reader. But it led to the increased sale of the original sermon, which seems to have been very carefully prepared, and the spirit and wit of the reply have been as much admired as its minute exhaustiveness. The original sermon was maintained by additional reasons and arguments, and to give the reader some idea of the exhaustive nature of the reply as well as the soundness of Fuller's Church Principles, we append the following particulars of it :—

I. That the doctrine of the impossibility of a Church's perfection in this world being well understood, begets not laziness but the more industry in wise reformers.

II. That the Church of England cannot justly be taxed with superstitious innovations.

III. How far private Christians, ministers, and subordinate magistrates, are to concur to the advancing of a public reformation.

IV. What parts therein are only to be acted by the supreme power.

V. Of the progress and praise of passive obedience.

VI. That no extraordinary excitations, incitations, or inspirations are bestowed from God on men in these days.

VII. That it is utterly unlawful to give any just offence to the papist, or to any men whatsoever.

VIII. What advantage the Fathers had of us in learning and religion, and what we have of them.

IX. That no new light, or new essential truths are, or can be revealed in this age.

X. That the doctrine of the Church's imperfection may safely be preached, and cannot honestly be concealed.

It must be evident to see from these points, which were pressed home with all the power and wit at the command our author, what his views really were upon ecclesiastical regimen ; and that for soundness and moderation they synchronize with the views of Church government laid down by the judicious Hooker in his immortal work on Ecclesiastical Polity.

In after life, Fuller thus speaks of his conduct in this controversy, wherein he challenged a reply from Saltmarsh, which, however, never came. " I appeal to such who knew me in the University, to those who have heard my many sermons in London and elsewhere, but especially to my book called *Truth Maintained*, made against Mr. Saltmarsh ; wherein I have heartily (to place that first), largely, to my power, strongly indicated " *non licet populo, renuenti magistratu, reformationem moliri*—(it is not lawful for the people, against the will of the magistracy, to undertake a reformation)."

Before leaving this controversy, we must mention an amusing story told in connection with Mr. Charles Herle, who licensed Saltmarsh's production. " I know the man full well," says Fuller in his " Worthies " (5th chapter), " to whom Mr. Charles Herle, President of the Assembly, said, somewhat insultingly, '*I'll tell you news—last night I buried a Bishop* (dashing more at his profession than person) *in Westminster Abbey.*' To whom the other returned with like latitude to both—'*Sure you buried him in hope of resurrection.*' This our eyes at this day see performed, and it being the work of the Lord, may justly seem marvellous in our sight."

Whilst at Oxford, all Fuller's property, including his valuable library (in quality if not quantity), fell into the hands of the Parliament, and another was appointed in his place at the Savoy (probably Dr. Bond, to whom allusion has been made), so that our author was brought into as great poverty as it was possible for his enemies to bring him to. The sequestrators laid their hands upon all they could get. He afterwards spoke of "sequestration as a yoke borne in our youth, hoping that more freedom is reserved for our old age—a rod formerly in fashion, but never so soundly laid on as of late."

This loss of his books and manuscripts—especially the parchments—affected our author much, and put an end to those studies in which he took so great a delight. It is not clear whether the bulk of his library was in London or Broad Windsor, but no doubt the confiscation took place at the former place. When Fuller quitted the Savoy, it was only as he thought for a time, for he expected soon to be restored to his dear parishioners. But, like many of his compatriots, he was mistaken, and had to endure the full brunt of poverty, although nominally a prebend, a rector, and a lecturer. His books were not only seized but disfigured by mischievous ignorance. "Was it not cruelty," he says, "to *torture* a library by *maiming* and *mangling* the *authors* therein? Neither leaving nor taking them entire. Would they had took *less* that so what they *left* might have been *useful to me*, or *left less*, that so what they *took* might have been *useful to others*. Whereas now, *mischievous ignorance* did a prejudice to me, without a profit to itself or any body else.

"But would to God all my fellow brethren, which with me bemoan the loss of their books, with me might also rejoice for the recovery thereof, though not the same numerical volumes. Thanks be to your honour,* who have

_____

*Rt. Hon. Lord Cranfield, Earl of Middlesex.

bestowed on me (the *treasure* of a Lord *Treasurer*) what remained of your father's library : your father who was the greatest honourer and disgracer of students, bred in learning ; honourer, giving due respect to all men of learning ; disgracer, who by his mere natural parts and experience acquired that perfection of invention, expression and judgment, to which those who make learning their sole study do never arrive."

His loss he thus notices in his *Meditations on the Times* (17th), " One Nicias, a philosopher, having his shoes stolen from him, '*May they,*' said he, '*fit his feet that took them away ;*' " a wish at the first view very harmless, but there was that in it which poisoned his charity into a malicious revenge. For he himself had hurled or crooked feet, so that in effect he wished the thief to be lame. " Whosoever hath plundered me of my books and papers I freely forgive him, and desire that he may fully understand and make good use thereof, wishing him more *joy* of them than he hath *right* to them. Nor is there any snake under my heels, nor have I, as Nicias, any reservation or latent sense to myself, but from my heart do I desire that, to all purposes and intents, my books may be beneficial unto him ; only requesting him, that one passage in his (lately my) Bible (namely, Eph. iv. 28), may be taken into his serious consideration."

But his loss was not so bad as at first anticipated, as is clear from his dedication of part of his *Pisgah Sight* to Henry Lord Beauchamp, son of the Marquess of Hertford, ' Besides desire to shelter myself under your patronage, gratitude obligeth me to tender my service to your honour. For all my books, being my ' nether and upper millstone ' (and such by the Levitical law might not be 'taken to pledge' because a man's life.   Deut. xxiv. 6), without which I had been unable to grind any grist for the good of myself or others, had been taken from me in these civil wars, had not a letter from your lady-mother preserved the greatest part thereof.   Good reason, therefore, that the first handful of my finest meal should be presented in thankfulness to your family " (Book ii. p. 50).

From a state of comparative affluence, as we have said, Fuller had now fallen into a state of the greatest poverty. He might style himself " Prebendary of Sarum," but no income was derivable thereof ; Salisbury falling early into the hands of the Parliamentarian party, there being no means of defending it against them : he might be in possession of the legal benefice of Broad Windsor, but no tithe could be drawn from a parish, whose vicinity was dominated by the so-called popular party ; and his cure at the Savoy being no longer profitable to him, as the Parliament showed that they were fully alive to the importance of that post, by intruding without loss of time one of their own creatures. But all these privations, though coming so suddenly on him in the midst of his prosperity, Fuller bore with Christian resignation, acquiescing in the decrees of Providence, Who was justly, so he thought, punishing the nation for its sins. "God could no longer be just if we were prosperous. Blessed be His name that I have suffered my share in the calamities of my country.   Had I poised myself so politicly betwixt both parties that I had suffered from neither, yet could I have taken no contentment in my safe escaping. For why should I, equally engaged with others in sinning, be exempted above them from the punishment ?   And

R

seeing the bitter cup which my brethren have pledged to pass by me, I should fear it would be filled again, and returned double, for me to drink it. Yea, I should suspect that I was reserved alone for a greater shame and sorrow. It is therefore some comfort that I draw in the same yoke with my neighbours, and, with them, jointly bear the burthen which our sins jointly brought upon us." ("Good Thoughts in Bad Times : Mixt Contemplations," xvi. 19.)

And again, "I have observed that towns which have been casually burnt have been built again more beautiful than before : mud walls afterwards made of stone, and roofs formerly but thatched after advanced to be tiled. The Apostle tells me that I must 'not think strange concerning the fiery trial which is to happen' unto me. May I likewise prove improved by it. Let my renewed soul, which grows out of the ashes of the old man, be a more firm fabric and stronger structure : so shall afflictions be my advantage." (ix. 14.)

Fuller paid therefore a dear price for his flight from London to Oxford. He found the daily expenses of living at Lincoln College more than his purse could meet. There was "nothing coming in," and all hope of preferment, now that he lay under disgrace, was altogether taken away for the time. He was paying the penalty of being a moderate man, and had no refuge but trust in Providence.

Nor did he "score" with the Cavaliers, for his position was not so comfortable as he had anticipated. Here was a man who had defended with such pertinacity, power, and persistence, the Royal cause publicly in the London pulpits, now a "suspect" in the Royalist camp itself. He seemed to have fallen under the ban of both parties. Even suspicions of his loyalty were freely bandied about ; unpleasant remarks were jeeringly made of the motive of his visit to Oxford ; the cordiality which the centre of metropolitical thought and culture had evinced towards him was found wanting in the gay camp of Charles's soldiers. Perhaps the love of many, as in other cases, began to wax cold. Shall we be surprised to find our author writing thus, subsequently, of this unrelated attitude of the Court : " Courtesy gaineth. I have heard the Royal party (would I could say without cause) complained of, that they have not charity enough for converts, who came off unto them from the opposite side, who, though they express a sense of, and sorrow for, their mistakes, and have given testimony (though perchance not so plain and public as others expected) of their sincerity, yet still they are suspected as unsound, and such as frown not on, look but a squint at them. This hath done much mischief, and retarded the return of many to their side." (" Mixt Contemplations in Better Times," xxiii. 35.)

CHAPTER XV.

MILITARY CHAPLAIN, SIR RALPH HOPTON, AND BASING HOUSE.—(1643-4.)

> "He resolved, therefore, strenuously to evince his faithful loyalty to the *King* by another kind of argument, by appearing in the *King's* armies, to be a Preacher Militant to his Souldiers."
> *Anonymous Life*, p. 24.

E often hear of soldiers turning parsons; and the saying is, that the best black coat is the red coat dyed black; certainly, as far as our experience goes, some of the best clergymen the writer has known have been in the army, and laid aside the sword for the toga. It must not be supposed that they are all like the late Dean of Buryan, one of the soldiers who took up the Church as a profession at the close of the great Peninsular War, and whose case furnished the instance of the following laconic correspondence : "Dear Cork,—Ordain Stanhope.—Yours, York"; which elicited the rejoinder, "Dear York,—Stanhope's ordained.—Yours, Cork." We do not allude to such. Both on the side of the Royalists and the Parliamentarians, clergy were found in the ranks of the soldiery; and, as might have been expected, prelates and other dignitaries of the Church fought with all the ardour of Norman ecclesiastics for "Church and King." And no doubt their presence had a very salutary and highly moral effect. The fact of these "cavalier parsons," as they were called, is thus alluded to by the biographer of Jeremy Taylor, who, of course, is included among the number:

"Five of the most eminent of English theologians were brought into scenes of difficulty, that put their nerves as well as their piety to the proof. *Fuller* picked up stories of English Worthies in the rear of a marching column. *Pearson* was chaplain to the King's troops in Exeter, under Lord Goring; and *Chillingworth* acted as engineer at the siege of Gloucester in 1643, and was only prevented from trying on English fortifications the implements of Roman science by the sudden advance of the Parliamentary army. *Barrow* was not summoned to the standard of his Sovereign; but, much as he admired Horace, there is no reason to think that he would have imitated his flight. Upon one occasion, at least, he stood gallantly to his gun, and succeeded in beating off an Algerine privateer, sailing from Italy to Smyrna."

No wonder that Fuller, then, without preferment and without books, feeling keenly the reproaches of all parties, being a "suspect" on the side of the extreme men in both camps, thinking reconciliation farther off than ever, looked upon even by the Royalists somewhat coldly, and tired of an inactive life, at length betook himself to the King's army as a "preacher militant," and, in one single step, placed his loyalty above all suspicion.

In commencing his military duties, Fuller was naturally attracted to one of the best of the Royalists' leaders, General Sir Ralph Hopton, then at the King's headquarters at Oxford. Both parties unite in singing his praises. Clarendon, in his "History," says of him that he was "a man superior to any temptation, and abhorred enough the licence and the levities, with which he saw too many corrupted. He had a good understanding, a clear courage, an

industry not to be tired, and a generosity that was not to be
exhausted,—a virtue that none of the rest had." May also
thus writes of him, that Hopton, "by his unwearied industry and great reputation among the people, had raised
himself to the most considerable height." Fuller's anonymous biographer thus testifies of Lord Hopton: "This
noble lord, though as courageous and expert a captain, and
successful withal, as any the King had, was never averse to
an amicable closure of the war upon fair and honourable
terms, and did therefore well approve of the Doctor" (who
was his chaplain, having as a colleague Richard Watson, of
Caius) "and his desires and pursuits after peace. The
good Doctor was infinitely contented in his attendance on
such an excellent personage, whose conspicuous and noted
loyalty could not but derive the same reputation to his retainers, especially to one so near his conscience as his
chaplain, and so wipe off that stain which the mistakes of
those men had cast upon him. In this entendment God
was pleased to succeed the Doctor, and give him victory,
proper to the camp he followed, against this first attempt
on his honour."

The general and his chaplain were well matched, and
seem to have been mutually pleased with each other. It is
supposed the Marquess of Hertford brought about the introduction; and as Lord Hopton was desirous of selecting a
chaplain, recommended Fuller to his notice, and subsequent engagement. The following passage, written at the
close of his military career, may afford us some clue to
Fuller's taking this step. "It is recorded to the commendation of such Israelites as assisted Barak (against Sisera),
that they 'took no gain of money.' Indeed, they of Zebulun

were by their calling 'such as handled the pen' (Judges
v. 14), though now turned swordsmen in case of necessity.
And when men of peaceable professions are, on a pinch of
extremity, for a short time, forced to fight, they ought not,
like soldiers of fortune, to make a trade to enrich themselves, seeing defence of religion, life, and liberty, are the
only wages they seek for in their service."

"During the campaign, and while the army continued,"
says his biographer, "he performed the duty of his holy
function according to the order and ritual of the Church of
England, preaching on the Lord's Day and exhorting the
soldiery. On his adopting this military career, he has left
his own feelings on the subject in one of his 'good thoughts
in bad times.' Lord, when our Saviour sent His apostles
abroad to preach, He enjoined them in one gospel, 'Possess
nothing, neither shoes nor a staff.'—Mat. x., 10. But it is
said in another gospel, 'And He commandeth them that
they should take nothing for their journey, save a staff
only."—Mark vi., 8. The reconciliation is easy. They
might have a staff to speak them travellers, not soldiers:
one to walk with, not war with; a staff which was a wand,
not a weapon. But oh, in how doleful days do we live:
wherein ministers are armed, not as formerly, with their
nakedness, but need staves and swords, too, to defend them
from violence."—("Good Thoughts.")

Besides Fuller, who would be naturally attracted to
Hopton's service, and attached themselves to the same
general, were Roger Clark, fellow Prebendary of Sarum and
Rector of Ashmore, Dorset, and the famous William Chillingworth.

This Lord Hopton, under whom Fuller took service,

presented our author with his portrait of "the good soldier,"
and seems to have been one of King Charles's most loyal
and successful generals. In the whole west country his
name was a potent spell everywhere, and at the head of
"the Cornish army" did the Royalist cause much good
service, both in Devon and Cornwall. From Liskeard to
Exeter, and from Stratton to Modbury, nay, even to Bath
and Bristol, and in the county of Dorset, his name was a
tower of strength. He is said to have fortified *thirty*
important strongholds on behalf of the King. Hopton was
the son of a Somersetshire squire, though born in Mon-
mouthshire, and was educated at Lincoln College, Oxford,
under the celebrated Dr. Robert Sanderson, the eminent
casuist. From Oxford he passed over to the Low Countries,
where he learnt the art of war, and this in company with
Waller, his future antagonist and great Parliamentary
general, who, as Lloyd says, "learned in one camp what
they practised in two." But his name is chiefly identified
with the West of England. He represented Somersetshire in
the short, and Wells in the long, Parliament, and had the
reputation of being an effective speaker and ready writer.
Although much respected on both sides, he ultimately
embraced the Royalist cause, and at the opening of the year
1642 we hear of him raising troops in Cornwall, and
"mastering all unquiet spirits in that county," the ultima
Thule of England. Hopton's military successes were chiefly
gained in the westernmost counties, so that he received the
soubriquet of "Hopton of the West," and his influence was
very great, "second to no man's."

Cornwall has always been remarkable for its virtue, and
strong religious proclivities and devotional instincts. Nor

was the time we are considering any exception to the rule. Clarendon speaks of the "extraordinary temper and virtue of the chief officers of the Cornish," commending the virtue and valour of their men. Hopton was considered one of the most religious of the King's generals, and no doubt his earnest piety told upon the men. He also made it a point to give God public thanks after his victories; conduct on the part of generals much eulogised by our author; "and because all true valour is founded in the knowledge of God in Christ, such generals may and must, to raise the resolutions of their soldiers : by inserting and interposing passages of Scripture, animating them to depend on God, the just maintainer of a right cause. Thus Queen Elizabeth, in '88, at Tilbury Camp, inspirited her soldiers with her Christian exhortation."

Hopton, we are informed by an old memoir, kept "strict communion with God all the while he was engaged in a war with men. He was reckoned a Puritan before the wars for his strict life, and a Papist in the wars for his exemplary devotion : entertaining serious and sober Nonconformists in his house, whilst he fought on foot against the rebellious and factious in the field." Both at home and in the army, he enforced "the strictest observation (observance) of the Lord's Day, the encouragement of good ministers and people throughout his quarters. He was also very strict in deprecating rapine and acts of violence on the part of his soldiery, saying that 'the scandal of his soldiers should neither draw the wrath of God upon his undertaking, nor enrage the country against his cause.'"

Some of Lord Hopton's most important victories were gained about the time that Fuller threw in his lot with his cause ; and, in his description of them, he tells us that they are founded " not on the floating sands of uncertain relations, but on the rock of real intelligence, having gotten a manuscript of Sir Ralph Hopton's (courteously communicated to me by his secretary, Master Tredin) interpolated with his own hand, being a memorial of the remarkables in the west, at which that worthy knight was present in person."

Hopton's first victory was at Liskeard, in the county of Cornwall (January 19th, 1643) and his chaplain tells us "He first gave orders that public prayers should be had in the head of every squadron, and it was done accordingly ; and the enemy, observing it, did style it saying of Mass." In this engagement the Parliamentarian forces under Stamford and Ruthven were defeated, and many prisoners fell into the hands of the Royalists. Marching that night to Liskeard, the King's forces first gave God public thanks, and then took their own private repose." Hopton's next great victory was at Stratton (near the present favourite rising watering place of Bude, with its bracing air, good bathing, and strong Atlantic tide) where on May 16th, in spite of great disadvantage, he routed the Parliamentarians, under the Earl of Stamford, taking much booty and many prisoners. They returned the usual thanks on the summit of the hill, which they had won. The " Cornish army " followed Stamford to Exeter, whither he had retired, after his " great defeat" so called in the Roundheads' Remembrancer. Troops were despatched from Oxford to reinforce Hopton's, under Prince Maurice, Hopton still remaining the real commander " whom the people took to be the soul of that army, the other names not being so well spoken of, or so we known."

But the detachment from Oxford does not seem to have kept up the reputation of the army of the West for its sobriety, especially at Taunton. " For whereas the chief commanders of the Cornish army had restrained their soldiers from all manner of licence, obliging them to solemn and frequent acts of devotion, insomuch as the fame of their religion and discipline was no less than of their courage (these Oxford troops), were disorderly enough to give the enemy credit in laying more to their charge than they deserved." (Clarendon vii, 400.)

On July 5th an indecisive battle was fought near Bath on an open plain at Lansdown, which Fuller describes as " a heap of skirmishers huddled together," with Waller, the Parliamentarian general, who had been dispatched from London with a fresh army. Here Hopton, who is described by Clarendon as "the soldiers' darling," was wounded twice; he was shot through the arm, and subsequently visiting the wounded on the field of battle, which was held by his own troops, he was so much hurt by an explosion of gunpowder that he was taken up at first for dead, a misfortune which much dispirited the Royal troops. This accident somewhat disfigured the appearance of his sedate but comely countenance. For he had a clear eye, his nose was that desiderated by Napoleon for his generals, and he had short cut hair; his beard, which was of a reddish hue, being closely cut.

The Royalist forces were then marched upon Devizes, in Wilts, where Waller followed them. It was settled for Hopton to defend this place, and hold the old Castle till relieved, and for Maurice to break through the Parliamentarian lines, and reach Oxford. On July 11th, Waller made an unsuccessful attack upon the town, and while terms of capitulation were being arranged, the beseiged were relieved by some Royalist forces under Wilmot two days afterwards, whereupon the army of the Parliament withdrew to Rounday Down, near to which Waller was defeated, and which became jocularly known as *Runaway* Down. Clarendon tells us that this victory redeemed the whole of the King's affairs for a time. Bath was taken. Bristol was surrendered (July 27th) to Prince Rupert by Colonel Fiennes. "The terror of Sir Ralph Hopton's name, and of his adjutant, Sir Francis Doddington, appears to have been sufficient to keep all Wilts and Somerset in awe." Hopton was now made Governor of Bristol, being "most popular and gracious to that city and the country adjacent"; but Prince Rupert claimed the important position for himself: the matter being compromised by Rupert being the nominal governor, but Hopton the actual governor, which unfortunate dispute (not of Hopton's creating) consumed a good deal of valuable time.

It was here Hopton remained for the purpose of establishing a magazine for arms and men, and to recover the effects of his wounds, while Prince Maurice advanced westwards to Exeter, taking the ever faithful city, "*semper fidelis*," in September.

Before leaving Bristol for Gloucester, the King, on account of his eminent military service and remarkable successes, created Hopton, Baron Hopton of Stratton, in the county of Cornwall. Fuller thus gives the account in his "Worthies":
" Being chaplain to this worthy lord, I could do no less than

(in gratitude to his memory) make this exemplification."
The news of these continued successes gladdened the closing
hours of Fuller's old friend and tutor, Dr. Ward (of Sydney
College), " whose dying words were breathed up to Heaven
with his parting soul " in benediction of the King and his
general. But Lord Hopton had no easy task to garrison
Bristol, which the King obliged him to do, as the main body
of the army had gone to the west. However, by his
indomitable zeal and personal influence, this indefatigable
soldier collected a good force of both arms.

It was about this time Fuller joined Lord Hopton's
division, and if our author had remained at Oxford, roughly
speaking, about seventeen weeks, we may conclude he left
that University about the month of December, and went
away with the general to his military commandantship at
Bristol.

We do not know much of Fuller's life, nor have we any
details to our hand, during the years in which he followed
the fortunes of Baron Hopton, *i.e.*, from the year 1643 to
1647, but it was the life of a campaigner. Our author,
when excusing the non-appearance of his promised ecclesiastical history, thus speaks of it : " For the first five
years during our actual civil wars, I had little list or leisure
to write, fearing to make a history, and shifting daily for my
safety. All that time I could not live to study, who did
only study to live." All we know is that he was in close
attendance on the General.

Lord Hopton had been ordered by the King to collect a
force out of the Bristol garrison to act apart in the Western
Counties, and be ready to meet Waller at any point, who
had been despatched to the West Country. This army he

led to Salisbury, and then on to Winchester, where he was met with a contingent of Devonshire soldiers, under Sir John Berkeley. At this time he was persuaded, the King consenting, to advance into Hampshire and Sussex, as the King's adherents wished to form, at all events, the nucleus of an army in those parts, and so break up the combination which had gathered under Waller's standard, and massed in the vicinity of Farnham.

Meanwhile, Lord Hopton passed into Sussex, and proceeded to Arundel Castle, one of the most charming spots in the county, and the seat of the Duke of Norfolk, one of the old English Roman Catholic families. On the march he was joined by the famous William Chillingworth, author of the "Religion of Protestants," who was attracted by the fame and excellence of the Royalist leader, and no doubt, like Fuller himself, he was glad of this favourable opportunity of putting his Royalist principles (which had been characterised by a little hesitancy and lukewarm preaching) beyond further suspicion. Chillingworth had made himself useful at the seige of Gloucester by his constructive power in the engineering department, having invented some musket-proof shelters—testudines cum pluteis—which were filled with marksmen and run out on wheels. From these and other contrivances he earned the soubriquet of the King's Little Engineer and Black-art-man. It was getting on into winter (Dec. 9th) when Arundel Castle (which was a place of great strength, and as well protected by nature as fortified by art) fell into the Royalists' hands. Hearing of Waller's advance, Lord Hopton hastily returned to Winchester, leaving a garrison at Arundel. Here Chillingworth, on account of the severity of the winter weather, was left behind. Waller, attending his motions, suddenly fell on Lord Hopton's rear near Alton, so that the Royal troops retired into Winchester in some disorder, Arundel Castle falling into the hands of the Parliamentary party. Among the prisoners was Chillingworth, who being unable to follow Waller to London, was consigned to Chichester, where he was so barbarously treated, that he died from the effects (according to Clarendon) in a few days, about January 30th, in the new year. Francis Cheynell at that time usufructuary of the rich rectory of Petworth, his old antagonist, has given us an interesting account of his closing days, which throws considerable light on the manners and customs of the military chaplains of those days. The "malignants" were allowed to attend his funeral, which was arranged as Cheynell observes "by men of a cathedral spirit." A curious scene took place at the grave. During the burial service, Cheynell solemnly walked up to the grave, holding in his hand what he called *the mortal book* of his dead brother ("The Apostolical Succession of Christianity"), abused the volume, and thus denouncing it, flung it on the coffin. "But his book," says Clarendon, "will live and declare him to be a man of admirable parts to all posterity." Fuller doesn't seem to have been present on this occasion, nor are his remarks those of an eyewitness. He merely tells us that Chillingworth had been taken prisoner, "and not surprised and slain in his studies as Archimedes, at the sacking of Syracuse (as some have given it out), but was safely conducted to Chichester, where, notwithstanding, hard usage hastened his dissolution." ("Worthies", Oxford, 340.) Chillingworth succeeded Dr. Duppa in the Chancellorship of Sarum, where he had been a Prebend since 1638, and he was selected to attend the Convocation of 1640. "He was put into the roll" says Wood, to be created Doctor of Divinity, with some others, "but he came not to that degree, nor was he diplomated."

Fresh troops were sent from the King to reinforce Lord Hopton's forces (who was much troubled by his defeat at Alton, and the capitulation of Arundel Castle) at Winchester under the King's general, the Earl of Brentford. Clarendon tells us that "Hopton was exceedingly revived with the presence of the general, and desired to receive his orders, and that he (the Earl) would take upon him the absolute command of the troops, which he as positively refused to do ; only offered to keep him company in all expeditions, and to give him the best assistance he was able." (Bk. viii. 479.) This was agreed upon, and Brentford took the lead.

With these reinforcements the Royal forces moved out from Winchester to meet Waller, who was descending upon Alresford. Lord Hopton, however, pushed forward with a party of horse, leaving the remainder of the troops to follow, and seized the village, where some of Waller's troops had been quartered. Some skirmishes took place that day, and on the next (Friday) they had a pitched battle. It was March 29th when Hopton drew up his forces, about seven miles from Winchester, upon Cheriton Down. The watchword on both sides happened to be the same in both armies : "God with us," but when Waller discovered this he changed that of the Parliamentary army to "Jesus help us." The battle was hotly contested, but the King's troops (which as usual got the best of it at first) were utterly worsted, two Irish regiments being the first to run off the field. In spite of the most obstinate resistance, the Royal forces were completely routed, and dispersed. Many Royalist notables were killed, and among them Lord John Stewart (the Duke of Richmond's brother) who had followed Hopton "to observe his conduct, and attain his other great virtues." Hopton managed his forces soldier like, and with a party of horse kept facing the enemy as well as he could to secure his rear. His troops tried to fire the village in their retreat. Waller failed to capture Lord Hopton's artillery, but continued the pursuit towards Winchester. But Hopton, favoured by the darkness, turned off to Basing House, where it is clear that Fuller must now have been in the general's company, for his biographer writes: "my Lord Hopton drew down with his army and artillery to Basing House, and so reached that way to Oxford, intending to take up winter quarters as soon as he had consulted with the King, and left the Doctor (Fuller) in that as courageously manned as well fortified house." From Basing House Hopton first of all advanced to Reading, and then got to Oxford.

Waller (after taking Andover and Christchurch) returned to Winchester, where he found the gates shut, which, however, he battered down, giving up the town to plunder to his soldiers, who behaved most disgracefully with the tombs and monuments of the Cathedral, throwing down images and escutcheons. This fanatical zeal of the Republican army Fuller alludes to in his reference to "crest-fallen" churches. Waller considered his reverses the next year a judgment upon him for this sacrilegious irreverence on the part of his troops. These military events are regarded by Clarendon as a doleful beginning to the year 1644, and as breaking up the King's measures. Waller now proceeded, and not for the first time, to the assault of Basing House, in which stronghold our hero now lay.

Basing House—where Fuller spent some time—was the very extensive and magnificent seat of the Marquis of Winchester. In his "Worthies," Fuller thus notices the valour with which the inmates so long warded off the attacks of the insurgents: "The motto, *Love Loyalty* (*Aymez Loyaulté*), was often written in every window thereof, and was well practised in it, when for resistance on that account it was lately levelled to the ground." Once a magnificent mansion, it was then a fort, and attained unexpectedly, as other strongholds have done under similar circumstances, great notoriety for its gallant defence. Even in the time of Henry III. it was a strong place, and its ruins form one of the most interesting relics of the civil wars. When it had come into the hands of Sir William Pawlet he was created by Edward the first Marquess of Winchester. The original structure was added to by him, until, as Fuller says, "it became the greatest of any subject's house in England; yea, larger than most (eagles have not the biggest nests of all birds) of the King's palaces." This Marquess was succeeded by his third son, John, who was sorely pinched in keeping up such a large establishment, whose rooms were all richly furnished.

By the time the Civil War broke out, John Pawlet had contrived to free his establishment from all pecuniary embarrassments, owing to his painstaking frugality. Dryden describes this nobleman, who was a Roman Catholic, as "a man of exemplary piety towards God, and of inviolable fidelity towards his Sovereign." Hugh Peters, who went through the house some three weeks after its final storming, was not only amazed at its elaborate decorations, but scandalised at the relics of Romanism : " Popish books many, with copes, utensils, &c." The old house had stood (as it was reported) two or three hundred years, a nest of idolatry : the new house surpassing that in beauty and stateliness : and either of ‚them fit to make an emperor's court. It was as much against the religion of the owner as to his faithful allegiance to the cause of the King, that the severity of the Puritan was directed. When the war broke out, its owner at once declared for the King and offered him both house and savings, which were gladly accepted, as it was an important place, situate on rising ground, two miles N.E. of Basingstoke ; a commercial centre, where five roads met. This, with Donington Castle, near Newbury, another Royalist stronghold, enabled the King to dominate the great western highway. Many efforts were therefore made to capture Basing House on account of its great importance, whose surroundings had been considerably strengthened by the inmates, a space of about fourteen acres being enclosed with the earthwork, consisting of deep dry ditches or moats, with high strong ramparts made of brick and lined with earth —not easily pierced with shot.

The house, which was first defended only by the Marquess and his retainers by way of a garrison, subsequently reinforced by 100 musketeers under Sir Robert Peake, sent from Oxford by the King, was first invested by the Round-head General Waller, in August, 1643. It was by him unsuccessfully stormed thrice in nine days in the month of November, who was compelled to retire with loss to Farnham on the 19th. The garrison, which never seems to have exceeded 500 men and 10 pieces of cannon, was of course much weakened by these assaults—but during the next few months the besiegers tried to starve them out, instead of storming the stronghold. Fuller arrived at the fortress, between the time that Waller left, and his next visit in March, probably bearing some important letters, or despatches, which at such critical times were usually confided to such trusty parsons. No doubt, the Doctor would receive a hearty welcome at Basing House, as its owner was relation to the Paulets, who were Fuller's patrons. And if we are to believe his biographer, he was neither an unemployed nor unacceptable guest in that loyal stronghold. The Marquess was an ardent littérateur, and subsequently wrote some pious works and adaptations of foreign devotional treatises. Dryden wrote his epitaph in Englefield Church, where he was buried, 1647.

While entering into the spirit of the scene, and doing his best to stimulate the courage of the defenders, our author, with his marvellous power of abstraction, commenced to arrange the materials for his "Worthies" or "Church History," and other antiquarian and literary work. This work was rudely interrupted by the return of Waller's besieging forces, fresh from the capture of Winchester, which gave birth to some of those incidents inseparably connected with the history of Basing House. " He had scarce begun," says his biographer, "to reduce his marching observations into form and method, but Sir William Waller, having taken in Winchester, came to besiege the Doctor's sanctuary. This no way amazed, or terrified him, but only the noyse of the cannon playing from the enemy's leaguer interrupted the prosecution of digesting his notes, which trouble he recompensed to them by an importunate spiriting of the defendants in their sallies : which they followed so close and so bravely, suffering the besiegers scarce to eat or sleep, that Sir William was compelled to raise his seige and march away, leaving about a thousand men slain behind him : and the Doctor the pleasure of seeing that strong effort of rebellion, in some way by his means, repulsed and defeated, and in being free to proceed in his wonted intendments."

Whether this account is exaggerated or not, we cannot say, but it is only right to mention that none of Fuller's other biographers mention it, nor does the Doctor allude to it himself in any of his works. That he must have been mixed up with the frequent sallies is evident, and his presence may or may not have been noticed, but whether so or no, his modesty is shown by his silence about himself. We may therefore say of him as he did of Samson : " His silence was no less commendable than his valour. But indeed the truest prowess pleaseth more in doing than repeating its own achievements."—(" Pisgah-Sight" ii., 215.)

Among other notabilities who assisted at the siege, and gave their assistance to the garrison, Col. Johnson, the herbalist, may be mentioned, and Inigo Jones, the architect. Johnson, however, fell a victim during the siege, which is thus alluded to by our author :—" A dangerous service having to be done, this Doctor, who publicly pretended not to valour, undertook and performed it. Yet afterwards he lost his life (1644) in the siege of the same house, and was (to my knowledge) generally lamented of those who were of an opposite judgment. But let us bestow this epitaph upon him :—

Hic Johnson jacet, sed si mors cederet herbis,
Arte fugata tua cederet illa tuis,
' Here Johnson lies : could physic fence Death's dart,
    Sure death had been declined by his art.'

Inigo Jones was also there at the last seige, " an excellent
architector to build, but no engineer to pull down." So
also the celebrated engraver, Wentzell Hollar, who
afterwards illustrated some of Fuller's works, for he
engraved the west front of Lichfield Cathedral in his
" Church History," and also etched the frontispiece of the
Doctor's collected sermons, published in 1657. Hollar is
also supposed to have executed a portrait of Lord Winchester, and to have made an etching of " The Siege of
Basinge House," from which the engraving is taken. " In
a window," says Mr. Bailey, " at the Rectory of Basingstoke are two quarries of domestic character, which were
found in a cottage in that town some years ago, and are
supposed to have come from old Basing House. One
bears the crest of the Pawlet family (a falcon gorged), the
other Lord Winchester's badge as Chamberlain (namely, a
key surrounded by a cord). This device occurs repeatedly
on brackets and shields in Basing Church, and also upon a
stone corbel, now at Basingstoke Rectory, which appears to
have come from Basing Church, as it resembles others
which are still *in situ.* The Rector of Basingstoke also
has one of Cromwell's cannon balls (a large one), and the
marks of others are to be seen in the walls of the
Church."

Several other attempts were made subsequently to reduce
this Royalist stronghold, under various Parliamentary
leaders, Morley, Harvey, and Waller, but without success,

nor was their military reputation thereby improved. Its ultimate reduction, however, took place under Oliver Cromwell (Oct. 4th, 1645), who described its fall in a letter to the Speaker, beginning in these words : "I thank God, I can give you a good account of Basing." A tradition in the neighbourhood says that the garrison were surprised while playing at cards, and there is a local saying among whist players, "Clubs trumps, as when Basing House was taken." Altogether, 2,000 men are said to have been slain before the place, which had received two soubriquets, one wittily that of "Basting House," on account of the many repulses of the besiegers, and the other "Loyalty House," from the pronounced loyal devotion of its inmates. It is a place described by Sanderson, seated and built as if for royalty, and Fuller's biographer says, in his notice of this princely edifice, "in spight of their potent arms," in his time still standing, "afterwards through the fortune of war, being fallen into their hands and razed by their more impotent revenge, he doth heartily lament in his 'Worthies General,' preferring it, while it flourished, for the chiefest fabric in Hantshire. This his kindness to the place of his refuge, though no doubt true and deserved enough, yet no questionless was indeared in him by some more peculiar obliging regards and respects he found during his abode there, though indeed his worth could want and miss them nowhere."

How long our author proved himself a doughty member of the Church Militant, and assisted the gallant defence in this palatial and loyal stronghold of "Basing" we cannot accurately determine ; and all we can glean is from the account given of Fuller's biographer. "What time the Doctor continued here is very uncertain ; sure we may be, he was not unemployed or an unacceptable guest to that loyal garrison, and that as noble as honourable Marquis, the Proprietary of the place, and his next removal was to his charge in the army, and his particular duty of chaplain to the said lord."

Although Fuller's movements just now seem a good deal shrouded in obscurity, he would appear about this time to have gone back to Oxford, where Lord Hopton was busily engaged in collecting materials for a new departure to the West country, where the chief hope of the Royalist cause apparently lay. These Royalist troops were massed about Marlborough ; it was thought that Sir William Waller would be moving in that direction down West. Lord Hopton usually held a command apart, and about April 16th, 1644, was quartered at Merlinsborough, with a force exceeding 10,000 foot and horse. Subsequently, he removed to Newbury, Fuller still being in his train, waiting to discover the movements and intentions of the enemy. At this time our author occasionally visited Oxford, and probably witnessed the scene which took place there, at the dissolution of the " Mongrel " Parliament, as it was called, and final parting of the King and Queen in the Cathedral Church of Christ Church. The King having, in the presence of the Peers, received the Sacrament of the Lord's Body and Blood at the hands of Ussher, Archbishop of Armagh, rose up from his knees and made the following declaration : " My lord, I espy here many resolved Protestants, who may declare to the world the resolution which I do now make. I have to the utmost of my power prepared my soul to become a worthy Receiver ; and may I so receive comfort by the blessed Sacrament, as I do intend the establishment of the true Reformed Protestant religion, as it stood in its beauty in the happy days of Queen Elizabeth, without any connivance at Popery. I bless God that in the midst of these public distractions I have still liberty to communicate, and may this Sacrament be my damnation if my heart do not join with my lips in this protestation." Fuller again, by some influence, came under the notice of the King, and hearing that he was either in the city or neighbourhood, King Charles made a special request that the witty divine should preach a second time before him. This request was complied with, and Fuller not only preached before the King, but the sermon was subsequently published, though without dedication, according to his wont. It was preached on one of the monthly fast days, on Friday, May 10th, the Royalists keeping Fridays and the Parliamentarians Wednesdays, as days of humiliation and deprecating the wrath of God, during this unhappy civil warfare. It was held on the second Friday in each month in all churches and chapels, and there was a special form of prayer drawn up for use on these occasions, besides which there was usually a sermon to edify the faithful Royalists. On the first of these days (October 13, 1643) Chillingworth preached a sermon on 2 Tim. iii. 1-5, which was published the year after his death. There were therefore two fasts in each month, which fact is alluded to by Fuller in the following terms.* "During these

---

* When the Jewish Sabbath in the primitive times was newly changed into the Christian Lord's Day, many devout people twisted both together in their observations, abstaining from servile works, and keeping both Saturday and Monday wholly for holy employments.

civil wars Wednesday and Friday fasts have been appointed by different authorities. What harm had it been if they had both been generally observed? Do not our two fasts more peremptorily affirm and avouch our mutual malice and hatred? God forgive us! we have *cause* enough to keep ten, but not *care* enough to keep one monthly day of humiliation." ("Good Thoughts in Worse Times: Med on Times, No. xvii.")

Fuller's Fast sermon, which he preached at St. Mary's, before the King and the Prince, was on the subject of "Jacob's vow" (Genesis xxviii, 20-21). It is thus given in Mr. Bailey's life, and is extremely rare and almost unknown before. The preacher describes the general circumstances under which the vow was made, dividing it into two parts (1) Petitio, a request which he desired of God; (2) Promissio, a duty which he promised to perform to God. (1) Jacob asked not for all the four things God had promised him, but for bread for necessitie. Fuller then asks why Isaac, being exceedingly rich, had sent forth his son so poore, when he had sent for his very servant on the same journey so richly attended. He gives four reasons (1) That his brother might not so easily miss him, or know which way to go after him; (2) that his misery might move his brother to compassion and reconciliation; (3) that, having no money to maintain him, he might have more mind to return home again; and (4) that he might have better experience of God's mercy. He then deduces that Adversitie is the blessing of God's children as well as Prosperitie. Jacob's moderate petition was designed to teach *us* moderation, "having once seen God in Bethel, and set his heart upon Him, who is the true treasure, he neither admired nor much desired (more than was necessary) this worldly trash." " Earthly honours and riches are the shadow of heavenly, and the pleasures of sinne not so much as shadows of heavenly pleasures."

But in addition to this moderate request for worldly goods he desires the Divine Protection, "which is the staffe of bread and blessing, without which a man may starve for hunger, with bread in his mouthe, and die like the children of Israel, with the flesh of quails between their teethe."

(2) He comes to the duties he promiseth to perform to God. " Jacob having received but even the promise of a benefit, presently voweth the performance of a dutie, to teach all true Israelites that beneficium postulat officium ; and that the thankfulness of the receiver ought to answere unto the benefit of the bestower as the eccho answereth to the voice." He concludes, " that we all having received the same spiritual and temporal mercies are bound to the like thankfulnesse." He reminds his congregation that " many of them have passed over, not Jordan, but the river of *Trent*, or *Thames*, or *Severne*, with their staves in their hands, in poor estates in comparison, and are now laden with riches and honours, and yet have not vowed with Jacob to have the Lord for their God. One religious vow you see weekly paid in this place by our Royal Jacob, I mean our Tuesday's exercise : which was devoutly vowed upon as just an occasion as ever vow was made. And hitherto (God be thanked) it hath been religiouslie performed. God grant that this our *Jacob* may long and long live a happie King of this happie island, even as long (if it be His will) as the old Patriarke Jacob did, to pay his tribute and the rest of his vows to the King of

Kings.   And   thus   much   for   the   generall of Jacob's
vow."

In the next division of the discourse Fuller discussed the
particular duties vowed by the Patriarch : these are three :
(1) " That the Lord should be his God.   (2) That the stone
he had set up as a pillar should be God's house, *i.e.*, that
he would   dedicate that place to the publique worship of
God.   (3) That for the maintenance of both these he would
give the tenth of all that he had."   (1) He describes as the
summe of the first commandment and the duty of everyone not an atheist : " How they perform this dutie, who
bestowe more cost even upon points and shoe strings in
one day than upon the worshipping of God a whole yeere,
judge ye."

(ii) This duty necessarily depends on the former, " For if
God must be worshipped, then must He have a place to be
worshipped in, here called a House."   He called the
place Bethel because (1) God had manifested His presence
here in an extraordinary manner ; and (2) because Jacob
had consecrated the place to His service, To teach us,
that as our first care should be of the worship of God, so
our second care should be of the place of His worship. "He
distilleth the drops of His mercie upon every part of the
earth : but He poureth it down upon that holy ground
which is dedicated to His service."

Fuller then refers to the existing condition of the parish
churches : " Some of these houses which they (our fore-
fathers) have built, and even the fairest of them, since their
buttresses and pillars (I mean their maintenance) have been
pluckt away, begin to droop alreadie, and in time (if it be not
prevented) will moulder away and drop down.   And yet

who pitieth the ruines of Zion, or repaireth any one wall or window thereof? As we need not therefore vow to build, let us vow to beautifie, or at least to keep up those houses which are built to our hands."

(iii) Jacob in the third place "voweth for himself and all the posteritie, as well of his faith as flesh, unto the end of the world the payment of Tithes." Why does he vow *the tenth ?* Because he knew, that by the light of nature or the tradition and practice of his ancestors, that this quota, the tenth, and no other part, was, is, and for ever must be, due as unto God, as either His house or His worship. That God, from the very creation of the world, reserved to Himself (1) a form of Divine Worship; (2) a time for this worship, the Sabbath Day; (3) a place for this worship, which is His House (4) a priesthood, which may never bow the knee to Baal; (5) Tithes, for the maintenance of all these). He suggests that Cain and Abel may have been taught to offer Tithes by Adam—names the payment to Melchesidech —the practice of the Levitical priesthood—and challenges any man " to show when and where they were abrogated by the Gospel." Not by Christ (Matt. xxiii.) ; not by St. Paul (Gal. vi., 6); though he nameth not the very *quotum*, but took it for granted. He then refers to I. Cor. ix., and lastly ("which in mine opinion is the most impregnable place ") Heb. vii. He goes on, " It is absurd to say that these Tithes were only Leviticall, and that there is now nothing but a competencie due by a morall equitie." Having shown that they were more than Levitical, he proceeds: To speak of a competencie now, is a mere conceit, for who shall presume to set down an uncertain competencie when God Himself hath set down a perpetual certaintie, which

He never yet altered." Or why should any man think that God, who provided a standing, certain, and liberal maintenance for the Levitical priesthood in the time of the Law which was less honourable, should leave the Ministerie of the Gospel, which exceedeth in honour, to a beggarlie and uncertain competencie: especially foreknowing and foretelling that in these days charitie should wax cold and men be lovers of themselves and their pleasures more than lovers of God and His Church ; and yet he requireth hospitalitie at our hands, too, which He knew the world's competencie could not afford." He advises the nobility not only to pay their own tithes, but to redeem the captive tithes out of the hands of those who have usurped the same, "than which they cannot almost offer a more acceptable sacrifice unto God." He says the competency of ten pounds a year left in some parishes is " scarce a competency for a Hog-heard," and that "the poor Levite has in some places, not the tenth, in some not the twentieth part of the tithes." In conclusion, he prays God "that the body of the Honourable Parliament were as willing as the religious and Royal Head hereof, to take this grievance into their serious considera tion " and enact "some wholesome law for the honour of God, the advancement of His Church, the peace of their own consciences, and the reliefe of the poor clergie in this behalf, that so we might all (as we are all bound) pray *Jacob's* vow unto the God of *Jacob*, and receive from Him *Jacob's* blessing."

The King's vow, which seems so prominently brought before our notice in this discourse, points to the promise publicly and weekly commemorated to give back to the Church all the Abbey lands which he then held. There

are no records on the subject, but if we correlate the
protestation made by the King before the celebrant, Archbishop of Armagh (Ussher) with this vow, we shall probably approximate to the truth of the facts. It was not till
April 13th, 1646, a few days before the King left the city in
disguise, that this vow "concerning the Restoring Church
Lands" was committed to writing. Here it is, as quoted
by the author of the "Fasts and Festivals of the Church,"
Robert Nelson :—" I, A. B. do here promise and solemnly
vow, in the presence, and for the service, of Almighty God,
that if it shall please His Divine Majesty, of His Infinite
goodness, to restore me to my just Kingly Rights, and to
re-establish me in my Throne, I will wholly give back to
His Church all those impropriations which are now held
by the Crown ; and what lands soever I now do, or should
enjoy, which have been taken away, either from any Episcopal See, or any Cathedral or Collegiate Church, from any
Abbey or other Religious House. I likewise promise for
hereafter to hold them from the Church, under such reasonable fines and rents as shall be set down by some conscientious Persons, whom I promise to choose with all upright-
ness of heart, to direct me in this particular. And I most
humbly beseech God to accept of this my vow, and to bless
me in the designs I have now in Hand, through Jesus
Christ our Lord.—Amen.—CHARLES R." The vow is also
to be found in that remarkable volume, "*Spelman's History
and Fate of Sacrilege,*" which is signed and attested as true
by Bishop Sheldon. There is also additional evidence to
prove that it was the King's fixed determination to restore
to the Church all that the exigencies of the times required
him to give up, and this especially in the case of the

Bishops' lands. "Here," says Fuller, "some presumed to know His Majesty's intention, that he determined with himself in the interim (within the period of the lease for 99 years) to redeem them, by their own revenues, and to refund them to ecclesiastical uses, which is proportionable to his large heart in matters of that nature."

Our author's movements become again obscure, but we shall not be wrong in assuming that, in company with Lord Hopton, he went first to Newbury, and then, after the skirmish with Captain Temple at Islip, near Oxford, proceeded to Bristol, where the general was sent by the orders of the King. "The war was then at its zenith," says Fuller's biographer, "hotter and more dilated, raging everywhere, both in this and the two neighbouring kingdoms, so that there was no shelter or retirement, which it had not invaded and intruded into by unruly garrisons, while the country became a devastated solitude, so that the Doctor's design (writing his " *Worthies* ") could proceed nowhere. This, therefore, is the most active part of Fuller's life as ' cavalier parson.' "

The King, pursued by the Parliamentary forces under Waller, and feeling uncomfortable as to the future of the Queen, who was then at Exeter, determined to get to Exeter by forced marches.   He met some of Hopton's detachment, who had received orders to levy troops in South Wales at Yeovil (intending to form a junction with Prince Maurice, in North Devon) and arrived at Bath (where he heard of Marston Moor) on July 15th.   During his march the King heard of the Queen's flight from Exeter, which made him slacken his pace, the Royal army not reaching the "everfaithful" city till July 26th, Essex having gone to the relief

Plymouth. Here, then, for the first time, Fuller took up his temporary abode at Exeter, for, as his biographer says, "he took refuge there" betimes, *i.e.* before the Royal forces had been driven into Cornwall at the end of February, 1646, adding that "he took his congé and dismission of his beloved lord."

We may, then, contemplate our author during this portion of his career, performing his duties of military chaplain with zeal and much painstaking regularity. He was, in the highest and best sense of the word, "a painful and pious priest": not one who gave pain to his hearers, but one who took great pains, gave himself much trouble in the discharge of his solemn responsibilities. "During the compania," his biographer goes on to say, "and while the army continued in the field, he performed the duty of his holy function with as much solemn piety and devotion as he used in places consecrated to God's worship, and according to the form used and appointed by the Church of England, in all emergencies and present enterprises, using no other prayers than what the Fathers of the Church had in those miserable exigencies newly direct." This, of course, refers to those *Royalist* liturgies, like all our modern State prayers, of very unequal merit, which had at that time come into use. Forms were drawn up under considerable excitement : first, the monthly fasts on Fridays had to be provided for, and then there was a *Collection* of *Prayers* and *Thanksgivings* put out at Oxford, for "use in His Majesty's Chapel, and in his armies." These contained special thanksgivings for victories over the Rebels at Edgehill, and in the North and West, and for the Queen's safe return, which provoked, as might be expected, the ridicule of the Puritans.

Constant preaching was added to these prayers by our chaplain on the Lord's Day. He especially animated the soldiers " to fight courageously, and to demean themselves worthy of that glorious cause with which God had honoured them," which stirring addresses must often have inspirited the besieged at Basing. To be busied in God's service was— in the preacher's opinion—the surest armour against the darts of death; "no malice of man can antedate my end a minute whilst my Maker hath any work for me to do." In his daily services he used to read David's Psalms, and in a collection of prayers, bearing date 1648, there are certain Psalms given as being suitable for certain occasions (with proper prayers) as setting the guards, marching forth, &c.

His biographer thus gives the account of the way in which Fuller spent the many leisure hours of time, and his taste for antiquarian researches : " With the progress of the war he marched from place to place, and wherever there happened (for the better accommodation of the army) any reasonable stay, he allotted it with great satisfaction to his beloved studies. Those cessations and intermissions begot in him the most intentness and solicitous industry of mind ; which, as he never used to much recreation or diversion in times of peace, which might loose and relasch *(sic.)* a well disciplined spirit : so neither did the horror and rigidness of the war stiffen him in such a stupidity (which generally possessed all learned men) or else distract him, but that in such lucid intervals he would seriously come to himself and his designed business."

" Indeed, his business and study then was a kind of Errantry, having proposed to himself (in addition to his Ecclesiastical History) a more exact collection of the

Worthies General of England, in which others had waded
before, but he resolved to go through. In what places
soever therefore he came, of remark especially, he spent frequently most of his time in views and researches of their antiquities and church monuments, insinuating himself into the
acquaintance (which frequently ended in a lasting friendship)
of the learnedest and gravest persons residing within the
place, thereby to inform himself fully of those things he
thought worthy the commendation of his labours. It is an
incredible thing to think what a numerous correspondence
the Doctor maintained and enjoyed by this means.

"Nor did the good Doctor ever refuse to light his
candle in investigating truth from the meanest persons'
discovery. He would endure contentedly an hour's or more
impertinence from any aged church-officer, or other super-
annuated people, for the gleaning of two lines to his purpose.
And though his spirit was quick and nimble, and all the
faculties of his mind ready and answerable to that activity
of despatch, yet in these inquests he would stay and attend those CIRCULAR rambles till they came to a *point:*
so resolute was he bent in sifting out abstruse antiquity.
Nor did he ever dismiss any such feeble adjutators or
helpers (as he pleased to style them) without giving them
money and cheerful thanks besides." (" Life," pp. 26-29).

This was indeed a strange sort of life for a Royalist
Chaplain, but it was one which the good Doctor took delight in, and one not (witness Cæsar's Commentaries) altogether without precedent even in secular history. In collecting materials for his historical work, Fuller made diligent
use of the parish registers, which we need not say cannot be
kept too carefully by the beneficed clergy, and other paro-

chial records, and these were useful in certain " nativities."
With great justice he bemoans the " μέγα χάσμα, that 'great
gulph ' or broad blank, left in our registers during our civil
wars, after the laying aside of bishops, and before the restitution of his most sacred majesty : yea, hereafter, this sad
vacuum is like to prove so thick, like the Ægyptian darkness,
that it will be sensible in our English histories. I dare
maintain, the wars betwixt York and Lancaster, lasting, by
intermission, some *sixty* years, were not so destructive to
church records as our modern wars in *six* years ; for during
the former their differences agreed in the same religion,
impressing them with reverence of all sacred muniments,
whilst our civil wars, founded in faction and vanity of pretended religions, exposed all naked church records a prey
to their armed violence."*

When, then, our chaplain pursued his antiquarian researches, it must have been under difficulties, and we hardly
know which to admire more—the fact itself or its results.
He not only filled up the long gaps of idleness, incident to a
soldier's life, but this mental activity had the approval of his
own conscience. " More than anything else, perhaps," says
one who has successfully delineated his portrait, " besides the
approval of his own conscience, did it tend to what appears
so remarkable in studying his works—that unmurmuring
acquiescence in the decrees of Providence, even when they
were most averse to his own earnest hopes and most
cherished desires—a feature in his character not enough
noticed by his biographer, but which is very strikingly
apparent when his works are read with a recollection of his

---

* "Worthies," c xxiii., p. 65.

times and the circumstances in which they were severally written.   And that there is no assumed resignation here, every reader of them will feel assured ; for never was the character of an author more impressed on his writings than that of Fuller on his.   That they are perfectly natural, it is as impossible to doubt as to doubt their perfect honesty."

By these pursuits Fuller acquired that marvellous skill in descents and pedigrees which characterises his *Worthies*, and enabled him from his own experience and antiquarian lore to write thus in his essay on "The Good Herald ":—"To be able only to blazon a coat doth no more make an Herald than the reading the titles of Gallipots makes a physician. Bring our Herald to a monument *ubi jacet* Epitaphium, and where the arms on the tombs are not only crest-fallen, but their colours scarce to be discerned, and he will tell whose they be, if any certainty therein can be rescued from the teeth of time."*

We see our author's reverence for antiquity, and the same shrewd delineation, where he pourtrays the companion portrait of " The True Church Antiquary," illustrating the maxim of *baiting* at middle antiquity, but *lodging* not till he came to that which is ancient indeed.   "Some scour off the rust of old inscriptions into their own souls, cankering themselves with superstition, having read so often *Orate pro animâ*, that at last they fall a-praying for the departed, and they more lament the ruins of monasteries than the decay and ruin of monks' lives, degenerating from their ancient piety and *painfulness*.   Indeed, a *little* skill in antiquity inclines a man to Popery ; but *depth* in that study brings

---

* " Holy State," p. 115 (Pickering's Edition.)

him about again to our religion. A nobleman who had heard the extreme age of one dwelling not far off, made a journey to visit him, with admiration of his age, till his mistake was rectified, for ' Oh, sir ' said the young old man, ' I am not he whom you seek for, but his son ; my father is farther off in the field.' The same error is daily committed by the Romish Church, adoring the reverend brow and grey hairs of some ancient ceremonies, perchance but of some seven or eight hundred years' standing in the Church, and mistake these for their fathers, of far greater age in the primitive times." (" Fuller's Holy State," p. 54.)

> A little learning is a dangerous thing ;
> Drink deep, or taste not the Pierian spring.
> There shallow drops intoxicate the brain,
> And drinking largely sobers us again."
> —*Pope's Essay on Criticism.*

CHAPTER XVI.

SIEGE OF EXETER, THE EVER FAITHFUL CITY (*semper fidelis*).—1644-6.

" How many churches and chapels of the God of St. Lawrence have been laid waste in England by this woeful war! and which is more (and more to be lamented) how many living Temples of the Holy Ghost, Christian people, have therein been causelessly and cruelly destroyed! How shall our nation be ever able to make recompense for it? God of His goodness forgave us that debt which we of ourselves are not able to satisfy."—*Good Thoughts in Bad Times.* (" Historical Application," vii.)

WE now accompany our author to the capital of the West Country, without rival—beautiful for situation, the joy and pride of fair Devon, Exeter— the ever faithful city. At the time of his sojourn there, it was very different to the description he gives of it in 1660, when he spoke of it as one of the sweetest and neatest cities in England. One of the Canons of the Cathedral, Dr. Kellett, thus writes of it in his " Incœnium" (1641), that " whereas the city of Exeter by its natural situation is one of the sweetest cities in England, yet by the ill use of many is one of the nastiest and noysommest cities of the land; but for my love to that city I do forbear to say more." Although there were a dozen churches (now there are twenty-one) they never had a churchyard but the Cathedral, and Bishop Hall made the remark that the accumulation of corpses was so great, buried within the walls, that they threatened to bury the Cathedral itself.

From the earliest times, owing to its natural position, Exeter has been a most important place, a centre of all military enterprises, eventuating westwards, and therefore the key of the strategical position. It was, no doubt, a British stronghold, and known as the "city on the river" (Caer Isc). It was built on the head of the estuary of the Exe, just where the river ceases to be navigable, and no doubt was the great emporium with the western tin trade. The Romans also established themselves here, as is evidenced by many coins of Claudius, which have been found.

Even after the departure of the Romans, it long remained the capital of the British kingdom of Damnonia, which included the counties of Devon, Cornwall, and part of Somerset. When, however, Athelstan came westward, about 926, he found the town, which was called *Exanceaster* (the English name—the "chester," or fortified town on the Exe, which has been shortened into Exeter), occupied by both Britons and English. William of Malmesbury says that Athelstan held a gemote there, when certain laws still in existence were promulgated, and fortified the city with towers, surrounding it with a wall of square stones. These defences were not only raised against the Britons of "West Wales" but against the Danes, who had wintered in Exeter, 876, and again beset the burgh in 894, when King Alfred marched against them and compelled them to fly to their ships. These walls protected the city in 1001, when the Danes ravaged the whole of that south coast of Devon, and enabled the burghers to beat off their assailants. It was taken and plundered in 1003, but only through the treachery of the Norman Hugh, "reeve" of the Lady Emma, Queen of Æthelred, who had received the royal rights over Exeter, as part of her "morning gift." The Danes then broke down the walls, having before this ravaged the whole of the surrounding county, in consequence of which " the Bishop's stool," of Devonshire, then at Crediton (to which Cornwall had been previously united), was removed by the Confessor in 1050 to the walled " burgh " of Exeter—which gave its name for some hundreds of years to the See, dominating the two westernmost counties, till its division again a few years ago (1877) into the Dioceses of Exeter and Truro (Cornwall), which has been followed by such happy and marvellous results, surpassing even the most sanguine expectations.

From its physical position, its increased importance as a Cathedral city, Exeter soon developed into a considerable local centre, just as York and Norwich had done, and the chief stronghold and key of the Western Peninsula. Even after the battle of Hastings it remained a long time independent, Gytha, the mother of Harold, taking refuge there with her own daughter, and some say the children of Harold. The burghers rallied round the Saxon, and prepared to resist the intrusion of an " alien king," and it was not till the spring of 1068 that William the Conqueror reduced it to submission, after a siege of 18 days. He then erected a strong castle on the Rougemont, "red mount," overlooking the city, which had been indifferently fortified before. This castle was in 1137 held out for Queen Matilda by Baldwin, Earl of Devon, and it was taken by Stephen after a siege of three months, during which the Cathedral of St. Peter was partly burned. Exeter was all this time a great commercial city, and the small craft then in use were able to come right up to the city, and land their cargo on its quays. This, however, was no longer possible after the powerful Countess of Devon, Isabella de Fortibus, built a weir (still called Countess Weir) right across the river, about a mile above Topsham, in 1284. There was much excitement in and around Exeter during the wars of the Roses, when this land was long wasted with civil war, "till the *red rose* became white with the blood it had lost and the *white rose* red with the blood it had shed," as our author puts it.

The city took the side of the House of Lancaster, and in 1469 received within its walls some of the most prominent of the partisans of King Henry, and although it was besieged by Sir William Courtenay, of Powderham Castle, for 12 days, and the Yorkists, it held out against all assaults. The celebrated Earl of Warwick, and Clarence, fled to Exeter after the battle of Losecote, in Lincoln, and thence to Dartmouth, so that when Edward IV. arrived in Exeter (April, 1470) he found no enemy to fight with. The burghers presented him with a purse of 100 nobles, and he walked in procession to the Cathedral on Palm Sunday. Perkin Warbeck, in 1497, after landing in Whitsand Bay, near Plymouth, marched on to Exeter in ten days, but was stoutly resisted by the citizens, and in spite of many assaults was compelled to raise the siege, and fly before King Henry VII. to Beaulieu, in Hampshire. He was, however, taken at Taunton, and led back to Exeter. Here the rebels were led out with halters round their necks before the King, to enable whom

to have a better view of them as they passed along before
him, eight large trees were felled in the Cathedral yard.
Henry pardoned them, but many had been already executed
in Southernhay, which is hard by the Cathedral.

The next siege of the city was in 1549, when the Western Counties rose in defence of what was called "the old
religion," the Catholic faith. Exeter exerted itself
vigorously in 1588, during the alarm of the great Spanish
Armada, and Queen Elizabeth then granted to the city the
motto attached to its shield of arms—"Semper fidelis."

We have been led to make these historical remarks about
Exeter, to point out its extreme importance to the Royalist
cause, in a strategical point of view, as the metropolis of the
west. The city, too, was compact and surrounded with walls.
It was defended by the castle or stronghold of Rougemont,
"red mount," so called from the colour of the soil, and
which dominated the whole city itself, and indeed the entire
neighbourhood. Fuller describes it thus in his time : "The
houses stand sideways backward into their yards, and only
endways with their gables towards the street. The city
therefore is greater in content than appearance, being bigger
than it presenteth itself to passengers through the same."*
And again, in his " Church History," he speaks of it as a
"round city, on a rising hill most capable of fortification, both
for the site and form thereof. Her walls, though of the old
edition, were competently strong, and well repaired."†

When the Civil War broke out, a city enjoying such natural
advantages was of course much coveted by the partisans of

---

* " Worthies," Exeter, p. 273.
† " Church History," Book vii., 293.

either side, but faithful to her old motto, Exeter remained staunch, true and loyal to the cause of " Church and King," and her four gates were frequently shut against the foe. The Earl of Stamford, at the head of the Parliamentarians, attacked it, and contrived to maintain a garrison there (Oct., 1642), which contributed not a little to the successes of the following year. After the loss of the battle of Stratton, where the Earl held the chief com mand, he hastened to Exeter with the news of his defeat, and expecting a siege, destroyed all the houses in the suburbs, and ordered the trees on the walls, and in the northern and southern Hays to be cut down. After the capture of Bristol (July 24, 1643), Sir John Berkeley was sent by Charles I. to hold the command in Devonshire, and take measures for blockading Exeter. About the middle of the following month Prince Maurice came with his army before Exeter, and found Sir John Berkeley besieging the city, with his guards close to the gates. The siege continued till after the loss of the Parliamentarian garrison on the north coast, when the Earl of Stamford, after an eight months' siege, was induced to surrender, which considerably diminished the power of the Parliamentarians in the west. Sir John Berkeley was then made Governor, to the great joy of the major part of the citizens, who were zealous Royalists "deservedly appointed," as Fuller says. From this time and throughout the war, Exeter was the principal garrison and chief hope of the Royalists, after this, its ninth siege in its history

Exeter being regarded as a place of great security, and the Governor of the city being a man in whom confidence could be safely placed, the Queen, then far advanced in pregnancy, was sent there, and was joyfully received by the citizens, who conducted her to Bedford House. The " ever faithful" city was regarded as not only one of the strongest garrisons belonging to the Royalists, but was conveniently situated in case a retreat was necessary to France, a contingency not to be overlooked, as she lay under a charge of high treason, for conveying money and arms into England. The Queen had left Oxford, April 17, 1644, and was escorted on her journey by her husband the first day, which proved the last time the King ever saw her.

The Queen who had rested one night at Bath—that charming old Roman city, with its mineral springs, destined one day to be the centre of gaiety and fashion—on her way, and was suffering from the effects of rheumatic fever, caught in the previous summer's campaign, arrived at Exeter on May day. Here she took up her quarters at Bedford House, a large secluded and quiet mansion, occupied as the residence of the Governor. This old building had been a Dominican convent, which Edward IV. had made his headquarters when in Exeter, and at the dissolution of the monasteries, had been conferred upon John Russell, afterwards Earl of Bedford, Lord-Lieutenant of Devon, a family much enriched, especially at Tavistock, with lands and buildings originally belonging to the Church. This dwelling-house having been pulled down, the site was covered by the present Bedford Circus, from which there is an outlet into Southernhay, where the theatre stands, and from which, too, another one has quite recently been made into High-street itself, which certainly has not improved the appearance of that famous and picturesque street, whatever convenience it may be for traffic, although the new arcade is a decided success, erected on the site of the old Grammar School.

The Mayor and Corporation voted the Queen a sum of two hundred pounds the day after her arrival "as a testimonie of the respect of the cittie unto her Matie. nowe in this cittie," which was gratefully accepted by her. As the city was threatened with a blockade, the Queen was much perturbed at the prospect of being besieged, till she was reassured by a demonstration of the strength of the place, on the part of the citizens, and by the personal influence of the Governor. Here, then, at Bedford House the whilom Convent of the Black Friars, the Queen held her court, and, according to Clarendon, recovered her spirits to the reasonable convalescence. Her physician arrived in attendance at the end of May, and on Monday, June 16th, 1644, she gave birth to a princess, her fourth child. The good people of Exeter were ever afterwards proud of this circumstance, as it was the only case of a Royal birth having taken place in their city. In the old Guildhall may still be seen Sir Peter Lely's portrait of the Duchess of Orleans, it having been presented by Charles II. to the Corporation of Exeter, in 1672, as a souvenir of his sister's connection with the old city, and a very good picture it is.

Meanwhile, the forces of the Earl of Essex were drawing closer to the beleaguered city, and the more so, that it now harboured, so they called her, a Popish Queen. In vain she sought the permission of their leader to retire to Bath or Bristol until after her recovery, and she therefore determined, although it was only a little more than a fortnight after the birth of her child, to flee from the city, to which, such being the position of the King's affairs, he could not bring an army to its relief. The royal infant was entrusted to the care of Lady Dalkeith, on the understanding that she should be removed elsewhere in case of a siege taking place. Strict directions were also given to the Governor, Sir John Berkeley, not to overlook the necessities of the Princess, come what might. She then left the city, speeding westwards. We read of her first reaching Okehampton, on July 1st, whence she made her way to Plymouth. Her next refuge was Pendennis Castle, at the entrance of the river Fal, in Cornwall, whence she escaped to France, in a Dutch vessel, sent by the Prince of Orange to fetch her.

The news of the birth of the Princess reached the King at Buckingham, who sent off an immediate despatch that she should be baptised in the Cathedral Church at Exeter, according to the rites and ceremonies of the Church of England. The ceremony was performed accordingly in the Cathedral, on Sunday, July 21st, by Dr. Laurence Burnell, Chancellor and Canon Residentiary, and it is said that a font, under a rich canopy of state, was purposely erected in the body of the church. These preparations, under the circumstances, an attack being imminent, had to be made in great haste. The name given to the child was Henrietta Anne, after her famous grandfather and her aunt, the Cathedral register of her baptism running thus : " Henrietta, daughter of our Soveraigne Lord, King Charles and our gracious Queene Mary, was baptized the 21st July, 1644." The sponsors of the child were Sir John Berkeley, the Lady Poulett, of Hinton St. George, and the Lady Dalkeith, who were personal friends of Fuller, and he was often in their company. Berkeley, who heartily enjoyed the society of our author, was the son of Sir Maurice Berkeley, likewise devoted to the King's cause. This family was a younger branch of the Berkeleys, of Berkeley Castle, whose head was George Lord Berkeley, one of Fuller's most munificent patrons. Besides Lady Poulett, other members of the family, with whom Fuller had been intimate since 1639, were present in the city at this time. Sir John Poulett and his eldest son were assisting Prince Maurice at Lyme Regis, but they don't appear to have acquired much glory.

Lady Annie Dalkeith—the great beauty of those times— had been designated by the Royal mother as the principal guardian of the young Princess. This lady was one of the "numerous and beautiful female kindred" of the Buckingham family, being the daughter of Sir Edward Villiers, the Governor of Munster. Her husband was Robert Lord Dalkeith, who became ninth Earl of Morton, 1648. To use Fuller's expression, this lady was matched with "little more portion than her uncle's smiles," the forerunner of some good office or honour to follow on their husbands. The Queen was entirely under the care of Lady Dalkeith during her stay in Exeter, and she was unremitting in her guardianship of the young child for many years. Fuller was "planted" in the Royal household through her instrumentality. This lady, owing to her beauty and the romantic surroundings of her companionship, became celebrated in verse by Waller, and also by the poet Herrick, in a sonnet to Lady Mary Villars :

> "For my sake, who ever did prefer
> You above all those sweets of Westminster ;
> Permit my book to have a free accesse
> To kisse your hand, most dainty governesse."

Not many days after the baptismal ceremony, on Friday, July 26th, the King, who was in pursuit of the forces under the Earl of Essex, came to Exeter from Honiton, and with him also Prince Charles. He was informed that the Queen had left the city before his arrival there. There came out to meet him Prince Maurice, Sir John Berkeley, the Governor, the Earl of Bristol, and Lord Poulett, and at the gates the Mayor, Aldermen, and many burgesses came to welcome him. He lodged at the Royal head-quarters, Bedford House, and here for the first time he saw the young Princess, then about six weeks old.

This loyal city was naturally delighted to welcome their Sovereign, and mindful of his " many gracious favours to the city," not only attended him, but the Corporation voted a sum of £500 to be presented to him, and £100 to Prince Charles "as a testimony of the citties service and the joy of his Majestie's presented here." Money was also given to the Royal servants, and a rate levied for the repairs of the city walls. The next day the King left the city, after reviewing Prince Maurice's troops, and holding a council of war. He pursued the Earl of Essex into Cornwall, where, being hard pressed, the greater part of his army were compelled to surrender (Sept. 1st), and on the 17th, the King returned to Exeter with the spoils he had captured. Once more he took up his quarters at Bedford House, and on this occasion he made suitable arrangements for the permanent establishment of his daughter's household.

It was about July in this year that our author took leave of active service under Lord Hopton, with a view to settling in the city. No doubt this alteration of his prospects was due to the King, who was interesting himself in his future, and who certainly held him in very great respect. And so, in acknowledgment of his loyalty and worth, and in token of services rendered to the good cause, he received from the

King, " during his stay at Exeter," the complimentary appointment of tutor or chaplain to the young Princess, an appointment which was also associated (if we may take Fuller's words) with Lady Dalkeith. " There was, un-doubtedly," says Mr. Bailey, " some policy on the King's part in selecting our hero for this merely nominal office. Fuller had been brought up at the feet of eminent divines, and was known for his staunch fidelity to the principles of his faith, for devotion to the Church, and for ability to give an answer to those who demanded a reason of the hope which was in him ; and the connections of such a divine with the household of the Princess, would be one testimony to the King's intention of educating the child in the faith of the Church of England. The appointment would also tend to disprove the rumours of the King's attachment to the Roman Catholic Faith—rumours, which were then, as here-tofore, injuring his prospects." The words of Fuller's biographer are : " Her royal father's intendment being, as he had educated the rest of his princely issue, to have her brought up in the Protestant religion " (p. 33). There are other testimonies to the King's carefulness in this respect. Thus Pére Cyprien, of Gamache, afterwards the tutor and spiritual adviser of the Princess, says that his Majesty would have the child kept " continually in the Protestant religion ; to counteract the ideas which several of his subjects enter-tained that he had himself a leaning towards Popery, and in the firm belief which he held, that salvation was not excluded from the Protestant or Catholic religion, and that one may be saved in either." This enabled Fuller, two or three years after this time, to vouch for the King's Protestantism, in opposition to the opinion of many persons. " His gracious

Majesty hath been suspected to be Popishly inclined. A suspicion like those mushrooms which Pliny recounts among the miracles in nature, because growing without a root. Well—he hath passed his purgation—a bitter morning's draught hath he taken down for many years together. See the operation thereof: his constancy in the Protestant religion hath not only been assured to such who were jealous of him, but also, by God's blessing, he daily grows greater in men's hearts, pregnant with the love and affection of his subjects."

To Fuller's loyal heart and nature, this new chaplaincy, taken in connection with other Royal favours, must have been highly gratifying. "It pointed only at his *merit*," says the *Life*, "which indeed was as much as the iniquity of those times would afford to any the most deserving personage" (p. 34). The King, further "to signify his approbation of the Doctor's excellent worth," offered Fuller a more substantial appointment. He pressed upon him " a patent for his presentation to the town of Dorchester, in Dorsetshire, a living valued to be worth £400 per annum" (p. 34). This living had been in the incumbency of Rev. John White, who was styled " the Patriarch of Dorchester." He was the grandfather of Charles and John Wesley, and was a man of great piety and sound learning, with a luminous grasp of Holy Scripture and great facility in expounding it. It is said that during these civil wars he had lost his library, and retired to London, where he became Minister of the Savoy, but "when the war was over he returned to Dorchester." This kind offer—this mark of Royal favour—our author saw fit to decline. He preferred to remain at Exeter, connected with the household of, and in close attendance upon, the infant Princess. Besides, he had no intention of burying himself in the country, but his ultimate intention was to come up to the metropolis, with the view of completing his literary compositions. As his biographer puts it, " London was in his eye." And so, whatever other arguments may have weighed with him, the King's offer was politely declined.

The King stayed in Exeter about a week, taking his final departure about September 23rd, previous to which he left an order upon the Excise revenues for the expenses of his daughter's household. In this household Fuller had now a place, and he remained in personal attendance upon his young charge during the two years the Princess remained in the city. From his own words we gather that he ate the King's bread for a much longer period He had been specially " designed to attend on her, to instil into her tender mind (if God had pleased to continue her with safety within the limits of this kingdom) the principles and belief of the English Catholic Church." Lady Dalkeith also discharged her responsibilities with great fidelity. Soon after this, the King, on his way to Oxford, after fighting a battle with Waller at Andover, relieved Donnington Castle, and Basing House. But Waller and Essex joining their forces, a second battle was fought at Newbury, which was hotly contested. In this battle Fuller says of his old comrades, " The Cornish, though behaving themselves valiantly, were conceived not to do so well, because expected to have done better." They returned in " a pace slower than a flight, and faster than a retreat."

After all these excitements, the good city of Exeter was glad of the rest, which it enjoyed for about a year. This was also most grateful to Fuller, who was glad of this lull in the storm, to devote himself to his professional pursuits and literary studies. He preached regularly every Lord's Day to "the truly loyal citizens," and by the assiduous discharge of his duties he won the goodwill of its Mayor and Corporation. The only fault they had to find was that the good Doctor too often spoke of the probability of the discourse he was then preaching being his last. But the times were stirring and uncertain. On August 6th, being " Observance Day," it fell to his lot to lead the devotions of the citizens on the anniversary of the defeat of the rebels in that city, in the reign of Edward VI. In his *Church History*, Fuller says, " It is an high day in the almanac of Exeter, good cheer, and (thereby I justly guess) their great gratitude being annually observed with a public sermon to perpetuate the memory of God's mercy unto them." We find our author thus praying during his absence from the House of God, " being in the spirit on the Lord's Day," in his *Personal Meditations* : " Lord—Thy servants are now praying in the Church, and I am here staying at home, detained by necessary occasions, such as are not of my seeking, but Thy sending, my care could not prevent them, my power could not remove them. Wherefore, though I cannot go to Church, there to sit down at Table with the rest of Thy guests, be pleased Lord to send me a dish of their meat hither, and feed my soul with holy thoughts. Eldad and Medad, though staying still in the camp (no doubt on just cause) yet prophesied as well as the other elders. Though they went not out to the Spirit, the Spirit came home to them. Thus never any dutiful child lost his legacy for being absent at the making of his father's will, if at the same time he were employed about his father's business. I fear too many at Church have their bodies there, and their minds at home. Behold, in exchange, my body here, and my heart there. Though I cannot pray with them, I pray for them. Yea, this comforts me ; I am with Thy congregation, because I would be with it." (x.)

Besides the discharge of his ministerial functions, he found learned leisure to pursue those literary works, which at that time he had "on the anvil." The compilation of the *Worthies of England* took up a good deal of his time, "not minding the cloud impending over the city." It was at this period he was engaged in composing, from time to time, that richly devotional manual, with the somewhat ambiguous title, "Good Thoughts in Bad Times," full of sweet—bitter reflections. In these he seems to make known his very inmost thoughts, and they contain passages which tend to illustrate his history. Many of his illustrations are borrowed from a soldier's life, and these quaint moralisings throw some light on the life and times of the beleagured citizens. They consist of personal meditations, Scripture observations, historical applications, and mixt contemplations.

"Whilst at Exeter," says Mr. Russell in his " Memorials," " Dr. Fuller's society was much sought (and by many of the titled Royalists). It is said that ' Old Doctor Vilvain of that city was pleasantly rallied by the Governor of Exeter, for inviting him so often, or detaining him so long from the society of others, as a cornholder, that hoardeth up the grain, to enhance the market and make a dearth.'" But it seems the Doctor had some uncommon manuscripts with a curious museum ; and being of a generous disposition, as his benefactions in that city may testify, notwithstanding his sufferings in those distracted times, as also of courteous comportment and communicative conversation, they were mutually agreeable to each other. John Digby, Earl of Bristol, offered to retain Fuller in his household, if he would go over and reside with him in France, protesting that while he was master of a loaf, Fuller should have half of it. But this offer he declined, 'for he loved liberty before the whole loaf,' as he did a similar one at another time from the venerable and most munificent Morton, Bishop of Durham (to whom is attributed an anonymous treatise on the Nature of God), whose liberality has found a place in the pages of honest Isaak Walton, there to survive (we may trust) to distant ages, the opening of his dialogue in the " Complete Angler " being borrowed from that work. Touching the charge that the Earl was a Papist, Fuller says : " The worst I wish such who causelessly suspect him of Popish inclinations is, that I may hear from them half so many strong arguments for the Protestant religion as I have heard from him, who was, to his commendation, a cordial champion for the Church of England."* Digby retired to France, on the surrender of Exeter, where he met with due respect in foreign, which he missed in his native, country.

There may have been also a patriotic reason for declining this kind offer, which, virtually, meant expatriation. Fuller never approved of this desertion of one's native country, which he, as a true-born Englishman, not only loved too well to leave, notwithstanding its unhappy distractions, but which he felt it his duty to serve with all his powers. "This

---

* " Worthies," Warwick, p. 124

running into the wilderness was but a bankrupt trick to defraud the Church and Commonwealth of their creditors, to both of which they stood bound." In fact, Fuller always urged his friends to remain at their posts. In one of his " Good Thoughts in Worse Times," he asks, " Do any intend willingly (without special cause) to leave this land, so to avoid that misery which their sins, with others, have drawn upon it? Might I advise them, better mourn in, than move out of, sad Zion." Fuller, therefore, preferred to remain at Exeter. Among his friends he now reckoned the Earl of Carlisle, and George Lord Berkeley; the latter name he thus gratefully records : "At this day there flourisheth many noble stems sprung thereof, though George Lord Berkeley, Baron Berkeley, Lord Mowbray, Seagrave, Bruce, be the top branch of this family : one who hath been so signally bountiful in promoting these and all other my weak endeavours, that I desire to be dumb if ever I forget to return him public thanks for the same." ("Worthies," Yorkshire, 222.) Leaving matters martial for the present, we contemplate Fuller in the more congenial light of Author and meditative Divine.

Whilst at Exeter in 1645, our author found a fitting opportunity of publishing this first of a series of meditations, very suitable to those disturbed times, under the title of " Good Thoughts in Bad Times," which was followed in 1647 with his " Good Thoughts in Worse Times." This book is most interesting, both from a literary and antiquarian point of view, not only by reason of its contents and authorship, but as being *the first book printed in the city,* Fuller, alluding to it as " *the first fruits of Exeter press.*" There was no daily *Telegram* in those days; no weekly

Exeter and Plymouth *Mail*. It was printed by Thomas
Hunt of that city, and the *Thoughts* contained about 250
pages, which made a volume small enough for the pocket,
for which it was intended. It was the first book which our
author put out, after a considerable interval, for a literary
man, possibly owing to the distracted life he had led as a
" Wandering Divine," or it may have been, as he says in
this book, " Once in the mind never to write more, for fear
lest my writings at the last day prove records against me."
" Here it is greatly to be regretted," says Mr. Russell in
his " Memorials," " in spite of the beauties with which his
' Good Thoughts ' abound, that they are in some instances
unhappily degraded by a quaintness that is never so much
out of place as in religious meditations. In like manner the
bidding prayers of Bishop Andrewes savour as well of his
defects as of his excellencies." (P. 155.)

Fuller, one of the most gallant and courteous of men
and who was courted as an accomplished and agreeable
companion, thus dedicates this Manual of Meditation to
his patroness, the beautiful Lady Dalkeith, Lady-Governess
to Her Highness the Princess Henrietta : " Madam,—It is
unsafe in these dangerous days for any to go abroad
without a convoy, or, at the least, a pass. My book hath
both in being dedicated to your Honour. The Apostle
saith, who planteth a vineyard and eateth not of the fruit
thereof. I am one of your Honour's planting, and could
heartily wish that the fruit I bring forth were worthy to be
tasted by your judicious palate. Howsoever, accept these
grapes, if not for their goodness, for their novelty ; though

---

* Mixt Contemplations, xxv.

not sweetest relished, they are soonest ripe, being *the first fruits of Exeter press*, presented unto you. And if ever my ingratitude shall forget my obligation to your Honour, these black lines will turn red, and blush his unworthiness that wrote them. In this pamphlet your Ladyship shall praise whatsoever you are pleased but to pardon. But I am tedious, for your Honour can spare no more minutes from looking on a better book, her infant Highness, committed to your charge. Was ever more hope of worth in a less volume? But O! how excellently will the same, in due time, be set forth seeing the paper is so pure, and your Ladyship the overseer to correct the press! The continuance and increase of whose happiness here and hereafter is desired in his daily devotions, who resteth, your Honour's, in all Christian service, THOMAS FULLER."

In this little devotional manual—it may be formed after the model of Donne's " Devotions and Meditations," or Bishop Hall's " Occasional Meditations "—we are admitted into the innermost thoughts and feelings of our quaint and witty author. There are to begin with twenty-five " Personal Meditations," illustrating principally his own chequered career. Next we have the same number of " Scriptural Observations," which tend to elucidate some of the difficulties of the sacred text. These are again followed by the same number of " Historical Applications," where episodes in history are happily and witilly applied, either to his own self-edification, or the circumstances of the times. Nineteen " Scripture Observations " follow these, and after them again come nineteen " Meditations on the Times." These are followed by nineteen " Meditations on all kinds of Prayer," and seventeen " Occasional Meditations." We then find, in two sets of fifty each, "Mixt Contemplations on these times." No doubt many, if not most, of these topics, formed illustrations, which the preacher used in his sermons. They are, as Mr. Russell says, the most characteristic of Fuller's writings. "In them we have a living portrait of their author, both as a politician and a Divine."

As might have been expected, many of these devout musings have not only reference to the "bad times" in which our author lived, but his own personal participation in them. Take the very first as a specimen, expressing gratitude for his hairbreadth escapes in the late campaign : "Lord—How near was I to danger, yet escaped ! I was upon the brink of the brink of it, yet fell not in ! They are well kept who are kept by Thee. Excellent Archer ! Thou didst hit thy mark in missing it ; as meaning to fright, not hurt me. Let me not be such a fool as to pay my thanks to blind Fortune, for a favour which the eye of Providence hath bestowed upon me. Rather let the narrowness of my escape make my thankfulness to Thy goodness the larger, lest my ingratitude justly cause, that whereas this arrow but hit my hat, the next pierce my head." Again, in the second, he says: "Lord, when Thou shalt visit me with a sharp disease, I fear I shall be impatient, for I am choleric by my nature, and tender by my temper, and have not been acquainted with sickness all my life-time. I cannot expect any kind usage from that which hath been a stranger unto me. . . . Teach me the art of patience whilst I am well, and give me the use of it when I am sick. In that day either lighten my burden, or strengthen my back. Make me, who so often in my health have discovered my weakness, presuming on my own strength, to be strong in sickness when I solely rely on Thy assistance."

What would Fuller have done in these days of musical services, when, if the priest's part be not inflected or intoned, it must at least be monotoned? "Lord," he says, " my voice by nature is harsh and untunable, and it is vain to lavish any art to better it. Can my singing of Psalms be pleasing to Thy ears, which is unpleasant to my own? Yea, though I cannot chant with the nightingale, or chirp with the blackbird, I had rather chatter with the swallow, yea, rather croak with the raven, than be altogether silent. Hadst Thou have given me a better voice, I would have praised thee with a better voice. Now, what my music wants in sweetness, let it have in sense, singing praises with understanding. Yea, Lord, create in me a new heart (therein to make melody), and I will be contented with my old voice, until, in Thy due time, being admitted into the choir of Heaven, I have another more harmonious bestowed upon me."

Fuller was a dear lover of peace; and he not only never wearied of singing his Eirenicon, but ever prayed "for the peace of Jerusalem." "Lord," he says (xiv.), "when young, I have almost quarrelled with that petition in our Liturgy, 'Give peace in our time, O Lord': needless to wish for light in noonday: for then peace was plentiful, no fear of famine, but a suspicion of a surfeit thereof. And yet how many good comments was this prayer then capable of! 'Give peace,' that is, continue and preserve it; 'give peace,' that is, give us hearts worthy of it, and thankful for it: 'in our time,' that is, all our time; for there is more besides a fair morning to make a fair day. Now I see the mother had more wisdom than her son. The Church knew better than I how to pray. Now I am better informed of the necessity of that petition. Yea, with the daughters of the horseleech I have need to cry, 'Give, give peace in our time, O Lord'" (Prov. xxx. 15).

We have a personal meditation (xvi.) on his own absent-mindedness, consequent on his scholarly habits, which was growing upon him. "Lord, when I am to travel, I never used to provide myself till the very time; partly out of laziness, loth to be troubled till needs I must; partly out of pride, as presuming all necessaries for my journey will wait upon me at the instant. (Some say this is scholar's fashion, and it seems by following it I hope to approve myself to be one.) However, it often comes to pass my journey is finally stopped, through the narrowness of time to provide for it. Grant, Lord, that my confessed improvidence in temporal, may make me suspect my providence in spiritual matters. Solomon says, 'Man goeth to his long home.' Short preparation will not fit for so long a journey. Oh let me not put it off to the last, to have my oil to buy, when I am to burn it; but let me so dispose of myself, that when I am to die, I may have nothing to do but to die."

Touching the putting off of repentance, and the intention of correlating it with some particular date, our author pertinently observes: "Lord, I do discover a fallacy, where I have long deceived myself, which is this: I have desired to begin my amendment from my birthday, or from the first day of the year, and from some eminent festival, that so my repentance might bear some remarkable date. But when those days were come, I have adjourned my amendment to some other time. Thus, whilst I could not agree with myself when to start, I have almost lost the running of the race. I am resolved thus to befool myself no longer. I see no day but to-day; the instant time is always the fittest time. In Nebuchadnezzar's image, the lower the members, the coarser the metal; the farther off the time, the more unfit. To-day is the golden opportunity, to-morrow will be the silver season, next day but the brazen one, and so long, till at last I shall come to the toes of clay, and be turned to dust. Grant, therefore, that to-day I may hear Thy voice. And if this day be obscure in the Calendar, and remarkable in itself for nothing else, give me to make it memorable in my soul, thereupon, by Thy assistance, beginning the re-formation of my life."

We will give one more " Personal Meditation" about daily prayer (xxi.) : " Lord, I confess this morning I re-membered my breakfast, but forgot my prayers. And as I have returned no praise, so Thou mightest justly have afforded me no protection. Yet Thou hast carefully kept me to the middle of this day; entrusted me with a new debt before I have paid the old score. It is now noon; too late for a morning, too soon for an evening sacrifice. My corrupt heart prompts me to put off my prayers till night, but I know it too well, or rather too ill, to trust it. I fear if till night I defer them, at night I shall forget them. Be pleased, therefore, now to accept them. Lord, let not a few hours the later make a breach; especially seeing (be it spoken, not to excuse my negligence, but to implore Thy pardon) a thousand years in Thy sight are but as yesterday. I promise, hereafter, by Thy assistance, to bring forth fruit in due season. See how I am ashamed the sun should shine on me, who now newly start in the race of my devotions, when he, like a giant, hath run more than half his course in the heavens."

Most of Fuller's "Historical Applications" refer to the disordered condition of the times, and between the lines we may often read some political purpose latent. Speaking of the summits of the Welsh mountains, from which shepherds might have discoursed, though parted by valleys, he says: "Our Sovereign and the members of his Parliament in London seem very near agreed in their general and public professions. Both are for the Protestant religion; can they draw nearer? Both are for the privileges of Parliament; can they come closer? Both are for the liberty of the subject; can they meet evener? And yet, alas! there is a great gulf and vast difference betwixt them, which our sins have made; and God grant that our sorrow may seasonably make it up again." (iii.)

Speaking of Henry VII.'s Chapel at Westminster, he breaks out with a parenthetic wish: "God grant I may once again see it, with the saint who belongs to it, our Sovereign, there in a well conditioned peace." (vi.)

Of almshouses he thus writes: "We are likely neither in bye-ways or hedges to have any works of mercy till the whole kingdom be speedily turned into one great hospital, and God's charity only able to relieve us." And again: "Now he who would formerly sue his neighbour for *pedibus ambulando*, can behold his whole field lying waste, and must be content. We see our goods taken from us, and can say nothing; not so much as seeking legal redress, because certain not to find it." And of the ruin of many houses of prayer: "How many churches and chapels have been laid waste in England by this woful war! And which is more

(and more to be lamented), how many living temples of the
Holy Ghost (Christian people) have been cruelly and causelessly destroyed !" (vii.) In all these Meditations our
author justifies God in His doings, counsels moderation,
and urges a prayerful attitude for Church and country.

We could multiply quotations, but enough have been
given as specimens of these meditations, which we can well
believe proved a comfort to many, and a solace to the
beleaguered citizens of the ever faithful city. It may seem
strange that a book of this character, meditative, should
have been composed at such a busy, not to say bellicose
period ; but extremes meet, and no doubt thoughtful minds
turned for inward peace as a set-off against these outward
distractions. At such times the soul falls back on itself,
and, in the spirit of the text appended to the original
edition, a man will love " to commune with his own
heart and be still," and gain that inward peace which
passeth understanding.

In connection with these *Good Thoughts* the following
is related by Oldys : " We have seen an account or description of a collection of moral and divine contemplations
written seemingly in a woman's hand, by either the said
Princess Henrietta Maria (Anne) as it was said, or for her
use (among the MS. collection of the late Mr. T. Coxeter),
having on its blue Turkey leather cover the two first letters
of her name in cypher, surrounded with palm branches, and
crowned with a coronet, in which there are several of the
curious thoughts of this book."

And upon this passage, Miss Strickland has the following
remarks, " The baby-Princess had the honour of frequently
giving audience to her loving and faithful chaplain, the Rev.

Thomas Fuller, who during his attendance on her wrote several of his beautiful little tracts, full of quaint stories, for her use. He had them printed in loyal but suffering Exeter. The first of these is supposed to be 'Good Thoughts in Bad Times.' One day there was a little festival among the sad circle of the loyal ladies˜ in the besieged city, when the little Princess gave audience in the arms of her governess and godmother, Lady Dalkeith, and received a copy of this work, for her use and early training in the reformed Catholic Church of England, from the venerable hands of its best historian, as 'the *first fruits of Exeter Press.*' This is told in her 'Lives of the Stuart Princesses.'"

There can be no question this habit of meditation, or interior recollection, was a very decided characteristic of Fuller. We remember Aubrey's story of him when quite a boy, which shows he was "the father of the man." The art of meditation is too much neglected in these busy days, but there can be no question that its results are most beneficial. In fact, no one can possibly imagine how useful it is for deepening the interior life, till it has been fully tried. Fuller was both thoughtful and observant ; this is stamped on his features : and we doubt not was evidenced in his very carriage. The elder D'Israeli has observed that the faculties, whatever they may be, are considerably enlarged by this habit. In those days of sundered friends and parted acquaintances, he was often forced to turn "solitariness into society." "A Christian's eyes," Fuller would say, "ought to be turned inward, and chiefly reflected on himself. Yet how many are there whose home is always to be abroad. It is a tale of the wandering Jew, but it is too much truth of many wandering

x

Christians, whose thoughts are never resident on their own souls, but ever searching and examining of others. These say not with the soldiers 'And what shall *we* do ?' but are questioning always as St. Peter is of John, 'And what shall *this man* do ?'" These "Thoughts" were composed in moments of solitariness, which encouraged meditation. He comments upon Matt. iv. 11 : "There is no purgatory condition between hell and heaven ; but instantly, when *out* devil, *in* angel. Such is the condition of every solitary soul. It will make company for itself. Grant, therefore, that my soul, which ever will have some, may never have bad company." Again, he quaintly observes, "One may make himself *three*, offender, accuser, judge, so that he should *never be less alone than when alone*, being always in the company of heavenly discourses in himself." In his " Essay on Books," one of his maxims is, " *Proportion an hour's meditation to an hour's reading of a staple author.* This makes a man master of his learning, and dis-spirits the book into the scholar." He again alludes to the advantages of meditation in his sermon "The Snare Broken," " Had people this art of entertaining a time to discourse with themselves, it would prevent much mischief. Thou mayest divide thy soul into several parts, and thou mayest discourse, if thou wilt, with every faculty—with thy understanding, memory, fancy, and the several affections of thy soul. Ask that question of thy *understanding* which Philip asked of the eunuch, ' Understandest thou what thou readest ?' Call your understanding to account whether you understand what you read or not. Ask thy *fancy* that question which Achish once propounded to King David, ' Where hast thou been roving all this day ?' Bring thy fancy to account.

Ask that of thy *memory* which the master did of the unjust steward, ' Give an account of thy stewardship.' Ask thy memory, what good thou hast treasured up. When thou findest thyself transported with *mirth*, ask thy soul that question God did to Sarah, ' Why laughest thou ? ' When thou seest the passion of *anger* grow too violently upon thee, ask of it that question God did to the prophet Jonah, ' Dost thou well to be angry ? ' "

Meantime matters were not looking bright for the Royalist cause. In the spring of 1645, Lord Hopton had returned to Bristol, where he was visited by Prince Charles, who subsequently went on to Barnstaple, described as a " miraculously fortified town." During August (the Battle of Naseby having been fought June 14th, 1645), Prince Charles visited Exeter, with the view of settling some dispute there, and took up his headquarters in the city, where he remained till September 15th. Soon after his departure, the Parliamentarian forces (under Fairfax and Waller) suddenly approached the city. The " dainty governess," the Lady Dalkeith, made an attempt to escape with her charge, the young princess, now about twelve-months old, but without success, so that they were compelled to remain and endure the rigours of the siege. The Clubmen of Devonshire at this crisis declared for the Parliament, which did not improve the prospects of the King ; and Fairfax, everywhere victorious, prepared to invest Exeter. Fuller has preserved reminiscences of his intercourse with the disorderly troops of Goring who were compelled to retreat to the city, Dr. Pearson being with them, "This day casually I am fallen into a bad company and know not how I came hither, or how I get hence. I was not wandering in any base by-path, but walking in the highway of my vocation, wherefore, Lord, Thou that calledst me hither, keep me here. Stop their mouths that they speak no blasphemy, or stop my ears that I hear none ; or open my mouth soberly to reprove what I hear." Making Mary Autree (Heavitree) his headquarters, Fairfax began his investment by erecting garrisons on the East side, but was much impeded by the inclemency of the weather. Meantime, Prince Charles was mustering his forces at Okehampton, on the western escarpment of Dartmoor, on the river Okement, another strong place with a castle, and holding the main road to Plymouth, through Lydford, only eight miles distant, where was a castle and a place naturally strong, made stronger by earthworks, commanding also the high road into Cornwall.

Fairfax marched against the Prince, fortifying this strong position in the valley of the Okement, "Castrum prenobile de Okehampton," as William of Worcester calls it, now lying in ruins, but turned southwards and took Dartmouth, the quaint and picturesque town at the mouth of that beautiful river, which has been called the English Rhine. On his return, he summoned the garrison, which was now almost entirely surrounded, to surrender (Jan. 27th, 1647), but the Governor, Sir John Berkeley, replied that they could not in honour do so, while they were in no worse condition, and had less probable hope of relief from the Prince. The occupation of the western side now completed the investment of the city.

During this winter the inhabitants seem to have suffered much from the want of provisions, and it was at this time the following remarkable occurrence took place, recorded by Fuller in his "Worthies of England":* "When the city of Exeter was besieged by the Parliament forces, so that only the south side thereof towards the sea was open unto it, incredible numbers of larks were found in that open quarter, for multitude like quails in the wilderness, though (blessed be God) unlike them both in cause and effect, as not desired with man's destruction, nor sent with God's anger, as appeared by their safe digestion into wholesome nourishment. Hereof I was an *eye* and *mouth* witness. I will save my credit in not conjecturing any number; knowing, that herein, though I should stoop below the truth, I should mount above belief; they were as fat as plentiful, so that being sold for two pence a dozen and under, the poor (who could have no cheaper, as the rich no better meat) used to make pottage of them, boiling them down therein. Several natural causes were assigned hereof. (1) That these fowl, frightened with much shooting on the land, retreated to the *seaside* for their refuge. (2) That it is familiar with them in cold winters (as that was) to shelter themselves in the most southern parts. (3) That some sort of seeds were lately sown in these parts, which invited them thither for their own repast. However, the *cause of causes* was *Divine Providence*, thereby providing a feast for many poor people, who otherwise had been pinched for provision."

Events in the west now followed in quick succession. Leaving Waller in command of the besieging force at Exeter, Fairfax went to meet the King's troops under the command of Lord Hopton, whose army had been reinforced by levies from Cornwall. They had marched 7000 strong

---

* Worthies of England, vol. ii., p. 304.

from Stratton to Torrington in one day, expecting to be joined with other troops from Barnstaple, and stores for the relief of Exeter, which did not come. Fairfax engaged Hopton, having the advantage of numbers, at Torrington, and gained a victory (Feb. 19th). "The stand of pikes," as Fuller says, "being oft-times no stand, and the footmen, so fitly called, as making more use of their feet than their hands. Torrington Church, which was used as a powder magazine, was blown up, destroying many on both sides, especially Royalists, and Lord Hopton's banner was captured among the spoils, which bore this loyal device, 'I will strive to serve my sovereign King.' The débris of the royal forces fled, but rallied again on the Cornish side of the river Tamar, which divides the two counties of Devon and Cornwall, about 6000 in number, chiefly cavalry. They were hotly pursued as far as Truro (now the seat of the new Cornish bishopric), where proposals of surrender were made (March 6th). Honourable mention was made of Lord Hopton, "whom we esteem and honour above any of your party," in these proposals, which being of such a character, Lord Hopton finding he could not assist the King any further, determined to accept these honourable conditions, and March 14th the whole army was disbanded." Thus, as Fuller said, "The King's cause verged more and more westward, until it set in Cornwall."

Fairfax returned to the siege of Exeter. Fuller was still preaching to the beleaguered citizens with "great satisfaction and content;" but the fall of the city was imminent. The good doctor received a token of the good feeling of its citizens towards him just before its surrender. On the 21st March the Chamber bestowed on him the *Bodleian*

Lectureship, which was in their gift. This lectureship had been founded by a brother of Mr. Bodley (Sir Thomas) who gave the famous library to Oxford—Dr. Laurence Bodley, formerly Canon of Exeter. This Canon had left £400 to the Mayor and Corporation of Exeter, to be invested in lands, bringing in £20 per annum, to provide a preacher to preach every Sunday in Exeter as they might direct. There are many notices in the *Act*-book of the city touching this lectureship. The following are some of the minutes, 29th Nov., 1643. "Mr. Henry Painter, having neglected the lecture, is dismissed, and Mr. William Fuller appointed." And 21st March, 1645-6. "Whereas Mr. William Ffuller, clark, about two yeers since was elected to preach the lecture heretofore founded by Dr. Bodlie, who hath now lefte this cittie, it is this day approved by xiii. affirmative votes that the grante made to hym shall ceasse, which is intimated by Sir John Berkeley, Knight, our Governor, to be the desire of the said Mr. William Ffuller. Also, this Mr. Thomas Ffuller, Bachelor of Divinitie, according to the direction of the foresaid Doctor Bodley to have and exercise the same att the will and pleasure of the Maior and Comon Counsell of this Cittie and noe longer."

As long as the Royalists held the city, Fuller retained his position as Bodleian Lecturer. In that capacity, and not long before the surrender of the city, our divine preached one of his most effective and earnest discourses, which was listened to with much interest by the Mayor (Mr. Cooper) and Corporation, to whom he dedicated it. In this dedication he says, " I must acknowledge my engagement unto you to be great. Is not Exeter a little one ? and my soul shall live, where I safely anchored in these tempestuous

times : it is a high advancement in this troublesome age
for one with a quiet conscience to be Preferred to life and
liberty : it fared better with me : for whilst her infant
Highness (on whose soul and body God crowd all blessings,
spiritual and temporal, till there shall be no room to receive
more), though unable to feed herself, fed me, and many
more of her servants. Other accommodations were bestowed upon me by your liberality." He prays for his
friends that God Himself would "stand watchman at the
gates of your city to forbid the entrance of anything
that may be prejudicial unto you, and give full and free
admittance to whatsoever may tend to the advancement
of your happiness both here and hereafter."

The sermon is entitled "Fear of loving the old light," and
is founded upon Revelations ii., 5 : "And will remove thy
candlestick out of his place except thou repent." Speaking
of the Church of Ephesus referred to in the text, he avers
that "no church in this world can be free from faults.
Even Ephesus, the best of the seven, had somewhat amiss
in it. As long as there be spots in the moon, it is vain to
expect anything spotless under it." "Here," says Mr.
Russell, "as in his sermon of Reformation, he remarks upon
the folly of looking for perfection in a church. He notices
the sovereignty of the Divine will in visiting some with the
light of the Gospel, and passing by others." He it is that
vouchsafed the Gospel unto unrepenting Corazin and
Bethsaida, and denied it to Tyre and Sidon ; bestowed it on
unthankful Capernaum, and withheld it from Sodom, which
would have made better use of it. God alone it was who
forbad Paul to preach the Word in Asia ; yea, when he
assayed to go into Bithynia, the Spirit suffered him not, but

he was diverted with a vision, " Come over to Macedonia and help us."

Discussing the conversion of the heathen, he deals with the results of the missionary enterprises of his days. " We shall find more impressions and improvement of the Gospel in these latter ages on Paganism. I have not heard of many fish (understand me in a mystical sense) caught in New England; and yet I have not been deaf to listen, nor they I believe dumb to tell of their achievements in that kind. I speak not this (God knoweth my heart) to the disgrace of any labourers there, being better taught than to condemn men's endeavours by the success : and am so sensible how poorly our ministry prevaileth here at home on professed Christians, that I have little cause and less comfort to censure their preaching for not taking effect upon Pagans. The fault is not in the religion, but in the profession of it, that of late we have been more happy in killing of Christians than happy in converting of Pagans ;" and alluding to the "favourable inclination" of the Gospel to verge westwards, he says : " This putteth us in some hopes of America, in God's due time; God knows what good effects to them our sad war may produce : some may be frighted therewith over into those parts (being more willing to endure American than English savages), or out of curiosity to see, necessity to live, frugality to gain, may carry religion over with them into this barbarous country. Only God forbid we should make so bad a bargain as wholly to exchange our Gospel for their gold, our Saviour for their silver, fetch thence *lignum vitæ* and deprive ourselves of the Tree of Life in lieu thereof. May not their planting be our supplanting, their founding in Christ

our confusion ; let them have of our light, not all our
light ; let their candle be kindled at ours, ours not removed
to them."

As to the objection that there was no danger of the
departure of the Light which was then daily increasing,
preaching, like silver in the reign of Solomon, being so
plentiful that it was nothing accounted of, he replies : " As
all is not gold that glitters, so all is not light that shines,
for glow-worms and rotten wood shine in the dark.   Firebrands also do more harm with their smoke than good with
light.   Such are many incendiaries, which without either
authority of calling, or ability of learning, invade the
ministerial function.   Whose sermons consist only of two
good sentences, the first as containing the text, and the last,
which must be allowed good in these respects, because it
puts an end to a tedious, impertinent discourse.   Notwithstanding all pretended new lights and plenty of preaching,
I persist in my former suspicion."

Then reminding his hearers of that place where they
would need no candle, and sermons should cease, and God
alone be the text, the hallelujahs of saints and angels being
the comment upon it, he concludes : " And now I am to
take my final farewell of this famous city of Exeter.   I have
suffered from some for saying several times that I thought
this or this would be my last sermon, when afterwards I
then preached again.   Yet I hope the guests are not hurt,
if I bring them in a course more than I promised, or they
expect.   Such would have foreborne their censures had they
consulted with the Epistle to the Romans.   In xv. 33, the
Apostle seems to close and conclude his discourse : ' Now
the God of peace be with you all. Amen.'   And yet

presently he beginneth afresh, and continueth his Epistle a whole chapter longer. Yea, in xvi. 20, St. Paul takes a second solemn *vale* : 'The grace of our Lord Jesus Christ be with you all. Amen.' And, notwithstanding, still he spins out his matter three verses further, till that full and final period, verse 27 : 'To God the only wise be glory through Jesus Christ, for ever. Amen.' Thus *loath* to depart is the tune of all loving friends : so same I plead for myself so often taking my farewell, wherein if any were deceived, none I am sure were injured."

Soon after this the garrison, seeing no hope of relief, and straitened for provisions, capitulated. This was March 31st, 1646, on the renewed summons from Fairfax. Fair and honourable terms were the basis of the negotiations. Fuller mentions, with lively satisfaction, that the loyalty of the inhabitants (of the ever faithful city) was unstained and unsullied in this siege. In the preface to the life of Andronicus, Mr Nicholls states that " Fuller's services were of great importance in procuring favourable terms for the garrison and the inhabitants."

The Princess and her household (which included her chaplain, Dr. Fuller) are the first persons alluded to in the Articles (4th) drawn up by six Commissioners on either side : " That the Princess Henrietta, and her governess, with her household, shall have full liberty to pass with their plate, money, and goods within twenty days after the conclusion of this treaty (when she shall desire) to any place within the continent of England or dominion of Wales, at the election of the governess, and these to remain until His Majesty's pleasure be further known touching her settling ; and that the governess shall have liberty to send

to the King to know his pleasure herein ; accordingly to
dispose of Her Highness within the aforesaid limitation of
places ; and that fit and convenient carriages be found for
their passage at reasonable rates." Then Article 5 stipulated for the preservation of the Cathedral and churches,
which was much insisted on. The next that the governors, lords, and clergymen, gentlemen, &c., "should march
out with colours flying," others being of a similar character,
which Fuller considered as "very honourable and comprehensive for the conscience and estates of all concerned."
The governor and his troops marched out, April 13th, when
the city was taken possession of by the enemy, with all the
honours of war,' and dispersed. Fuller spoke of these
Articles in the following terms : " I must not forget the
Articles of Exeter, whereof I had the benefit, living and waiting there on the King's daughter, at the rendition thereof ;
articles which, both as penned and performed, were the
best in England, thanks to their wisdom who so worthily
made, and honesty who so well observed them."

Fuller remained a few weeks longer, when he resigned his
lectureship and left the city he had taught so wisely and
loved so well ; a restful haven, full of sweet and bitter
memories. His royal charge, the young princess, after a
time was by Lady Dalkeith taken across to France, where
she fell into other hands. To Fuller, unfortunately, there
succeeded a very different tutor in the person of Père
Cyprien, the Capuchin friar. She was a girl of 16, when at
the Restoration she visited London. Like her mother she
was fond of intrigues, and she was considered at the French
Court the fairest princess in Christendom, and one of the
wittiest women in France. She married in 1661 the Duke

of Orleans, brother of the French King, but after an unhappy life, she died at the early age of 26.   The city of Exeter did not forget her, and the Chamber voted her £200 at the Restoration, for purchase of plate, which was presented to her in the name of the city.   Her portrait now adorns the walls of the Guildhall, although it is hung in a very bad light.

CHAPTER XVII.

UNSETTLED AND TROUBLOUS TIMES.

"This nation is scourged with a wasting war. Our sins were ripe; God could no longer be just if we were prosperous. Blessed be His name that I had suffered my share in the calamities of my country. Had I poised myself so politicly betwixt both parties, that I had suffered from neither, yet could I have taken no contentment in my safe escaping. . . . It is therefore some comfort that I draw in the same yoke with my neighbours, and with them jointly bear the burden which our sins jointly brought upon us."---(*Mixt Contemplations*, xvi.)

E must now accompany the whilom and witty tutor of the Princess Henrietta and Ex-Court Chaplain from Exeter to the metropolis. Things were going from bad to worse. Times were indeed bad, and out of joint. Politically, the Royalist cause was fast waning, and the monarchy was tottering to its destruction. The Church fared little better, ecclesiastically and socially all was confusion and disorder. "England doth lie desperately sick of a violent disease in the bowels thereof," wrote Fuller. And here is his picture of the morals of the day. "We have," he said, "taken the saint-ship from those in heaven, but have no more holiness in ourselves here on earth. What betwixt the sins which brought this war, and the sins which this war hath brought, they are sad presages of '*better times.*' Never was God's name more taken in vain by oaths and imprecations. The Lord's Day, formerly profaned with mirth, is now profaned

with malice, and now as much broken with drums as formerly with tabor and pipe. Superiors never so much slighted, so that what Nabal said sullenly and (as he applied it) falsely, we may say sadly and truly, 'There be many servants now-a-days that break away every one from his master.' Killing is now the only trade in fashion, and adultery never more common, so that our nation (in my opinion) is not likely to confound the spiritual whore of Babylon, whilst corporal whoredom is in her everywhere committed, nowhere punished. Theft so usual that they have stolen away the word of *stealing* and hid it under the name of plundering. Lying both in word and print grown epidemical, so that it is questionable whether guns or printing (two inventions of the same country and standing), do more mischief in this kingdom. It is past ' coveting of our neighbours houses,' when it is come to violent keeping of them. He, therefore, that doth seriously consider the grievousness and generality of these sins, will rather conclude that some *darkness of desolation* than any 'great light' is likely to follow upon them." And again, writing three years later, " Vice, these late years, hath kept open house in England."

The articles connected with the "rendition" of the good and faithful city of Exeter to the Parliamentarian forces under Fairfax, provided our divine (included in the terms under the head *clergymen*) with a safe conduct to London. This enabled him to be an eye-witness of the dismal state of the country through which he journeyed, as well as that of the metropolis itself. He passed by the scenes of former labours, and his former refuge, the stronghold of Basing, then a heap of ruins. His journey to town must have been very melancholy to one of his loving and patriotic nature, seeing on all sides the disjecta membra of this internecine warfare. His horizon was gloomy in the extreme, and everything seemed against him. The Royal cause was completely lost, the King himself was practically a captive. The liturgy and Book of Common Prayer, the living voice of his "dear mother," the Church of England, had been prohibited, both in public and private; and the same Parliamentary ordinance, which had abolished Episcopacy and silenced the Church's voice in the Prayer Book, established the Presbyterian form of Church polity, and sanctioned extempore prayer. Church and Monarchy therefore (and in this country they will always stand or fall together), both lay in the dust, and the political outlook was of the gloomiest. Fuller must have noticed great changes since his three years' sojourn in the Royalist camp. His own prospects were anything but bright. Without preferment, without any chance of professional employment for the present in the National Church, without means, and for the time almost friendless, he set his face to go to London, yet hardly knowing whither he went. What kind of a welcome would he get there? Would his old friends receive him now that he had declared so emphatically for Church and King? Would his congregation and parishioners of the Savoy recognise their former pastor and popular minister of happier days? Like the patriarch of old he went up, full of faith it may be, but low in spirits and much depressed.

Our author found a temporary home with his publisher, John Williams, arriving at his house about the end of May. Williams may have had some balance in hand as the results of the sale of his two very popular works the "Holy War" and the "Holy State." "No stationer ever lost by me," Fuller says in another place: and no doubt there must have been something due to him, which would in all probability have been forestalled by debts, contracted in this unsettled period, and which item figures largely in the various petitions for composition. That of our author's is still extant at the Record office, but there is nothing to show the state of his monetary affairs, or literary prospects, at the time.

When Fuller visited the Savoy, he found his former hearers dispersed, and the parish much changed, socially and ecclesiastically. He may be said to have "come to his own, but his own received him not." The pulpit of the Savoy Chapel was occupied by one Mr. Bond, formerly of Exeter, before Fuller's time, and previously to his acceptance of the Bodleian lectureship there; so he and the Doctor may be said to have exchanged pulpits all this time. Bond was a native of Dorchester, evidently possessed considerable powers as a popular preacher, though a setter forth of "strange positions, rebellious conceits, and religious cantings; and on his return to his lectureship at Exeter was rewarded with a piece of plate for his services. But for Fuller there was no return to his Savoy preferment. Fuller, it may be, was reflecting his own thoughts as to his desolate condition when he wrote about Josiah Shute, the rector of St. Mary Woolnoth, "the most precious jewell that was ever shown or seen in Lombard Street," in the following terms : " He was for many years, and that most justly, highly esteemed of the parish ; till in the beginning of our late civil wars, some began to neglect him, distasting wholesome meat well dressed by him, merely because their

Y

mouths were out of taste by that general distemper which in his time (he died 1640) was but an *ague*, afterwards turned to a *fever*, and since is turned to a frenzy in our nation.   I insist hereon the rather for the comfort of such godly ministers, who now suffer in the same nature wherein Mr. Shute did before.   Indeed, no servant of God can simply and directly comfort himself in the sufferings of others (as which have something of envy therein) ; yet may he do it consequentially in this respect, because thereby he apprehends his own condition herein consistent with God's love and his own salvation, seeing other precious saints taste with him of the same affliction, as many godly ministers do now-a-days, whose sickles are now hung up as useless and neglected, though before these civil wars they reaped the most in God's   harvest."   ("Worthies, Yorkshire," p. 211).

As to the relations between pastor and people, Fuller has some very pertinent remarks : "Some clergymen who have consulted God's honour with their own credit and profit could not better desire for themselves than to have a Lincolnshire church, as best built; a Lancashire parish, as largest bounded ; and a London audience, as *consisting of most intelligent people.*"   And again : " Protestants in some kind serve their living ministers as Papists their dead saints : for aged pastors, who have borne the heat of the day in our Church, are justled out of respect by young preachers, not having half their age, nor a quarter of their learning and religion.   Yet let not the former be disheartened, for thus it ever was, and will be,—English Athenians, all for novelties, new sects, new schisms, new doctrines, new disciplines, new prayers, new preachers."

He thus speaks with contempt of those who were put
into the priest's office of the ejected clergy during the interregnum without a university education, or proper training:
"How many now-a-days (1655), without any regret, turn

pr $\begin{cases} \text{aters} \\ \text{eachers} \end{cases}$ without any commission from the Church! It

is suspicious on the like occasion, some would scarce follow
Bilney to the stake, who run so far before him into the pulpit."
And again on the same topic he writes, anent the case of
Paul and Barnabas being solemnly separated for the ministry (Acts xiii. 15); "They behaved not themselves in
God's house during the exercise of God's ordinances like
some spiritual clowns now-a-days, whose unreverend deportment bewrays their ignorance: but so decently they
demeaned themselves, that they struck the beholders into a
reverent opinion of their persons, and conjecture at their
profession to be preachers of God's Word." Like Hooker
(who regarded the reading the lessons as part of preaching,
and the most important part too), he speaks very highly of
the written Word: "Some conceive that the Word *preached*
is as much holier than the Word *read* as the pulpit is
higher than the desk. But let such know that he which
doth not honour all, doth not honour any of God's
ordinances."

Fuller's opinion with regard to preachers may be gathered
from these words: "None are to preach but such as are
lawfully called thereunto. The rulers of the synagogue gave
a license to Paul and Barnabas, who intrude not without
their leave or desire. How many now-a-days (1654),
despight of the rulers of the synagogue, the undoubted
patron, the lawful incumbent, the guardians of the Church

publicly chosen—storm the pulpit by their mere violence, without any call or commission thereunto."

Again: "Should such a person appear, commencing *per saltum*, complete in all sciences and languages, so that all the tongues which departed from Babel in a confusion, should meet in his mouth in a method, it would give assurance to others that these his gifts came down from the Father of Lights, if willingly submitting to the examination and ordination of such, to whom it properly doth belong. Otherwise, if amongst all other gifts, the essential grace of humility be wanting, it will render the rest suspected from what fountain they do proceed.

"But let us survey what gifts those are, which generally are most boasted of by *opposers* in this point. God is my witness, I speak it without bitterness or any satyrical reflection. Are they not for the most part such as may be reduced to boldness, confidence, memory, and volubility of tongue? Might they not truly say of many of their sermons what the sons of the Prophets said of their axe (2 Kings vi. 5), 'Alas! it's borrowed'—venting chiefly the notes and endeavours of others. But grant their gifts never so great, graces so good, parts so perfect, endowments so excellent, yet mere gifting without calling makes not a lawful preacher." ("Hist. Camb.," p. 94.)

Want of charity, however, was the chief failing of the preachers of his time. "In my father's time," he writes, "there was a Fellow of Trin. Coll., Cambridge (Joseph Mede), a native of Carlton, in Leicestershire, where the people (thorow some occult cause) are troubled with a wharling in their throats, so that they cannot plainly pronounce the letter *r*. This scholar, being conscious of his

infirmity, made a Latin oration of the usual expected
length without an *r* therein ; and yet did he not only select
words fit for his mouth, easy for pronunciation, but also
as pure and expressive for signification, to show that men
might speak without being beholding to the dog's letter.
Our English pulpits for these last eighteen years (1642—
1660) have had in them too much caninal anger, vented by
snapping and snarling spirits on both sides. But if you bite
and devour another (saith the Apostle, Gal. v. 15), take
heed ye be not devoured one of another. Think not that
our sermons must be silent if not satirical, as if divinity did
not afford smooth subjects enough to be seasonably insisted
on in this juncture of time (1660); let us try our skill whether
we cannot preach without any dogletter or biting word;
the art is half learned by intending, and wholly by serious
endeavouring it."

In his occasional Meditations he says, " Our age (1647)
may seem sufficiently to have provided against the growth of
idolatry in England. Oh, that some order were taken for
the increase of CHARITY ! It were liberty enough if for the
next seven years all sermons were bound to keep residence
on this test, " Brethren, love one another" (vii., p. 210).
Clarendon speaks of the numbers of ministers who preached
from their favourite text in Judges v. 23, "Curse ye Meroz,"
&c., touching which Fuller remarks, " If it were a city, new
queries are engendered where it is to be placed. For the
exact position thereof we refer the reader to those of our
learned divines, which in these unhappy dispensations have
made that text so often the subject of their sermons."
(Pisgah Sight, ii.)

How sad it is that in all ages of the Church, ministers

have been prone to forget that beatitude, " Blessed are the peace makers," and instead of looking upon the Gospel as an εἰρηνικὸν have made it an arena of strife, being carried away with that bitterest of all enmities, the *odium theologicum.*"

Soon after his arrival in town, Fuller set about endeavouring his composition for his estates, which no doubt mainly occupied the few months he remained in London. This was a very delicate matter, and according to the articles agreed upon at the rendition of Exeter (xii) it was stipulated that the composition should not exceed two years' value of any man's real estate : and for personal or similar proportion, "which composition being made, they shall have indemnity for their persons and enjoy their estates, and all other immunities, without the payment of any fifth." To arrive at the desired consummation our author penned the following document about May :

"To ye Honorable Comittye at Goldsmythes' Hall.

"Your petitioner Thomas Fuller, late of ye Savoy in London, and since attendant in Exeter on ye Princess Henrietta, beeing there present at ye rendition of ye Citty.

"Requesteth that late coming to this Cittye, and now lodging at ye Croune in Pauls' Churchyeard, hee may have ye benefit of Exeter Articles, to endeaour his composition, according to same articles confirmed by ordinance of Parliament, until ye expiration of ye four monethes, from ye date of those articles, and he shall, &c.

"Regd. pximo Junij, 1640.

"THOMAS FULLER."

Touching this document, it would seem that Fuller did not write the word honourable, which the clerk inserted, also it was addressed first of all by him to the Haberdashers. The word Crown is also "writ large," as if to show the writer's lingering loyalty for the then falling Monarchy. Other peculiarities may also be detected in this letter, which no doubt effected its purpose.

All this time Fuller was endeavouring "to be restored to the exercise of his profession on terms consisting with his conscience." The Savoy chaplaincy had slipped out of his grasp, but he was trying to secure the lectureship of St. Clement's, Eastcheap (with the concurrence of the parishioners) which he actually did obtain the following year. It was impossible to get a living, such was the temper of the times, and Fuller would not, we may believe, certainly consent to give up the use of the liturgy. The penalty for using it was £5 for the first time, £10 for the second, and a year's imprisonment for the third. Fuller, therefore, was thrown back on other resources, and to his pen and literature. He refers to his straitened means in the following meditations, "How shall God make my bed, who have no bed of my own to make? Thou fool! He can make thy not having a bed to be a bed unto thee," instancing Jacob's sleep on the ground. And again, "Small are my means on cash. May I mount my soul the higher in heavenly meditation, relying on Divine Providence. He that fed many thousands with 'five loaves,' may feed me and mine with the *fifth part* of that one loaf, which once was mine." This last fraction has reference to an order whereby the sequestrators had the power of setting part one fifth (not more) of the sequestered estates for the use of delin-

quents' wives and children.   But inasmuch as Clergymen
were not mentioned, they were supposed to be outside the
order, which Fuller much complained of, averring that,
" Covetousness will wriggle itself out at a small hole."
This led to much altercation, and when they were paid,
the fifths were paid at *sixes* and *sevens*.   Walker says when
paid, they were at the rate of *tens* and *twelves*.

During this time also, while living under his publisher's
roof, he took up his pen the more vigorously, as he was
debarred the carrying on the duties of his clerical profession.
He fell back on literature, stirring up that gift that was in
him, intending to spend the residue of his days in composing useful books and edifying stories.   Here he published
his Exeter sermon, and brought out another edition of his
" *Good Thoughts.*"   He also published a little work, intending it as a lampoon upon the bad times, called " *Andronicus ;
or, the Unfortunate Politician.   Shewing Sin, Slowly
Punished.   Right, Surely Rescued.*"   Two editions of this
popular work appeared the same year, and the third in
1649, and it is the only work of Fuller's which was ever
translated into a foreign language.   There is a Dutch
edition to be seen at the British Museum, dated Amsterdam,
1659, which no doubt, was owing to the exertions of some
of the cavalier refugees in Holland, whither many had
betaken themselves, " Lately written in English by the
Reverend, learned, and ingenious Dr. Thomas Fuller, Court
Preacher to Charles I., King of Great Britain, H.L.M.,
Translated by Johannes Crosse."   This curious work, which
the Dutch edition entitles " Andronicus, or Unfortunate
Subtilty : containing a true account of the short but cruel
and tyrannical Government, sudden downfall and fearful

death of Andronicus Comnenus, Emperor of Constantinople," was embodied in the 1648 edition of the " Profane
State," where, without the preface and index it has remained
ever since. It is to be found in one of Pickering's reprints.

It is the supposed life of the Grecian Emperor Andronicus Comnenus, who reigned from A.D. 1163 to 1185.
The biography was printed in a small-sized volume, under
two hundred pages, and divided into six books, with a full
index. Mr. Nicholls, one of Fuller's editors, thus gives
his reasons why he thus expanded his brief memoir and
published it at the time he did. " During these four years
of active service in the war (1643-46) he had ample
opportunities of becoming acquainted, through friends and
foes, with the views of both the belligerent parties: and
knew many clever men whose culpable cupidity was then
excited, and who did not attempt to dissemble their
eagerness to derive personal profit and aggrandisement from
our national convulsions. He was induced therefore to
enlarge this article, and with all the appendages of a true
historical narrative, to form into a kind of *Menippean satire*
on the ambition, avarice, cruelty, and other destructive vices
which had then sufficiently developed themselves in the
leading characters of the Republican movement. It has
been regarded by moderate men of every party as a
salutary and reasonable warning to all those who were engaged
in ambitious unpatriotic projects, during that distressing
season of domestic warfare. In reference to many curious
events which subsequently occurred, Fuller's broad
intimation proved to be eminently prophetic: but in none
of his anticipatory delineations was he afterwards accounted
to have been more felicitous, than in the speech of

Andronicus on the eve of his being elected to be join. Emperor with the youthful Alexis Comnenus, which might have been purposely indited a pattern for that of Cromwell, when he reluctantly declined the faintly-proffered sovereignty of these realms, and with much apparent coyness accepted the Protectorate. Other then uncontemplated coincidences will be obvious to everyone who is acquainted with the historical records of those times of civil discord (Nicholl's *Holy State*, p. 400).

There is a brief notice of Andronicus himself in our author's history of the *Holy War*, where he records that the usurper succeeded his cousin Alexis, whom he strangled. "A diligent reader, and a great lover of St. Paul's Epistles, but a bad practiser of them : who (rather observing the devil's rule, that it is the best way for those who have been bad to be still worse) fencing his former villainies by committing new ones, and held by tyranny what he had gotten by usurpation : till having lived in the blood of others, he died in his own, tortured to death by the headless multitude, from whom he received all the cruelties which might be expected from servile natures when they command." These full details into which Fuller entered were, however, taken "from the black copy of his wicked actions."

There are some, who have risen from the perusal of this and his other stories, with the regret that Fuller did not (from finding subsequently professional employment as a preacher) pursue his intention of writing more of these entertaining and felicitous stories, to which, especially at this break in his official career, he seems to have fully determined to devote himself.

Before giving a few extracts from this remarkable work, which attained such sudden and deserved popularity, we will give the preface to the original edition, containing, as it does, much of personal interest :

"We read of King Ahasuerosh, that having his head troubled with much business, and finding himself so indisposed that he could not sleep, he desired the *Records* to be called for, and read unto him, hoping thereby to deceive the tediousness of the time (an honest fraud), and that the pleasant passages in the Chronicles would either invite slumber unto him, or enable him to endure waking with less molestation.

" We live in a troublesome and tumultuous age : and he needs to have a very soft bed who can sleep soundly now-a-days amidst so much loud noise, and many impetuous rumours. Wherefore it seemeth to me both a safe and cheap receipt to procure quiet and repose to the mind, which complains for want of rest, to prescribe unto it the reading of History. Great is the pleasure and profit hereof. Whereupon until such times as I shall by God's providence, and the Authority of my superiors, be restored to the open exercise of my profession, on terms consisting with my conscience (which welcome minute I do heartily wish, and humbly wait for : and will greedily listen to the least wisdom sounding thereunto), it is my intent, God willing, to spend the remnant of my days in reading and writing such stories as my weak judgment shall commend unto me for most beneficial.

" Our English writers tell us of David, King of the Scots, that whilst he was a prisoner in a cave in Nottingham Castle he, with his nails *(carved,* shall I say ? or) scratched

out the whole history of our Saviour's passion in the wall.
And although the figures be rough and rude, yet in one
respect they are to be compared unto, yea, preferre d before
the choicest pieces and most exact platforms of all en-
gravers, being done at such disadvantages, cut out of a
bare rock, without any light to direct him, or instrument to
help him, besi les his bare hands.

"The application of the Story serves me for manifold
uses.   First, here I learn, if that princes, then meaner
persons, are l und to find themselves some honest employment.   Secol lly, that in a sad and solitary condition,
a Calling is a comfortable companion.   Thirdly, when men
want necessa: s, fit tools and materials, the work that they
do (if it be iy degree passable) deserves, if not to be
praised, to l ardoned.   Which encourageth me to expect
of the charit: le reader favour for the faults in this tract
committed, w a he considers the author in effect banished
and bookless. il wanting several accommodations requisite
to the comple ig an history.

"Noah, to ke an essay whether 'the waters were abated
from the face the earth' before he would adventure to
expose the w e fraught of his Ark to danger, dispatched
a dove to ma discovery, and report unto him the condition of the v ld, intending to order himself accordingly.
A deep delug hath lately overflowed the whole kingdom
to the drown ; of many, and dangering of all.   I send
forth this s l treatise to try whether the swelling
surge and bo ng billows in men's breasts (flowing from
the distance their judgments, and difference in their
affections) be now to assuage, and whether there be a
dry place for s my innocent dove safely to settle her-

self. If she find any tolerable entertainment, or indifferent approbation abroad, it will give me encouragement to adventure a volume of a more useful subject and greater concernment in the view of the world. (Probably referring to his 'Church History.') Thine in all Christian offices, THOMAS FULLER."

We will now present our readers with one or two sketches of this remarkable book, which may partly explain its rapid popularity. It begins thus : " Alexius Comnenus, only son of Manuel Comnenus, succeeded his father in the empire of Constantinople 1179. A child he was in age and judgment: of wit too short to measure an honourable sport, but lost himself in low delights. He hated a book, more than a monster did a looking-glass, and when his tutor endeavoured to play him into scholarship, by presenting pleasant authors unto him, he returned, that learning was beneath the greatness of a prince, who, if wanting it, might borrow it from his subjects, being better stored ; for, saith he, *if they will not lend me their brains, I'll take away their heads.* Yea, he allowed no other library than a full-stored cellar, resembling the butts to folios, barrels to quartos, smaller runlets to less volumes, and studied away his time, with base company, in such debauchedness."

Here is a gloomy picture of the body politic. " The body of the Grecian State, at this time, must needs be strangely distempered under such heads. Preferment was only scattered among parasites, for them to scramble for it. The Court had as many factions as lords, save that all their divisions united themselves in a general viciousness, and that Theodorus, the patriarch, was scoffed at by all as an antic, for using goodness when it was out of fashion : and was adjudged impudent for presuming to be pious alone by himself."

This is a portrait of Xene, Alexius' mother, the regent Empress. "But he could not be more busy about his war than Xene was employed about her wantonness, counting in life all spilt that was not sport, who, to revenge herself on envious death, meant in mirth to make herself reparation for the shortness of her life. That time, which flieth of itself, she sought to drive away with unlawful recreations, and though music did jar, and mirth was profaneness, at this present time, when all did feel what was bad, and fear what was worse, yet she, by wanton songs (panders to lust), and other provocations, did awaken the sleepy sparks of her corruption into a flame of open wickedness." On the other hand, we have a more pleasing picture of Anna, the Empress. "Daughter she was to the King of France, being married a child (having little list to love, and less to aspire) to the young Emperor Alexius, whilst both their years put together could not spell thirty. After this she had time too much to bemoan, but none at all to amend her condition : being slighted and neglected by her husband. Oft-times being alone (as sorrow loves no witness), having room and leisure to bewail herself, she would relate the chronicle of her unhappiness to the walls, as hoping to find pity from stones, when men proved unkind to her. Much did she envy the felicity of those milkmaids, which each morning pass over the virgin dew and pearled grass, sweetly singing by day, and soundly sleeping at night, who had the privilege freely to bestow their affections, and wed them which were high in love, though low in condition, whereas royal birth had denied her that happiness, having neither liberty to choose nor leave to refuse, being compelled to love, and sacrificed to the politic ends of her potent parents."

This is a description of what Andronicus (now possessed of power) did for Constantinople. "Thus all Constantinople was brought within the compass of her walls, as she remains at this day, not like many ill-proportioned cities of Europe, which groan under over-great suburbs, so that the children overtop the mother, and branch themselves forth into out-streets, to the impairing of the root, both weakening and impoverishing the city itself. He bestowed great cost in adorning the porphyry throne, which a usurper did provide and beautify for a lawful prince to sit upon. He brought fresh water, a treasure in that place, through a magnificent aqueduct into the heart of the city, which, after his death, was spoiled out of spite (as private revenge in a furious fit oft impairs the public good), people disclaiming to drink of his water, who had made the streets run with blood. His benefactions to the Church of Forty Martyrs amounted to almost a new founding thereof, intending his tomb in that place, though it was arrant presumption in him, who had denied the right of sepulture to others, to promote the solemnity thereof unto himself."

The following is a graphic account of the fate of Andronicus :—" Two heavy iron chains were put about his neck, in metal and weight different from those he wore before, and laden with fetters and insolencies from the soldiers who in such war seldom give scant measure, he was brought into the presence of Isaacius. Here the most merciful and moderate contented themselves with tongue revenge, calling him dog of uncleanness, goat of lust, tiger of cruelty, religion's ape, and envy's basilisk. But others pulled him by the beard, twitched his hair left by age on his head, and proceeding from depriving him of ornamental excrements, dashed out his teeth, put out one of his eyes, cut off his right hand : and thus maimed, without surgeon to dress him, man to serve him, or meat to feed him, he was sent to the public prison amongst thieves and robbers."

All these were but the beginning of evil unto him. Some days after, with a shaved head, crowned with garlick, he was set on a scabbed camel, with his face backward, holding the tail thereof for a bridle, and was led clean through the city. All the cruelties which he, in two years and upwards, had committed upon several persons, were now abbreviated and epitomised on him in as large a character as the shortness of time would give leave, and the subject itself was capable of : they burnt him with torches and firebrands, tortured him with pincers, and threw abundance of dirt upon him."

We must draw a veil over this picture, and hasten to his end.

" After multitudes of other cruelties, tedious to us to rehearse, and how painful then to him to endure, he was hanged by the heels between two pillars. In this posture he put the stump of his right arm, whose wound bleeded afresh, to his mouth, so to quench, as some suppose, the extremity of his thirst with his own blood, having no other moisture allowed him, when one ran a sword through his back and belly, so that his very entrails were seen, and seemed to call, though in vain, on the bowels of the spectators to have some compassion on him. At last with much ado, his soul, which had so many doors opened for it, found a passage out of his body into another world."

Speaking of his stature, our author says "he was higher than the ordinary sort of men. He was seven full feet in length, if there be no mistake in the difference of measure : and, whereas often the cockloft is empty in those which nature hath built many stories high, his head was sufficiently stored with all abilities."

It is supposed that our author had London in view in picturing the prosperity of Constantinople "enjoying happiness so long, that now she pleaded prescription for prosperity."

"Because living in peace time out of mind, she conceived it rather a wrong to have constant quiet denied, than a favour from heaven to have it continued unto her. Indeed she was grown sick of a surfeit of health, and afterwards was broken with having too much riches. But instead of honest industry and painful thrift, which first caused the greatness of the city, now flowing with wealth, there was nothing therein but the swelling of pride, the boiling of lust, the fretting of envy, and the squeezing of oppression, so that, should their dead ancestors arise, they would be puzzled to see Constantinople for itself, except they were directed thereto by the ruins of St. Sophie's temple. True, it was some years since, upon a great famine, some hopes were given of a general amendment, during which time riot began to grow thrifty, pride to go plain, gluttons to fast, and wantons were starved into temperance. But forced reformation will last no longer than the violent cause thereof doth continue. For soon after, when plenty was again restored, they relapsed to their former badness : yea, afterwards became fouler for the purge, and more wanton for the rod, when it was removed."

Although Fuller was one of the most moderate of men, he thus writes of those who belonged to neither party: " Neuters are of that lukewarm temper, which heaven and hell doth hate. . . . They hoped, though the vessel of the State was wracked, in the private fly-boat of neutrality to waft their own adventure safe to the shore. Whoever saw dancers on ropes so equally to poise themselves, but at last they fell down and brake their necks ? "

We do not know, nor can we glean from his writings, how long our author remained in London, which in those troublous times could not have been the most pleasant place in the world. Some time would have been spent in effecting his composition, which was no easy task, and in trying to get clerical duty, which in those proscribed days of the Anglican Liturgy was a matter of considerable difficulty. Besides this, an ordinance had passed both Houses (December 11th) to put out of the city for two months all " delinquents," *i.e.*, Royalists and Papists, of which there was an extraordinary confluence.

Things being thus unpleasant in the metropolis, having arranged with his publisher about his books being brought out—new works, and fresh editions—we are not surprised to learn that when we next hear of him (January, 1647), he is far away from the city's strife and turmoil, and near his old home in Northamptonshire. Under the well-known hospitable roof of Edward Lord Montagu, a gentleman of great position, and in the confidence of Parliament, and not far from our author's birthplace, Fuller, homeless and distressed, spiritless and troubled, found a welcome asylum and warm reception in the retirement of Boughton House. Here, then, he spent his Christmas, which, if not a merry one, was at all events quiet and restful; supported by the sympathy of the old friends of his youthhood, and cheered with the prospect of better times.

Two deaths had occurred in this family which now received our author, since he had been there. They were that of his old literary associate, Christopher Montagu, who died in 1641, "that he might not be entangled in the evils to come." The old baron, too, who had fallen under the displeasure of the Parliament in 1642, was taken prisoner at Boughton House. Clarendon describes him as "a person of great reverence, being above fourscore years, and of great reputation." At first it was arranged for him to have been consigned, as his prison, to the house of his daughter, the Countess of Rutland; but this he refused, as she was busily engaged in the Parliament cause, which was irksome to him. Ultimately he was lodged in the prison of the Savoy, where he died June 15th, 1644. Fuller thus alludes to his death: "To have no bands in their death (Ps. lxxiii. 4.) is an outward favour many wicked have, many godly men want; amongst whom this good lord, who died in restraint in the Savoy, on the account of his loyalty to his Sovereign. Let us not grudge him the injoying of his judgment, a purchase he so dearly bought and truly paid for." ("Worthies, Northampton," p. 292.) He it was who said to his daughter-in-law, whose Puritanism caused her to disparage the Liturgy, which was daily read in his household, "Daughter, if you come to visit me, I will never ask you why you come not to prayers: but if you come to cohabit with me, pray with me, or live not with me."

Fuller was not unmindful of the kind hospitality which he had received from this noble family, which he much needed, and was so grateful to him. His acknowledgment was made some four years after to a son of the old baron, in the dedication of the " Plan of Jerusalem " ; " Who when I was feeble, an exile, a nobody (*i.e.,* undone and good for nothing), was the first to take care of me, to receive me under his roof, to restore me by his munificence to my former self, and (as the sum of all) to provide generously for the education of my darling boy, the solitary hope of my old age."

This timely retreat at *Boughton House* in his jaded and dejected state, and his return to his own native air and hospitable scenes and surroundings of former times, seems to have restored our author to his "former self." The mansion was well placed in a spacious park, covered with avenues of trees ; it was richly wooded, watered with streams, and the grounds were of an undulating character— a sylvan retreat, calculated to inspire peace and induce repose. It belongs to the Duke of Buccleuch (the lineal descendant of the first Lord Montagu), and is situated on the road to Stamford, three miles to the north of Kettering. The old house, which was much smaller than the present one, which has been arranged in the French manner, contains many portraits of the Montagus who were Fuller's contemporaries. The park extends up to the village of Weekley—in which parish Boughton is—which is about a mile distant from the house. This was the parish church of the Montagus, and in the parochial registers are to be found many of the baptisms, marriages, and deaths of this family. It is just possible, Fuller, complying as far as he could with the law, may have preached in this church ; but there was no " preacher's book " in those days, as the ministers were under the protection of the lord of the manor, Lord Montagu.

Our author, during his stay at Boughton House, was once more brought into the neighbourhood of royalty, and not far from the person of his beloved Sovereign. The King had been brought by the Commissioners to Holmby House in Northamptonshire, and was right loyally received. So much so, that Fuller at this time wrote of the King that he daily "grew greater in men's hearts, pregnant with the love and affection of his subjects." Lord Montagu was in close attendance on the King during the four months he spent at the mansion, passing his time in study, hawking, with occasional visits to Lord Spencer's house at Althorp for games at bowls. Upon the King's arrival he made a request (which had been before refused) for the attendance of two or more of his chaplains, "for the exercise of his conscience, and the assistance of his judgment, in deciding upon the present differences respecting religion." In the list of names furnished by the King himself was Dr. Sheldon and "Dr. Fuller" (this was probably the Dean of Ely, who at that time was busy in London about his composition), but the royal request was refused.

Among Fuller's friends at this time we may mention a sister of Lord Montagu, Frances, Countess of Rutland, who was making her old home again in Boughton House, which was then a safer retreat than Belvoir Castle, the seat of her husband, the Earl. Our author for many years, especially during their sojourn in London, was well known to the Countess, who possessed not her father's spirit, but strong royalist proclivities, which prompted her to befriend Dr. Fuller, and other eminent royalist clergymen. Amongst

these, also a friend of his, was the venerable Bishop of
Durham, Dr. Thomas Morton; of him Fuller records that
" in the late long Parliament the displeasure of the House
of Commons fell heavy upon him, partly for subscribing the
Bishop's protestations for their votes in Parliament, partly
for refusing to resign the seal of the bishopric, and baptising
a daughter of John, Earl of Rutland, with the sign of the
cross; two faults which, compounded together, in the
judgment of honest and wise men, amounted to a *high
innocence.*" This infant was one of the daughters of Frances
Montagu. He was imprisoned for six months, and on his
release became the charge of the Earl and Countess of
Rutland, at Exeter House. "He solemnly professed,"
added Fuller, " unto me (pardon me, reader, if I desire
publicly to twist my own with his memory, that they may both
survive together), in these sad times to maintain me to live
with him, which courteous offer, as I could not conveniently
accept, I did thankfully refuse. Many of the nobility
deservedly honoured him, though none more than John,
Earl of Rutland, to whose kinsman, Roger, Earl of Rutland,
he formerly had been chaplain." This aged Bishop, who
had befriended many good men, and raised the tomb in
Westminster Abbey to Casaubon, died in 1659.

It was under the hospitable roof of this Northamptonshire retreat that our author wrote his deservedly popular
work and pious treatise, which he called, in his fondness for
alliteration, " The *Cause* and *Cure* of a Wounded *Conscience*"
(1646), which contains an analysis of his mental depression,
after the manner of Burton's " Anatomy of Melancholy."
It is dedicated to the Right Honourable and Virtuous Lady
Frances Manners, Countess of Rutland, sister of Edward,

the second Lord Montagu of Boughton, touching which pleasing surrounding and scenery one writes : " Some of his most touching and beautiful utterances seem to owe much of their charming power to his own happy sense of harmony between the beauty of nature and loveliness of grace. Surrounded by the quiet joys of an unfolding Creation, he looks as if he could feel nothing but love for his bitterest foes : and now he murmurs forth his devout thoughts, the very thoughts which he bequeaths to us for ' the cure of the wounded conscience.' "*

The dedication runs as follows, and is very Fullerian in form and feeling : " Madam, by the judicial law of the Jews, if a servant had children by a wife which was given him by his master, though he himself went forth free in his seventh year, yet his children did remain with his master as the proper goods of his possession.   I ever have been, and shall be, a servant to that noble family, whence your Honour is extracted.   And of late in that house I have been wedded to the pleasant embraces of a private life, the fittest Wife and meetest helper that can be provided for a student in troublesome times: and the same hath been bestowed upon me by the bounty of your noble brother, Edward Lord Montagu : wherefore, what issue soever shall result from my mind, by his means most happily married to a retired life, must of due redound to his honour as the sole proprietary of my pains during my present condition.   Now this book is my eldest offspring, which, had it been a son (I mean had it been a work of masculine bigness and beauty), it should have waited as a Page in dedication to

* " Worthies, York," p. 229.
* " Homer of Old English Writers."

his honour.   But finding it to be of the weaker sex, little
in strength and low in stature, may it be admitted (Madam)
to attend on your Ladyship, his honour's sister.   I need
not remind your Ladyship how God hath measured outward
happiness unto you by the cubit of the sanctuary—of the
largest size, so that one would be posed to wish more than
what your Ladyship doth enjoy.   My prayer to God shall be
that, shining as a pearl of grace here, you may shine as a
star of glory hereafter."

A sustained gravity, as befits the subject, marks this
much-esteemed work, our author remarking, that as it
would be out of keeping to wear gaudy clothes at a funeral,
so in "this sad subject" he had endeavoured "to decline
all light and luxurious expressions."   The work consists of
twenty-one separate dialogues, well constructed and connected together, which contain many beautiful and soothing
passages, familiar to most.

Mr. Russell, in his comments on this work, evidently
claims Fuller as Calvinistic in his tendency, if not teaching.
" Let those who object to what some ignorantly call even
yet solifidianism and fatalism, as being doctrines of licen-
tiousness, mark the following passage : ' Sorrow for sin
exceeds sorrow for suffering, in the continuance and dura-
bleness thereof : the other, like a landflood, quickly come,
quickly gone ; this is a continual dropping or running river,
keeping a constant stream.   *My sins*, saith David, *are ever
before me ;* so also is the sorrow for sin in the soul of a
child of God—morning, evening ; day and night ; when
sick, when sound ; feasting, fasting ; at home, abroad—ever
with him.   This grief beginning at his conversion ; continueth all his life ; endeth only at his death."

After glancing at the Antinomian error of many in those days, who were utterly opposed to all *marks* of sincerity, counting it needless for preachers to propound, or people to apply them, he proposes the following test : " Art thou careful to order thy very thoughts, because the infinite Searcher of the hearts doth behold them ? Dost thou freely and fully confess thy sins to God, spreading them open in His presence without any desire or endeavour to deny, dissemble, defend, excuse, or extenuate them ? Dost thou delight in an universal obedience to all God's laws, not thinking with the superstitious Jews, by overkeeping the fourth commandment to make reparation to God for breaking all the rest? Dost thou love their persons and preaching best who most clearly discover thine own faults and corruptions unto thee ? Dost thou strive against thy vindictive nature, not only to forgive those who have offended thee, but also to wait an occasion with humility to fasten a fitting favour upon them? Dost thou love grace and goodness even in those who differ from thee in point of opinion in civil controversies ? Canst thou be sorrowful for the sins of others, no whit relating unto thee, merely because the glory of a good God suffers by their profaneness ?" On signs of sincerity in repentance he says : " As I will not bow to flatter any, so I will fall down as far as truth will give me leave, to reach comfort to the humble to whom it is due. Know to thy further consolation, that where some of these signs truly are, there are more, yea, all of them, though not so visible and conspicuous, but in a dimmer and darker degree. When we behold violets and primroses to fairly flourish, we conclude the dead of the winter is past, though as yet no roses or July flowers appear, which long after lie hid in their leaves, or lurk in their roots; but in due time will discover themselves. If some of these signs be above ground in thy sight, others are underground in thy heart; and though the former started first, the other will follow in order; it being plain that thou art past from death unto life, by this hopeful and happy spring of some signs in thy heart."

He thus points the moral of a wounded conscience by the example of Adam : " When Adam had eaten the forbidden fruit he tarried a time in Paradise, but took no contentment therein. The sun did shine as bright, the rivers ran as clear as ever before, birds sang as sweetly, beasts played as pleasantly, flowers smelt as fragrant, herbs grew as fresh, fruits flourisht as fair, no punttilio of pleasure was either altered or abated. The objects were the same, but Adam's eyes were otherwise : his nakedness stood in his light: a thorn of guiltiness grew in his heart before any thistles sprang out of the ground : which made him not to seek for the fairest fruits to fill his hunger, but the biggest leaves to cover his nakedness. Thus a wounded conscience is able to unparadise Paradise itself." (P. 27.)

Fuller urges the continuance of prayer and of reading the Scriptures, in spite of inward deadness of heart, that in due time discomfort may be removed; and the sure result of a steadfast adherence to the appointed aids. *He commends the discreet use of confession of sin to some godly minister, who, by absolution, may pronounce and apply pardon to the afflicted spirit.*

But whilst the sincerity of our faith may be surely proved and known by its effects, as the life of a tree by its fruit, in despair, or rather, when we are strongly tempted to it (and no, or but few, sincere Christians are there but will be so tempted), it is our only resource to " look upwards to a gracious God " then " it is not thy faith but God's faithfulness thou must rely upon : casting thine eyes downward on thyself, to behold the great distance betwixt what thou deservest and what thou desirest, is enough to make thee giddy, stagger, and reel into despair." This true broken-heartedness is that which all need, and which a thorough self-knowledge would impart to all, to all who know the mystery of redemption, and whose hearts are all touched by it. And how can those esteem the physician who know not their own wounds? He Himself said, " To whom little is forgiven, the same loveth little." It is not for sinners proudly to refuse the comfort of this truth."

This excellent manual concludes with this poetical passage : " Music is sweetest near or over rivers, where the echo thereof is best rebounded by the water. Praise for pensiveness, thanks for tears, and blessing God over the floods of affliction, makes the most melodious music in the ear of Heaven."

Fuller was not long in preparing, in his rural retreat, for the press another devotional manual, reflecting his own mentally depressed state, and taking its complexion from the perturbations of the times. It is not dedicated, as the author remarks : " Dedications begin now-a-days to grow out of fashion." But in his remarks to the " Christian reader " he laments over the " worse times " which form his gloomy subject : " How many thousands know as little why the sword was drawn, as when it will be sheathed. Indeed (thanks be to God), we have no more *house* burnings, but many *heart* burnings ; and though outward *bleeding* be

The Life of Fuller.

stanched, it is to be feared that the broken vein bleeds inwardly, which is more dangerous." Under these circumstances he considered that controversial writing (sounding somewhat of drums and trumpets) did but make the wound the wider. "Meditations are like the minstrel, the prophet called for (2 Kings, iii. 15) to pacify his mind discomposed by his passion." On this account he "adventures on this treatise"—a smaller treatise—as the most innocent and inoffensive manner of writing, and putting off for the present his larger-sized promised work on *Church History*.

These "Good thoughts in Worse Times" are like those written and published as the "First Fruits of Exeter Press," divided into four sets of twenty in each—" Personal Meditations," "Scriptural Observations," "Meditations on the Times, and all sorts of Prayers"; in all a hundred exactly.

Turning to his "Personal Meditations," we find him saying of himself: "These last five years have been a wet and woeful seedstime to me, and many of my afflicted brethren. Little hope have we as yet to come again to our own homes; and in a literal sense how to 'bring our sheaves,' which we see others daily carry away on their shoulders. I have endeavoured, in these distemperate times, to hold up my spirits and steer them steadily. A happy peace here, was the port whereat I desired to arrive. Now, alas, the storm grows too sturdy for the pilot. Hereafter all the skill I will use, is no skill at all, but even let my ship sail whither the winds send it. This comforts me that the most weather-beaten vessel cannot properly be seized on for a wrack which hath any quick cattle remaining therein. My spirits are not forfeited to despair, having one lively spark of hope in my heart, because God is even where He was before."

Alluding to his seeking peace, and illustrating his position from David's history, he says : " Peace did long lie languishing in this land. No small contentment that, to my poor power, I have *prayed* and *preached* for the preservation thereof. Seeing, since it is departed, this supports my soul, I having little hope that peace here should return to me. I have some assurance that I shall go to peace hereafter." He prays that God in due time would send " such a peace in this land, as Prince and people may share therein." And he concludes boldly : " May I die in that Government, under which I was born, where a monarch doth command."

In his " Scripture Observations " the following passage occurs in " Prayer may preach " ; " When before sermon I pray for my Sovraign and master, King Charles of Great Britain, France and Ireland, Defender of the Faith, in all causes and over all persons, and some (who omit it themselves) may censure it in me for superfluous. But never more need to teach men the King's title, and their own duty, that the simple may be informed, the forgetful remembered thereof, and that the affectedly ignorant, who will not take advice, may have all excuse taken from them. Wherefore, in pouring forth my prayers to God, well may I therein sprincle some by-drops for the instruction of the people."

Fuller's views on the course of events are seen in his " Meditations on the Times." " There was not long since a devout but ignorant Papist dwelling in Spain. He perceived a necessity of his own private prayers to God, besides the Pater-nosters, Ave Maries, &c., used, of course, in the Romish Church. But so simple was he that how to pray he knew not, only every morning humbly bending his knees, and lifting his eyes and hands to heaven, he would deliberately repeat the alphabet. 'And now,' said he, 'O, good God, put these letters to spell syllables, to spell words, to make such sense, as may be most to Thy glory and my good.' In these distracted times, I know what *generals* to pray for: God's glory, truth and peace, his Majesty's honour, privileges of Parliament, liberty of subjects, &c. But when I descend to *particulars*, when, how, by whom I should desire these things to be effected, I may fall to that poor pious man's A. B. C. D. E., &c."

Our author's " Observations on all kinds of Prayers," are very characteristic ; " of *groans* which never knew their own meaning" he says that "God knows the meaning, and that He understood those *Sighs*, which never understood themselves. *Ejaculations* are short prayers darted up to God on emergent occasions; their principal use is against the fiery darts of the devil. In *extemporary prayer*, what we most admire, God least regardeth, namely the volubility of the tongue. He gives such prayers their full dues, and frees them from a causeless scandal." He exalts the *Lord's Prayer*, which, "in this age we begin to think meanly of." He concludes, " Oh, let us not set several kinds of prayer at variance betwixt themselves, which of them should be most useful, most honourable. All are most excellent at several times. No ordinance so abused as prayer. Prayer hath been set up against preaching, against catechising, against itself. See how St. Paul determines the controversy πάσῃ προσευχῇ with all manner of prayer (so the Geneva translation) and supplication in the spirit."

This, then, was the great period of Fuller's literary activity, when he was debarred from preaching, and unofficially correlated in regard to his sacred profession. Notwithstanding that he was cut off from his books and manuscripts, he contrived to collect materials for, and push on the compilation of, his celebrated *Church History.* He also published a translation of Archbishop *Ussher's Annales*, with whom he was on very friendly terms. Ussher was chosen preacher of Lincoln's Inn, in June, 1646, and while he was in London the most eminent divines were wont to resort to him as to a father. It was there, too, that our author, his partner in misfortune, again met the prelate, who gave him valuable assistance in his compilation of the *Church History.* In the early portion of that work, Fuller refers to his "engagement" with Ussher as to the religion of the early British, saying that from him he had "borrowed many a note." Fuller also acknowledges that his "wares" were from the "storehouse of that reverend prelate, the Cape merchant of all learning." He says further, "Clean through this work, in point of chronology, I have with implicit faith followed his computations, setting my *watch* by his *dial*, knowing his *dial* to be set by the *sun.* Long may he live for the glory of God, and good of His church. For whereas many learned men, though they be deep abysses of knowledge, yet (like the Caspian sea, receiving all and having no outlet) are loth to impart aught to others, this bright sun is as bountiful to deal abroad his beams, as such dark dales as myself are glad and delighted to receive them."* We are told that Archbishop Ussher intended to publish a third part of his "Chronicle," but death put an end to his design.

* Book ii. 150.

CHAPTER XVIII.

ROYALIST EXILE, AND MENDICANT DIVINE (1647-49).

"How do many (exiles in their own country) subsist now-a-days on nothing : and wandering in the wilderness of want (except they have manna miraculously from Heaven) they have no meat on earth from their own means. At what ordinary, or rather extraordinary, do they diet, that for all this have cheerful faces, light hearts and merry countenances? Surely some secret comfort supports their souls. Such never desire but to make one meal all the days of their lives on the 'continual feast' of a good conscience. The fattest capons yield but sad merry thoughts to the greedy glutton in comparison of those delightful dainties which this dish daily affords such as feed upon it."— (*Meditations on the Times*, viii.)

IT was hard times now with the Royalist partisans, and especially the divines and clergy, with their livings in the hands of the opposite party, and their tithes sequestrated. They had to lead a wandering life, and vagabond existence. With the Patriarch of old, "they went out not knowing whither they went" : with the great Apostle they might truly say " in journeyings often." This was pre-eminently the case with our author. The time came for him to leave the hospitable retreat and charming surroundings of Boughton House, and to seek a fresh asylum amongst those patrons of the ejected clergy, the munificent laity of the day, scattered up and down the land, endeavouring to find employment outside, but not unsuitable to, his clerical profession. Thus he writes of him-

self : " How do many exiles in their own country subsist now-a-days of nothing, wandering in a wilderness of want (except they have manna miraculously from heaven) they have no meat on earth from their own means. At what *ordinary*, or rather, *extraordinary*, do they diet, that for all this have cheerful faces, light hearts, and merry countenances ? Surely some secret comfort supports their souls. Such never desire but to make one meal all the days of their lives on the ' continual feast ' of a good conscience." (Prov. xv. 15.) Alluding to the statute against wandering scholars (1388), he says : " Indeed, I have ever beheld begging scholars as the most improper objects of charity : who must be vicious, or else cannot be necessitous to a mendicant condition. *But since*, I have revoked my opinion, the calamity of this age falling so heavily on scholars, that I am converted into a charitable conceit of such who beg the charity of others."

We have seen that Lord Montagu was one of the first who befriended our wandering Divine. Others also are mentioned, who possibly gave, about this time, protection and relief to the poor clergy, a temporary shelter to those upon whom—as the whilom staunch supporters of Church and King, with tongue, pen, and means—this political storm of internecine warfare beat most pitilessly. Thus Fuller thus writes to Mr. Thomas Rich, of Sunning, Berks, in 1655 : " You are, sir, the Entertainer-General of all good men. Many a poor minister will never be wholly sequestered whilst you are living, whose charity is like to the wind, which cannot be seen, but may be felt." This patron had made a considerable fortune in the Turkey trade, and like Fuller was an exceedingly corpulent person. He not only liberally assisted the poor clergy, but furnished Prince Charles with funds. Again, Fuller says, in his dedication of *Ruth* to Lady Ann Archer, in 1654, quoting the verse "none communicated with me concerning giving and receiving but ye only" : * "Should I apply the same in relation of myself to your ladyship, I should be injurious to the bounty of many of my worthy benefactors. However (not exclusively of others, but) eminently I must acknowledge you a great benefactor of my studies." Another of Fuller's patrons was Mr. Thomas Adams, Lord Mayor of London, 1646, who had in 1632 founded a professorship of Arabic in Cambridge, "a man of great length in his extraction, breadth in his estate, and depth in his liberality," and "deservedly commended for his Christian constancy in all conditions."

Among his other patrons may be mentioned Dr. Hammond, and Bishop Jeremy Taylor. Both these eminent Divines were much respected. Dr. Hammond was the learned commentator on the Scriptures "well versed in all modern pamphlets touching Church Discipline," and is described by Fuller as "the tutelar angel to keep many a poor Royalist from famishing ; it being verily believed that he yearly gave away more than £200." His friendship "had an especial place for sequestered divines, their wives and orphans, for young students in the Universities, and also those divines that were abroad in banishment." Jeremy Taylor, the celebrated preacher, and author of " Life of Christ," " The Golden Grove," " Holy Living and Dying," was also a great friend of the ejected clergy, and

---

* Phil. iv., 15.

being so trustworthy, much of the private contributions passed through his hands. There is a good story told of this marvellous prelate. Once preaching before Laud, the Archbishop remarked that it was " too good a sermon for such a young Divine !" to which the preacher made the rejoinder " that if he lived, he would easily cure *that* fault." His learning, too, was so prodigious that it was said at his death, that if it had been bequeathed to the whole of his diocese, each of his clergy would then be richly endowed. Besides these patrons of the poor clergy, we may mention Thomas Palmer, the sequestered minister of St. Bride's, Fleet Street, and Dr. Scarborough, who, on leaving Oxford, 1647, practised in London, where his hospitable board was " always accessible to all learned men, but more particularly to the distressed Royalists, and yet more particularly to the scholars ejected out of either of the Universities."

Other friends of the ejected Royalist clergy were Dr. Warner, Bishop of Rochester, John Crane, a Cambridgeshire worthy, William Chappell, Milton's College tutor at Christ College, Bishop of Cork and Ross, who, coming over here to escape the rebellion, says Fuller, "rather exchanged than eased his condition, such the woefulness of our civil wars. He died Anno 1649, and parted his estate almost equally betwixt his own kindred and distressed ministers, his charity not impairing his duty, and his duty not prejudicing his charity": then there was Dr. Warmistry, Fuller's associate, the Dean of Worcester, who lived mostly in London, distributing alms collected from the Royalists to the clergy. The Dean was chief confessor to loyal martyrs, a constant and indefatigable visitor and comforter of sick and distressed cavaliers. He was also a great preacher.

But Fuller's chief benefactor was Sir John D'Anvers, who for many years treated our Divine with the most generous bounty ; a name, unfortunately, mixed up with the Regicides at a subsequent period of our history, and therefore not in good odour with the Royalists. However, at this period he was very kind to Dr. Fuller, with whom he had probably been acquainted in his native county. Whether our author applied to him for assistance remains in obscurity ; but this is quite clear, that Sir John encouraged him with favour and patronage ; and being of the same school of thought—the moderate section—and a favourer of Episcopacy, from this epoch a close intimacy sprung up between the two, which considerably relieved our author from his temporary embarrassments.

It must be borne in mind that the portrait-sketch given of Sir John, drawn by Clarendon, belongs to a later period of the history ; but at the time we are writing he was, as far as we can gather, loyal to Church, if not to King. It should therefore be read in connection with the event which generated it. Our author's intimacy with Sir John, who, leaving his office in the King's household, joined the Parliamentary forces, attained to some eminence in that party, and painted as black as he has been by Clarendon, Bates, and others, has been much discussed. But it must be remarked that very often the *social* intercourse of families remained uninterrupted during these civil wars, in spite of those political feuds and theological animosities which divided the nation into two hostile camps, and moreover a good deal of courteous civility obtained even among opponents. At all events, Fuller seems to have had a good opinion of his benefactor, towards whom he evinced lively feelings of gratitude for his protection. Besides this, the " Worshipful " Knight, by an annual and ample exercise of bounty, raised our author's fortunes at a time when they were, as he himself expresses it, not only tottering, but actually prostrate (*non modo nutantes sed plane jacentes*). These particulars are set out in the dedication of his " Pisgah Sight " to Sir John's son, and a friend.

Sir John D'Anvers seems to have been a jovial, open-hearted man, one who could enjoy a good joke and hearty laugh. In appearance he was very fair, of a beautiful complexion, small but intelligent eyes, a well formed nose, slightly retrousé, a round face and open forehead. Whatever their political relationships, or even theological proclivities, may have been, no doubt there was much in common between the two men, if they were not altogether kindred spirits. Fuller did not probably hold the office of " chaplain " to his household, though he may have preached occasionally in his private chapel, but he would be a frequent visitor, not to say resident, and a very pleasant companion at all times. We can well imagine our witty Divine's spirits rising under the genial influences, and the depression of spirits and melancholy wearing off, would, such was his fund of humour and inexhaustible good nature, become the life and soul of the party, keeping the table in fits of laughter. If, after the manner of Coleridge's "Table Talk," the witticisms of this quaint Divine—the outcome of the feast of wit and flow of soul—had been taken down, what a fund of entertaining anecdotes, punning alliterations, piquant sayings, and interesting *repartee*, we should have had, for it has been well said Fuller was

"Formed by his converse happily to stir
From grave to gay."

One of Fuller's ardent admirers writes: "How delightful must have been the conversation of Fuller, varied, as it was, with exuberance of knowledge, enlivened with gossiping, chastened by good sense, and sparkling with epigrammatical sharpness of wit, decorated with all its native fantastical embroidery of humorous quaintness! We verily declare for ourselves, that if we had the power of resuscitating an individual from the dead to enjoy the pleasure of his conversation, we do not know anyone on whom our choice would sooner fall than Fuller."* Fuller, no doubt, knew full well how to comport himself both in grave and gay hours in the household of his protector. He himself says of such positions: "God's prophets are no lumber, but the most profitable stuff wherewith an house can be furnished. Landlords prove no losers by such tenants (though sitting rent-free), whose dwelling with them pays for their dwelling with them.† Sir John D'Anvers lived at Chelsea, of whom saith John Bates, in his *Lives of the Regicides*, "Though he lived some years in his disloyalty without repentance, yet, drawing near the time of his death, I have cause to believe that he repented of the wickedness of his life: for that then Mr. (now Dr.) Thomas Fuller was conversant in his family, and preached several times at Sir John Danvers, his desire, in Chelsea Church: where I am sure all that frequented that congregation will say he was instructed to

---

* "Retrospective Review," ii, 51.
† Pisgah ii. 161.

repent of his misguided and wicked consultations, in having
to do with the murder of that just man, the King ;" thus
proving himself a model chaplain after George Herbert's
pattern.

It was at this time Fuller was bestirring himself to take
a more energic part in public matters, and becoming more
eager to resume the active duties of his profession. Jeremy
Taylor was calling public attention to the freedom of the
silenced clergy in his *Liberty of Prophesying*, and was doing
his utmost to restore them to their official responsibilities.
Fuller's friends and patrons, such as the Montagus and
Danvers, were also busily engaged in pushing him forward,
till at last we find him obtaining employment. Once again,
we find our Divine in possession of a metropolitan pulpit,—
the pulpit he loved so well,—preaching to a London
audience. But we must not forget the altered condition of
London life in these two hundred years. The metropolitan
pulpit had more weight in those days than it has now, both
in London and the provinces, and that is why there was
such a contention between the two rival political parties to
secure the city churches, and "tune the pulpits." The influence was incalculable, and went far towards deciding the
political problems of the day. In fact, London was then
more to England at large, what Paris has always been to
France.* Now we have changed all this. The City
churches, except in a few remarkable instances,

---

* The London of Whittington, surrounded by its grey walls,
two miles and a quarter in length, has been described as a small,
compact town—smaller, for instance, than the modern Jerusalem—smaller than Hyde Park. Modern London is a vast
congeries of cities, towns, boroughs, hamlets, and villages, which

are nowhere; some have been pulled down, and the audiences are to be found in the principal centres of suburban life. London, too, has become a congeries of suburbs; it is a county rather than a city, and no one can tell where it begins and where it ends; its population, too, has grown out of all proportions, and equals that of a small kingdom. But we are talking of the London of 1647, when it was compact, not an overgrown city—a measurable community; and the word fitly spoken would make itself heard and felt through the town. It was the end of March of that year when our Divine preached with such acceptance, that he became *lecturer* of St. Clement's, East Cheap. This was the first of those many lectures which Fuller held from time to time, for which he was indebted to his friends, merchants and residents, who had not forgotten him. The rector of this parish, Benjamin Stone, appointed by Laud in 1637, appears to have been ejected and imprisoned, and finally sent to Plymouth, driven away by the political troubles of the period. During his absence, the churchwardens managed the temporalities, and the entries in the vestry book make it probable that the services of the church were during this time entirely discharged by various lecturers. In the vestry minute book there is an entry, dated July 22, 1647, to the

---

threaten to fill up the valley of the Thames from Hampton Court to Gravesend. Still, there are those who believe that the London of 1881 is as small as the London of 1381. According to a great wit, London is a place bounded on the south by Pall Mall, on the north by Piccadilly, on the west by St. James's Street, and on the east by the Haymarket. Within the bills of mortality there are, of course, other Londons. There is the commercial London, the mercantile London, the literary London, the art London, and above all the political London. Every one of these is a world to those sojourning therein.

effect that the *tithes* should be kept by the churchwardens, and paid to such ministers *as should be appointed:* " Paid for four sermons preached by ,Mr. ffuller, 00I. 06. 08.," sermons from eminent divines being then paid at the rate of a lawyer's fee in modern times. Fuller is said to have preached also a lecture on the Thursday afternoon, at St. Bride's, Fleet Street, but the books of this parish were destroyed, or lost, in the great fire of 1666. Probably he also was permitted to preach again in these churches about or after 1652, as also at the Mercer's Chapel, for he commemorates that company among his benefactors subsequently in his "Church History." These city lecturers, among whom we find the name of Pearson as well as Fuller, were due to the parishioners in vestry assembled, and did not imply compliance with the times. The Puritan party were therefore hoisted by their own petard. For, in opposition to Laud's measures to promote conformity, an ordinance had been passed in 1641, authorising the parishioners "to set up a lecture, and to maintain an orthodox minister at their own charge, to preach every Lord's day when there is no preaching, and to preach one day in every week when there is a weekly lecture." About this time Fuller became *Lecturer* of St. Clement's, and afterwards the old clergy, who had been ejected, began to avail themselves of this ordinance, which thus cut both ways ; and in this way upwards of forty London churches, which in 1648 were without any settled pastorate, became gradually filled with them. Our Divine was probably one of the first of " the old Cavalier parsons " who was again, to his great satisfaction, enabled to resume the active duties of that profession so dear to his heart, by means of a decree of his political opponents. Fuller would seem to have retained his connection with St. Clement's in the two following years, 1648-9, for citations from his sermons during those two years are extant, as well as during the preceding year, when he began his ministrations. And although the names are not specified, no doubt Fuller's name would be covered in the following entry in the parish accounts for 1648: "Paid diverse ministers for preachinge 22 Sabbath daies, beginige the 12th of Nov., 1648.—0.22. 00. 00." Besides which, there were the Wednesday afternoon lectures, which our Divine always delivered. This proves that Fuller's suspension did not last long, for he tells us he was silenced by the prevailing faction. Indeed he informs us in his Dedication of his *Sermon on Assurance:* "It hath been the pleasure of the present authority (to whose commands I humbly submit) to make me mute, forbidding me, till further order, the exercise of my public preaching : wherefore I am fain to employ my fingers in writing, to make the best signs I can, thereby to express, as my desire to the general good, so my particular gratitude to your honour (Sir John Danvers)."

In addition to these lectures we find from a passage in his *Appeal,* that Fuller was also lecturing at St. Dunstan's East, and it was here that the following laughable incident took place in connection with his wonderful *memory,* which even by that time had become remarkable. We have it from Fuller himself in his *Church History* in a rejoinder to his great antagonist, Dr. Peter Heylin, who had written thus of our author : "If our author be no better at a pedigree in private families than he is in those of kings and princes, I shall not give much for his art of *Memory,* for his *History* less, and for his *Heraldry* just nothing." To this

Fuller replied, writing in 1659, "When I intend to expose them to sale, I know where to meet with a franker chapman. None alive ever heard me pretend to the art of memory, who, in my book ("Holy State") have decreed it as a trick, no art, and indeed is more of fancy than memory. I confess, *some ten years since*, when I came out of the pulpit of St. Dunstan's East, one (who since wrote a book thereof) told me in the vestry, before *credible* people, that he, in Sydney College, had taught me the art of memory; I returned unto him that it was not so : *for I could not remember that I had ever seen his face*, which I conceive was a real refutation." This certainly was a *Roland* for his *Oliver.* Who these *credible* people were, we are not told, possibly the churchwardens, or sidesmen, or some leading persons in the congregation, came into the vestry, as was usual in those days, to pay their respects to the Doctor, but, whoever they were, they must have keenly relished the joke.

We must not, however, suppose that Fuller was not grateful for his splendid endowment of a good memory (apart from any memoria technica) which he undoubtedly had, for he concludes thus : "However, seeing that a natural memory is the *best* flower in mine, and not the worst in the animadvertor's (Dr. Heylin's) garden, let us turn our competitions herein unto mutual thankfulness to the God of heaven," and, "thankfulness to God for it," he says elsewhere, "continueth the memory."

In his chapter on "Memory" in his *Holy State*, Fuller says : "It is the treasure house of the mind, wherein the monuments therefrom are kept and preserved. Plato makes it the mother of the muses. Aristotle sets it one degree further, making experience the mother of arts, memory the parent of experience. Philosophers place it in the rear of the head, and it seems the mine of memory lies there, because there men naturally dig for it; scratching for it when they are at a loss. This, again, is two-fold : one the simple retention of things, the other regaining them when forgotten. After illustrating, by the Bee, his contention that the *brute creatures equal if not exceed man* in a *bare retentive memory*, he says that *artificial memory is rather a trick than an art,* and *more* for the gain of the *teacher than profit* of the *learners.* Like the tossing of a pike, which is no part of the postures and motions thereof, and is rather for ostentation than use, to show the strength and nimbleness of the arm, and is often used by wandering soldiers as an introduction to beg. Understand it if the artificial rules, which at this day are delivered by memory-mountebanks, for sure an art thereof may be made, wherein as yet the world is defective, and that no more destructive to natural memory than spectacles are to eyes, which girls in Holland wear from twelve years of age."

These are some of the *plain rules* which our author insists on : " *Soundly infix in thy mind what thou desirest to remember.* What wonder is it if agitation of business jog that out of thy head which was there rather tacked than fastened? Whereas those notions that get in by violenta possessio will abide there till ejectio firma, sickness or extreme age, dispossess them. It is best knocking in the nail over night, and clinching it the next morning. *Overburthen not thy memory to make so faithful a servant a slave.* Remember, Atlas was weary. Have as much reason as a camel, to rise when thou hast thy load full. Memory, like a purse, if it be over-full that it cannot shut, all will drop out of it. Take heed of a gluttonous curiosity to feed on many things, lest the greediness of the appetite of thy memory spoil the digestion thereof. *Marshal thy motions unto a handsome method.* One will carry twice more weight, trussed and packed up in bundles, than when it lies untowardly flapping and hanging about his shoulders. Things orderly fardled up under heads are most portable."

He also gives other plain rules: " Sport not thy memory with thine own jealousy, nor make it bad by suspecting it. Adventure not all thy learning in one bottom, but divide it betwixt thy memory and thy notebooks. Moderate diet and good air preserve memory"; but what air is best he does not define ; "some say a pure and subtle air is best, another commends a thick and foggy air. For the Pisans, sited in the fens and marshes of Arnus, have excellent memories, as if the foggy air were a cap for their heads."

How long our Divine held the lectureship of St. Clement's, and what was the duration of prohibition from preaching, which assuredly was levelled against him about this time, seems involved in some obscurity, but his anonymous biographer informs us in what spirit, and with how much con-scientiousness he recommenced his ministrations. " A living was not the design of the good doctor, who knew how incompatible the *times* and his *doctrine* must needs be. However, as he had private opportunities, he ceased not to assert the purity of the Church of England, bewailing the sad condition into which the grevious abominable sins of the nation had so far plunged it as to make it more miser-able by bearing so many reproaches and calumnies grounded only upon its calamity. But some glimmering hopes of a settle-

ment and understanding betwixt the King and the pretended
Houses appearing, the pious doctor betook himself to
earnest prayers and petitions to God that He would please
to succeed that blessed work, doing that privately as a
Christian, which he might not publicly do as a subject, most
fervently imploring in those families where his person and
devotions were alike acceptable, the blessing of a restoration on his afflicted Church, and its defenceless defender the
King" (pp. 37-8).

We can well imagine Fuller's difficulty at this time. He
was too pronounced a churchman, he was too prominent a
divine, he was too popular a preacher, he was too methodi-
cally orthodox, though moderate a theologian, to hold his anomalous position as lecturer long. Attracted by the fame of his
preaching, select and rapt audiences would gather round the
well-known and deservedly popular lecturer at St. Clement's
on Wednesday mornings, and St. Bride's on Thursday
afternoons, as we have remembered to have seen gather
round Melvill, and heard used to come from all parts to hear
Watts Wilkinson in the last generation, on Tuesday mornings, at the Golden Lectureship of St. Margaret's, Lothbury,
in the City, hard by the Exchange. There they would listen
to his eloquent addresses, and recognise the true ring of his
doctrine as a fearless exponent of the Catholic doctrines of
his beloved Mother, the National Church, in which he had
been brought up, and the patriotism of his aspirations for
his country, the loving allegiance towards his sovereign lord,
King Charles, of glorious memory. But he was too outspoken for the times, and his Royalist proclivities were too
well ascertained. The Parliamentarian party, with its two rival
factions of Independents and Presbyterians—struggling for

mastery in its womb—took knowledge of him ; that he was *among* them, but not *of* them. They remembered his whilom influence at the Savoy, when minister thereof, his flight to Oxford, his enthusiasm at Basing, his influence at Exeter, as Court-chaplain, and tutor to a scion of the Royal house. They knew his stubborn implacable character as a "Church and King" man. This could not be endured, a popular Royalist preacher, in spite of his influential friends, and so they got him silenced. He had to thank the rendition Articles of Exeter that nothing worse followed his so great freedom of speech, and potential utterance. We have Fuller's own words to this effect (in a preface to a sermon of 1641):— "We read how Zechariah, being struck dumb, called for table books thereon to write his mind, making his hands to supply the defect of his mouth ; it hath been the pleasure of the present authority (to whose commands I humbly submit) to make me mute, forbidding me till further order the exercise of my publick preaching." It is evident that Fuller had given offence, and was one of the malignants referred to in the following gravamen, addressed to the House of Commons (December 25th, 1647)—if the House really sat on Christmas-Day—in reference to "countenancing of malignant ministers in some parts of London, where they preach and use the Common Prayer Book contrary to the ordinance of Parliament ; and some delinquent ministers were invited, and did preach on this day, being Christmas Day. The House upon debate ordered that the committee for plundered ministers have power given them to examine and punish churchwardens, sequestrators, and others that do countenance delinquent ministers to preach, and to commit them if they see cause."* This, of course, referred to *public*

---
* Rushworth vii. 944.

ministrations, for he might do that privately as a Christian, which he could not do publicly as a subject. But this drove our Divine to officiate and preach amongst those families which gave him and other of his brethren the protection and privilege of doing so. Thus Evelyn says in his diary (March 18th, 1648-9) :—" Mr. Owen, a sequestered and learned, minister, preached in my parlour ; he gave us the blessed Sacrament, *now wholly out of use in the parish churches*, on which the Presbyterians and fanatics had usurped."

London, at this time, was full of many ejected clergymen, who had been driven from their cures as parish priests, their livings sequestrated, and had made their way up to town, drawn thither by their common misfortunes. We do not know if they sunk so low as many of the ex-curés in France have done, who to the number of scores and hundreds may be met with in Paris driving cabs, and as conductors of omnibuses, but they had to get their living as best they could, some by teaching and keeping schools, or in other ways, many being supported by the bounty and liberality of wealthy Royalists, who relieved them privately. Among these worthies we again meet with Dr. William Fuller, Dean of Ely, who was well known to our Divine, and many others of his contemporaries. He was then a great sufferer for the Royal cause, and helped, being in London at that time, his son-in-law, Dr. Walton, who had come up from Oxford to proceed with his work, the Polyglot, or many-languaged Bible, which had been projected at that University, being also assisted by the advice of the learned and religious Dr. Ussher, Primate of Ireland, and with the permission therein of Dr. Juxon, Bishop of London. The Dean signed this work as a coadjutor. Our Divine in 1655, adding this "excellent work," which was published in 1657, "happily performed as it is worthily undertaken." Dean Fuller died two years later, aged 79, and was buried at St. Vedast (which has become somewhat notorious for the ritualistic persecution of its rector, Mr. Dale), in Foster Lane, where a decent monument was raised to his memory by his daughter, Jane Walton.

The character of Dean Fuller has been given in the following eulogistic terms : "He was famous for his prudence and piety, was an excellent preacher, and without doubt he would have risen higher, had it not been for the iniquity of the times." And Lloyd says of him " that he was a general scholar, well skilled in his own and former times, a good linguist: those languages which parted at Babel in confusion met in his soul in a method : a deep divine, a grave man, whose looks were a sermon, and affable withal. Such a pattern of charity himself, and so good a preacher of it, that he was (with S. Chrysostom) called the poor man's preacher."

Our author, with more learned leisure than usual, betook himself to his literary labours and pen with redoubled energy. His anonymous biographer says "he presently recommenced his laborious enterprise (*i.e.* his "Worthies"), and by the additional help of books, the confluence and resort of learned men (his acquaintance) to their fleecing and tyrannical Courts and Committees newly erected, it made such a progress that from thence he could take a fair prospect of his whole work." Again, "that desired affair (the agreement of the King and Parliament) went on slowly and uncertainly, but so did not the Doctor's book: for having recommended the first to the Almighty wisdom, he stood not still expecting the issue, but addressed himself to his study, affording no time but the leisure of his meals (which was short) to the hearing of news, with which the minds and mouths were full employed by the changeableness of the army, who played fast and loose with the King and Parliament, till in conclusion they destroyed both." *

During this time Fuller was engaged also on his *Church History*, the first three books of which were mainly written in the reign of Charles I.

It was at this period of his life that Fuller, prohibited from the exercise of his public preaching, published some of his smaller sermons, the first being his *Sermon of Assurance*, which he had preached in Cambridge in 1633. It was "exposed to public view (1647) by the importunity of his friends," and the preacher gave his style as *late* Lecturer of Lombard Street. Speaking of this place, having critically examined the register and examined into the circumstances of the case, he tells us of the finding (Feb. 16th, 1647) of a coffin and a corpse, underneath two skeletons, both complete and unconsumed. "Had this happened," he says, "in the time of Popery, what a stock had been here to graft a miracle upon." He dedicates this Sermon on Assurance to that " honourable and nobly accomplished Knight, Sir John D'Anvers," in the following terms: "Wherefore I am fain to employ my fingers in writing to make the best signs I can, thereby to express as my desire to the general good, so my particular gratitude to your honour. May this treatise but find the same favour from your *eye* as once it did from your *ear*, and be as well accepted when read as formerly when heard. And let this humble dedication be interpreted a weak acknowledgment of those strong obligations your bounty hath laid upon me. Well may you taste the fruits of that tree whose roots your liberality hath preserved from withering. Sir, these hard times have taught me the art of frugality, to improve everything to the best advantage : by the same rules of thrift this my dedication, as returning thanks for your former favour, so begs the continuance of the same. And to end, as I began, with the example of Zechariah, as his dumbness was but temporary, so I hope by God's goodness and the favour of my friends, amongst whom your honour stands in the highest rank, the miracle may be wrought, that the dumb may speak again, and as well by words publicly profess, as now by his hand he describes himself, your servant in all Christian offices, Thomas Fuller."

In his address "To the Christian Reader" we get a glimpse, not only of our author's relations to the "powers that be," but his prospects about his future predicatorial career. "I shall be short," he says, "in my addresses unto thee : not only because I know not thy disposition, being a stranger unto thee, but chiefly because I am ignorant of my own present condition, remaining as yet a stranger to myself. Were I restored to the free use of my Function, I would then request the concurrence of thy thanks with mine to a gracious God the Giver, and honourable Persons the dealers, of this great favour unto me. Were I finally interdicted my calling, without hope of recovery, I would bespeak thy pity to bemoan my estate. But, lying as yet in the Marshes between Hope and Fear, I am no fit subject to be condoled for, or congratulated with. Yet it is no piece of Popery to mantain that the prayers of others may be beneficial, and available for a person in my Purgatory condition. Which moves me to crave thy Christian suffrages that I may be rid of my present torment on such terms as may tend to God's glory, mine own good, and the edification of others. However matters shall succeed, it is no small comfort to my conscience that in respect of my Ministerial Function I do not die Felo-de-se, not stabbing my profession by my own laziness, who hitherto have and hereafter shall improve my utmost endeavours, by any lawfnl means to procure my restitution. When the Priests would have carried the ark after David, David forbad them to go further. ' If,' said he, ' I shall find favour in the eyes of the Lord, He will bring me again, and show me both it and His habitation. But if He thus say, I have no delight in thee : behold, here am I, let Him do to me as seemeth good unto Him.' Some perchance would persuade me to have my pulpit carried after me, along with me to my private lodgings : but hitherto I have refrained from such exercise as subject to offence, hoping in due time to be brought back to the pulpit, and endeavouring to compose myself to David's resolution. And if I should be totally forbidden my Function, this is my confidence: that *that great pasture* of God's Providence, wherein so many of my Profession do daily feed, is not yet made so bare by their biting but that, besides them and millions more, it may still comfortably maintain thy friend and servant in Christ Jesus, Thomas Fuller."

Our Divine takes his text from II Peter, i., 10., "Wherefore the rather, brethren, give diligence to make your calling and election sure," a well-known controversial passage. Referring to the description of curious but needless points, he wittily compares them to *Ehud's dagger,* "short, but sharp: and although it be now fallen into a lame hand (the unworthiness of the Preacher in this place) to manage it, yet, enforced with the assistance of God's arm, it may prove able to give the deadly blow to four *Eglon sins* tyrannizing in too many men's hearts; (1) Supine negligence in matters of Salvation; (2) Busy meddling in other men's matters; (3) Preposterous curiosity in unsearchable mysteries; (4) Continual wavering, or Scepticalness concerning our calling and election.

"*Supine negligence* is despatched in those words *give diligence.* This grace of Assurance is unattainable by ease and idleness. *Busy meddling in other men's matters* is destroyed by the particle *your.* Each one ought principally to intend his own assurance. *Preposterous curiosity* is stabbed with the order of the words *calling and election,* not election and calling. Men must first begin to assure their calling, and then *ascendendo* argue and infer the assurance of their election. *Continual wavering* is wounded under the fifth rib in conclusion of my text *sure.* We will but touch at the three first and land at the last (man's apprehension concerning his assurance) as the chief subject of our ensuing discourse." The sermon deals with the momentous question 'Am I His, or am I not?'

The discourse treats of this topic with great tenderness and charity, and admirably illustrates the scriptural soundness of his views. The grace of assurance he shows had been subject to the extremes of fanaticism and Romanism. But in opposition to the former Fuller shows from his text that the assurance of our "calling and election" may be

attained in this life without any miraculous revelation. On
the other hand, he insists that those cannot enter into its
enjoyment who make Christianity a life of worldly conformity, or luxurious ease. " Christianity," he observes, " is a
laborious profession. Observe God's servants clean through
the Scriptures resembled to men of painful vocations : to
Racers, who must stretch every sinew to get first to the
goal : to *Wrestlers* a troublesome employment, so that I am
unresolved whether to recount it amongst toils or exercises
(at best it is but a toilsome exercise) : to *Soldiers*, who are in
constant service and daily duty, always on the guard against
their enemies. Besides, we ministers are compared to *Shepherds*, a painful and dangerous profession amongst the Jews :
to *Watchmen*, who continually wake for the good of others ;
so that, besides the difficulties of our Christian calling, we
are encumbered with others which attend our Ministerial
function."

To those who made this assurance " to be the very being,
essence, life, soul, and formality of faith itself," our Divine
charitably says, " Far be it from me, because dissenting from
their opinions to rail on their persons, and wound with
opprobrious terms the memories of those which are dead ;
rather let us thank God for their learned and religious writings left behind them, knowing that the head of the knowledge of this age stands on the shoulders of the former, and
their very errors have advantaged us into a clearer discovery
of the truth in this particular." (Pp. 5, 10.)

The next sermon we have to notice is one on " Contentment," which was preached in Sir John D'Anvers' private
chapel, and belongs to the year 1648. It is upon the short
text (1 Timothy vi., 6) " Godliness with contentment is great

gain." This sermon is one of the least known and rarest of Fuller's works, nor is a copy to be found in the British Museum. It is for Fuller a very short one, preached to a small but select auditory in a small chapel, and its author calls it Zoar, for is it not a little one? The preaching of this sermon in the knight's "private chapell" throws some light upon our author's relationship with Sir John, who must have opened his pulpit to his friend a Royalist clergyman of ecclesiastical status, rather than to his Parliamentarian preachers. It was not intended for publication, but owing to the importunities of his patron he had it printed. " Good was the counsel which Iaash (Joash) gave Amaziah (2 Chron. xxv., 19), "Abide now at home," especially in our dangerous days, when all *going* is censurable for *gadding* abroad without a necessary vocation. But the next " mainest motive " which put him on that public adventure was the consideration of " my engagements to your noble bounty, above my possibility of deserving it. The Apostle saith it is the part of a good servant (Tit. ii., 9) μὴ ἀντιλέγοντας ' not answering again.' I must confess myselfe your servant, and therefore it ill beseemed me to dislike or mutter against anything you was pleased I should doe. Thus desiring the continuance and increase of all spiritual and temporal happiness on your honour, I commend you to the Almighty. —T.F." *

As the writer cannot meet with a copy of this sermon,† he must be indebted to Mr. Bailey for this account of it, which

---

* Bailey's Life, p. 423.

† Since writing the above, the author has procured a transcript of the only copy, that at Emmanuel College, Cambridge, through the courtesy of the librarian, Mr. Pearson.

he wishes gratefully to acknowledge. He (Fuller) says in the verse preceding his text, ". St. Paul sets forth the worldling's prayer, creed and commandments, which is their daily desire, belief, and practise, and all contained in three words —*gain is godliness*, but the text countermines their opinion or raiseth our antiposition to break down their false conceit," most elegantly crossing and inverting their words. "Take notice," he continues promptly, " of the unaffected elegancy of the Apostle, how clearly and naturally, with a little addition, he turns the worldling's Paradox into a Christian Truth. Though sermons may not laugh with light expressions, yet it is not unlawful for them to smile with delightfull language, alwaies provided that the sweetness of the sawce spoile not the savouriness of the meat. 'The Preacher sought to find out acceptable or pleasant words,' that so his sound matter might be more welcome to his auditors."

The sermon is as quaintly divided as the former. He says that his text presented his auditors with (1) a *Bride*, " Godliness " ; (2) with a *Bridesmaid*, " Contentment " ; (3) with her *Great Portion*, " Gain " ; and (4) with the *present payment thereof*, down on the nail " is." Godliness and Contentment he beautifully likens to Saul and Jonathan, "lovely and pleasant in their lives, and in their death they are not divided. These twin graces always go together." The discourse abounds with passages of interest. He refers to the wild religious extravagancies of the sects of that time. " Ask the tenacious maintainer of some new upstart opinions what Godliness is, and he will answer it in the zealous defending with limb and life of such and such strange tenets, which our fathers perchance never heard of before ; yea, which is worse, such a person will presume so to confine

Godliness to his opinion as to ungodly all others who in the least particular dissent from him. Oh! if God should have no more mercy on us, than we have charity one to another, what would become of us ? Indeed, Christ termeth His own a little flock. 'Fear not, little flock.' (Luke xii., 13.) But if some men's rash and cruel censures should be true, the number of the Godly would be so little it would not be a flock."

In the sermon on " Assurance " he had pointedly censured those who spent much precious time in needless disputes, "the conclusions thereof are both uncertain and unprofitable," and he also here condemns the same class. "It is a true but sad consideration how in all ages men with more vehemency of spirit have stickled about small and unimportant points than about such matters as most concern their salvation. So that I may say (these sorrowful times having tuned our tongues to military phrases) some men have lavished more powder and shot in the defence of some sleight outworks which might well have been quitted without any losse to Religion than in maintaining the main platform of piety, and making good that Castle of God's service, and their own salvation. Pride will be found upon enquiry the principal cause hereof."

As to the vital efficacy of Church ceremonies, etc., his old opinions had undergone no change. "As for all particular forms of Church government, Ceremonies, and outward manner of divine worship, most of them admitting of alterations upon emergencies, and variation according to circumstances of time, place, and persons (though these be more or less ornamental to godlinesse, as they neerer or further off relate to Divine institution). Yet it is erroneous to fixe or place the life or essence of godlinesse therein : we conclude this point with the words of St. Peter :—'Of a truth I perceive that God is no respecter of persons.' But in every nation he that feareth Him and worketh righteous-ness, is accepted with Him : yea, in one and the same nation he that feareth Him and worketh righteousness, of what Sect, Side, Party, Profession, Opinion, Church, Congregation, soever he be, is accepted with Him, as having true godliness in his heart, which, with contentment, is great gain."

The following is a specimen of our author's peculiar eloquence :—"*Great gain* : of what? Let Saint Paul himself, who wrote this Epistle, tell us, when he cast up his audit, what profit he got by the profession of Piety. 'In labours more abundant, in stripes above measure, in prisons more frequent, in deaths oft !' Where is the gain all this while ? Perchance it follows. We will try another verse : 'In journeyings often, in perils of water, in perils of robbers, in perils by mine own countrymen, in perils by the heathen, in perils in the city, in perils in the wilderness, in perils in the sea, in perils amongst false brethren !' Where is the gain all this while ? You will say, these were but the Apostle's adventures, his rich return (slow, but sure) will come at last. Once more we must try. ' In wearinesse and painfulnesse, in watchings often, in hunger and thirst, in fast-ings often, in cold and nakedness.' The further we go the less gain we find. Cushai said unto David 'May all the enemies of my lord the king be as the young man Absalom is.' But if this be given : ' May all the enemies of God and goodness have plenty thereof,' it will never sink into a worldling's head that godliness is gain. Whilst the grandees of piety are found so poore, Eliah begging food of a widdow, Peter without gold or silver, our Saviour himself 'not having where to lay his head.'"

From a perusal of these extracts it will be seen that in Fuller's discourses there was, as usual, plenty of wit, wrapped up in "delightful language," but with him it was always the vehicle of practical divinity. In his case, wit was invariably allied to its sister wisdom ; and, in the witticisms he indulges in, no one can detect the slightest soupçon of irreverence and want of devotion. To use his own words, he "never wit-wantoned it with the Majesty of God." Craik avers that there is not to be found in Fuller's writings probably neither an ill-natured nor a profane witticism. It is the sweetest-blooded wit that was ever infused into man or book. And how strong and weighty, as well as how gentle and beautiful much of his writing is." The author of the *Holy State* could never be profane. In that work there is more than enough to free our author from any suspicion of levity or irreverence, and to him might fairly be applied Rosaline's words of Biron :—

> " A merrier man,
> *Within the limits of becoming mirth*,
> I never spent an hour's talk withal."

"Harmless mirth," says Fuller, "is the best cordial against the consumption of the spirits. Wherefore jesting is not unlawful if it trespasseth not in quality, quantity, or season." "It is good to make a jest, not to make a trade of jesting." "Jest not with the two-edged sword," he says (μάχαιραν δίστομον) of God's word." "Will nothing please thee to wash thy hands in but the font? or to drink healths in but the church chalice?" "And know the whole art is learnt at the first admission, and profane jests will come

without calling." " Wanton jests make fools laugh, and wise
men frown." " Scoff not at the natural defects of any,
which are not in their power to amend. Oh ! 'tis cruelty
to beat a cripple with his own crutches." " Let not thy
jests, like mummy, be made of dead men's flesh." And
again, " It is unnatural to laugh at a natural." " No time
to break jests when the heart-strings are about to be broken."
Of the character entitled, " A Faithful Minister," he would
" not use a light companion to make thereof a grave application, for fear lest his poison go further than his antidote."
Again he says, " Indeed, reasons are the pillars of the
fabric of a sermon, but similitudes are the windows which
give the best lights." He avoids such stories whose mention may suggest bad thoughts to his auditors. Thus the
philosopher Bacon and Fuller are on this subject in the
fullest accord.

Archdeacon Churton was rather hard on our preacher
in calling him " the jester," for his jokes are often full of true
wit. Lloyd's judgment upon our author was that he was not
so skilled where to *spare* his jests, as where to *spend*.
Though Fuller's wit was mainly under his direction, yet on
some occasions he certainly did come " within measurable
distance " of the limits laid down for the province of harmless mirth. He may have sometimes offended both in
quantity and quality, even if his sallies were always " in
season." The ingenuous reader will, however, very readily
make allowance for their cheerful-minded favorite, who has
repeated his opinion that besides entailing a " vigorous
vivacity," an ounce of mirth, with the same degree of grace,
will serve God more, and more acceptably, than a pound of
sorrow. Fuller invariably commended those of a cheerful

spirit, and it is not therefore singular that among such men almost the whole of his intimate acquaintances are to be found.

Fuller's exuberant wit and piety went hand in hand. He is therefore classed with Bishop Earle, La Fontaine, and others, who, as the richest in wit and humour, were also the simplest and kindest hearted of men. Thus their piety never suffered on account of their cheerfulness and wit, but rather commended it ; for, to quote Addison's words, "they make morality appear amiable to people of gay dispositions, and refute the common objection against religion, which represents it as only fit for gloomy and melancholy tempers."

But to return to what Fuller's biographer says of his preaching : "For his ordinary manner of teaching, it was in some kind different from the usual preacher's method of most ministers in those times, for he seldom made an excursion into the handling of common places, or drew his subject-matter out at length by any prolixly continued discourse. But the main frame of his public *sermons*, if not wholly, consisted (after some brief and genuine resolution of the context, and explications of the terms where need required) of notes and observations, with much variety and great dexterity drawn immediately from the text, and naturally without restraint, issuing and flowing, either from the main body or from the several parts of it, with some useful application annexed thereunto ; which, though either of them long insisted upon, yet were wont with that vivacity to be propounded and pressed by him, as well might, and oft did, pierce deep into the hearts of his hearers, and not only rectify and clear their judgments, but have a powerful work also on their affections." (P. 80.)

It was the preacher's opinion that, if surprised with a sudden occasion, a good minister would count himself to be rather excused than commended, if premeditating the bones of his sermon he clothes his flesh *extempore.* Fuller was scrupulously careful in preparing for the pulpit, on which account he appears to have approved of preaching the same sermon often, preferring, like Dean Colet, the meat well done, to that half raw and fresh from the spit. His biographer tells us that " in spite of his prodigious memory, it was not Fuller's habit to quote many Scriptures, finding it troublesome to himself, and ;supposing it would be to his auditors also ; besides deeming it the less needful in regard that his observation being grounded immediately on the Scripture he handled, the necessary consequence, thence deduced, seemed to receive proof sufficient from it." " Heaping up of many quotations," said Fuller, himself free from a vice of his day, "smacks of a vain ostentation of memory."

Nor must we omit to mention that although to a modern audience, which wearies of a sermon over a quarter of an hour, Fuller's sermons would seem of inordinate length, these were remarkably short for his age. As now it is all music, so then it was all preaching, and the " hour glass " was often turned again. Yet he himself says, the faithful minister " makes not that wearisome which should ever be welcome." Wherefore his sermons are of an ordinary length, except on an extraordinary occasion. What a gift had John Halsebach, Professor at Vienna, in tediousness, who to expound the prophet Esay to his auditors, read twenty-one years on the first chapter, and yet finished it not." *

* " Holy State," p. 66.

CHAPTER XIX.

" REGICIDE, AND THE JUST MAN'S FUNERAL " (1649).

" Honour to their memories is more certaine, being sometimes paid them very abundantly, even from those who formerly were so niggardly and covetous, as not to afford them a good word in their life-time.

Defunctus amabitur idem.

So such as rail at, revile, curse, condemne, persecute, execute pious people, speake other language of them, when such men have *passed the Purgation of Death,* and confesse them faithfull and sincere servants of God."—*Abel Redevivus* (Epistle to the Reader).

Praise to our God ! not cottage hearths alone
And shades impervious to the proud world's glare,
Such witness yield : a monarch from his throne
Springs to his Cross and finds his glory there."

KEBLE.

E again find the efforts of Fuller's friends successful, and he was allowed the exercise of his public profession once more, and resumed the duties of his sacred calling. But this permission was given, and liberty was regained at a very gloomy, if not the gloomiest, period in the annals of this country. Our author himself characterised it as " the midnight of misery!" and he tell us in his "Mixt Contemplations" that "it was questionable whether the law should first draw up the will and testament of dying *divinity*, or *divinity* should first make a funeral sermon for expiring *law*. Violence stood ready to invade our property ; heresies and schisms to oppress our religion." The King and Parliament could not come to

terms, and having been taken prisoner, Charles was brought from the Isle of Wight up to London. Here he underwent the mockery of a trial, for his doom was a foregone con- clusion. The spirit of regicide was abroad, which found its expression and concrete embodiment in the "Commons" House of Parliament ; the ungodly and worldling had it all their own way.

"Having received in himself (says Fuller, in his "Church History") the sentence of death, Dr. Juxon, Bishop of London, preached privately before him on the Sunday following, January 28th ; his text, Romans ii, 16, " In the day when God shall judge the secrets of men by Jesus Christ, according to my gospel."

Next Tuesday, January 30th, being the day of his dis- solution, in the morning alone he received the Communion from the hands of the said bishop, at which time he read for the second lesson, the twenty-seventh chapter of St. Matthew, containing the history of the death and passion of our Saviour. Communion ended, the King heartily thanked the Bishop for selecting so seasonable and comfortable a portion of Scripture—seeing all human hope and happiness are founded on the sufferings of our Saviour. The Bishop modestly disavowed any thanks due to himself, it being done merely by the direction of the Church of England,* whose

---

*" True son of our dear Mother, early taught
  With her to worship and for her to die,
Nurs'd in her aisles to more than kingly thought,
  Oft in her solemn hours we dream thee nigh,
For thou did'st love to trace her daily lore,
  And where we look for comfort or for calm,
Over the self-same lines to bend, and pour
  Thy heart with hers in some victorious psalm.

Rubric appointed that chapter the second morning lesson for the thirtieth of January.

His hour drawing nigh, he passed through the park to Whitehall. As he always was observed to walk very fast, so now he abated not any whit of his wonted pace. In his passage, a sorry fellow (seemingly some mean citizen) went abreast along with him, and in an affront often stared his Majesty in the face, which caused him to turn it another way. The Bishop of London, though not easily angered, was much offended hereat, as done out of despiteful design, to discompose him before his death, and moved the captain of the guard he might be taken away, which was done accordingly." (Vol. III., pp. 563-4.)

"Before his own gate at Whitehall," says Baxter, "they erected a scaffold, and before a full assembly of people beheaded him: wherein appeared the severity of God, the mutability and uncertainty of worldly things, and the fruits of a sinful nation's provocations, and the infamous effects of error, pride and selfishness." ("Life," i., 63.)

We take the following graphic description of the death of this saint-king and martyr, "our own, our royal saint," the unfortunate Charles I., from Dr. Lingard's pages: "About two o'clock the King proceeded through the long gallery, lined on each side with soldiers, who, far from insulting the fallen monarch, appeared by their sorrowful looks to sym‑pathize with his fate. At the end, an aperture had been made in the wall, through which he stepped at once upon

---

> And well did she thy loyal love repay ;
> When all forsook, her Angels still were nigh,
> Chain'd and bereft, and on thy funeral way,
>   Straight to the Cross she turned thy dying eye."

KEBLE.

the scaffold. It was hung with black : at the further end were seen the two executioners, the block and the axe ; below appeared, in arms, several regiments of horse and foot, and beyond, as far as the eye was permitted to reach, waved a dense and countless crowd of spectators. The King stood collected and undismayed amidst the apparatus of death. There was in his countenance that cheerful intrepidity, in his demeanour that dignified calmness which had characterized, in the hall of Fotheringay, his royal grandmother, Mary Stuart. It was his wish to address the people; but they were kept beyond the reach of his voice by the swords of the military, and therefore confining his discourse to the few persons standing with him on the scaffold, he took, he said, that opportunity of denying, in the presence of God, the crimes of which he had been accused. It was not to him, but the Houses of Parliament, that the war and all its evils should be charged. The Parliament had first invaded the rights of the Crown by claiming the command of the army, and had provoked hostilities by issuing commissions for the levy of forces, before he had raised a single man. But he had forgiven all, even those, whoever they were (for he did not desire to know their names) who had brought him to his death. He did more than forgive, he prayed that they might repent. But for that purpose they must do three things : they must render to God His due by settling the Church according to the Scripture ; they must restore to the Crown those rights which belonged to it by law ; and they must teach the people the difference between the Sovereign and the subject; those persons could not be governors who were to be governed ; *they* could not rule, whose duty it was to obey. Then, in allusion to the offer formerly made him by the army, he concluded with these words : "Sir, it was for the liberties of the people that I was come here. If I would have assented to an arbitrary sway, to have all things changed according to the power ot the sword, I needed not to have come hither; and therefore I tell you (and I pray God it be not laid to your charge) that I am the martyr of the people."

Having added, at the suggestion of Dr. Juxon, " I die a Christian according to the profession of the Church of England, as I found it left me by my father," he said, addressing himself to the prelate, " I have on my side a good cause and a gracious God."

Bishop : "There is but one stage more ; it is turbulent and troublesome, but a short one. It will carry you from earth to heaven, and there you will find joy and comfort."

King : " I go from a corruptible to an incorruptible crown."

Bishop : "You exchange an earthly for an eternal crown —a good exchange."

" His speech ended, he gave that small paper (some four inches square, containing heads whereon in his speech he intended to dilate) to the Bishop of London."*

Being ready, he bent his neck on the block, and, after a short pause, stretched out his hands as a signal. At that instant the axe descended : the head rolled from the body, and one deep dismal groan, a groan which is said by bystanders to have been something dreadful, beyond human imagination, burst from the multitude of the spectators. But they had no leisure to testify their feelings : two troops

---

* Fuller's " Church History," iii., p. 564.

of horse dispersed them in different directions. One good man, Dr. Fell, after seeing that sight, went home and died.

A man in a vizor performed the office of executioner; another, in a like disguise, held up to the spectators the head streaming with blood, and cried out: "This is the head of a traitor." (Jan. 30th, 1649.)

Such was the end of the unfortunate Charles Stuart; "an awful lesson," says Dr. Lingard, "to the possessors of royalty, to watch the growth of public opinion, and to moderate their pretensions in conformity with the reasonable desires of their subjects. . . . . The men who hurried him to the scaffold were a small faction of bold and ambitious spirits, who had the address to guide the passions and fanaticism of their followers, and were enabled through them to control the real sentiments of the nation. Even of the Commissioners appointed to sit in judgment on the King, scarcely one half could be induced to attend his trial, and many of those who concurred in his condemnation sub-scribed the sentence with feelings of shame and remorse: But so it always happens in revolutions : the most violent put themselves forward; their vigilance and activity seem to multiply their number, and the daring of the few wins the ascendancy over the indolence or the pusillanimity of the many."*

The corpse, embalmed and coffined in lead, which was followed by the Duke of Richmond, the Marquis of Hertford, the Earl of Southampton, and the Earl of Lindsey (to three of whom Fuller was not unknown), was buried a few days after in St. George's Chapel at Windsor,

----

* Lingard's " History of England," vol. viii., 120.

and he who in his life was called the *White King*, from his great purity and because he had been crowned, at his own desire, in white robes, had his coffin, as it passed to the chapel, covered with snow which fell at that time.

This is not the time to discuss the character of Charles, but even Hallam, in his "Constitutional History," who charges the Martyr-King with want of sincerity, is bound to add, "Few personages in history, we should recollect, have had so much of their actions revealed and commented upon as Charles. It is, perhaps, a mortifying truth that those who have stood highest with posterity have seldom been those who have been most accurately known." But we may pray with our Church, "that according to the example of this God's blessed martyr, we may press forward to the prize of the high calling before us, in faith and patience, humility and meekness, mortification and self-denial, charity and constant perseverance to the end." (ii., 229.)

It was intended to use the burial service of the Church over the body, but this, says Fuller, who was not an eye-witness, but received his account from the Duke of Richmond himself, the governor refused. "Coming into the Castle, they showed," writes Fuller, "their commission to the governor, Colonel Wichcot, desiring to inter the corpse according to the Common Prayer Book of the Church of England: the rather because the Parliament's total remitting the manner of the burial to the duke's discretion, implied a permission thereof. This the governor refused, alleging, it was improbable the Parliament would permit the use of what so solemnly they had abolished, and therein destroy their own act."

"All things being then in readiness," with which words,

concludes Fuller his "Church History,"—"the last sheet of my history" he calls it—" Friday, February 9th, the Corpse was brought to the vault, being borne by the soldiers of the Garrison. Over it a *black velvet herse cloth*, the four labels whereof the four Lords did support. The Bishop *of London* stood weeping by, to tender that his service which might not be accepted. There was It deposited in silence and sorrow in the vacant place in the vault (the herse-cloth being cast in after it) about three of the clock in the afternoon, and the lords that night (though late) returned to London." (Book xi., 238.)

Fuller wrote this *last sheet* of his History from the mouth of the Duke of Richmond, "his grace endeavouring to be very exact in all particulars." ("Appeal" ii., 430.)

Within two days of the funeral, the House of Lords and office of King were abolished by votes of the Commons. By taking the life of Charles his enemies exalted his fame. The execution of a King was a thing unheard of, and Royalist and Presbyterian alike stood aghast. The mass of his subjects, forgetting the mistakes he might have made, only remembered that he had been illegally condemned, and that free institutions seemed to have fallen with him. The Church, which, throughout his many negociations with the Puritans, he had ever striven to maintain, styled him her *Martyr*, and the Cavaliers well nigh worshipped his memory.

Fuller was indeed violently affected by this terrible deed. Its first effect on him was to cause him to surcease from his literary labours, and in particular the compilation of his " Worthies " was abruptly abandoned. It is said that "such an amazement struck the loyal pious Doctor when he first heard of that execrable design intended against the King's person, and saw the villainy proceed so uncontrollably, that he not only surceased, but resolved to abandon that luckless work (as he was then pleased to call it) ; " For shall I write," said he " of the 'Worthies of England,' when this horrid act will bring such an infamy upon the whole nation, as will ever cloud and darken all its power, and suppress its future rising glories." Fuller's grief at this tragic event must have been very intense, judging from the numerous and touching references to it in his various works.

To the very last he remained staunch and loyal to the King and his cause. And he makes a most pointed allusion to this fact in a powerful figure with which he illustrates his unchangeable attitude thereto, in reply to one of Peter Heylin's sarcasms. "My loyalty did not rise and fall with his Majesty's success, as a rock in the sea doth with the ebbing and flowing of the tide. I had more pity, but not less honour, for him in his deepest distress." Fuller's bio- grapher thus touches on his devotion and loyalty, and his deep grief at the King's death. : " But when, through the seared impiety of those men, that parricide was perpetrated, the good Doctor deserted not his study alone, but forsook himself too. Not caring for nor regarding his con- cerns (though the Doctor was none of the most providential husband by having store beforehand) until such time as his prayers, tears, and fasting, having better acquainted him with that sad dispensation, he began to revive from that dead pensiveness to which he had so long addicted himself." (Pp. 39, 40.) He once more found solace in his pen, and renewed his literary labours, putting out another joint edition of his " Good Thoughts," which their popularity demanded, and the then condition of the country called for and warranted

It was no doubt to alleviate his great grief, and externalize his thoughts, on the death and execution of his beloved Sovereign, that he composed a sermon thereon. This sermon was published after delivery at the close of this sad year, and was intended to be a vindication of the Divine Providence in the misfortunes and deaths of good men. It was entitled *The Just Man's Funeral*, and although the King's name is not mentioned, it was generally understood to refer to his death, and to be accentuated by recent sorrowful events, being preached, as the title-page states, "before several persons of Honour and Worship." The sermon, which when published had a black border round it, was publicly delivered in Chelsea Church owing to D'Anvers' influence, who seems to have come very badly out of the affair touching the king's condemnation and execution, and earning for himself the soubriquet of "the regicide" from the part he took, or was supposed to have taken, in it. This sermon is based on the text, Ecclesiastes vii., 15, "All things have I seen in the days of my vanity; there is a just man that perisheth in his righteousness, and there is a wicked man who prolongeth his life in his wickedness."

In the explication of Solomon's remarks, he marshals his thoughts under four heads, to prove (1) That it is so, (2) Why it is so, (3) What abuses wicked men make because it is so, (4) What uses good men should make because it is so. Very characteristic of the preacher is the commencement. "The world is a volume of God's works, which all good people ought studiously to peruse. Three sorts of men are to blame therein ; first, such as observe nothing at all, seeing but neither marking nor minding the daily accidents that happen ; with Gallio, the secure deputy of Achaia, *they care for none of these things.* Secondly, such as observe nothing observable. These may be said to *weed the world.* If any passage happeneth which deserves to be forgotten, their *jet memories* (only attracting straws and chaff unto them) registereth and retaineth them : fond fashions and foolish speeches is all that they charge on their account, and only empty cyphers swell the notebooks of their discoveries. Lastly, such who make good observations but no applications. With *Mary* they do not *ponder things in their heart,* but only brew them in their heads, and presently breathe them out of their mouths, having only a rational understanding thereof (which renders them acceptable in company for their discourse), but never suffering them to sink into their souls, or make any effectual impression on their lives."

In this sermon Fuller touches upon the various senses of the term *righteous,* as applied to men in this life, "*intentionally,* desiring and endeavouring after righteousness with al their might ; *comparatively* in reference to wicked men ; *imputatively* having the righteousness of God in Christ imputed unto them: *inhesively,* having many heavenly graces and holy endowments, sincere thoughts not perfect. He observes that good men of all others are most envied and maligned, having the fiercest adversaries to oppose them. With the most in this world it is quarrel enough to hate a good man because he is a good man. Righteous men, as they have more enemies, so they are themselves less wary than other men, as being less suspicious, whilst wicked men, partly out of policy, more out of guiltiness, sleep like Hercules with their club in their hand, stand always on their guard, and are jealous of their very shadows. And again, the righteous are given unwisely indeed to hope that their very innocency will suffice without other means for their protection. Lastly, the righteous man is restricted in his use of means, preferring to die many times rather than to save himself once by unwarrantable ways."

Under the second head he asserts that the wicked make religion itself a cloak and a weapon. "Yea, we may observe in all ages that wicked men make bold with religion, and those who count the practice of piety a burden find the practice thereof an advantage, and, therefore, be the matter they manage never so bad (if possible) they will intitle it to be *God's cause*. Much was the substance in the very shadow of St. Peter, which made the people so desirous thereof as he passed by the streets. And the very umbrage of religion hath a sovereign virtue in it. No better cordial for a dying cause than to overshadow it with a pretence that it is God's cause ; for, first, this is the way to make and keep a great and strong party. No sooner the watchword is given out, *for God's cause*, but instantly, 'GAD, behold a troop cometh,' of many honest but ignorant men, who press to be listed in so pious an employment. These may be killed but cannot be conquered, for till their judgments be otherwise informed, they will triumph in being overcome, as confident, the deeper the wounds got in God's cause gape in their bodies, the wider the gates of heaven stand open to receive their souls. Besides, the pretending their cause is *God's cause* will in a manner legitimate the basest means in pursuance and prosecution thereof, for though it be against God's word to do evil that good may come thereof, yet this old error will hardly be beaten out of the heads and hearts of many men, that crooked ways are made direct, by being directed to a straight end ; and the lustre of a bright cause will reflect a seeming light on very deeds of darkness used in tendency thereunto. This hath been an ancient stratagem of the worst men (great politicians) to take piety in their way, to the advancing of their designs. The priests of Bel were but bunglers which could not steal the meat of the idol, but they must be discovered by the print of their footsteps. Men are grown more cunning thieves nowadays. First, they will put on the shoes of him they intend to rob, and then steal, that so their treadings will tell no tale to their disadvantage. They will not stride a pace, nor go a step, nor stir a foot, but all for *God's cause*, all for the good and glory of God. Thus Christ Himself was served from His cradle to His cross ; Herod, who sought to kill, pretended to worship, and Judas kissed Him who betrayed Him." There can be no mistake respecting the people here pointed at. Everyone is aware who those were that always had religion in their mouths, the men who acted any part indicated by policy and expediency, the men who brought the King to the scaffold, and were branded ever after with the name of "regicide." With further reference to his own times he says, under the last head, " It is also the bounden duty of all pious people, in their several distances and degrees, to improve their utmost for the preservation of dying innocency from the cruelty of such as would murder it. But if it be impossible to save it from death, so that it doth expire, notwithstanding all their cares to the contrary, they must then turn lamenters at the funeral thereof. And if the iniquity of the times will not safely afford them to be *open*, they must be *close* mourners at so sorrowful an accident. O, let the most cunning chyrurgeons not begrutch their skill to unbowel, the richest merchants not think much of their choicest spices to embalm, the most exquisite joiner make the coffin, the most reverend divine the funeral sermon, the most accurate marbler erect the monument, and most renowned poet invent the epitaph to be inscribed on the tomb of Perishing Righteousness. Whilst all others, well wishers to goodness in their several places, contribute to their sorrow at the solemn obsequies thereof, yea, as in the case of Josiah his death, let there be an Anniversary of Mourning kept in remembrance thereof. However, let them not mourn like men without hope, but let them behave themselves at the interment of his righteousness as confident of the resurrection thereof, which God in His time will raise out of the ashes : it is sown in weakness, it is raised in power ; it is sown in disgrace, it shall be raised in glory." Referring to the King, our preacher adds, "Solomon, speaking of the death of an ordinary man, saith, 'the living will lay it to heart.' But when a righteous man is taken away, the living ought to lay it to the very Heart of their heart, especially if he be a Magistrate or Minister of any note. When the eye-strings break, the heart-strings hold not out long after, and when the *seers* are taken away, it is a sad symptom of a languishing Church or Commonwealth."

In this proposal for an "Anniversary of Mourning" we have the first public indication of a national and annual fast-day, to be kept as a sad memorial of the death of the Martyr King, which was afterwards appointed by authority for January 30th, in each year

It very soon began to be kept by Archbishop Ussher among the clergy, and Evelyn the diarist, among the laity, the service used being that printed in our own Prayer Books, until recently, but which has now disappeared with all the other so-called State services, *e.g.*, Gunpowder Treason, and the Restoration of the Royal Family, with the exception of that for Accession Day, the 20th of June, the day on which our beloved Sovereign began her happy reign. It is entitled "A Form of Prayer, with Fasting, to be used yearly on the thirtieth of January, being the day of the martyrdom of the blessed King Charles the First, to implore the mercy of God, that neither the guilt of that sacred and innocent blood, nor those other sins, by which God was provoked to deliver up both us and our King into the hands of cruel and unreasonable men, may at any time hereafter be visited upon us or our posterity."

> " And yearly now, before the Martyrs' King,
>   For thee she offers her maternal tears,
> Calls us, like thee, to His dear feet to cling,
>   And bury in His wounds our earthly fears.
> The Angels hear, and there is mirth in Heaven,
>   Fit prelude of the joy when spirits won
> Like thee to patient Faith, shall rise forgiven,
>   And at their Saviour's knees thy bright example own."

Thus concludes our great Christian poet of the Nineteenth Century, the saintly Keble, author of the " Christian Year," in his poem on King Charles the Martyr, composed before the service (which had not, it is true, the sanction of Convocation), had been eliminated with a view to its discontinuance, from our Book of Common Prayer, by the authority of the State ; " Given at our Court at St. James's this seventeenth day of January, 1859, in the twenty-second year of our Reign, by Her Majesty's command.—S. H. WALPOLE."

This very pointed sermon, upon this pointed text was publicly preached by Fuller in the private chapel of Sir John Danvers, at Chelsea, where he had preached that unusually quaint sermon, commented upon in our last chapter, "On Contentment." It is another and more observable instance of his integrity, in that he preached it before one, under whose roof he had been so often welcomed, and who was, presumably, one of the misguided regicides who signed the King's death-warrant. But it was a very bold proceeding, and must have made the Preacher apprehensive of a renewed suspension, if not of being interrupted by some of the auditors, who may have had crypto-sympathies with the young nascent republic.

Then again, the prayers of those ministers who used the prohibited Book of Common Prayer, were particularly obnoxious, as in the case of Dr. Saunderson. Walton, in his "Lives," tells the story that when he was reading the old Church Prayers at Boothby Pagnell to his parishioners, the soldiers "forced his book from him, or tore it, expecting extempore prayers." No doubt it would have gone hard with him, but he was shrewd enough to follow the advice of some influential members of Parliament, and did not read *all* the prayers, or varied them in their sequence, thus throwing dust in their eyes. It was thus the Royalist clergy, and those who remained staunch members of the National Church, had to be on their guard, and when they saw they were watched and marked by the hired spies of persecution, "being crafty, caught their hearers with guile." Whether Fuller was annoyed or molested in any of his public predicatorial preachments we are not told, nor in what way they were accentuated, if so manifested, but we have the

following incident from his own pen. This is the paragraph :
" KEEP YOUR CASTLE. Soon after the King's death, I
preached in a church near London, and a person then in
great power, now (1660) levelled with his *fellows*, was present at my sermon. Now I had this passage in my prayer :
' God, in due time, settle our nation on the *true foundation*
thereof.' The (then) great man demanded of me what I
meant by *true foundation.* I answered, that I was no
lawyer nor statesman, and therefore skill in such matters
was not to be expected from me.' He pressed me further to
express myself whether thereby I did not intend the King,
Lords and Commons. I returned that it was *part* of my
prayer to God, who had more knowledge than I had
ignorance in all things, and that He knew what was the *true
foundation*, and I remitted all to His goodness. When such
men come with nets in their ears, it is good for the preacher
to have neither fish nor fowl in his tongue. But, blessed be
God, now we need not lie at so close a guard. Let the
gent now know that what he *suspected* I then *intended* * in
my words ; and let him make what improvement he pleaseth
thereof."

Fuller's anonymous biographer quotes this as a very
excellent passage of the Doctor's, and as a " kind of his ex-
periments in prayer, which were many and very observable :
God often answering his desires in kind, and that immediately when he was in some distresses : and God's
providence, in taking care and providing him in his whole
course of life, wrought in him a firm resolution to depend
upon Him, in what condition soever he should be : and he

* " Mixt Contemplations in Better Times," xl.

found that providence to continue in that tenour to his last end. Indeed, he was was wholly possessed with a holy fear of, and reliance in, God." *

We find Fuller attending in August of this year (1649) the death-bed of his old friend Dr. Richard Holdsworth, Dean of Worcester, upon whom the tragic death of the King had such a fatal effect, having been his chaplain at Hampton Court, and the Isle of Wight.

His preaching was very acceptable, and seems to have produced a very deep impression, for when he preached "the church rang not with the preacher's raving, but with the hearers' groans." "Skill in school divinity and practicable profitable preaching seldom agreed in one person : but if ever they were reconciled to the height of any in our nation," says Fuller, "it was in Holdsworth." He was imprisoned, when the tide turned, in the Tower, in a small room of which Laud betook himself, after receiving his sentence of death, to desire his prayers in particular. These two prelates had been fellow prisoners for a year and a half. Laud was beheaded, but Holdsworth was released, and waited on the King, who rewarded him with the Deanery of Worcester, and also offered him the Bishopric of Bristol. Fuller was with him when he died, and was thus a witness of "his pious life and patient death." He thus speaks of him—"How eminent an instrument he was of God's glory and the Church's good, is unknown to man, who in the least degree were acquainted with his pious and profitable pains. They knew him to be composed of a learned head, a gracious heart, a bountiful hand, and (what must not be

---

* "Life," 97, 99.

omitted) a patient back, comfortably and cheerfully to endure much heavy afflictions as were laid upon him." Shortly
after his death, some twenty-one reputed sermons of his
were published, under the title of "The Valley of Vision,"
1651 ; Fuller being induced to write one of his characteristic prefaces to the volume. He there regrets the Dean
left no works of his own, accounting for the fact thus :—
"rather it proceeded partly from his modesty, having his
highest parts *in* himself, and the lowest opinion *of* himself,
partly from his judicious observations that the world nowadays surfeits with printed sermons." The supposed manuscript of Holdsworth was scarcely legible, and it turned out
afterwards that our ingenuous doctor had been imposed upon,
only one sermon "The People's Happiness," being really his,
that preached, 1642, on the anniversary of the King's inauguration, which brought him into trouble, being printed by
command of the King, to whom it was dedicated.

Some clergymen know to their cost that, such is the law,
anyone has a right to take down their sermons, and print
them to their own profit. This is sucking their brains and
sweating their purses with a vengeance, but there is no help
for it. Thus it was with the sermons of the preachers of
those days. Fuller complains of the shorthand writers of
his age, who pretended to print his sermons on Ruth from
imperfect notes, "to their profit, but my prejudice." The
practice of taking notes of sermons of famous divines and
great preachers, in shorthand, was very prevalent. Earle
tells us of his "young raw preacher," that his "collections
of study are the notes of sermons, which, taken up at St.
Mary's, he utters in the country." And if he write brachi-
graphy, his stock is so much the better. Many of the

divines of the period animadvert on the practice of "scrib-blers, stationers, and printers," who traded upon the names of eminent theologians. But all this points to a state of things long passed away, for who, except in the case of Robertson's, of Brighton, was ever known to take shorthand notes of modern sermons ; and is not this too often the remark of our modern æsthetic congregations, "the shorter the better." It may be very lamentable, but it is the fact nevertheless.

CHAPTER XX.

INISTER OF WALTHAM—HOLY CROSS, OR ABBEY (1649-50).

"Providence, by the hands of my worthy friends, having planted me for the present at *Waltham-Abbey*, I conceive that in our general work of *Abbies* I owe some particular description to that place of my abode. Hoping my endeavours therein may prove exemplary to others (who dwell in the sight of remarkable monasteries) to do the like, and rescue the observables of their habitations from the teeth of time and oblivion."—(*History of Waltham Abbey*, p. 7.)

BETTER times and happier thoughts were now in store for our old "Cavalier Parson, and wandering Divine." He had had a hard struggle in the metropolis, and the opportunities for his literary labours were often unceremoniously interrupted. Now all was changed, and a welcome piece of preferment fell to his lot, which gave him just what he wanted, a settled home, a definite sphere, an opportunity of renewing his literary avocations and study, and that quiet and repose which his nature had so long desiderated. It restored him also to the pleasures of a parochical charge, and the sweets of social life. This was the perpetual curacy of Waltham Abbey, or Waltham Holy Cross. The patron was the Earl of Carlisle, whose attention had been attracted to Fuller before 1649, and who became much attached to him subsequently. This nobleman bestowed his living "voluntarily and desirously" upon the homeless parson, who was "highly beloved of that noble lord, and other gentlemen and inhabitants of the parish." *　This Earl of Carlisle was the son of the first gay and profligate Earl, and at the breaking out of the civil war had taken up the side of the King, and was present at the battle of Newbury (1643), where he was wounded. He appears to have gone over to the Parliamentary side in the spring of the following year, and compounded for his estate. He also seems to have been very liberal, " giving what he could save from his enemies in largesses to his friends, especially the learned clergy, whose prayers and good converse he reckoned much upon, as they did upon his charities, which completed his kindness with bounty, as that adorned his bounty with courtesy."

It is a fact worthy of remark that the right of patronage, *i.e.*, the right of next presentation to a vacant benefice, was in the majority of cases, even in those troublous and unsettled times of the Civil War, retained by the original holders. This says a great deal for the legal rights of patronage, and the stability of even the temporal side or accidents of spiritual things, in connection with the old historical and National Church of our country. The exercise of this patronage on the part of the Earl of Carlisle was in virtue of his holding the barony of Waltham and Sawley, which enabled him to present Fuller to the vacant perpetual curacy. Royalists and Roundheads alike, being the original patrons, kept their rights, and exercised the privilege of nominating to livings as a rule. Sometimes the Presbyterians (and Essex at that time was very Presbyterian, and mostly under that form of ecclesiastical polity) objected to the

---

* " Life," pp. 40-41.

selection, and we find Fuller complaining, under the Commonwealth, that ministers were thrust into parishes against
the wishes of the patron. But, on the whole, there was less
unsettlement, under the circumstances, than might have
been expected. Certainly these livings at that time proved
an asylum to many of the eminent episcopal clergy, as
Fuller and Jeremy Taylor, saving them from the common
ruin, and possible dispersion of their order. Waltham Abbey,
now in the new diocese of St. Alban's (which has recently
been carved out of the old diocese of Rochester, its episcopal jurisdiction being over the counties of Herts and Essex,
and the Bishop's residence being Danbury Palace, Chelms-
ford), was formerly in the diocese of Rochester, whose then
bishop, Dr. Warner, was remarkable for his able advocacy
of Episcopacy in the House of Lords, and his generosity to
the ejected clergy. He therefore became not only Fuller's
diocesan, but, as far as his influence permitted, his fast and
faithful friend.

Doubtless many of the ejected clergy were finding a
shelter in the houses of the aristocracy and landed gentry,
but Fuller's appointment to a legal benefice was exception-
ably fortunate. The exact date in which he was instituted
cannot be discovered from documentary evidence, nor, indeed, do any available local sources throw any light upon
the subject. The customary signature of the newly inducted
incumbent is not forthcoming, nor do the old churchwardens' accounts exhibit any proof. Our Divine was
probably appointed in 1648, towards the end, or at all
events the beginning, of the year following. His appointment is referred to in his " Pisgah-Sight," part of which was
published during that year, and one of the quaint maps

bears the inscription "Apud Waltham, 1649." In a manuscript in the British Museum, belonging, it would seem, to
the year 1650, and containing an account of certain Church
livings, mention is made of a "Mr. ffuller" under Waltham, as being at that time the perpetual curate, and "an
able godly preaching minister," which terms point to a
continued residence among the parishioners on his part.
Every one, therefore, seems to have been delighted to have
had so able and witty a Divine in their midst, a residential
fact, as their neighbour. For Fuller was not only greatly
approved of by the patron who had made the selection, but
also much esteemed by the local celebrities, and other gentlemen of the parish. This, therefore, must have made the
incumbency very agreeable to him, as in his capacity of
Vicar he gave satisfaction to all alike, being a good all round
man, to Presbyterian as well as Churchman.

Besides presenting Fuller to Waltham Abbey, the Earl of
Carlisle made him also his private chaplain. In every way
this nobleman showed his appreciation of him, and with
such a genial and hearty nature as Fuller possessed, we are
not surprised to find grateful mention of him in our author's
publications, more particularly and publicly expressed in
the first of his literary offspring ("Pisgah-Sight"), which
emanated from his new parsonage and official residence at
Waltham. Fuller tells us there that the Earl set him over
the flock at Waltham when he had no fixed habitation, and
gave him a higher salary than that usually apportioned to the
benefice. For all which he prays, that his patron might
have the fivefold happiness of Benjamin in this life, and
everlasting happiness in the world to come.

The perpetual curacy of Waltham Abbey had been well

endowed by the Earl of Norwich, being raised from eight
to one hundred pounds. But for this increase the Vicar
must have kept, as Fuller has it, more fast days than ever
were put in the Roman Calendar, and would have accentuated the saying anent the " difference between a curate and
a perpetual curate, that the one was an income straightened
and the other an income bent (incumbent)," a fact only too
patent to the majority of those whose names appear in the
eleven hundred and seventy-seven pages of Crockford. Yet
the gross amount of the revenues of the Abbey, when its
Abbots were mitred peers of the realm and spiritual barons
of Parliament, was upwards of one thousand pounds. It is
said that Fuller was not long left unmolested in his new
cure, but that before he had been settled in Waltham many
weeks, he was here once more called before the Triers, *i.e.*,
the local Ecclesiastical Board, or Committee of Sequestrators, who examined and dispossessed such ministers as they
judged to be unfit on any ground. These gentlemen desired
some proof of our author's extraordinary memory, upon
which he promised them, if they would restore a certain
poor sequestered minister, never to forget that kindness as
long as he lived. " 'Tis true, gentlemen, that fame has given
me the report of a memorist, and if you please, I will give
you an experiment of it. Gentlemen" (said he), "I will give
you an instance of my good memory in that particular.
Your worships have thought fit to sequester an honest poor
but cavalier parson, my neighbour, from his living, and
committed him to prison ; he has a great charge of children
and his circumstances are but indifferent : if you please to
release him out of prison and restore him to his living, I
will never forget the kindness while I live." 'Tis said the

jest had such an influence upon the committee, that they immediately released and restored the poor clergyman.

The report goes that our author applied to the celebrated John Howe for advice touching this ordeal, and Dr. Edmund Calamy, in his "Memories of Howe," says, "Howe freely gave him his advice which he promised to follow, and when he appeared before them they proposed to him the usual question, whether he had ever had experience of a work of grace in his heart : he gave this in for answer, that he could appeal to the Searcher of hearts that he made conscience of his very thoughts, with which answer they were satisfied, as indeed they might well."

One of Fuller's predecessors at Waltham Abbey was Bishop Hall, preferred thence from Suffolk by Lord Denny, about whom our author writes (and the good effects of his zealous labours were apparent when Fuller came into the parish) :—"Here I must pay the tribute of my gratitude to his memory, as building upon his foundation, beholding myself as his great-grandchild in that place, three degrees from him in succession, but oh ! how many from him in ability. His little catechism hath done great good in that populous parish, and I could wish that ordinance more generally used all over England."*

Bishop Hall, the "English Seneca," who had been beneficed at Waltham for twenty-two years, was not unlike Fuller in genius and disposition. In Waltham Abbey he had preached those charming *Contemplations*, which are still perused by the Anglican Churchman with such delightful interest. He was one of the

---

* "Worthies."

divines who represented our Church at the synod of Dort (1619), and on his return from ill-health was successively Dean of Worcester, Bishop of Exeter, and thence translated to Norwich. He, too, with other Anglicans, felt the brunt of the times, and, besides suffering in other ways, was imprisoned with the protesting bishops. Like Fuller, he saw " the sky thicken, and heard the winds whistle and hollo afar off, and felt all the presages of a tempest." Fuller, writing of Bishop Hall's illness at Dort, tells us in his *Church History* that the Bishop was then " so far recovered, not to say revived, that he hath gone over the graves of all his colleagues there ; and what cannot God, and good air do ? --surviving in health unto this day, three and thirty years after, may well, with Jesse ' go amongst men for an old man in these days ;' and living privately, having passed through the bishoprics of Exeter and Norwich, hath now the opportunity, in these troublesome times, effectually to practise those precepts of patience and contentment which his pen hath so eloquently recommended to others." Of his many valuable writings Fuller has said, " Not unhappy at controversies, more happy at comments, very good in his character, better in his sermons, best of all in his meditations."

In the History of "Waltham Abbey," our author says "it was then (1655) "the inheritance of this Earl (his patron), grandchild (by Honora, his daughter), of James Hay, Earl of Carlisle, who married Margaret, daughter to Francis, Earl of Bedford, by whom as yet he hath no issue ; for the continuance of whose happiness my prayers shall never be wanting." Among others of Fuller's works which he patronised was "The Infants' Advocate " (1653), inscribed to "this most bountiful patron." Elsewhere he says that the shadow of the least of the in-escutcheons in his patron's arms, with his favourable reflection, was sufficient to protect and defend his weak endeavours. The History of Waltham Abbey is dedicated to this same Mecænas, about whom Fuller subsequently writes, " All will presume me knowing enough of the orthography of his title, who was my patron when I wrote the book ("Church History"), and whom I shall ever whilst I live deservedly honour for his great bounty unto me."* To Francis, Lord Russell, son to the Right Hon. William, Earl of Bedford, Fuller dedicates the fourth volume of his *Pisgah Sight.* " Far be it from your Honour to be listed among those noblemen, of whom it may be said, in a bad sense, that they are *very highly descended*, as being *come down many degrees* from the worth and virtues of their noble progenitors." Nor does our author fail, on a fitting occasion, in his "Church History," to do honour to the virtues of that tried and admirable person, Anne, Countess of Bedford, "as chaste and virtuous a lady as any of the English nation," the daughter indeed of an unhappy parent, happy had her name been handed down to us only as the mother of such a daughter."†

Waltham Abbey, or more correctly Waltham Holy Cross, is situated in Essex, on the east side of the river Lea. Its name was derived from the miracle-working rood or cross, which being discovered in the West in the time of Cnut, was transferred to Waltham, with which it was supposed to surround its minister with a circumambient aroma of sanctity. It must not be confounded with Waltham Cross,

---

* "Appeal" (1659.)
† ("Church History," bk. x.)

a village about a mile distant, where a large cross had been erected by Eadward the Confessor, in memory of his consort Eleanor—a monument which had received some rough treatment at the hands of the iconoclastic Puritans, who had also destroyed a stained glass window in the Abbey, representing King Harold, besides doing other damage to it. This action of the "deforming reformers" of the previous reign was much censured by Fuller, who, commenting on this iconoclastic spasm of zealotry, wrote in 1650, "No zealot reformer (whilst Egypt was Christian) demolished *the Pyramids* under the notion of Pagan monuments." Again, while lamenting the destruction of Paul's Cross, he remarked that while "idle crosses, standing only for show, were punished for offenders, this useful one, which was guilty of no other superstition save accommodating the preacher and some about him with convenient places, might have been spared, but all is fish which comes into the net of sacrilege."* Fuller, who was "a great lover and preserver (properties never parted) of antiquities," affectionately regarded this old Cross of Waltham in its depressed condition.

The river Lea—dear to the disciples of Isaac Walton—is crossed two or three times before reaching Waltham Abbey. No doubt, thereabouts, the great and complete Angler himself, who has written such a charming work on his favourite sport, often fished and threw the fly, and it is not unlikely that in that locality the acquaintance of "my deservedly honoured master," Isaac Walton, with Fuller may have begun. These two men were not unlike; in their dis-

---

* "Worthies"—Kent, p. 72.

positions they were bright and cheery, their minds were exceedingly active and industrious, and they both were acquainted with the great Divines of the day. Both, too, were fond of antiquarian lore, and if Fuller wrote his Worthies, Walton wrote his Lives—which if they don't include that of our author, is no disparagement to his friend, who was not unworthy to stand by the side of Donne and Sanderson. They both belonged to the same Church, and were in great repute for their devotion to the Royal cause, counting among their friends in common many of the ejected clergy, and the adherents of the Monarchy. Besides, they were both lovers of peace and quietude, and their respective meditative treatises had the same blessed end—an *eirenicon*, a message of peace to all parties in the body politic. On this stream, mayhap, Fuller and Walton often met—to whose piscatorial lore and culture, as an authority, our author always bowed—about which Fuller remarks that it "not only parteth Hertfordshire from Essex, but also seven times parteth from itself: whose septemfluous stream, in coming to the town, is crossed again with so many bridges."

The town of Waltham was partly surrounded by rich meadows, and partly by the great forest—portion of the extensive Weald of Essex, "when, fourteen years since (in 1642, circiter), one might have seen whole herds of red and fallow deer. But these late licentious years have been such a Nimrod—such 'an hunter'—that all at this present are destroyed, though I could wish this were the worst effect which our woful wars have produced." The well-known Epping Forest is now the only relic of this extensive forest. The town was formerly within the perambulation of the Weald, as its name Waltham implies. This is Fuller's description of the old town and neighbourhood : " The air of the town is condemned by many for over moist and aguish, caused by the depressed situation thereof : in confutation of which censure we produce the many aged persons in our town above three-score and ten years of age ; so that it seems we are sufficiently healthful, if sufficiently thankful for the same. Sure I am, what is wanting in good air in the *town* is supplied in the *parish,* wherein as many pleasant hills and prospects are, as any place in England doth afford."* The streets are irregular and narrow, which are adorned by many old and quaint buildings. A great admirer of Fuller's, who visited the town as a pilgrim would a shrine, remarked of it, " Everything about it looks as if it had a sort of sympathy with his quaint, good-natured, and witty spirit. Humorous turns, bo-peep corners, unexpected street-vistas, architectural 'quips and cranks,' queer associations, grotesque groupings—all varieties in good-tempered unity, told of their former pastor." The Abbey itself is, of course, the chief point of interest, and is connected with Harold, under whose fostering care the original foundation developed into a considerable monastery. It was to this shrine that the remains of Harold, who had fallen on that fatal mound now shown to the visitor in Battle Abbey, were finally conveyed and buried. The foundation suffered much at the hands of the Norman kings, but it was befriended by Stephen, and re-founded and enlarged under Henry II. At the dissolution of the larger monasteries it was entirely destroyed except the nave, which escaped owing to its belong-

---

* " Hist. Waltham," p. 6.

ing to the parishioners, and the land and revenues passed
into the hands of Sir Anthony Denny, one of the executors
of the King. The edifice underwent considerable restoration
during the reign of Queen Mary. But in Fuller's time the
sacred edifice was again much out of repair, and when
Charles I. visited the place in 1641, the Earl of Carlisle, who
entertained the King, requested him to grant a moderate toll
of cattle coming over the bridge (with their great drifts
(droves), doing much damag to the highways), and therewith
both the town might be paved, and the church repaired.
The King graciously granted it, provided it were done with
the privity and consent of a great prelate (not so safe to be
named as easy to be guessed), with whom he consulted on
all Church matters. But when the foresaid prelate (Laud)
was informed, that the Earl had applied to His Majesty before
addresses to himself, he dashed the design ; so that poor
Waltham Church must still be contented with their weak
walls and worse roof, till Providence secure her some better
benefactors." But in spite of its dilapidated condition, its
worthy minister, and ' painful and pious ' parish priest, found
there, Sunday after Sunday, that ' best commendation of the
Church,' its being filled with a great and attentive congregation.*

Fuller thus describes the Abbey as existing in his time,
" a structure of Gothish (Gothic) building, rather large than
neat, firm than fair: very dark (the design of those days to
raise devotion) save that it was helped again with artificial
lights, and is observed by artists to stand the most exactly
east and west of any in England. The great pillars thereof

---

* " History of Waltham," p. 22.

are wreathed with indentings, which vacuities, if formerly filled up with brass (as some confidently report), added much to the beauty of the building. But it matters not so much their taking away the brass from the pillars, had they but left the lead on the roof, which is but meanly tiled at this day."

The size of the edifice had been much reduced, the west end only being the church. It may have been on the destruction of the choir that the old central tower, with its "five great tuneable bells," tumbled down. In the year 1558 the present square tower was erected, and the old bells, which had been hung meanwhile on a framework in the graveyard, had to be sold to raise money. This excited the remark of Fuller that Waltham, which formerly had " steeple-less bells, now had a bell-less steeple." The Earl and the parishioners bought six, which used to chime every four hours in Fuller's time. The great bell was rung at 4 a.m. to rouse the apprentices to their work, and again at 8 p.m. when the work of the day (*usque ad vesperum,* until the evening) was ended. The treble bell was (during Fuller's pastorate) purchased by the maids and bachelors of his congregation for £13 12s. 8d., and another was purchased by the parish about the same time. All this was, doubtless, done at Fuller's suggestion, who was evidently very fond of bell-ringing and chiming from his frequent allusions to them. He tells us in his time England was called " the ringing island." Upon the south side of the church there was a side chapel, with its separate altar, formerly our Lady's, now a schoolhouse, and under it an arched charnel-house, the fairest that ever I saw. Here a pious fancy could make a feast to itself on these dry bones, with the meditation of mortality." This Lady Chapel has never been restored, but after many years of neglect, the main sacred building—one of God's houses in the land—underwent a substantial restoration, and was in 1860 re-opened for Divine worship.

The parishioners, who were mostly poor, found their chief occupation in tending the large herds of cattle, which depastured on the broad meadows which surrounded the town. Fish was one of the chief commodities at the market, but its trade was insignificant owing to the contiguity to the metropolis, because, as Fuller puts it, "the *golden* market at Leadenhall made *leaden* markets in all places thereabouts." But much gunpowder was made in the neighbourhood. "More powder," he says, "was made by mills of late erected on the river Ley, betwixt Waltham and London, than in all England besides." Fuller also adds that it "is questionable whether the making of gunpowder be more profitable or more dangerous, the mills in my parish being *five* times blown up within *seven* years, but, blessed be God, without the loss of any one man's life."

Waltham was not only the nearest mitred Abbey to London, but it had in former times entertained illustrious guests. Hard by, at the house of "one Mr. Cressie," Cranmer was introduced to Henry VIII., then returning from one of his ' progresses,' and it was then the future Primate broached the subject of the possible post-futurum abolition of the Pope's supremacy. Fuller tells* us that Cranmer came to the town attended by two of his pupils, "the sons of Mr. Cressey, a name utterly extinct in that town (where God hath fixed my present habitation) long before the memory of any alive.

---

* "Church History," ch. v.

But consulting Weever's *Funeral Monuments* of Waltham Church (more truly than neatly by him composed), I find therein this epitaph :

> ' Here lieth Jon and Jone Cressy,
>   On whose soulys Jesu hav mercy.'   Amen.

It seems paper is sometimes more lasting than brass, all the ancient epitaphs in that church being defaced by some barbarous hands, who, perchance, one day may want a grave for themselves."

This may account for the fact that Fuller was unable to find the arms of the Abbey, which, he says, " appear in this day neither in glass, wood, nor stone, in or about the town or church thereof.*   At last we have recovered them (*unus homo nobis*) out of a fair deed of Robert Fuller's, the last Abbot, though not certain of the metal and colours, viz., *gules* (as I conjecture), two angels (can they be less than *or ?*) with their hands (such we find them in Scripture, Matt. iv., 6), holding between them a cross *argent*, brought hither, saith our antiquary, by miracle."

These passages abundantly prove that our author was beginning to collect materials for writing " some particular description " of his abode, and picturing himself Waltham Abbey " in the olden time."   Reflecting on the lives of the Regulars of the old foundation, he drew a very vivid picture of their " painful and pious " lives, which could turn " solitariness into society."   " It would do one good even but to think of their goodness, and at the rebound and second hand to meditate on their meditations.   For if ever poverty was to be envied it was here."   The refuge which they

---

* "Church History," ch. vi., 312.

E E

enjoyed, seemed to be the haven to which the moderate men of his day might wish to repair.*

It was in this town that Foxe wrote his famous *Book of Martyrs*, which, especially with its weird illustrations, has done more to excite and stimulate the young Protestant mind and apprehensions of this country, than any other book in our language. There was a tradition that he wrote it in a garret (which was pointed out) under the roof of the old building opposite the south wall of the churchyard, and which was once, it is said, his tenement. When the new vicar came into residence, Foxe's descendants still lived in the parish.

When a man is getting on, or up, in the world, there are always plenty of people who would like to pull him down again. Not only are there to be found detractors, who will, if they can, take away a man's good name and character (and a clergyman's character is the life of his life, as the Lord Chief Justice has lately said), but there are those who look with jealous and envious eyes on the successful ones. Aristotle calls this somewhere in his Ethics " ἐπιχαιρεκακία," which is a species of spitefulness, and we fear is not unknown to some even of the clergy. Be that as it may, we find that Fuller's peaceful enjoyment of this well-earned preferment began to excite the jealous envy of some of his brethren, who were not so advantageously placed. Some thought they detected a want of loyalty to the fallen monarchy, or a lukewarm attachment to the National Church, with its episcopal regimen. Dr. Heylin, his doughty antagonist, advanced the direct charge that "he complied

---

* "Church History," bk. vi., 263.

with the times." This taunt has been often repeated, and Hearne, the antiquarian and Bodleian librarian, said of his anonymous life, " A great character of the Doctor is in it, *yet he was certainly a Trimmer.*" In other words, what the great Halifax was in the political sphere (for he, too, was called a *Trimmer*), that our Fuller was in the theological. But Heylin's insinuations were not allowed to pass unanswered, and his reply is embodied in one of his most characteristic works, the *Appeal of Injured Innocence*, published 1659. In this he exhibits the difficulties which beset the path and dogged the steps of even the shrewdest of the ejected clergy, under those critical circumstances, and he not only illustrates his moderation of character, but explains the kindliness, wherewith he was regarded by all classes.

Fuller says that there is a *sinful* and *sinless* compliance with the times. After having explained the former, he passes on to the latter, which he says is lawful and necessary. Commenting on the text, " Serving the time " (Rom. xii., 11), he says the doctrine was true if the rendering were false ; " though we must not be slaves and vassals, we may be servants to the times." Lawful agreeableness with the times was partly passive, partly active. *Passive*, consisting in bearing and forbearing ; *bearing*, in paying the taxes imposed ; *forbearing* (1), by silence, "using no provoking language against the present power," and (2) by " refraining (though not without secret sorrow) from some laudable act which he heartily desireth, but dares not do, as visibly destructive to his person and estate being prohibited by the predominant powers. In such a case a man may, to use the apostle's phrase, διὰ τὴν ἐνεστῶσαν ἀνάγκην, " for the present necessity (1 Cor. vii., 26) ; omit many things pleasing to, but not commanded by, that God who preferreth mercy before sacrifice." Lawful compliance, again, was *active*, doing what was enjoined "as being indifferent, and sometimes so good that our own conscience doth or should enjoin the same." In such a case, where there is a concurrence of both together, it is neither dishonesty nor indiscretion for one in himself to conceal his own inclinations, and publicly to put his actions (as fasting, thanksgiving, preaching, &c.) on the account of conformity to the times ; it being (as flattery to court so no less) folly to condemn and reject the favour of the times—when it may be had without the least violation—yea, possibly, with an improvement of our own conscience.

"I have endeavoured to steer my carriage by the compass aforesaid : and my main motive thereunto was, that I might enjoy the benefit of my ministry, the bare using whereof is the greatest advancement I am capable of in this life : I know all stars are not of the same bigness and brightness ; some shine, some only twinkle : and allowing myself of the latter size and sort, I would not willingly put out my own (though dim) light in total darkness, nor would bring my half talent, hoping by putting it forth to gain another half talent thereby, to the glory of God, and the good of others."

" But it will be objected against me, that it is suspicious (at the least) that I have bribed the times with some base compliance with them, because they have reflected so favourably upon me. Otherwise, how cometh it to pass, that my fleece, like Gideon's, is dry, when the rest of my brethren of the same party are wet with their own tears ?

I being permitted preaching and peaceable enjoying of a Parsonage ?

"I answer, First I impute this peacefulness I enjoy to God's undeserved goodness on my unworthiness. 'He hath not dealt thus with all my brethren,' above me in all respects. God maketh people sometimes *potius reperire quam invenire gratiam*, to find the favours they sought not for. If I am one of them whom God hath made 'to be pitied of those who carried me away captive' (Ps. cvi. 46), I hope I shall be thankful unto Him; and others, I hope, will not be envious at me for so great a mercy.

"Next, to the fountain of God's goodness, I ascribe my liberty of preaching to the favour of some great friends God hath raised up for me. It was not a childish answer, though the answer of a child to his father, taxing him with being proud of his new coat, 'I am glad,' said he, 'but not proud of it.' Give me leave to be glad, and joyful in myself, for my good friends; and to desire and endeavour their continuance and increase. 'A friend in the court' hath always been accounted 'as good as a penny in the council, as a pound in the purse.' Nor will any rational man condemn me for making my addresses to, and improvement of, them, seeing the Animadverter himself (as I am informed) hath his friend in the Council; and it is not long since he had occasion to make use of his favour."

Having referred to the advantages which he derived from the rendition Articles of Exeter, of which he had the benefit, he adds, "Nor was it (though last named) least casual of my quiet, that (happy criticism to myself as I may call it) I was never formally sequestered, but went, before driven away, from my living, which took off the edge of the

Ordinance against me, that the weight thereof fell but slantingly upon me. Thus when God will fasten a favour on any person (though never so unworthy) He ordereth the concurrences of all things contributive thereunto."

"All I will add is this, that hitherto (1659), and I hope He who hath kept me will keep me—I speak it in the presence of God—I have not by my pen or practice, to my knowledge, done anything unworthily to the betraying of the interest of the Church of England; and, it it can be proved, let my Mother Church 'not only spit in my face' (the expression, it seems, of parents amongst the Jews, when they were offended with their children for some misdemeanour (Num. xii. 14), but also 'spue me out of her mouth.' Some will say, 'Such a vaunt savoureth of a Pharisaical pride.' I utterly deny it. For even the publican, after he came from the confession in the Temple 'God be merciful to me a sinner' (Luke xviii., 13), had he met one in the outward court, accusing and taxing him with such particular sins whereof he was guiltless, would no doubt have replied in his own just defence. And seeing I am on my purgation in what the Schools term *justicia causæ* (though not *personæ*), I cannot say less (as I will no more) in my justification.

"Thus have I represented to the reader with the true complexion of my cause; and though I have not painted the face thereof with false colours, I hope I have washed from it the foul aspersion of temporizing or sinful agreeableness with the times, which the Animadvertor causelessly casts upon it.

"So much," adds he, "for my outward carriage in reference to the times: meantime, what the thoughts of my heart have been thereof, I am not bound to make a discovery to my own danger. Sure I am, such who are 'peaceable and faithful in Israel' (2 Sam. xx. 19) may nevertheless be mourners in Zion (Isaiah lxi. 3), and grieve at what they cannot mend, but must endure. This also I know, that that spoke in the wheel which creaketh most, doth not bear the greatest burthen in the cart. The greatest complainers are not always the greatest sufferers; whilst as much, yea, more, sincere sorrow may be managed in secret silence, than with querulous and clamourous obstreperousness: and such who never print nor preach satires on the times, may make elegies on them in their own souls." *

There are many passages which are to be found scattered up and down in our author's writings, about this time, which are very much in the same strain with the foregoing remarks, and with which they naturally connect themselves. From a few extracts it may be gathered that he did not always endeavour to conceal his real principles. These bifurcated citations prove the general freedom accorded to reputed Royalists during the interregnum, and they exhibit our hero to be what he is supposed to typify, "that stout Church-and-King man." Many of them are to be found in the "Pisgah Sight," one of his most carefully digested and critically arranged works, published the year after the execution of King Charles, and the others are taken from his "Church History," published later on. Thus he says, of the death of Absalom, that "It was Joab which despatched him with three darts through his heart. Wherein, through

---

* "Appeal," p. I, ch. xxv.

a treble orifice, was discovered disobedience to his parent, treason to his prince, and hypocrisy to his God; pretending a sacrifice, and intending a rebellion." And he adds, of Absalom's tomb, that it consisted of "a great pit to hold, and a great heap of stones to hide, a great traitor under it. May they there lie hard and heavy on his corpes, and withal (if possible) sink down his rebellious example from ever having a resurrection! No methodical monument but this hurdle of stones was fittest for such a causer ot confusion."

Elsewhere, of Absalom's pillar, he remarks: "Pilgrims at this very day, passing by the place, use every man to cast a stone upon it, and my request to the reader is, if ever he should go thither, that when he hath first stood himself and satisfied his own revenge, he would then be pleased to cast one more stone upon that heap, in my name, to express my detestation of so damnable a rebellion. Rebellion," he adds, "though running so at hand is quickly tired, as having rotten lungs, whilst well breathed Loyalty is best at a long course."

There are also other glances at his own times in the same book. He refrains from giving the title "Holy Land" to Palestine, "lest while I call the land holy, this age count me superstitious." "Such as take down our church before fully furnished to the setting up of a new, making a dangerous breach for profaneness and atheism to enter in thereat. No such *regnum* for Satan, as in the *interregnum* between two religions."

He alludes to the Rechabites as constantly dwelling in tents—"so to entertain all turnings of the times with less trouble to themselves. Provident birds, only to perch on the boughs, not to build their nests on that tree which they suspected would suddenly be cut down, foreseeing, perchance, the captivity of Babylon. Indeed, in all fickle times (such as we live in), it is folly to fix on any durable design, as inconsistent with the uncertainty of our age, and safest to pitch up *tent-projects*, whose alteration may be with less loss, and a clear conscience comply with the change of the times."

We perceive his agitation of mind under certain emergent circumstances, as in his description of Issachar (whose resemblance to an ass should not, he says, depress the tribe too low in our estimation : the strength of his back, not the stupidity of his head, gave the occasion thereunto) where he says that the inhabitants were men that had "understanding of the times to know what Israel ought to do" (1 Chron., xii, 32), and then exclaims : "Oh, for a little of Issachar's art in our age to make us understand *these* intricate and perplexed times, and to teach *us* to know what we ought to do, to be safe with a good conscience."*

Our biography has to do more with Fuller than his friends, and therefore our space does not permit us to do more than give the names, and sketch very briefly the histories of some of Fuller's principal friends, with whom he was a frequent and welcome guest, during the pleasant time he spent at Waltham, the Cure which gave our author such a quiet home, and undisturbed lettered ease.

The first to notice will be the Earl of Middlesex. Here Fuller enjoyed the friendship of Lionel Cranfield, second son of Lionel the displaced and unjustly persecuted Lord Treasurer of James. Fuller "was frequent in his house at Copt Hall"—a mansion now no more, but which

---

* Book ii, 158.

derives an interest from its having been erected by Abbot
Fuller, and since enlarged and occupied by Sir Thomas
Heneage and others.   The house also possessed a long
gallery "as well furnished " says Fuller, "as most ; more
proportionable than any in England."   Its chapel, moreover,
was beautified with the richly painted glass windows, which
were afterwards removed and placed in the chancel windows
of St. Margaret's, Westminster.   This nobleman died in
1651, and was succeeded by his younger brother Lionel, the
third Earl, who seems to have been very fond of his parish
priest.   Knowing his pastor's love of literary pursuits, and
his hard lot in being a "library-less scholar," this Earl, by
a rare generosity, bestowed upon him the remains of his
father's library at Copt Hall.   This welcome gift is gratefully
and graciously acknowledged in his Dedication of his first
book of "Pisgah Sight," which is inscribed to his kind patron.
In one part of this dedication he says " And this hath God,
by your bounty, equivalently restored unto me what 'the
locusts and the palmer-worm have devoured,' so that now I
envy not the Pope's Vatican for the numerousness of books
and variety of editions therein : enough for use, being as
good as store for state, or superfluity for magnificence.
However, hereafter I shall behold myself under no other
notion than as your lordship's library keeper, and conceive
it my duty not only to see your books dried and rubbed (to
rout those moths which would quarter therein) but also to
peruse, study, and digest them, so that I may present your
Honour with some choice collections out of the same, as
this ensuing History (Reign Henry VIII.) is for the main
extracted thence, &c."

There is also another passage which shows Fuller's

intimacy with this noble family. "Some three years since,"
he says (about 1656), "walking on the Lord's Day into the
park at Copt Hall, the third son (a child in coats) of the
Earl of Dorset desired to go with me, whereof I was unwilling, fearing he should straggle from me, whilst I meditated
on my sermon, and when I told him, if he went with me he
would lose himself, he returned: 'Then you must lose
yourself first, for I will go with you.'" Fuller relates this
episode for the purpose, illustrating "this rule I always
observe, when meddling with matters of law ; because I myself am a child therein, I will ever go with a man in that
faculty, such as is most eminent in his profession, *a cujus
latere non discedam*, &c., that if he lose me he shall first lose
himself."

Fuller was also intimate with another nobleman in Essex :
Robert, the "pious old Earl of Warwick," the Admiral
under the Long Parliament. He held the presentation to
many livings in this county. Besides being noted for
integrity of character and manliness of bearing, he was "of
a pleasant and companionable wit and conversation, of an
universal jollity."

Here also he enjoyed the friendship of Sir Henry Wroth,
of Durance (near Ponder's End) or Durands. This seat
had been in the possession of that family from the reign of
Henry IV., by the marriage of John Wroth, to Matilda, the
daughter of Thomas Durand. Sir Henry's great-grandfather
was much esteemed by Edward VI., who died in his arms.
He fled in the next reign to Germany, but returned and was
restored to his possessions, when the terrors of Romanism
were at an end. "It was almost observable," relates Fuller,
"that the family of this man, who went away from his

conscience, was the only family in Middlesex, out of all those mentioned by Morden, which was not extinct in his time."

Perhaps the most intimate and truly paternal of all Fuller's friends was Matthew Gilly, Esq., of Waltham. To him he thus dedicates the tenth book of his " Church History " (section 11.), " Solomon saith, '*and there is a friend that is nearer than a brother.*' Now though I have read many writers on the text, your practice is the best comment which hath most truly expounded it unto me. Accept this, therefore, as the return of the thanks of your respectful friend."

Edward Palmer, Esq., was also another of Fuller's parishioners and tried friends. He was an accomplished scholar, and became Fellow of Trinity College, Cambridge, 1614, succeeding Andrew Downes.

At Cheshunt he enjoyed also the friendship of Sir Thomas Dacres. Fuller makes mention of a lively picture of Cranmer, which he had seen at Sir Thomas Dacre's house, done, as I take it, by Hans Holbein. To Cheshunt, also, belonged William Robinson, Esq., of the Inner Temple, who likewise patronised our author's works. This anecdote may interest those whose minds are somewhat exercised about the component elements of our present Court of Final Appeal, which succeeded (*per incuriam*) the High Court of Delegates in 1832. After relating an anecdote of Sir Edward Coke (who said that he never knew a Divine meddle with a matter of law, but therein he committed some grave error), Fuller, presuming that " you lawyers are better Divines than we Divines are lawyers," states that having cause to suspect his own judgment in that particular section of *Church History* wherein was so much of law he submitted it to his patron's. Among others of Fuller's friends we may mention Robert Abdy, Esq., of London and Albyns, Essex; and William Cooke, Esq., of Gidea Hall, near Romford; Sir Thomas Trevor, of Enfield ; and R. Freeman, Esq., of Aspeden, Herts.

These facts speak for themselves, and show that Fuller's official life must have had most charming social surroundings. The intimate way in which he addresses his friends and neighbours points to a parochial residence of a very agreeable character. His biographer tells us that he had the happiness of a very honourable, and that very numerous acquaintance, so that he was no ways undisciplined in the arts of civility, yet he continued *semper idem*, which constancy made him always acceptable to them."* And another contemporary notice observes that he "was so good company, that happy the person that enjoyed him, either citizens, gentlemen, or noblemen, he removing up and down out of an equanimous civility to his many worthy friends that he might so dispense his much desired company among them, that no one might monopolise him to the envy of others."†

With regard to his general bearing towards his friends and neighbours, his unknown biographer writes thus : " To his neighbours and friends he behaved himself with that cheerfulness and plainness of affection and respect as deservedly gained him their highest esteem. From the meanest to the highest he omitted nothing what to him belonged in his station, either in a familiar correspondency or necessary visits, never suffering entreaties of that which either was

---

* " Life," p. 69.
† " Lloyd," 524.

his duty or in his power to perform. The quickness of his apprehension, helped by a good nature, presently suggested unto him (without putting them to the trouble of an *innuendo*) what their several affairs required, in which he would spare no pains, insomuch that it was a piece of absolute prudence to rely upon his advice and assistance. In a word, to his superiors he was dutifully respectful, without neglect or unsociableness, and to his inferiors (whom indeed he judged Christianly none to be) civilly respectful, without pride or disdain."*

" He was so engaging," says another, "and had such a fruitful faculty of begetting wit in others when he exerted it himself, that he made his associates pleased with their own conversation as well as his ; his blaze kindled sparks in them till they admired at their own brightness ; and when any melancholy hours were to be *filled* up with merriment it was said in the vein he could sometimes descend to, that the doctor made everyone *Fuller*."† In other words, our facetious Divine was, as Falstaff puts it, " Not only witty in himself, but the cause that wit is in other men." That wit, whose essence is its conciseness, as Shakespeare says :

" Brevity is the soul of wit,
And tediousness the limbs and outward flourishes."
Hamlet ii., 2.

---

* " Life," pp. 74-5.
† Biog. Brit. iii., 2057.

CHAPTER XXI.

FULLER'S "PISGAH-SIGHT OF PALESTINE" (1650)

" It is safest for such (waverers) to insert conditional clauses in their prayers, *if it may stand with God's good will and pleasure*, used by the best men (not to say the best of bests) in their petitions, *Lord, if Thou wilt, Thou cans't make me clean.* Such wary reservations will not be interpreted in the Court of Heaven, want of faith, but store of humility, in such particulars where such persons have no plenary assurance of God's pleasure. Yea, grant the worst, that God never intended the future conversions of the *Jews*, yet whilst He hath not revealed the contrary (as in the case of *Samuel's* mourning for *Saul*) all men's charitable desires herein cannot but be acceptable to the God of Heaven."—(*Pisgah-Sight*) Land of Canaan, p. 201.

NOTHING strikes us more in the life of Fuller than his indomitable literary industry. Under the most untoward as well as more favourable circumstances, with his books or libraryless, we find him collecting materials for present or future works, if not engaged in actual composition. Whether as the popuar minister of the Savoy chapel, or as Cavalier Parson with the King at Oxford, or at the siege of Basing-house, or Exeter, or again as the popular lecturer of some city church, or the beloved parish priest at Waltham, it is still the same well-sustained character. We see not only the *painful* and *pious* preacher, but the plodding and industrious author A list of his many voluminous works, issuing from the press at regular intervals year by year, show a concentrated power of composition, which is truly marvellous and surprising. It is not easy to be at once an active parochial clergyman, and

affect the *rôle* of an author.   Waltham was indeed a most
congenial sphere in more ways than one, and there was, so
to speak, an aroma of literature about it.   This literary fame
of his new parish seems to have attracted his notice,
charmed his sentiment, and stimulated his energies.   He
dwells upon the fact with peculiar pride and satisfaction·
Thus in his *Infants' Advocate*, dedicated to his parishioners,
he says, " For first the book of *Mr. Cranmer* (after Archbishop of Canterbury and martyr), containing the reasons
against Henry the Eighth and his marriage with Queen
Katherine, Dowager, was compiled in *our* parish, whilst the
said Cranmer retired hither (in the time of a plague at
Cambridge) to teach his pupils.   Thus did Waltham give
Rome the first deadly blow in England, occasioning the
Pope's primacy to totter therein, till it tumbled down at
last.   The large and learned works of the no less religious
than industrious *Mr. Foxe*, in his 'Book of Martyrs,' was
penned here, leaving his posterity a considerable estate, at
this day possessed by them in this parish.   What shall I
speak of the no less pleasant than profitable pains of
Reverend Bishop Hall (predecessor in my place), the main
body of whose books bears date from Waltham."

It was here, then, that our author devoted himself with
recreated enthusiasm to the composition and publication of
some 'worthy books,' which became correlated with the same
locality.   The mantle of ·his illustrious predecessors fell on
no unworthy shoulders, and Fuller himself added to the
literary laurels of his parish.

The first great work which he published, connected with
Waltham, was an entertaining description of the Holy Land,
not that he would call it by that name, as some might think

it savoured of superstition. It was entitled "*A Pisgah-Sight of Palestine, and the Confines thereof, with the History of the Old and New Testament acted thereon,* by Thomas Fuller B.D." It is dated Waltham Abbey, July 7th, 1650, and is a large folio of some 800 pages, but has been reprinted by William Tegg, London, 1869.

It is supposed that the work had been planned as far back as when our author was at Broad Windsor composing his *Holy War*, of which Palestine was its principal theatre. Indeed, the 18th chapter of that work bears the very same title as this bigger work does—"A Pisgah-Sight, or Short Survey of Palestine in General"—one of Fuller's fascinating chapters about which Professor Rogers remarks in his Essay, —" What in other hands would have proved little more than a bare enumeration of names, sparkles with perpetual wit, and is enlivened with all sorts of vivacious allusions." The happy selection of the name of this new work was a most felicitous one, but for a time the title was undecided, and we find it entered in Stationers' Hall, dated April 15th, 1649, as "a booke called a Choragraphicall Cōment on the History of the Bible, or the description of Judæa, by Thomas Fuller, B.D." Perhaps his manuscript and collected topica may have fallen into the hands of the Sequestrators, and subsequently were returned to him about the time of his settling in his new home, which would account for his utilising them at once without further delay, putting off for the time his more ambitious work, which he was composing, on the "Ecclesiastical History of Great Britain." This is his own account of the matter : "So soon as God's goodness gave me a fixed habitation, I composed my 'Land of Canaan, or Pisgah-Sight.'"

F F

After his dedication to the Right Honble. Esme Stuart, Earl of March and Darnley, he has a few words to say " To the Reader "—in which he sets out the reasons why his promised *Church History* had not appeared.

After alluding to the substitution of Leah for Rachel at the end of Jacob's seven years' servitude, he continues : " Many have long patiently waited that I should now, according to my promise, set forth an Ecclesiastical History, who now may justly complain that their expectation is abused, finding their Changeling in the place thereof. And should I plead with Laban the custom of the country, that it is not fashionable to give the younger before the first-born (Gen. xix, 26), should I allege for myself that this book, containing matter of more ancient date, ought to precede the other, yet this, like Laban's answer, will be taken rather as a sly evasion than solid satisfaction." And again, referring to his promise, he says : " true it is we have no wars at this instant, yet we have rumours of wars, and though the former only doth destroy, the latter also doth distract. Are their gloomy days already disclouded (to use my own expression in my promise), or rather, is it not true in the Scriptnre phrase, that the clouds return after the rain (Eccles. xii, 2) ? Indeed, I am sorry I cannot say so much in my own defence, and should account myself happy if all other breaches were made up, and I only to be punished for my breach of promise ; which, notwithstanding all the difficulties of the subject, and distractions of our days, I hope in God, in competent time to effect, might but my endeavours meet with a quiet residence and proportionable encouragement for such undertakings."

He thus quaintly concludes : " Meantime, accept of these

my labours, which, by God's blessing, and the bounty of my friends, are brought into the light; useful, I hope, for the understanding of the Scriptures. What I have herein performed, I had rather the reader should tell me at the end of the book than I tell him at the beginning. For the manifold faults therein, I doubt not but that the ingenious reader (finding in Palestine six cities of refuge, by God's own appointment for the safeguard of such as slew one unawares without *malice prepense* (Josh. xx, 9), will of his own bounty build a seventh in his own bosom for my protection when guilty of involuntary mistakes in so great a work. If thou reapest any profit thereby, give God the glory; to whose protection thou art committed by, thine in Christ Jesus, Thomas Fuller."

The completion of the *Pisgah-Sight* was made about the autumn of 1650, nearly twelve months after it had been registered. The cause of the delay was doubtless the engraving of the plates, which in those days was as slow producing as quaint. Of these the title page is the most artistic, but we need hardly caution the reader not to judge of them from a nineteenth century standpoint. The art of engraving has much improved even in our own days, but what strides it has made during two centuries these quaint, not to say grotesque, pictorial efforts will enable us to judge. How would our author (who took almost as much interest in the maps of his engraver, as he did in the letter-press of his own hand) have revelled in the marvellous art productions of our age—this age of the *Art Journal*, brought to such perfection under the masterful conduct of my friend Mr. S. C. Hall, during the last half century—in these days of illustrated papers, as the " Graphic" and the " Illustrated " (with their wonderful Christmas numbers), of comic papers, as " Punch " and " Judy," and the maps of Wyld and Stanford.

How would Clein (for that was the name of Fuller's principal engraver) have craned his neck in delightful astonishment over the etchings, engravings, oleographs, or chromos of this artistic and hyper-æsthetic nineteenth century. One sight of these humble, but then very successful pictures, will well make a man reckon up his artistic "mercies" in these so-called prosaic days ! This Francis Clein was a native of Nostoch, and became connected with the tapestry works of Mortlake, in the county of Surrey, which were established by James I, in 1616, with which establishment he became connected as a designer of new patterns. Clein picked up his art-skill in Copenhagen, and subsequently at Venice, where he met Sir Henry Wotton, through whose influence he was invited by Prince Charles to England. Here he was liberally entertained by King James, who sent the artist back to the King of Denmark with a letter, described by Fuller "for the form thereof, I conceive not unworthy to be inserted, transcribing it with mine own hand." Returning the year following to this country, he was pensioned in £100 per annum, which was duly paid him till the breaking out of the civil wars, when the manufactory at Mortlake was destroyed, Holland House contains specimens of his painting, and so does Petworth of his designs. Clein had a son, who assisted him in making drawings for a pictorial edition of Virgil and Æsop (Ogilby's), which were published about the time of *Pisgah*. Clein's style is supposed to be like that of Hollar, and having spent his last days in Waltham, died in the year 1658 ; but his son died eight years before him.

Another of Fuller's "gravers" was J. Goddard, who is credited with the plate which contains the armorial bearings of those intimate friends of the author's, who so kindly encouraged him in his literary undertakings. And in the address to the reader, as we have already seen, our author makes the assertion, and couples it with a grateful acknowledgment that, but for the assistance of his numerous patrons, he could not possibly have composed so expensive and difficult a work. And he subsequently (1659) made the remark, with reference to such and similar difficult undertakings, that "of late some useful and costly books, when past their parents' power to bring them forth, have been delivered to the public by the midwifery of such dedications." "(Appeal.)" On the top of the plate the upper row is occupied by Fuller's favorite patrons.

Another of these "gravers" was Rob, Vaughan, who signs seven of the maps. He lived at Waltham, and although an indifferent illustrator, seems to have been on very good terms with his parish priest ; and they both worked their jokes into the plates ; as, for instance, where one place is jocularly called " Fuller's field." Vaughan's enthusiasm for his art no doubt incited Fuller to do what lay in his power to encourage him in his work. Fuller's other assistant " gravers" were W. Marshall, P. Cross, and J. Fuller. Eight of the maps are without signatures, but four were executed by the first of these, who is said to have been a laborious artist: three, by Cross, whose work is not well spoken of; and the plate description of the Jewish dresses was cut by the last named, though he was no relation of our author's. Oldys suggests that he may have been a son, or other kinsman, of Isaac Fuller, the history painter, if not

himself.   Isaac Fuller was a man of some note in his time,
and was "much employed to paint the great taverns of
London."   At Oxford is still to be seen some of his work,
including his portrait by himself, and his Altar-piece at
Magdalen College is celebrated by Addison.

Some have supposed that our author himself held the
graving tool at times, but there is nothing to prove this.
Indeed, a discrepancy appears in more than one case
between the letter-press of the author, and its accompanying
illustration.   Whatever suggestions he may have made, and
doubtless he made many, he left this externalised digital
expression to the manual labour of the workman.   Besides,
in some places he censures or excuses, as best he can,
oversights and blunders.   Thus, in the Map of Judah, an
objection is raised to Goddard's engraving of the Dead
Sea.   "Would it not affright one to see a *dead* man *walk ?*
and will not he in like manner be amazed to see the *Dead*
Sea moving?   Why have you made the surface thereof
waving, as if, like other seas, it were acted with any tide ? "
" I will not score it," replies Fuller, " on the account of the
Graver, that it is only *lascivia* or *ludicrum cœli*, the over
activity of his hand.   In such cases the flourishes of the
Scrivener are no essential part of the bond : but behold
Mercator's and other authors' maps, and you shall find
more motion therein than is here by us (*us, we* gravers)
expressed."   (Book v, 166.)

Fuller also amusingly answers another objection : " The
faces of the men which bear the great bunch of grapes are
set the wrong way !   For being to go south-east to Kadesh-
Barnea, they look full west to the Mediterranean Sea."
" You put me in mind," replied Fuller, " of a man who,

being sent for to pass his verdict on a picture, how like it was to the person whom it was meant to resemble, fell a finding fault with the frame thereof (not the *Limner's*, but the *Joiner's* work), that the same was not handsomely fashioned. Instead of giving your judgment on the map (how truly it is drawn to represent the tribe), you cavil at the *History-Properties* therein, the act of the *Graver* not the *Geographer*. Yet know, Sir, that when I checkt the Graver for the same, he answered me, that 'it was proper for *Spies*, like *Watermen* and *Ropemakers*, for surety sake, to look one way and work another.'" And this same simile is used by Fuller of the Romanizing clergy of the reign of John, " Looking at London, but rowing to Rome : carrying Italian hearts in English bodies."

No doubt these maps and engravings very much enhanced the costliness of the work,* for not only were these arts in their very infancy, they were on that account the more expensive to produce. Besides a very large map of Palestine and the two plates already referred to, there are twenty-seven double-paged maps, all closely filled, illustrating each of the tribes, the City of Jerusalem, surrounding nations, Jewish dresses, and idols. The different Biblical events are depicted in the places where they are reported to have happened, and remind one of the story of the Cambridge undergraduate, who, being called upon to draw a map of the Holy Land, after making a straggling outline, and putting the capital, Jerusalem, in the centre,

---

* To get a good idea of these engravings, the plates in the old folio edition of 1650 should be inspected. This edition is both scarce and costly, and the writer has consulted the folio in possession of his own family, being one of its heir-looms.

placed a big asterisk close by, referring to a foot-note, which informed the examiners, with N.B., that this was the exact spot where the poor man fell among thieves. Thus the progress of the Israelites into Canaan is pictorially delineated; a ship in a storm off Joppa, and a big whale, represent Jonah's history; the cities of refuge are marked by fugitives making their way there, followed by avenging pursuers; the four cities of the plain are in flames; Moses "views the prospect o'er" from Pisgah's lofty top (which looks like one of the tors of Dartmoor); even "middle earth" is given. The different cities, towns, and villages are marked with walls, coronets, double circles, turrets, asterisks, banners and little flags, and the camp of the chosen people is pourtrayed by the tents of the various tribes, ranged geographically according to the points of the compass, with the Tabernacle in their midst; Moses is seen pointing to the brazen serpent; and the whole map bristles with every imaginable quaint and weird device, which our author calls " History-properties." We can well imagine how his child-patrons must have revelled in these eccentric pictures, and the delight the children of the period (if their parents could afford so costly a work) must have experienced in these object-lessons. This was indeed teaching through the eye, and must have proved most attractive to the youthful student on Horace's principle—

" Segnius irritant animos demissa per aurem,
Quam quæ sunt oculis subjecta fidelibus."
(Hor. Art Poet. 180.)

or that of Herodotus (i. 8)—

" ὦτα γὰρ τυγχάνει ἀνθρώποισι ἐόντα ἀπιστότερα ὀφθαλμῶν."
or Seneca's—

" Homines amplius oculis quam auribus credunt."

(Ep. vi.)

And our author to the same effect: " Nor can knowledge herein be more speedily and truly attained, than by particular description of the tribes, where the eye will learn *more in an hour from a map, than the ear can learn in a day from a discourse.*" But with regard to these plates Fuller gravely cautions the reader, " For the further management of our scale of miles we request the reader not to extend it, therewith to measure all the properties or History-pictures in our maps (for then some men would appear giants, yea, monsters many miles long), expecting him rather to carry a scale in his own eyes for surveying such portraitures. Nor would I have the scale applied to cities drawn in per[pro]-spective." Adding, " Yea, in general, I undertake nothing in excuse or defence of those pictures, to be done according to the rule of art, as none of my work, ornamental, not essential to the maps: only this I will say, that eminency in English Gravers is not to be expected till their art be more countenanced and encouraged." And again : " Such towns as stand on tiptoes (as one may say) on the very umstroke or on any part of the utmost line of any map (unresolved in a manner to stay out or come in), are not to be presumed placed according to exactness, but only signify them there or thereabouts." And referring to any discrepancies, he adds: " Such motes not being before the sight, but in the corner of the eye, will little, if at all, hinder the light of a geographical truth. Surely, as in the strictest law of horse racers, some waste of weight is allowed to the riders ; so methinks some favour ought to be afforded an author in measuring and making many maps, were it but for the shaking of his weary hand in so tedious a work."*

In the opening chapter of the first book he begins by asserting his design from causeless cavils, in which he likens his condition to the Israelites at Kadesh-Barnia (Numb. xiii, 23–8), "who were much pleased with the report that the spies brought of the fruitfulness of the country, until they told them of Ahiman, Sheshai, and Talmai, the three sons of Anak, which quite appalled their courage, and "deaded" their desire thereof. In the like manner, whilst I am invited with several pleasing considerations, and delightful motives, to adventure on this work, three giant-like objections, which must be encountered, do in a manner dishearten me from further proceeding. For some will lay to my charge that the description of this country—

(1) Hath formerly been done by many.

(2) Cannot perfectly be done by any.

(3) If exactly done, is altogether useless, and may be somewhat superstitious.

To the *first* cavil Fuller makes answer that it "is not planted particularly against my endeavours, but is levelled against the industry of all posterity, in any future design. Solomon saith there is no new thing under the sun (Eccles. i, 9). Except, therefore, men were gods to create new subjects to write upon, groundless is the first exception against us. It never disheartened St. Luke to write his Gospel, for as much as many had taken in hand to set it forth before. Yet the former endeavours of many in the

---

* Book I. ch. xvi.

same matter, argue the merit of the work to be great. For sure there is some extraordinary worth in that face which hath had so many suitors. Wherefore, although we cannot, with Columbus, find out another new world, and bring the first tidings of an unknown continent or island, by us discovered, yet our labours ought not to be condemned as unprofitable, if setting forth an old subject in a new edition enlarged and amended. This I dare say, though many have written discourses without maps, and more maps without discourses, and some both (yet so that three tribes are joined in one map), none have formerly in any tongue (much less in English) presented us with distinct maps and descriptions together."

With regard to the *second* cavil, he replies, " I could wish that the objection also lay against the work in hand, and might not also equally be enforced against other liberal undertakings : for he that holds a reed in one hand to mete the topography, and an hour-glass in the other to measure the chronology of the Scripture, shall meet with as many, if not more, uncertainties in the latter, as in the former. And yet the learned pains of such as labour therein, justly merit commendation. If all conjectural results should be cast out for weeds, few herbs would be left in the gardens of most arts and sciences. St. Paul hath a passage, " We know in part and we prophesy in part " (1 Cor. xiii, 9), which is a good curb for our curiosity ; and the same apostle hath a precept, " Prove all things ; hold fast that which is good " (1 Thess. v, 21), which is as good a spur for our diligence. As for the difference betwixt geographers, they ought not to make us careless to follow any, but careful to choose the best ; except with the sluggard's drowsy fancy we tune the Alarums to our industry to be Lullabies to our laziness."

Answering the last objection, he says, " It matters not to any man's salvation to know the accurate distance between Jericho and Jerusalem : and he that hath climbed to the top of Mount Libanus is not, in respect of his soul, a hair's breadth nearer to heaven. Besides, some conceive they hear Palestine saying to them, as Samuel to Saul, endeavouring to raise him from his grave, ' Why hast thou disquieted to bring me up ? ' (1 Sam. xxviii. 15.) Describing this country is but disturbing it, it being better to let it sleep quietly, entombed in its own ashes. The rather because the New Jerusalem is now daily expected to come down (Rev. xxi. 10), and then corporal (not to say carnal) studies of the terrestrial Canaan begin to grow out of fashion with the more knowing sort of Christians."

" It is answered, though these studies are not essential to salvation, yet they are ornamental to accomplish men with knowledge, contributing much to the true understanding of the history of the Bible. Remarkable is that passage of the Apostle—Acts xvii. 26, ' And hath made of one blood all nations of men for to dwell on all the face of the earth, and hath determined the times before appointed, and the bounds of their habitation,' wherein we may see Divinity, the Queen, waited on by three of her principal ladies of honour, namely skill in—

" (1) Genealogies : concerning the persons of men and their pedigrees ; ' of one blood all nations.'

" (2) Chronology : in the exact computation ' of the times afore appointed.'

"(3) Geography : measuring out the limits of several nations, 'and the bounds of their habitations.'

The *Pisgah Sight* of Palestine is divided into five books, of which the first is prefatory, and treats of the general description of Judæa. This book contains fifteen chapters, the last touching how the different qualities of places in our maps are distinguished by their several characters, and is dedicated to his child-patron the Right Honourable Esme Stuart, Earl of March and Darnley, Lord Leighton, son and heir to the illustrious James, Duke of Richmond and Lennox. Referring to the present incapacity of his patron deriving instruction from the book, he adds that " until such time as your lordship's judgment can reap profit from our descriptions herein, *may your eyes but take pleasure in the maps which are here presented unto you.*" After some quaint conceits on the family name and ancestry, Fuller concludes : " But I grow tedious in a long letter to a little lord, and therefore turn my pen into prayers that Christ would be pleased to take you up into his arms (whose embraces are the best swaddling clothes, as to straighten, so to strengthen you in the growth of grace), to 'lay his hands upon you and bless you,' that you may 'grow in stature and favour with God and man,' the daily desire of your Lordship's humble orator, THO. FULLER." Speaking of his innocence, Fuller beautifully remarked (a sentiment which attracted the notice of Charles Lamb, who inserted it among the specimens from the writings of Fuller), " Yea, some admiring what motives to mirth infants meet with in their silent and solitary smiles, have resolved (how truly I know not) that then they converse with angels, as indeed such cannot among mortals find any fitter companions." The second and largest book, which is occupied with the tribes, and contains fourteen chapters (the last being on the land of Moriah, with a fine plate) is dedicated to the Right Honourable Henry Lord Beauchampe, son to the Right Honourable William, Marquess of Hertford. The third book treats of the city of Jerusalem, and King Solomon's Temple (a subject dear to all free and accepted Masons), and contains four chapters, the last chapter a most interesting one, dealing with Zorobabel's temple, in twelve sections (the ninth being on "the Action of Christ in the Temple," and the tenth the "Acts of the Apostles in the Temple"), and is dedicated to the Right Honourable John, Lord Ros, son of the Right Honourable, John, Earl of Rutland. The fourth book contains seven chapters, and is devoted to Mount Libanus and adjacent countries, the tabernacle, clothes (with pictures of same), ornaments, vestments, and idols of the Jews (with a very graphic plate, showing the Pantheon, *Sive Idola Judeorum*). This part is dedicated to the Right Honourable Francis, Lord Russell, son to the Right Honourable William, Earl of Bedford. The fifth book contains two chapters, the first on the "Objections Answered Concerning this Description," and the latter "Ezekiel's Visionary Land of Canaan," and deals with a miscellaneous assortment of topics, so arranged that the former books might be, as the author says, more pleasant and cheerful in the lection. The objections are set out in a continuous dialogue between Philologus and Alethæus. This last book is dedicated to the Right Honourable John, Lord Burghley, son to the Right Honourable John, Earl of Exeter. In his dedicatory epistle he alludes to his birthplace. "Now the first light which I saw in this world was

in a benefice conferred on my father by your most honourable great-grandfather, and therefore I stand obliged in all
thankfulness to your family ; yea, this my right hand, which
grasped the first free air in a manor to which your lordship
is heir apparent, hath since been often catching at a pen to
write something expressive of my thankfulness, and now at
last dedicates this book to your infant honour. Thus, as my
obligation bears date from my birth, my thankfulness makes
speed to tender itself to your cradle." Alluding to the objection that his lordship was " infra-annuated " to be the
patron of a book in the first acceptation thereof, he has a
sly hit at the Church of Rome : " If they (Roman Catholics)
do, I refer them to a story confessed by their champion, a child
not fully five years old, consecrated Archbishop of Rheims
by Pope John the Tenth, since which time some children of
small age (but great birth) have been made Cardinals,
though long since their Church of Rome had been off the
hooks, had it no stronger hinges."

This book concludes with a beautiful Prayer for the
Conversion of the Jews, which had been considered in
the 4th, 5th, and 6th section of the last chapter " of the
general calling of the Jews : of the present obstructions to
the calling of the Jews " : and " how Christians ought to
behave themselves, in order to the Jews' conversion." On
this subject Mr. Russell observes, *" Fuller, and according
to him the majority of the learned in his day, were
against the opinion that the Jews would be put again in
possession of their ancient territory. The negation of
this opinion he grounds upon the ninth chapter of Amos,

---

* " Memorials of Life and Works," p. 176.

as interpreted in the fifteenth chapter of the Acts. The opinion of the general conversion of the Jews he shews to be conformable to Scripture, and to have been maintained in the first four centuries."

He proceeds to treat of the hindrances that opposed their conversion. The first he notices is " our want of civil society with their nation. There must be first conversing with them before there can be converting of them. The Gospel doth not work (as the weapon-salve) at distance, but requires some competent familiarity with the persons of probationer-converts. Whereas the Jews being banished out of England, France and Spain are out of the call of the Gospel and ken of the sacraments in those countries." This was a degree of genuine liberality beyond the age in which Fuller wrote. *Tempora mutantur.* Our generation has seen the Jews admitted to the Great Council of the nation, and such is the anomalous condition of things they might even vote on measures concerning the National Church itself, and perhaps they did vote on the Public Worship Regulation Act. Be that as it may, the Jews were then (1650) under the ban of those laws which forbad their setting foot upon our shores : and this state of utter outlawry they could not escape even by an appeal to Cromwell, who long deliberated on this point, but would not, or at least, did not, commit himself to a measure in his time so unpopular as the mere toleration of the Jews.

He notices also the scandal of image-worship in the Church of Rome, " and to speak out the plain truth the Romanists are but back-friends to the Jews' conversion, chiefly on this account, because the Rabbins generally interpret Dumah (especially on the burden of Dumah :

Isa. xxi, 11.) or Edom to be Rome, and Edomites Romans, in their expositions on the Old Testament. And therefore all those passages have (by order, no doubt, from their superiors) been lately purged out and expunged the Venetian edition of the Rabbins;* yea, there is a constant tradition, current time out of mind, that after the destruction of the city of Rome, their nation shall be put in a glorious condition. No wonder, then, if cold and dull the endeavours of the Romanists for the conversion of the Jews, who leave that task to be performed by Moses and Elias, whom the Papists fondly fancy, shall, toward the end of the world, personally appear, and by their powerful preaching persuade the Jewish nation unto the Christian religion." He adverts to the great joy of the godly Jews at the conversion of Cornelius, and probable expectation of the Scriptures themselves being better understood, when both Jew and Gentile shall unite their labours to the illustration of them. But upon whatever subject our Author treated, his piety was always ready to edify the heart, as his industry was incessant to instruct the mind of his readers. Witness his admirable chapters on the "Land of Moriah," and on "The Mysteries of Mount Calvary."

Strange ideas now-a-days obtain on the subject of property, especially Church and landed property. We have lived to see a sister Church disestablished, and, as to our country, the prophets tell us that the landlords will be disestablished before the parsons, the reverse of the prediction some twenty years ago. "Some there are in our own age," say

---

* Set forth by Daniel Bambergius.

Mr. Russell, "who hold no kind of property sacred except their own, that is private property. The property of the Church, they tell us, is the property of the State, and the property of the State is the property of the people,* so that if the Parliament do but alienate, there can be neither wrong nor robbery." " Indeed," says Dr. Fuller, "some hold that under the Gospel the sin of sacrilege cannot be committed. If so, it is only because nothing under the Gospel hath been given to God's service, or because God hath solemnly disclaimed the acceptance of any such donations; which, when, and where it was done, will be hardly produced. If this their position be true, we have cause, first, to rejoice in regard that God and His members are now-a-days grown so rich that they need not addition of human gratuities to be bestowed on them ; secondly, we can congratulate the felicity of our above former ages being not in a capacity of committing the sin of sacrilege, to which those were subject who lived before the time of our Saviour ; lastly, we may silently smile to see how Satan is defeated, having quite lost one of his ancient baits and old temptations : men now-a-days being secured from this sin, and put past a possibility of being guilty thereof. But before we go thus far, let us first be sure we go on a good ground, otherwise it is the highest sacrilege itself, and to deny that (which formerly was a grevious) to be any transgression."†

In the compilation of this exhaustive and *painful* work our author had in his hands and used, among other aids Jerome, Adrichomius, Villepandus, Bochart, Breidenbachius,

---

* " Memorials," p. 178.
† Pp. 403, 404.

of Mentz, Brochardus (who travelled in the Holy Land in
1283), Sandys, or Sands (the traveller whose famous Eastern
journey was made in 1600, and of whose description of the
Holy Land Fuller speaks so admiringly), Morison, Biddulph
(a late English divine), and Bunting's "Travels of the
Patriarchs." Of ancient authors, Josephus takes the first
place. "Pardon a digression," says he, "in giving a free
character of his writings, whereof, next Holy Writ, we have
made most use in this book. Notwithstanding all these
his faults, the main bulk of his book deserves commendation, if not admiration ; no doubt at the first compiled, and
since preserved, by the special providence of God, to reflect
much light and lustre upon the Scriptures."

He also quotes the Rabbins, and laid Pliny under contribution. And as to the spirit in which our author
utilized the labours of those who had gone over the same
ground, the following quotation will show : "We intend a
little, both upon the commodities and countries, of such as
hither (to Tyre) resorted. For though I dare not go out of the
bounds of Canaan to give these nations a visit at their own
homes, yet, finding them here within my precincts, it were
incivility in me not to take some acquaintance of them.
In setting down of their several places I have wholly followed (*let my candle go out in a stink when I refuse to confess
from whom I have lighted it*) Bochartus in his 'Holy
Geography.'"

His treatment of the work, and the design itself, is quite
original—we were tempted to say, Fullerian. Our author
gives this account of his literary production : "Our work in
hand is a parcel of geography, touching a particular description of Judæa: without some competent skill wherein, as

the blind Syrians, intending to go to Dothan, went to Samaria (11 Kings vi, 19); so ignorant persons discoursing of the Scripture, must needs make many absurd and dangerous mistakes. Nor can knowledge herein be more speedily and truly attained than by particular description of the tribes, when the *eye* will *learn* more in an hour from a map than the ear can learn in a day from discourse, and, if there were any fear of superstition, his works might go the way of the Ephesian conjuring books (Acts xix., 19), and not all the water of Kishon, of Jordan, of the Red, of the Dead, of the Middleland Sea should serve to quench the fire, but all be reduced to ashes."

This marvellous production is now over two hundred years old; but, in spite of fresh investigations, recent explorations on a grand scale, and more modern researches, it still holds its own against all comers, and is even now a book of reference, as luminous and sprightly as it is useful. It is worthy to stand on the same shelf as that truly delightful and brilliant book of Dean Stanley* on *Palestine* and Syria, with its very picturesque diction. As a proof of its popularity, fresh editions of the work were soon called for. And our author refers to its success with honest pride and satisfaction, when he was jeered at by Dr. Heylin for sallying forth into the Holy Land, when he should have been endeavour-

---

* "Fuller's pages are more fruitful of healthy influence than those of Stanley. Brilliant as Stanley is, he lacks steady, Christian warmth; and is very unlike Fuller, in that he so often makes his reader feel the presence of a subtle scepticism. Dear old Fuller, thine eye was single, and had too much the nature of Divine light in it to be dazzled or touched with the least uneasiness before the face of inspired truth." (Christopher's "Homes of English Divines," p. 179.)

ing a Church History (his adversary, perhaps, not liking this popularity, as he himself had lately put out a descriptive account of the same in his *Microcosmography*, which he may have wished to look upon as his own preserves). Fuller tells his critic that he can brook all such sarcastic remarks, " seeing (by God's goodness) that my book hath met with general reception, likely to live when I am dead ; so that friends of quality solicit me to teach it the Latin language."*

The very peculiar and attractive style of Fuller had no doubt much to do in deserving and securing this popularity. Some of their details—especially the chronological—are of the driest character, yet his pen lights them up, and makes them sparkle with verve and wit by a quaint fancy and luxurious facetiousness, brimming over at times, and hardly patient of being confined within reverent and duly subordinated limits, befitting the sacred profession of the author. We seem spell-bound by some literary wizard, and are riveted with the pictorial phantasmagoria and verbal transformation scenes, which delight the eye and ravish the imagination.

One writer says, speaking of this work : " No one could have expected the lavish display of every kind of wit and drollery which is to be found in the book. His fancy fertilized the very rocks and deserts ; the darkest and dreariest places he illumines and renders cheerful with his never-fail-humouring." † Another says that this book is a felicitous illustration of Fuller's strong point—sacred story ; " and no work of his better displays the riches of his mind, or the plenitude and fertility of its images."

---

* " Appeal," Pt. I., 317.
† Knight's "Cabinet Portrait Gallery," vii., 16.

But our readers by this time must be anxious for a few brief excerpts, as specimens of the lively spirit and witty pleasantry of the work. We cannot do better than quote some two or three citations, which are very apposite. *The Septenary Number* : " Seven years was this Temple in building. Here some will behold the sanctity and perfection of the Septenary Number, so often occurring in Scripture, whilst we conceive this the best reason why just seven years were spent on the building thereof, because it could not be ended in six, nor accomplished within a shorter compass of time." * *The Beautiful Gate* : " We will wait on the reader into the Temple, first requesting him to carry competent money, and a charitable mind along with him, for, as we shall enter into the Eastern gate (commonly called ' Beautiful ') we shall be sure to meet there with many creeples and beggars of all sorts, as proper objects of his liberality. Here daily lay that lame man on whom St. Peter, though moneyless, bestowed the best alms he could give, or the other receive, even the use of his limbs." †
Jerusalem : " As Jerusalem was the navel of Judæa, so the Fathers make Judæa the middest of the world, whereunto they bring (not to say how) those places of Scripture. 'Thou hast wrought salvation in the midst of the earth.' Indeed, seeing the whole world is a *round table*, and the Gospel the *food* for men's souls, it was fitting that this *great dish* should be set in the midst of the *board*, that all the guests round about might equally reach unto it ; and Jerusalem was the *center* whence the *lines* of *salvation* went out

* iii., 362.
† iii., 426.

into all lands."* " Modern Damascus is a beautiful city. The first Damask-rose had its root here, and name hence. So all Damask silk, linen, poulder, and plumbs, called *Damascens.* Two things at this day are most remarkable among the inhabitants : there are no Lawyers amongst them, no Advocates, or Solicitors of causes, no compacts being made for future performance, but *weigh* and *pay*, all bargains being driven with ready money. Secondly, physicians here are paid no fees, except the patient recover his health." †

" The once famous city of Capernaum, Christ's own city. Note by the way that Christ had three cities which may be called His own (if seven contended for Homer, well may three be allowed to Christ); Bethlehem, where He was born; Nazareth, where conceived and bred; and Capernaum, where He dwelt—more than probably in the house of Simon Peter. This Capernaum was the magazine of Christ's miracles. Here was healed the servant of that good centurion, who, though a Gentile, out-faithed Israel itself. Here Simon Peter's wife's mother was cured of a fever: and here such as brought the man sick of the palsy, not finding a door on the floor, made one on the roof (love will creep, but faith will climb where it cannot go), let him down with cords, his bed bringing him in, which presently he carried out, being perfectly cured. Here also Christ restored the danghter of Jairus to life, and in the way, as He went (each parenthesis of our Saviour's motion is full of heavenly matter, and His *obiter* more to the purpose than our *iter*) He cured the woman of her flux of blood, with the touch of His garment.

---

* iii., 315.
† iv., 9.

But, amongst all these and more wonders, the greatest was the people of Capernaum, justly occasioning our Saviour's sad prediction, 'And thou, Capernaum, which art exalted,' &c. O sad strapado of the soul, to be hoised up so high, and then cast down suddenly so low, enough to disjoint all the powers thereof in pieces !* Capernaum at this day is a poor village, scarce consisting of seven fishermen's cottages."

Bethlehem.—"But what gave the greatest lustre to Bethlehem (Bethlehem in Hebrew is 'The house of Bread,' principally so called in reference to Christ, the Bread of Life, who, in fulness of time, was here to be born) was that Jesus Christ, the Prince of Peace (Isaiah ix, 6), was born herein of the Blessed Virgin Mary, in a time of peace, to procure and establish a peace betwixt God and man, man and angels, man and man, man and his own conscience, man and other creatures. Public the place of his birth, an inn (Luke ii, 7) (every man's house for his money), and poor the manner thereof, so defeating the Jews' towering fancies of a temporal king, who long looking to see their Messiah sitting on a throne, would rather stumble at Him than stop to behold Him lying in a manger. The first tidings of the Lamb of God, by intelligence of angels, is told to poor shepherds watching their flocks by night (Luke ii. 8), whilst the priests, the pretended shepherds of Israel, were snorting on their beds of security. The place of this apparition not being far from the tower of Eder (or the tower of flocks), where Jacob sometimes pitched his tent (Gen. xxxv, 21-22) and kept cattle, and where Reuben defiled his father's concubine." Again, "As for their conceit that anti-Christ should be born

---

* ii., 109.

in *Chorazin,* I take it to be a mere monkish device, to divert men's eyes from seeking him in the right place where he is to be found."

We are tempted to make two more extracts from this interesting work. " Fuller's Field must not be forgotten, where they stretched and dried their clothes, which they had washed at the brook of Kedron. But all the soap used here by men of that trade could not scour the indelible stain of impiety out of the credit and conscience of King Ahaz, who, in the highway of the Fuller's Field (Isaiah vii., 12), peevishly refused a sign which God graciously proffered unto him. And men's several behaviour in matters of this kind deserved to be marked. For it was (1) commendable in Gideon (Jud. vi., 21) and Hezekiah (Isaiah xxxviii, 22) humbly requesting a sign for further strengthening of their weak faith ; (2) pardonable in Zacharias (Luke 1, 18) craving one out of a mixture of infidelity, therefore granted him in loving anger, his dumbness serving as well to correct as confirm him ; (3) damnable in the Jews, who, out of pride and presumption in a daring way (Mat. xvi, 1), and in Herod, who, out of curiosity, expected (Luke xxiii, 9) a sign from Christ, and therefore denied him. But most of all in Ahaz, in whose nostrils the very perfumes of heaven scented ill, because proferred unto him, refusing to accept a sign so freely tendered unto him." *

The conclusion of this third book is a sly hit against the Pope and some relics :—" For Vespasian and Titus his son, Roman emperors, anno Dom. 72, razed the temple, and utterly confounded all the utensils thereof. Indeed, they

---

* Book. III., c. i., sec. 13.

were first carried in triumph to Rome, but what afterwards became of them is altogether unknown. It is no sin to conceive that their property was altered, and they either converted to coin, or turned to plate for the use of the emperor or his favourites. Sure none are known to remain in specie at this day, and one may wonder that no impudent relic-monger hath produced a golden feather of a cherub's wing, or a knob, flower, bowl, or almond of the seven-branched candlestick, having pretended since Christ's time to improbabilities of as high a nature. Strange that no Pope hath gotten a piece of Aaron's mitre or breast-plate to grace his wardrobe, or a parcel of the manuscript commandments, written by God's finger, to adorn his Vatican. But Divine providence hath utterly razed all foundations for superstition to build upon, in the total abolition of these holy ornaments. And if those reasonable witnesses of God's truth were by His permission overcome, and killed by the beast when they had finished their testimony (Rev. xi, 7). no wonder if these senseless and inanimate types, having served their generation, the truth being come, were finally extinguished. Nor have I ought else to observe of those holy utensils, save that they were made of pure gold, and yet the Apostle is bold to term them and all other legal ceremonies beggarly elements (Gal. iv, 9), so debasing them in comparison of Christ, the Author of grace, and Giver of eternal life."

We have given sufficient specimens of Fuller's sprightly style and quaint allusions to send our readers to the work itself, and if they cannot procure a folio copy (now rare and costly) to get the reprint by Tegg, An admirer thus writes of the *Pisgah* : " His book really answers to its title. He

might be thought to have seen the ' Good Land,' so graphic
are some of its sketches, so lively his observations, and so
pleasantly does he keep the eyes and hearts of his hearers.
He is as painstaking, acute, discriminating and cautious as
Dr. Robinson himself, but where this tedious doctor is as
dull, dry, and monotonous as if he had never seen Palestine
from a nearer point than the United States, and was merely
describing it from a leaden model to a school of American
Surveyors, our old Fuller is all life and buoyancy, enticing
you by his company into long rambles over scenes which he
knows all about, upon which he looks lovingly, about which
he talks charmingly, and which he really photographs upon
your very soul by the light of his genial wit and hallowed
fancy.   His wit, however, is never out of tune with pure
and simple faith : his intellectual brightness never loses its
devout warmth, nor does any affectation of science ever
mar the loveliness of his meek and reverent spirit."*

The vagueness in the topography of this work was a
source of much anxiety to our author, but the rough and
ready way in which he settles some of these topographical problems is very amusing.   Thus the first syllable of
Gadara is to him argument enough for placing it in *Gad !*
When distances are in his original authorities stated
variously, he " umpires the distance by *pitching* on a *middle
number betwixt both.*   For instance, Seiglerus makes it
14,000 paces or 14 miles betwixt Zidon and Tyre (eminent
marts, and, therefore, the distance beween them might be
notoriously known), whilst Vadianus makes it 200 furlongs,
or 20 miles.   Here to part the distance equal we have

---

* " Homer of English Writers," p. 179.

insisted on 17 miles." Dibon, which the author finds sometimes assigned to Reuben (Josh. xiii, 17), sometimes to
Gad (Numb. xxxii, 34) is similarly treated.   "Some," he
says, "make them different and distant cities, which, in my
apprehension, is to set up two marks and have to hit the right
one.   For seeing these two tribes confine together, and
both lay claim to Dibon (like the two mothers challenging
the living child), we have only instead of a sword made use
of pricks, settling it *equally in the bounds of both*." Heshbon,
said in Scripture to be sometimes in Reuben, sometimes in
Gad, is also inserted "so equally between these tribes as
partially in both, totally in neither."   With regard to the
locality of the disputed altar Ed, our author, following the
customs of those very devout and Sabbatical Jews, who, when
the Sabbath or seventh day was transferred to the Lord's
day or first day of the week (Sunday), kept both Saturday
(a custom partially followed in the Eastern Church) and
Sunday holy, observing both *ex nimiâ cautelâ*, for more certainty *erects* "two altars, one on each side of the river,
leaving it to the discretion of the judicious reader to accept
or refuse which of them he pleaseth."

Other hints are thrown out as to the vagueness of the
then geographical knowledge by such expressions as that
the distance between Cyprus (about which we have heard
so much of late) and the Continent "cannot be great if it
be true what Pliny reports, that whole herds of deer used
to swim over thither."   Flags and banners are seen floating
over many of the towns and cities on the maps to indicate
that their position is *conjectural*, "one side of which flags
humbly confesseth our want of certainty, the other as
earnestly craveth better information." He often confesses his

want of exact topographical knowledge, and promises that all errors should be amended in his second edition (" God lending me life to set it out "), where he would give thanks to any reader convincing him of error, " or else let him conclude my face of the same metal with the plate of these maps."

Much of our author's writing and reasoning is very quaint and peculiar, and has earned for itself the sobriquet (for want of a better) of *Fullerian*. Professor Rogers thus refers to it (and the quotation is also given, from the difficulty of access to the original essay in the *Edinburgh Review*, 1851) : " If it be inquired what was the character of his wit, it must be replied, it is so various, and assumes so many different shapes, that one might as well define wit itself; and this, seeing the comprehensive Barrow has contented himself with an enunciation of its forms, in despair of being able to include them all within the circle of a precise definition, we certainly shall not attempt. Suffice it to say, that all the varieties recorded in that singularly felicitous passage are exemplified in the pages of our author. Of *his* wit, as of *wit* in general, it may be truly said, that sometimes it lies in pat allusion to a known story, or in seasonable application of a trivial saying, or in forging an apposite tale ; sometimes it playeth in words and phrases, taking advantage from the ambiguity of their sense, or the affinity of their sound ; sometimes it is wrapped in a dress of humorous expression ; sometimes it lurketh under an odd similitude ; sometimes it is lodged in a sly question, in a smart answer, in a quirkish reason, in a shrewd intimation, in cunningly diverting or cleverly retorting a question ; sometimes it is couched in a bold scheme of speech, in a tart irony, in a

lusty hyperbole, in a startling metaphor, in a plausible
reconciling of contradiction, or in acute nonsense ; sometimes a scenical representation of persons and things, a
counterfeit speech, a mimical look or gesture, passeth for
it ; sometimes an affected simplicity, sometimes a presump-
tuous bluntness giveth it being ; sometimes it riseth only from
a lucky hitting upon what is strange ; sometimes from a crafty
wresting obvious matter to the purpose.   Often it consisteth
in one knows not what, and springeth up one can hardly
tell how.   Its ways are unaccountable and inexplicable,
being answerable to the numberless rovings of fancy, and
'windings of language.'   Of all the preceding varieties of
wit, next to the 'play with words and phrases,' perhaps
Fuller most delighted in ' pat allusion to a known story';
in 'seasonable application of a trivial saying'; in 'a tart
irony and affected simplicity '; in the 'odd similitude,' and
'the quirkish reason.'"

   "In all respects," says Mr. Bailey, "the 'Pisgah Sight'
was worthy of Fuller's sacred calling. An ardent antiquary, he
carried his favourite pursuit into his profession.   To him, as
to his contemporary, Browne, of Norwich, 'the Ancient of
Days' was the Antiquary's truest object." The Pisgah
reverently sprang from his affection for the Bible : for (to
use his own expression) next to God the Word, he loved
the Word of God.   Hence, as has been well said, the work
is mainly illustrative of the Bible, with which book it often
ranged in the homes of the time.   Scripture is reverently
used as the *chief* authority.   "Let God be true and every
man a liar," says Fuller in one place.   "I profess myself a
pure Leveller, desiring that all human conceits (though built
on most specious bottoms) may be laid flat and prostrated,

if opposing the *Written Word.*"* No other of his books
evince so deep an acquaintance with the sacred volume.
He has probably extracted every topographical verse, besides
very many others. Like his friend, he was "an exact text-
man, happy in making Scripture expound itself by parallel
passages." "Diamonds," he would say "only cut diamonds." Hence the Pisgah has been called the exactest of
his works. Orme says this is one of the most curious books
ever written on the Scriptures, and incidentally illustrates a
number of passages of Scripture. "The learning which he
brings to bear on his descriptions is not only exact, but
deep."†

This work of Fuller's brought him into connection with
two learned men of that time, one was the celebrated Dr.
Lightfoot, and the other a Scotch minister, John Baillie, of
Glasgow. The former had been engaged in a similar work
to Fuller's for some years past, but our author had the start
of him. In his "Harmony," part 1st, he refers to the progress
he had made in a "Chorographical description of Canaan
from the Writings of the Jews, and prepared at great Pains,"
he says, "I went on in that work a great while, and that
with much cheerfulness and content: for methought a Talmudical survey and history of the Land of Canaan (not omit-
ting Collections to be taken up out of the Scripture and other
writers), as it would be new and rare, so it might not prove
unwelcome nor unprofitable to those that delighted in such
a subject. But at last I understood that another Workman, a
far better Artist than myself, had the *Description of the Land*

---

* Book v., 170.
† Bailey's Life, p. 483.

of Israel, not only in hand, but even in the press: and was so far got before me in that travail, that he was almost at the journey's end when I was but little more than setting out. Here it concerned me to think what I had to do. It was grievous to me to have lost my labour, if I should now sit down : and yet I thought it wisdom not to lose more in proceeding further when one in the same subject, and of far more abilities in it, had got the start so far before me. And although I supposed, and at least was assured, even by that Author himself (my very worthy and learned friend) that we should not thrust nor hinder one another any whit at all, though we both went at once in the perambulation of that land, because he had meddled with that Rabinick way that I had gone : yet when I considered what it was to glean after so clean a reaper, and how rough a Talmudical pencil would seem after so fine a pen, I resolved to sit down, and stir no more in that matter till time and occasion did show me more encouragement thereunto than as yet I saw. And thus was my promise fallen to the ground, nor by any carelessness or forgetfulness of mine, but by the happy prevention of another hand, by whom the work is likely to be better done."* And again, in his *Description of the Temple in the Life of the Saviour,* Lightfoot says, " When I had spent a good large time and progress in that Work I found that I was happily prevented in that subject by a more Learned and Acute Pen (Lightfoot's note is " Mr. Thomas Fuller, B.D."), which, though it went not in the same way in that Work as I had done, yet was it so far before me, both in progress and accuracy, that I knew it would be lost labour for me to proceed further."†

---

* Lightfoot's Works, Vol. i., 559.
† Works, Vol. i., 1048.

This work came out in 1650. Respecting the "Choro-graphy" Strype's appendix to the Life of Lightfoot says "The unhappy chance that hindered the publishing this elaborate piece of his, which he had brought to pretty good perfection, was the edition of Dr. Fuller's *Pisgah's Sight.* Great pity it was that so good a book should have done so much harm. For that book handling the same matters and preventing his, stopped his resolution of letting his labours see the light. Though he went a way altogether different from Dr. Fuller, and so both books might have shown their faces together in the world."*

Fuller also himself alludes to the learned labours of his brother Divine : " As for the remainder of the vessels of the Temple, with the manifold traditions concerning them, the reader is referred to the learned pains of my industrious friend, Mr. John Lightfoot, who, as I understand, intends an extire treatise thereof. Far be it from me that our pens should fall out, like the herdsmen of Lot and Abraham, 'the land not being able to bear them both that they might dwell together.' (Gen. xiii., 6.) No such want of room in this subject, being of such latitude and receipt that both we and hundreds more busied together therein, may severally lose ourselves in a subject of such capacity, the rather because we embrace several courses in this our description : it being my desire and delight to stick only to the written Word of God, whilst my worthy friend takes in the choicest Rabbinical and Talmudical relations, being so well seen in those studies that it is questionable whether his skill or my ignorance be the greater therein." †

---

* Vol. i, p. 12.
† " Pisgah-Sight," Book iii.., p. 95.

H H

Fuller, also alluding to Lightfoot's brilliant acquirements, speaks of him as one " who for his exact nicety in Hebrew and Rabbinical learning hath deserved well of the Church of England."

It is to this good feeling between these two painful and charitable Divines, Southey alludes in his " Doctor," where he says, " Lightfoot was sincere in the commendation which he bestowed upon Fuller's diligence and his felicitous way of writing.   And Fuller on his part rendered justice in the same spirit to Lightfoot's well known and peculiar erudition." [*]

The other Divine that Pisgah brought our author into notice with was Professor Robert Baillie, Principal of Glasgow University, who had been in London (1643) attending the assembly of Divines (Scotchmen being very popular then, and often asked to preach).   As a rule, Fuller didn't like Scotchmen, but the following letter from Dr. Baillie's *Letters and Journals* shows he was appreciated north of the Tweed :—

For Mr. THOMAS FOWLER.

REVEREND SIR,—

Having latelie, and but latelie, gone through your Holy Warr and Description of Palestine, I am fallen so in love with your pen that I am sorry I was not before acquaint with it, and with yourself, when from 1643 to 1647, I lived at Worcester House, and preached in the Savoy, that then, when I had some credite there, I might have done my best endeavours to have done your pleasure. You seem to promise an Ecclesiastick Storie : it were a pity, but it should be hastened. However, I am one of those who would gladlie consent to the burning of many thousand volumes of unprofitable writers, that burthens and harms the world ; yet there are some pens whom I wish did write much, of which yours is one. Mr. Purchase, in his

---

[*] Southey's " Doctor," vol. ii., p. 38.

Pilgrims, from the intelligence he had by English and Dutch travellers and merchants, together with the printed treatise of some late Italian, Spanish, and French writers, gave us a very good account of the world, the whole universe, the present condition of it, as in his time. I conceave no man were fitter than you to let us know, in a handsome. fyne, and wyse way, the state of the world as now it stands. If the Lord would put it in your heart to mend it, and give yow encouragement for such a performance, if yow would put out one part of it, were it the present state of Asia, I trust it should be so accepted of judicious men, that you should have from many all desirable encouragement, for the perfyting of the rest. Your cartes are very neatly and singularly well done ; yow would not be spareing of them. I wish in your Palestine, yow added some more, as one or two of Chaldæa, because of many scriptures relating to Nineve, Babylon, Ur, &c,; the voyage of Paul ; some cartes of the present state, joyned with those of the old scripturall state, as of Egypt, Jerusalem, &c. For these and the like happy labours, we at so great distance can but encourage yow with praise, love, and prayers to God, which you shall have, I promise yow, from me, as one who very highly pryses the two wrytes I have seen of your hand, and judges by these that the rest yow have done, or shall doe, will be of the same excellence. The Lord bless yow and all your intentions. So prays,

Your very loveing and much honouring brother,

R. B.

Glasgow in Scotland, August 22nd, 1654.

No answer can be found to this pithy and shrewdly critical letter, which we are sure Fuller would have quaintly answered with his usual politeness. We have described at somewhat a great length this most important and exhaustive of our author's works. But enough has now been said, we trust, to demonstrate the intrinsic merit of his " Pisgah-Sight," both from the internal evidence of the work itself, and the external testimony of its author's numerous friends, critics, contemporaries, confrères, and collaborateurs.

END OF VOL. I.

PRINTED BY
S. STRAKER & SONS, BISHOPSGATE AVENUE, LONDON;
AND REDHILL.

www.ingramcontent.com/pod-product-compliance
Lightning Source LLC
Chambersburg PA
CBHW032012110726
47901CB00004B/1053